DATE DUE

THE

CENTENARY EDITION

OF THE WORKS OF

NATHANIEL HAWTHORNE

Volume III

THE BLITHEDALE ROMANCE

and

FANSHAWE

NATHANIEL HAWTHORNE

THE BLITHEDALE ROMANCE

and

FANSHAWE

Ohio State University Press

ACKNOWLEDGMENTS

THE EDITORS of the Centenary Hawthorne are grateful for the generous assistance given by librarians, scholars, and bibliophiles. We are indebted to John Cook Wyllie and William H. Runge, Alderman Library, University of Virginia; William A. Jackson, William H. Bond, and Miss Carolyn Jakeman, Houghton Library, Harvard University; Herbert Cahoon, Pierpont Morgan Library; John D. Gordan, Berg Collection, Robert W. Hill, Manuscript Division, and Gilbert A. Cam, Reference Section, New York Public Library; Herbert C. Schulz, Huntington Library; Frederick R. Goff, Library of Congress; Kermit Cudd and Miss Jane W. Gatliff, Ohio State University Libraries; Marcus A. McCorison, American Antiquarian Society; Donald Gallup, Yale University Library; John Alden, Boston Public Library; Roger E. Stoddard, Brown University Library; Walter M. Whitehill, Boston Athenaeum; William Henry Harrison, Fruitlands Museum; Mrs. June Moll, University of Texas Library; the Bowdoin College Library; John S. Van E. Kohn, Seven Gables Bookshop; Henry W. Wenning, New Haven; Rollo Silver, Simmons College; Norman Holmes Pearson, Yale University; Nolan E. Smith and Robert C. Elliott, Ohio State University; Edward H. Davidson, University of Illinois; Lewis Leary and Miss Bette Statsky,

ACKNOWLEDGMENTS

Columbia University; Luther Mansfield, Williams College; Mrs. Kathryn Turner, Wellesley College; Donald Hyde, New York City; and C. Waller Barrett, Charlottesville. Special acknowledgment must be made for the work of Mrs. F. Russell Hart and Mrs. Robert Ratcliffe, Charlottesville. We are particularly indebted to C. E. Frazer Clark, Jr., Detroit, and Hyman W. Kritzer of the Ohio State University Libraries.

THE EDITORS

CONTENTS

CONTENTS

CONTENTS

ILLUSTRATIONS

The Ohio State University Libraries draft page from *The Blithedale Romance,* and the corresponding page from the Pierpont Morgan Library fair-copy manuscript (folio 35).
(facing page xvii)

Title page of the first edition of *Fanshawe* in the Ohio State University Libraries.
(facing page 30)

THE BLITHEDALE ROMANCE

INTRODUCTION TO
THE BLITHEDALE ROMANCE

A BUSINESS-LIKE NOTE in Hawthorne's *American Notebooks* reads: "Wrote the last page (199th manuscript) of the Blithedale Romance, April 30th, 1852. Wrote Preface, May 1st. Afterwards modified the conclusion, and lengthened to 201 pages. First proof-sheets, May 14th."[1]

We can estimate with fair certainty that it took him four months to shape the book in his mind. He had finished *The House of the Seven Gables* on January 27, 1851, and had let himself lie fallow for some six months. On July 22, he wrote Horatio Bridge, "I don't know what I shall write next," and was not even sure that the book would be a romance.[2] But two days later he made up his mind: "When I write another romance, I shall take the Community for a subject, and shall give some of my experiences and observations at Brook Farm."[3]

It was not until November 23 that he wrote a friend that

---

[1] Randall Stewart (ed.), *The American Notebooks by Nathaniel Hawthorne* (New Haven, 1932), p. 141. Hawthorne's pagination here indicates that he is referring to the combination fair-copy and final draft from which the Centenary Edition text derives.

[2] MS, Bowdoin College Library.

[3] Hawthorne to William B. Pike, July 24, 1851, quoted in Rose Hawthorne Lathrop, *Memories of Hawthorne* (Boston, 1897), pp. 150-54.

he was "about to engage in a longer work."[4] He had just moved from the Berkshires to a rented house in the Boston suburb of West Newton, and presumably he began composition soon after he was settled. If we take late November as the beginning date, the writing time for *The Blithedale Romance* was about the same as for *The Scarlet Letter* and *The House of the Seven Gables*—approximately five months.

Though he did not increase his usual work-pace, he was anxious to be finished with the book. His income from literature for 1851 was $1,430, his best record thus far,[5] but he was in need of money. A third child had been born the previous spring; and he wanted to buy a house. Encouraged by his prospects, he bought the house and nine acres in Concord belonging to Bronson Alcott,[6] paid $1,500, plus heavy expenses for alterations and redecoration, renamed it the "Wayside," and moved in while *Blithedale* was going through the press.

Meanwhile, on May 2, he had sent the manuscript to E. P. Whipple, who had been of all American critics the one most precisely to remark his genius and its strengths and limitations.[7] He wrote Whipple:

Behold a huge bundle of scribble, which you have thoughtlessly promised to look over! If you find it beyond your

[4] Hawthorne to John Sullivan Dwight, November 23, 1851, MS, Yale University Library.

[5] Randall Stewart, *Nathaniel Hawthorne: A Biography* (New Haven, 1948), p. 117.

[6] Hawthorne wrote Evert A. Duyckinck, June 15, 1852, that at the "Wayside" he felt "for the first time in my life, at home." Of the house he said, "It is no very splendid mansion . . . ; but Mr. Alcott, the Orphic Sage, of whom I bought it, had wasted a good deal of money in fitting it up to suit his own tastes, all which improvements I get for little or nothing. Having been much neglected, the place is the raggedest in the world; but will make, sooner or later, a comfortable and sufficiently pleasant house" (MS, Duyckinck Collection, New York Public Library).

[7] Cf. Hawthorne to Fields, May 23, 1851, MS, Huntington Library: "Whipple's notices have done more than please me; for they have helped me to see my book [*The House of the Seven Gables*]. Much of the censure I recognize as just. I wish I could feel the praise to be as fully deserveu.

powers, hand it over to Ticknor at once, and let him send it
to the Devil; but before that happens, I should be glad to
have it looked over by a keen, yet not unfriendly eye, like
yours. Nobody has yet read it, except my wife; and her
sympathy, though very gratifying, is a little too unreserved
to afford me the advantages of criticism. After all, should
you spy ever so many defects, I cannot promise to amend
them; the metal hardens very soon after I pour it out of my
melting-pot into the mould.[8]

By the spring of 1852, it would seem, Hawthorne characteristically needed not editorial advice but assurance. By now
he feared only the printer's Devil. Also, there was his usual
practical problem: finding an appropriate and attractive title.
He told Whipple that he had temporarily settled on "Hollingsworth," but also had thought of "Blithedale," "Miles Coverdale's Three Friends," "The Veiled Lady," "Priscilla," "The
Arcadian Summer," "Zenobia"—and of course "The Blithedale
Romance," which would do "in lack of a better."[9] Perhaps
Whipple helped him decide on a title which would, like
the ending of the novel, put the whole matter into the soft
focus of Coverdale's final lucubrations. In any case, it was
all done in a great hurry. On May 15, Hawthorne wrote
to his sister Maria Louisa: "My book is in press. We are
all well."[10]

Since all previous efforts to get London publishers to pay

[8] May 2, 1852, MS, Pierpont Morgan Library, now bound in with the
manuscript of The Blithedale Romance.

[9] Whipple's reply to Hawthorne has not been found. Randall Stewart
(American Notebooks, p. 309) conjectures that a "suggestion from Whipple
may have led to the modification of the conclusion," but offers no proof.
Fields, in London, reported to Mary Russell Mitford, May 21, 1852:
"Hawthorne has just finished another Romance. Whipple who has read
the Ms. says it is admirably done; that it is full of thought and beauty
and pathos and humour. . . . The sharp, penetrating, pitiless scrutiny of
morbid hearts which H. is so celebrated for appears in the new novel in
some transcending examples" (MS, Huntington Library, a copy said to be
in the hand of Sarah Orne Jewett). The tenor of Fields's letter, if it echoes
that of Whipple to him, suggests that Whipple may have considered
the book—to use a later word of Hawthorne concerning it—insufficiently
"genial."

[10] May 15, 1852, MS, Essex Institute.

for a work by Hawthorne had failed, it was fortunate that Fields was in Europe (he had sailed October 9) while *Blithedale* was being written and printed: he was able in person to supervise negotiations for the sale of British rights to the book. A letter to the firm's London agents on March 9 set £100 as the price—the sheets to be furnished the English publisher as they came from the press. Ticknor and Fields's English agent was instructed to "see Bogue (first) and then Routledge or Bohn." And the letter added that Hawthorne's "reputation now ought to command even a *higher* price than this but he is willing to do this with this vol."[11]

On May 21, Fields wrote Hawthorne from London that Whipple had given him a "most glowing account" of the "beauties" of *The Blithedale Romance*. Negotiations were progressing:

My plan with the London reprint is this. We must not announce it in America till terms are made for it here. The sheets must be sent over to me at once as fast as they come from the Stereotypers. And this business must be hurried too. I find on investigation that the London Pub[s]. who deal in Cheap issues (Routledge & others) are determined to get this book at £50 and they will not offer more. . . . altho' Bentley says he will publish it at ½ profits I do not think it politic to let him have it because his universal plan is to take all himself & say the expenses have eaten up the author's share. . . . It occurred to me to open a negotiation with C[h]apman & Hall the Pub[s]. of Bulwer & Dickens. I met Chapman at Dinner and poured into his ear the great merits of Somebody on the other side of the water. Before I left Paris I wrote him that you had finished a Romance and if he chose to add another great name to his list here was his chance. A correspondence ensued and to-day I have been closeted with him and the result is after reading E.P.W[.]'s letter and bringing forward the other evidences of what might be expected in this new Romance he says if we will send him the Mss. or the proof sheets and his literary adviser,

[11] Ticknor and Fields Letter Books, MS, Houghton Library, Harvard University. See W. S. Tryon and William Charvat (eds.), *The Cost Books of Ticknor and Fields, 1832-1858* (New York, 1949), p. 218.

(whom I know to be strongly y^r. admirer), agrees with my report he will purchase the copyright for the sum I offer it, which sum is *two hundred Pounds*. I put it high and spread it thick for I want you to make a fortune as fast as possible.[12]

Hawthorne had his doubts as to the possibility of getting so large a sum for the new romance.[13] But on June 3, Fields wrote him: "Nine cheers! I have sold The Blithedale Romance for Two Hundred Pounds to Chapman & Hall," and he added that the book would have to appear in England before its American publication.[14] Hawthorne replied, June 17:

> You have succeeded admirably in regard to the Blithedale Romance and have got just £150. more than I expected to receive. It will come in good time, too; for my drafts have been pretty heavy of late, in consequence of buying an estate!!! and fitting up my house. [15]

The English edition (which sold at a guinea for two volumes) appeared shortly before July 7.[16] Meanwhile, Hawthorne was instructing Ticknor to send complimentary copies to some of his friends—Longfellow, Hillard, Holmes, Melville, Tuckerman, Curtis, and others. He was beginning to plan his promised campaign biography of Franklin Pierce and was still worried about his financial condition.[17] Ticknor

[12] MS, Berg Collection, New York Public Library.

[13] He wrote Ticknor, June 8, 1852: "I rec'd a note from Fields, informing me of his hopes of getting £200. for the romance. I don't believe he will" (MS, Berg Collection, New York Public Library).

[14] MS, Berg Collection, New York Public Library.

[15] Hawthorne-Fields Letter Book, MS, Houghton Library, Harvard University.

[16] On this date Fields wrote Hawthorne: "The Romance is now fairly launched into the world of London" (MS, Berg Collection, New York Public Library). Fields cited the one guinea price in this letter.

[17] July 7, 1852, MS, Yale University Library; Hawthorne to Burchmore, July 7, 1852, quoted in an American Art Association auction catalogue, *The Stephen H. Wakeman Collection* . . . (New York, 1924), item no. 322; Hawthorne to Ticknor, July 13, 1852, MS, Berg Collection, New York Public Library; Hawthorne to George W. Curtis, July 14, 1852, MS, Fruitlands Museum.

and Fields published *The Blithedale Romance* on July 14, in an impression of 5,090 copies, and on August 12 issued a second impression of 2,350 copies. Another impression was not called for until September 5, 1855, and it was of only 536 copies. Subsequent impressions in Hawthorne's lifetime amounted to little more than a thousand copies. After its successful launching, then, *The Blithedale Romance* was no great success.

Fields was particularly disappointed, writing Miss Mitford, "I hope Hawthorne will give us no more Blithedales."[18] Hawthorne may have been partly serious when, at the height of the sale, he wrote Ticknor: "I am glad you have got rid of so many of the new books. Sweep them off as fast as you can. Don't let your shelves be disgraced with such trash."[19] Nonetheless, he seemed satisfied with his financial rewards. Writing of the difficulties of securing copyright protection for a serial which his friend George W. Curtis wanted him to do for *Putnam's Magazine,* he proclaimed flatly on October 28, 1852: "I received a thousand dollars [i.e., for the English rights] for Blithedale, and mean to get more (if I can) for the next one. . . ."[20] Earlier in the month he had written Bridge: "Just at this time, I rather think, your friend stands foremost there [in England], as an American fiction-monger. In a day or two, I intend to begin a new romance, which, if possible, I mean to make even more genial than the last!"[21]

As always, Hawthorne was bedeviled by the problem of being "genial." In spite of the hastily added ending, the book did not seem very genial to his admiring friends.[22] Hawthorne's severe attitude toward social reform in the romance simply would not allow him to be genial. Even

---

[18] Stewart, *Nathaniel Hawthorne,* p. 123.
[19] July 24, 1852, MS, Berg Collection, New York Public Library.
[20] MS, Houghton Library, Harvard University.
[21] October 13, 1852, MS, Bowdoin College Library.
[22] See Stewart, *Nathaniel Hawthorne,* pp. 122-23.

though the Preface contains a clear disclaimer (inspired perhaps by the difficulties which ensued from his using the name of a real family of Pyncheons in *The House of the Seven Gables*),[23] the characters in *Blithedale* invited comparison with people who had actually been associated with Brook Farm. Hawthorne seems to have begun with the intention of sticking fairly closely to his recollections of Brook Farm, but to have gradually moved away from these recollections in order to give himself the freedom which Romance permitted. As has been noted, his first intention was to "take the Community for a subject."[24] A notebook entry of July 30, 1851, shows that he had borrowed some volumes of Fourier, "with a view to my next Romance."[25] The matter was clear enough to Fields, who wrote Bayard Taylor, June 5, 1852, that the scene of Hawthorne's new romance "is laid at Brook Farm!"[26] Nevertheless, Hawthorne could justifiably write to George W. Curtis, who had belonged to the Community, "Do not read [*The Blithedale Romance*] as if it had anything to do with Brook Farm (which essentially it has not) but merely for its own story and characters."[27] He wrote more bluntly to an unnamed autograph seeker in 1852: "As regards the degree in which the 'Blithedale Romance' has a foundation in fact, the preface to the book gives a correct statement."[28]

Hawthorne's use of his experiences at Brook Farm is in accord with his "method" as a writer of fiction. For the romance he drew liberally on the extant notebook covering his final few weeks at Brook Farm, and perhaps on earlier notebooks which have not survived; moreover, many of the

[23] See Introduction to *The House of the Seven Gables*, Centenary Edition.
[24] See note 3.
[25] Stewart (ed.), *American Notebooks*, p. 219.
[26] MS, Huntington Library.
[27] July 14, 1852, MS, Fruitlands Museum.
[28] October 16, 1852, MS, St. Lawrence University Library.

persons, places, and things he mentioned in his long Brook Farm letters to Sophia Peabody got into the novel—transformed to make them appropriate to a narrative recounted by a man like Coverdale, essentially an outsider. Hawthorne had gone to Brook Farm in the hope of finding a place where he could eventually settle after his marriage. From the outset, as his letters to her reveal, he was simply not cut out for such a life. He was not unsympathetic toward those involved in the experiment; it was the *idea* of the experiment which he found inadequate. And so, as he modified his memories of places and persons for the purposes of story, he did indeed create a new world.[29] But it was not new enough: readers could not resist identifying Blithedale people with those of Brook Farm. Hollingsworth has been identified as Alcott, Brisbane, Brownson, Burritt, Channing, Dana, Emerson, Mann, Parker, and Pike; Zenobia as Margaret Fuller, Caroline Sturgis, Mrs. George Ripley, Mrs. Almira Barlow, and Fanny Kemble.[30] Coverdale, of course, has usually been taken to be Hawthorne—as, in some ways, he is. Perhaps the difficulty is that Hawthorne himself had not discovered just what his Brook Farm experience had meant to him. He did not regret having attempted the experiment, and he respected the people with whom he had been associated there; but even before he left the Farm he had rejected as impractical the theory on which it was based. The important point, however, is that he was unable to transform, for the purpose of his art, his memories of the Community. Thus those who sought to identify his fellows at Brook Farm did so not only out of

[29] The derivation of *The Blithedale Romance* from Hawthorne's experience is summed up correctly, though with inadequate documentation, in Hubert H. Hoeltje, *Inward Sky: The Mind and Heart of Nathaniel Hawthorne* (Durham, N. C., 1962), pp. 382-95. Mr. Hoeltje properly notes that Hawthorne used some of his Brook Farm (and other) experiences in his tales before he wrote *The Blithedale Romance*.

[30] This list, supported by abundant documentation, comes from Maurice A. Crane's unpublished dissertation, "A Textual and Critical Edition of Hawthorne's *Blithedale Romance*" (University of Illinois, 1953), pp. lxxvi-lxxvii.

their accustomed curiosity, but out of a sense that the particulars grounded in Brook Farm had not been quite absorbed into the whole and transformed in the absorbing. And surely many of his contemporaries, knowing that he had gone to law to recover the money he had put into Brook Farm, were justified in looking for what they found. Some of his revisions in the fair-copy manuscript were attempts to soften the "realistic" details which he remembered—to the end, as he noted in his Preface, of establishing "a theatre, a little removed from the highway of ordinary travel, where the creatures of his brain may play their phantasmagorical antics, without exposing them to too close a comparison with the actual events of real lives." Yet the Preface hardly succeeds in justifying Hawthorne's use of the final word in the title of *The Blithedale Romance.*

In the end, as at the beginning, there was something of the Coverdale in him. Away from Brook Farm, he had written his beloved Sophia, September 3, 1841:

> But really I should judge it to be twenty years since I left Brook Farm; and I take this to be one proof that my life there was an unnatural and unsuitable, and therefore an unreal one. It already looks like a dream behind me. The real Me was never an associate of the community. . . . [31]

About two months earlier, he had written his friend Hillard, "You cannot make a silk purse out of a sow's ear; nor must you expect pretty stories from a man who feeds pigs."[32] *The Blithedale Romance* is almost a "pretty story," but not quite. In *The House of the Seven Gables,* which he often claimed to be a better book than *The Scarlet Letter,* he had, in dealing with contemporary life, already strained his conception of the romance to its limits. Justify it as he might, the concept would

[31] *Love Letters of Nathaniel Hawthorne, 1839-1863* (Chicago, 1907), II, 36.
[32] July 16, 1841, MS, University of Virginia Library.

not quite hold in *The Blithedale Romance* and the books which followed. He had achieved his status as the foremost American "fiction-monger," only to discover that, without fully realizing it, he was writing the sort of fiction for which his taste, talent, and understanding had not prepared him.

R. H. P.

TEXTUAL INTRODUCTION:
THE BLITHEDALE ROMANCE

T HE BLITHEDALE ROMANCE, printed by Thurston, Torry and Company from type pages set for and stereotyped by Hobart and Robbins, was published on July 14, 1852, by Ticknor, Reed, and Fields.* The book collates, 8⁰: [1]⁸ 2-18⁸; 144 leaves, pp. [i-iii] iv-vi [vii] viii [9] 10-288. The title page is on p. i, the copyright and stereotyper's notice on p. ii, the Preface on pp. iii-vi, and the Contents on pp. vii-viii. The text begins with Chapter I on p. 9. Although book-advertisement inserts are not present in all copies, some contain catalogues dated April, 1852, and later.

The first impression was of 5,090 copies. A second printing, issued August 12, 1852, consisted of 2,350 copies. Collation on the Hinman Machine of an unbound set of 1852 sheets in the Clifton Waller Barrett Collection at the University of Virginia (perhaps final proofs or an advance copy of some nature) against the third impression of 1855 reveals no textual variants and thus no positive evidence for separating the first two impressions in 1852. However, Matthew J. Bruccoli in machine-collating multiple copies dated 1852[1] has discovered

---

* For a consideration of the evidence that seems to bear on such a division of typesetting and presswork, see the Note on the Typesetting in the Centenary *House of the Seven Gables.*

[1] The following Ohio State Libraries copies were completely machined: (1) PS 1855.A1.1852. copy 3; (2) PS 1855.A1.1854a. copy 2. The following University of Virginia copies were completely machined: (3) PS

five different bindings-up exhibiting pages in different stages of type-batter,[2] as follows (all references are to page and line of the 1852 plates; "r.t." means "running-title"):

	A	B	C	D	E
vi.14			x	x	x
16.15					x
57.26				x	x
69.6					x
97 r.t.			x	x	x
97.1			x	x	x
108.28		x	x	x	x
229.2			x	x	x

Because the publishing records for Ticknor, Reed, and Fields are complete in respect to this book, we may be certain that these bindings-up are representative only of two and not of five different impressions. At one extreme, a copy with no type batter (A) is almost certainly a member of the first impression. Correspondingly, a copy with all eight examples of batter (E) is almost surely a member of the second impression. If one were to hazard a guess, the copy with the single example of type-batter (B) is probably an example of the first impression, in which case we may suppose (a) the batter on p. 108 occurred during the course of printing the original copies, or (b) a second-printing sheet got bound up with first-printing sheets in this particular copy. Since batter can occur during the course of printing, as well as from rough handling of plates between impressions, it may be that

---

1855.A1.1852a (565914); (4) PS 1855.A1.1852 (535999); (5) PS 1855.A1.1852 (565924). The Ohio State third-impression copy of 1855 (PS 1855.A1.1855) was also completely machined as a control. The following Ohio State Libraries copies were thereupon spot-checked against the results: (1) PS 1855.A1.1852c; (2) PS 1855.A1.1852c. copy 2; (3) PS 1855.A1.1852c. copy 3; (4) PS 1855.A1.1853; (5) PS 1855.A1.1854a.

No textual differences were found in copies with states A and B of the spine imprint as noted in the *Bibliography of American Literature*; no copy in the extra-gilt binding was available for collating.

[2] "Concealed Printings in Hawthorne," *Papers of the Bibliographical Society of America*, LVII (First Quarter, 1963), 45.

copies in the C and D categories are actually representative of different stages of their respective sheets in the second impression; although it cannot be demonstrated that they did not receive their batter during the final impressions of the first-printing sheets. Fortunately, the matter is one of purely historical and book-collecting interest since no questions of text arise.

The original plates served for further impressions of 536 copies in 1855, 277 copies in 1859, 280 copies each in 1860, 1862, 1863, and 1864, 500 copies in 1865, 300 in 1866, 280 each in 1868, 1869, and 1870, and so on. The latest identified use of these plates is in the New Fireside Edition, first issued in 1886 and reprinted four times. Machine collation establishes that throughout the printings only three changes occurred: the alteration of "until" to "untill" in error as the result of resetting a line at 109.1 (Centenary 90.30); a resetting that inverted the "v" in "individual" at 196.33 (Centenary 166.33); and a resetting that inserted the "l" in "slow y" at 275.26 (Centenary 237.10).

The Little Classics Edition of 1876, published by James R. Osgood and Company, introduced a new typesetting (II) derived from the 1852 plates (I) with no infusion of fresh authority but with some slight corruption to be expected in a reprint. Various "editions" (i.e., impressions) were manufactured from these plates, including the Popular Edition (1891), the Salem (1894), and the Concord (1899). A few alterations in these plates made between impressions are recorded in the Historical Collation.

The famed Riverside Edition of 1883 (III), published by Houghton, Mifflin and Company, was set from the Little Classics text in a late state of the plates and was issued originally both in trade and in large-paper form.[3] The text of this edition is notoriously corrupt.

[3] Evidence from *The Scarlet Letter* (Centenary Edition, 1962, pp. lix-lx) suggests that the plates for the trade edition were made from the

The last of the collected editions collated for the Centenary text is the Autograph Edition of 1900 (IV) set from the Riverside text in a late state of the plates and published by Houghton, Mifflin and Company in a white binding with tipped-in signed illustrations; copies in a blue binding contain unsigned illustrations. Each appears to have been bound from sheets of the same impression.[4] The further history of these Autograph plates has not been investigated for the purposes of the Centenary text, although one may note an Old Manse impression printed from them in 1904.

The London edition of 1852 (E^1) published by Chapman and Hall preceded the American edition for copyright purposes and was published in two volumes shortly before July 7, 1852. Its copy was proof sheets from the American typesetting. The second London edition, in one volume, followed in 1854, a new typesetting without fresh authority. No variant in either English edition appears to result from a Hawthorne revision or correction not present in the final state of the text as represented by the first American printing. On the other hand, the first English edition preserves a few readings that can be identified as set from American proof sheets in a lost state intermediate between their original and final forms. This matter is discussed later.

Fields took possession of the printer's copy holograph manuscript of *The Blithedale Romance*, which, with his binding instructions on folio 200^v, is now preserved in the Pierpont Morgan Library. This manuscript is composed of 204 leaves, all (in the text enumeration) written on the recto except for a small addition on the verso of folio 188 and the conclusion, which is written on page 201, the verso

typesetting before printing and were thereupon corrected in a few details before reimpression in a second trade printing, followed by printing of the large-paper copies from type metal. This question has not been investigated in *The Blithedale Romance*.

[4] The Historical Collation for *The Blithedale Romance* has been prepared from a copy with the blue binding in the Ohio State University Libraries.

of folio 200 of the text. The paper is a light-blue wove, measuring 9⅝ by 7¾ inches, with a seal consisting of three plumes above the initials "B & G". This paper is identical with that in the printer's copy manuscript of *The House of the Seven Gables* written in the preceding year. The writing is in black ink, now mostly faded to brown. Unlike the manuscript of *The House of the Seven Gables*, the present manuscript exhibits no differences in the ink between the text and the chapter numbers and titles, thus indicating that they were inscribed at the same time as the text.

The first four leaves of the manuscript are preliminary. The recto of the first is occupied by the title, which reads "The Blithedale Romance, | By Nathaniel Hawthorne." The first line is a substitution written above the two deleted lines, "Hollingsworth: | a Romance." The verso is blank. The recto and verso of the second leaf comprise the list of chapter numbers and titles under the general heading "Contents." For the initial fifteen chapters the printer has added in pencil the page numbers according to the first edition.

The Preface starts on the recto of the third leaf (verso blank) and concludes on the verso of the fourth leaf. This fourth leaf is paged 2^d and 3^d, with "Preface" following in parentheses to distinguish these leaves from the independently numbered text leaves. The text begins, unnumbered, on the fifth leaf, but the foliation appears on the sixth as 2^d, followed by 3^d on the seventh, and thereafter by simple arabic numbers ending with 201 on the verso of text folio 200.

The numerous examples of false starts and corrected eye-skip in the inscription of the manuscript (recorded in the appendix Alterations in the Manuscript) would in themselves be sufficient to suggest that the Morgan manuscript does not represent the papers of the original composition. But, fortunately, inference is not required, for in November, 1962, the Ohio State University Libraries purchased at auction from Parke-Bernet Galleries a single leaf written on the recto of the same blue wove paper as in the Morgan manuscript and containing a version of the text in a manifestly earlier stage. The forty lines on this leaf run from Morgan MS text folio 34, line 27, to folio 35, line 36 (1852 edition 56.28-58.14), which is Centenary 46.16 ("picion, and") to 47.28 ("glances as").

Oddly enough, it is unnumbered, but a leaf must, at least, have preceded and followed it; and there is no reason to suppose that it is a discarded part of the Morgan MS inscription. Since the Morgan MS gives evidence of having been copied from some other document, this single leaf (although its history is unknown) would appear to represent the only known survivor of an earlier complete inscription of *The Blithedale Romance*. Whether a still earlier version in whole, or in part, underlies this lost manuscript from which the Morgan MS seems to have been copied, or whether we have in the Ohio State leaf a fragment of the initial composition is not to be determined, although the evidence of copying found throughout the later manuscript is not present in this single leaf.[5]

A full collation of the text of the leaf against the Morgan equivalent is provided in an appendix. In general, the Morgan form exhibits no far-reaching changes but only a more extensive stylistic alteration, plus general expansion of the same kind as the alterations within the printer's copy manuscript. Here, as in the manuscript of *The House of the Seven Gables*, Hawthorne's revisions are seldom condensations but almost invariably amplifications, whenever they go beyond simple substitution.

The Morgan manuscript holds, on an average, from thirty-seven to thirty-nine lines per page. Very few pages fail to show alteration of some variety made during the course of

---

[5] A further discussion, with an analysis of the textual variants, will be found in Bowers, "Hawthorne's Text," *Hawthorne Centenary Essays* (Columbus, O., 1964), pp. 401-25. See also illustration facing p. xvii, above.

the inscription or as part of a general review. Much of the alteration was made *currente calamo*, ordinarily by wiping out with a finger while the ink was still wet and writing over the same space. In the appendix Alterations in the Manuscript these changes are distinguished from the interlineations, which presumably were made at a later time, at least after the ink had dried.

The alterations over wiped-out letters and words offer the most serious difficulty in recovering the readings of the initial inscription, especially as no more than a letter or two, often, may have been written before the error was detected or a change decided on. Whenever anything of the original can be recovered, it is listed in the appendix, since sometimes even a single letter, in context, can suggest the probable word that was started. Less commonly, substitute words were written over the discarded original when little or no erasure had been attempted. The manuscript has scores of apparent cases of alteration which, on examination, prove to be no more than the tracing-over of an identical original word in order to make it more legible. Occasionally, the same word is interlined for clarity. No attempt is made in the appendix to record these tracings or interlined duplications, whether of words or of letters.

Some hand other than Hawthorne's has made in pencil a very few obvious and necessary additions of omitted words. These have been recorded also. The hand is not that of Hawthorne's wife and may be that of E. P. Whipple, to whom the manuscript was sent for criticism, or some publisher's reader. Whoever performed this office missed a number of mechanical faults, chiefly Hawthorne's dittography.

The five Hobart and Robbins compositors who set this book in type included Henderson and Fox who had worked on *The House of the Seven Gables*. One compositor, Innes, set only four pages in two stints. The four regular compositors worked in rough alteration: Henderson set 70 pages of the edition, Fox 68, Emery 63, and Munn 62.[6] The compositor of the Preface, Contents, and title page is not known.

The copy appears to have been distributed in "takes" of three to four folios for simultaneous setting by the four major compositors, each of whom would sign his name in the indention of the initial paragraph on the first leaf of his take, at which point he would start composition. When a type-page ended on the last folio of a take, the compositor (if there were enough material) might continue to set copy, ending his page with text from the first folio of the next take, above the compositor's name. More often, however, he would stop setting at the end of the type-page on his last folio, and the compositor of the succeeding take would thereupon complete his own stint by setting this remaining text on the folio and then continuing with the top of his own first folio until he reached the signed paragraph start where he had previously begun his composition. He could then page his galleys. What appears to be a foreman's pencil bracket and page number indicates the start of each compositor's adjusted stint, usually followed by the name of the compositor in the foreman's hand and occasionally by the running-title of the chapter. Ink step brackets with page numbers may relate to the imposition process; but these are in different hands from the foreman's brackets and pagination and have nothing to do with the notation of stints. For a more extended analysis of these various markings, see the Textual Introduction to *The House of the Seven Gables*.

Although the compositor always seems to have set a full page, reimposition to save a page when the end of a chapter consisted of only a few lines was several times employed, with the result that an extra line was added at the foot of two,

[6] In *The Boston Directory, For the Year 1852* James Henderson, printer, is listed as living at 8 Fayette; Frederick E. Fox, engraver, at 6 School; and Benjamin S. Munn, printer, at 10 State. No listing is found for Emery or Innes.

three, or four pages before the chapter end. This process occurred first in order to tuck in the ending of Chapter III on page 29 by adding a thirty-third line to the normal thirty-two on pages 28-29; in this instance two lines set by Emery were added at the foot of page 28 otherwise set by Fox. However, since this relining of the pages must have been performed immediately on the discovery that Chapter III would run over three lines on page 30, and since Emery then continued to set Chapter IV on page 30 instead, the printer's pagination numbers in the manuscript are not affected.

On the other hand, when Henderson ended Chapter XIX, originally, with four lines on page 198, and the manuscript was so marked, the stints continued on this basis up to the end of Chapter XX, which also was set originally with a four-line runover. Then setting continued to the very end of the book, when it was found that the final Chapter XXIX would need two pages over a full gathering to complete. At this point, the printer appears to have gone back to Chapters XIX and XX (ignoring the four-line ending of Chapter XXVII), and saved the two necessary pages by adding a thirty-third line to the final four pages of each chapter. Thus Chapter XX, in the final form of the book, began on page 198 (not 199), and Chapter XXI on page 204 (not 206). New pagination was substituted in the headlines, and the composition of the book was complete. From page 198 on, then, the pagination marked in the manuscript is off by one page; and starting with page 208 (the first page marked in the manuscript for Chapter XXI) the pagination is off by two and continues so to the end. In this stretch, several correctly numbered page beginnings are marked in ink, along with the distinctive bracket, seemingly as an aid to the revision of the pagination.

On the verso of folio 36, the recto of which had begun Chapter VII, a pencil computation calculates the number of pages of Chapter VI as 11⅓, by dividing 3,220 by 282. Comparable calculations appear thereafter, each dividing a number by 282. For example, on the verso of folio 43, the recto of which had begun Chapter VIII, the figure 2,670 is divided by 282, giving the result 9.5, which is the number of pages found in Chapter VII.

Thereafter, these calculations occur regularly for each chapter. On the verso of folio 71, Chapter X was calculated as 8 pages, whereas it is 9. On the verso of folio 78, Chapter XI is calculated at 9.8 although it is 10¼. On the verso of folio 84, Chapter XII is calculated at 8 pages although it is 8½. On the verso of folio 92, Chapter XIII is correctly calculated at 12 pages. The calculations then proceed correctly. No computation appears for Chapters XVII and XVIII. On folio 138 verso (facing the start of Chapter XXI), Chapter XX is calculated as 1,660 divided by 282 for the result "5, 6 nearly". It is a full six pages, and was originally 6⅛. And so on.

The computations represent a rough estimate, made before typesetting the chapters, of the number of pages that each would fill. The invariable figure 282 used as the divisor represents the estimated number of words in each page of the print. The figure that is divided is the total number of manuscript lines in the chapter multiplied by 10, as 267 lines in Chapter VII making 2,670 words estimated; and 366 lines in Chapter VIII making 3,660 words estimated. It is certain that the person making this estimate actually counted each line of the chapter in the manuscript and did not merely estimate the number of lines from averaging the pages. The hand making the computations is always the same. Whether the man worked ahead a chapter at a time, or whether this represents a rough casting-off of copy for the book at one operation in order to compute the approximate number of pages is not to be ascertained. If the latter, the omission of figures for three chapters is puzzling.[7]

The textual theory adopted for the Centenary Edition establishes the Morgan MS as the copy-text, that is, as the major basis of the edited text. Since this manuscript is a fair-copy holograph, it is clear that its "accidentals," or the forms of its spelling, punctuation, capitalization, and word-division, must be more authoritative than the house style imposed on this same copy by the Hobart and Robbins compositors. On the other hand, if Hawthorne can be conjectured to have corrected or revised any of the "substantives" (i.e., the words themselves) in the course of reading proof, such variant first-edition substantives would represent his final intentions and would become more authoritative than the corresponding manuscript readings.

Since indisputable evidence exists for Hawthorne's revisions in proof,[8] the present edition adheres to Sir Walter Greg's classic exposition of the theory of copy-text and has utilized, with only a few specific exceptions, the manuscript accidentals in preference to those of the first edition. In this general texture of authoritative accidentals from the manuscript, the editors have then placed all such variant substantive readings of the first edition as may be thought to represent Hawthorne's proof-alterations of the original typesetting from the manuscript.

Two points in this procedure need brief analysis. First, comes the question whether Hawthorne is, in general,

[7] Thomas MacKellar, *The American Printer* (Philadelphia: MacKellar, Smiths & Jordan, 14th edition, 1883), pp. 223-26, describes a similar system for estimating the length of printed books by dividing the number of words per MS (words per line × lines per page × pages per MS) by the number of words per printed page (words per line × lines per page). This book was first copyrighted in 1866 and again in 1878.

[8] In an unpublished University of Illinois doctoral dissertation (1953) entitled "A Textual and Critical Edition of Hawthorne's *Blithedale Romance*," Maurice A. Crane asserts that any first-edition reading variant from the manuscript is a compositorial error. But see below, pp. xli ff.

responsible for the numerous variants in the accidentals between the manuscript and the print. That he is not responsible for several large classes seems demonstrable. The major differences between the forms of the manuscript and of the first edition are similar in *The Blithedale Romance* to those between the manuscript and the print of *The House of the Seven Gables* set the preceding year in the same shop, partly by the same compositors. For instance, both prints use syntactical commas plus dashes in a sentence like the following, quoted in its first-edition form: "Nobody else in the world, I am bold to affirm,—nobody, at least, in our bleak little world of New England,—had dreamed of Paradise that day, except as the pole suggests the tropic" (9.22–10.2). In neither manuscript do commas precede dashes in such constructions. One would scarcely wish to argue that Hawthorne made hundreds of such proof-alterations in the *Seven Gables* sheets and then ignored the new system he had embraced and returned to his former ways in the manuscript of *The Blithedale Romance*, only to alter them again in proof.

Similarly, the invariable Hawthorne custom in manuscript is to place commas required by the syntax as follows in relation to parentheses: "The snow-fall, too, looked inexpressibly dreary, (I had almost called it dingy,) coming down through an atmosphere of city-smoke . . . " (11.19–23). But the prints of both romances punctuate this construction in the manner of the first edition here, "inexpressibly dreary (I had almost called it dingy), coming down. . . . "

House style, of course, has been imposed rigorously on both prints. In word-division, for example, it is impossible to believe that Hawthorne would forsake his invariable forms like "tomorrow" and alter them in proof to uncharacteristic "to-morrow". In spelling one would hesitate to argue that he revised in proof his invariable "Oh" to first-edition "O", "Aye" to "Ay", or "faulter" to "falter". Or in capitalization, as in 53.25–26, that he would find compelling cause to reduce to lower-case as in the first edition the manuscript capitals of "Unpardonable Sin" and "Devil".

All in all, probably at least two thousand differences exist in the accidentals between the manuscript and the print of *The Blithedale Romance.* That any great part of these should be taken as stemming from Hawthorne's proofreading is fantastic. Authors then as now were accustomed to accepting the printer's house style; and there was always the possibility that they would be charged for excessive alterations, especially alterations of details which a publisher considered correct.

On the other hand, the print does exhibit accidentals that vary from manuscript forms in ways that are not inconsistent with Hawthorne's characteristics. For instance, among the changes made during the process of writing out the fair copy, a certain number of commas in parenthetical constructions have been altered to dashes. The direction of change in the inscription of the manuscript is almost wholly from commas to dashes, whereas in the first edition such variants from manuscript are sometimes changes from commas to dashes, sometimes from dashes to commas. Moreover, even if one were to assume that house-styling were responsible for one treatment and authorial proof-alteration for the other, typographical evidence demonstrates that at least some of the dash substitutions in the print must have originated with the compositors. A typical and by no means uncommon example appears in Centenary 42.20 (52.5 in 1852). Here the manuscript "at hand, as most probably there will not, he had better make up" reads in the print, "at hand,—as most probably there will not,—he had better make up". However, the line with the dashes is so loosely spaced that it is quite impossible to believe that they were added in proof: with the narrower commas alone, the line would not have been at all properly justified. Another clear illustration occurs at 17.24, which reads in manuscript, "being women at all; their sex" but in the print (24.6) "being women at all;—their sex". Once again, although a dash in this construction is often characteristic of Hawthorne, the spacing of the line makes it evident that the dash must have been set originally by the compositor and cannot be a proof-alteration.

The matter comes down to the point, then, that whereas a critic can on literary grounds attempt to judge whether substantive alterations are authorial or not, no one can thus adjudicate the authority of most of the accidentals altered in the print. With comparatively few exceptions, therefore, a definitive edition must follow the forms of the manuscript, and not of the print. In doing so, the editor will perhaps lose some few Hawthorne alterations in the accidentals; but in these unknown and undeterminable cases he will at least preserve an authorial reading even though not a final one, and he will protect himself from accepting hundreds of printer's house-style variants as if they were the author's.

Hence the Centenary text reproduces Hawthorne's own accidentals in all their flavor and with all the literary intent that ordinarily governed his usage. A single example must suffice to illustrate the distortion that can accompany the imposition of compositorial styling on the author's delicate use of punctuation to define and limit meaning. At 202.7–9 the manuscript reads, "they perpetrated so hideous a clamor, that methought it might have reached, at least a little way, into the eternal sphere." This represents a different sense from the compositor's version in the first edition, "that methought it might have reached, at least, a little way into the eternal sphere", wherein "at least" modifies "reached" instead of "a little way" as in the manuscript.[9]

However, the case for the retention of the author's instead of the printer's forms of the accidentals does not rest only on

[9] A more difficult but more dangerous case occurs at 45.23–24, where the manuscript reads: " 'It is an idea worthy of a feverish poet,' said she, laughing, rather compassionately, and taking out the flower." In the first edition the compositor's removal of the comma after "laughing" silently

such evident distortions of meaning. An author's accidentals are an important part of his total style by which he conveys meaning. After surveying the difference between reading Hawthorne in the manuscript and in the first-edition versions, Professor William Charvat was moved to write in a private communication:

> It comes to me now, for the first time, that Hawthorne's style is essentially parenthetical, and that this characteristic reflects the basically essayistic, generalizing, and speculative quality of his fiction. His parentheses give him the latitude and flexibility that this quality requires. He modulates the degree of isolation of a unit by selecting (usually) just the right pair of separators: parentheses, or dashes, or commas. I don't think he did this selecting consciously, and probably the restoration of his own punctuation, after the compositors mangled it, looked like too much drudgery. Certainly, the compositors show very little sensitivity about his modulations.[10]

A number of substantive alterations do not carry the stamp of a compositor, as for instance the alteration of manuscript "agency" to first-edition "influence" (7.30), "to his credit" to "creditable" (30.2), "consider her his" to "recognize her as his" (74.32), "kiss" to "lips" (113.4), "useless" to "aimless" (133.22), or "season to season" to "autumn to autumn" (211.32). The one major addition—to the conclusion (247.26–32)—cannot be compositorial, of course.

---

enforces only one meaning, that Zenobia's laughter was compassionate. On the other hand, in the manuscript version it is equally possible that Hawthorne intended her words to be said "rather compassionately" although she spoke them laughing. The exact sense can perhaps be determined critically after examination of the numerous parallels where Zenobia's laughter is described, usually without modifying phrase. That such a problem exists in the manuscript, however, is effectively concealed by the compositor's interpretation.

[10] To this perceptive statement one can add only that the various examples of change exhibited in the manuscript in which Hawthorne usually weights more heavily, but occasionally lightens, the parenthetical punctuation might lead one to suppose that sometimes, at least, he had a pretty clear idea what he was doing and was consciously altering his original sense of the modulation.

The view that Hawthorne was a rapid and careless proof-reader originates chiefly in his treatment of material which was not creative (like the biography of Pierce) or which was being reprinted in collections, like the tales, from copy that had already seen print. The fact that the leaves of the manuscript of *The Blithedale Romance* have been folded is not necessarily evidence that copy was returned with proof, since this manuscript had been sent to Whipple and then to Ticknor, and the folds seem to form no pattern in large sections such as may be observed in the manuscript of *The House of the Seven Gables*. But whether or not copy was returned has little to do with the basic question of Hawthorne's care in reading proof; or with the problem that faces a textual critic: the authority of the first-edition substantive variants as representing authorial proof-alteration.

The full extent of Hawthorne's proof-correction of *The Blithedale Romance* sheets must always remain in doubt, wanting the evidence of the proof sheets themselves. Such correction would have been in four categories. First, the printer's errors that Hawthorne recognized and corrected. Since for these the manuscript and the 1852 text would agree, after correction, no evidence as to their extent can be recovered from the extant documents. Second, the alterations in proof that Hawthorne may have made of any readings in the accidentals. Some two thousand or more differences in the accidentals exist between the manuscript and the first edition. Certain categories of these can readily be attributed to house-styling by the compositors and not to Hawthorne's possible proof-alteration. Although large numbers cannot be identified with confidence as one or the other, the presumption is that any variant between the first edition and the manuscript in the accidentals must ordinarily be laid to the printer. In these circumstances, therefore, except for unusual cases it is folly to attempt to distinguish authorial proof-alterations from compositorial variants.

In the third category come variant substantive readings that an editor may fairly believe to be compositorial errors overlooked by Hawthorne in reading the proofs. In the fourth, the remaining substantive differences between manuscript and print must be taken to represent words that had originally been set by the compositors in accord with the manuscript but that were altered by Hawthorne to other words in the proofreading process. Allied with these, and perhaps indistinguishable from them except in case of error, are unauthorized alterations that could have been made in the proofs by the publisher's reader after Hawthorne had passed copy.

If we put aside the added passage in the final chapter, and do not count the first-edition correction of various dittographic manuscript errors (almost surely compositorial), collation discloses that forty-nine substantive variants exist between the manuscript and print. Of these, the Centenary editors believe that twenty-eight represent Hawthorne's revisions in the proof sheets of authoritative and satisfactory readings in the manuscript,[11] ten represent his correction in proof of his own manuscript errors (although some of these could be compositorial corrections),[12] and eleven represent printer's errors that he overlooked and that an editor must reject.[13]

Widely variant readings between manuscript and print like "recognize her as his" (74.32) for manuscript "consider her his", as noticed above, present no particular difficulty in identifying as the author's second thoughts despite the hypothetical possibility that they could be compositors' memorial errors that slipped by the proofreading. Much more difficult

[11] The readings are found in the Centenary Edition at 7.30, 15.30, 19.11, 19.33, 30.2, 30.30, 40.21, 63.13, 64.12, 65.18, 73.30, 74.32, 110.27, 113.4, 120.23, 133.22, 141.22, 144.18, 148.33, 169.29, 188.7, 194.7, 199.2, 203.10, 205.15, 211.32, 223.33, 232.13.

[12] These readings are found at 30.18, 101.4, 128.21, 146.10, 146.12, 150.17, 163.17, 178.5, 178.33, 196.29.

[13] These readings are found at 18.10, 37.25, 74.16, 85.11, 98.7, 132.31, 150.11, 178.29, 180.4, 213.18, 218.9.

are those readings, some of them discussed in the Textual Notes, like "roof" for manuscript "roofs" (148.33), or "near her" for manuscript "nearer" (169.29), with their suspicious sound-equations. Difficult as these are, however, they offer differences in meaning that can be subjected to critical scrutiny, just as one can, on grounds of meaning, reject first-edition "winter" for manuscript "wintry" (85.11), or as uncharacteristic usage reject the first edition's normalization of manuscript "nor" to "or" (132.31), or its vulgarization of manuscript "inspirited" to "inspired" (180.4). But the relatively indifferent variant causes serious trouble. Did Hawthorne intend to alter "I'm" to "I am" (232.13), "of a considerable" to "of considerable" (110.27), "hanging by" to "hanging up by" (144.18), or are these the inevitable by-products of compositorial eye or memory failure that Hawthorne did not notice in proof?

Faced with this problem, a textual critic is justified when dealing with a state of a document that clearly shows authorial revision (as does the first edition of this text) in holding that—indifferent readings and all—the reading in the revised document must be accepted unless, as in the eleven first-edition words rejected by Centenary, evidence of some weight exists to deny them to the author. That is, the variant readings of the first edition must be taken as innocent until proved guilty.

Unexpected support for this position comes in fragmentary form from the first English edition. We know that Chapman and Hall published this edition more than a full week before the American, and that their text was set up using as copy proof of the American typesetting rushed across the Atlantic in batches. We know that Fields, from England, had ordered these proof sheets to be pulled as the plates came from the stereotyper.

The interesting question then arises whether, in these circumstances, the English typesetting preserves any readings that at a later stage of proof-correction were altered in the American sheets before printing and publication. The evidence is sparse, but in a few specific examples no doubt can exist that when the English edition agrees with the manuscript against the American first edition, the reading of the American print must represent a proof-alteration. The most prominent example is the agreement of E^1 and MS at 74.32 in "consider her his" as against the first-edition "recognize her as his", a variant in the print that one would not wish to assign to compositor or to publisher's agent. Next, although the variant itself is largely indifferent, one would have trouble envisaging an independent reader altering the E^1 and MS agreement in "I'm" at 232.13 to first-edition "I am". The presence of a question mark after "Priscilla" in E^1 and MS as against a period in the first edition (86.32) may be fortuitous, the result of the English compositor's independent emendation of his American printed copy, but the question mark is not so mandatory as to make this a more probable explanation than proof-alteration in the punctuation. The case is much clearer for the fortuitous nature of the agreement of E^1 and MS at 59.28 in "squirrel!" versus the practically impossible "squirrel?" in the first edition. Here independent English emendation is very probable indeed.[14]

Chance may account for the E^1 and MS agreements in the spellings "behoved" (123.31) and "befal" (207.20) versus the first-edition "behooved" and "befall"; but the odds may well favor, at least for the second, the hypothesis that E^1

[14] In a different category are two E^1 errors that might represent misprints by the E^1 compositor or else his faithful rendition of American copy: "let" and "head" for MS and first-edition agreement in "lets" (90.4) and "heads" (144.18). In each case the final $-s$ in the manuscript is not clearly formed. But this evidence alone is insufficiently strong to support a conjecture that the English compositor here followed an original error in his American copy and that the two plurals were caught and added in a later state of the American proof. Nevertheless, this same sort of error, corrected later in English proof, may be seen in the second volume of the Boston 1860 edition of *The Marble Faun* set from uncorrected English proof sheets.

was following the spelling of the original American type-setting that was altered in a later state of the proof. Variants like these, however, might represent the publisher's proof-reading, such as took place in both the first and second editions of *The Scarlet Letter*.[15]

These few readings do not materially assist an editor in deciding on the authority of the forty-nine substantive variants between manuscript and first edition, but the conclusion that the English edition was set, even though in small part, from American proofs that had not been finally corrected does most interestingly require an editor to select the otherwise indifferent "I am" of the first edition (232.13) and to consider seriously the authority of the period in the first edition at 86.32.

On the other hand, the fact that E[1] follows the majority of what appear to be authentic proof-alterations in the American sheets (thirty-six of the thirty-eight substantive variants selected as authoritative, in fact) appears to confirm the hypothesis that normally Fields's instructions were followed and that the copy sent abroad consisted of proofs pulled from stereotype plates made from the finally revised typesetting. It is certain, for instance, that the passage added in proof at 247.26–32, present also in E[1], could not have been set in England from the original state of the proof sheet for gathering 18.

Three possible explanations can be advanced for the evidence that in at least two, very likely in four, and perhaps in five, sheets the English publisher must have been sent proof sheets in other than their final form: (1) The sheets in question were completely uncorrected and had not yet been returned by Hawthorne before proofs were pulled and sent to England; (2) the sheets had been returned by Hawthorne, but a publisher's reader made certain changes after proofs had

15 See Centenary, pp. liv-lviii, lxiii.

been pulled to be sent abroad; and (3) for at least some sheets Hawthorne sent in supplementary instructions after the return of the proofs and the pulling of the corrected sheets for England—if so, the variants of this nature in the first edition represent what amounts to a second round of authorial proof-alteration. (It is not known whether revises were submitted to Hawthorne.) No need exists, of course, for all the sheets under scrutiny to conform to the same hypothesis.

If the variant "squirrel?" in the first edition is actually a later alteration of original "squirrel!", we must assume either a clumsy repair of fallen or pied type (the reading is in the last line on the page), or, less likely, a singularly inept proofing by a publisher's reader. This occurs at 71.32 of the first edition, sig. 5_4. The text of sheet 5 runs from Centenary 53.9 to 67.11. In this stretch the only substantive variant between first edition and manuscript is the apparently authoritative "further" versus manuscript "longer" at 63.13. Thus if this reading be accepted as authoritative, the variant at 71.32 (Centenary 59.27) must be either a later alteration (possibly inadvertent) from Hawthorne's original proof-corrected state or else, as is just as possible, the English compositor's independent emendation of an American misprint.

The major variant at 74.32 of "recognize her as his" for manuscript and E^1 "consider her his" appears at 90.1 of the first edition, on sig. 6_5^v. Sheet 6 covers the text in Centenary 67.11 to 80.17. In this area appears the accepted first-edition variant of "to" for manuscript "of" (73.30) as well as the rejected "lessons" for manuscript "lesson" (74.16), a fairly obvious misprint. Either the variant at 73.30 is a compositorial error in the first edition and not an authorial proof-correction, or else the sheet has had two stages of proofreading. The variant at 73.30 is so relatively indifferent as to make critical decision almost impossible. The first-edition idiom is perhaps slightly the "harder," but this test is not always accurate and in a reading like this the interpretation may be subjective.

The doubtful variant of "Priscilla" with a period appears in the first edition at 104.24, sig. 7_4^v (Centenary 86.32). In this sheet 7 (Centenary 80.17–94.7) is the rejected first-edition variant at 85.11, an indubitable misprint, but there are no substantive differences. If the substitution of a period for a question mark is indeed a press correction, then either the first or the third hypothesis would be plausible.

The two spelling variants at 123.31 and 207.20 may represent a second round of correction, perhaps made by some agent after Hawthorne's return of the proof sheets, although the first variant may with equal plausibility be no American proof-correction at all but the preferential spelling both of Hawthorne and of the English compositor. A firm decision is quite impossible. This first variant, at 123.31, occurs at first-edition 148.2, sig. 10_2^v, in a sheet (Centenary 121.13–134.34) that contains the somewhat indifferent 128.21 addition of "a" omitted in the manuscript but the clearly authorial alteration at 133.22 of manuscript "useless" to "aimless". Another variant, at 132.31, has been editorially rejected as a compositorial sophistication.

The second spelling variant, at 207.20, which is perhaps more definitely to be assigned to a proofreader, appears at 242.3 in sig. 16_1^v in a sheet (Centenary 206.24–220.27) that incorporates the authorial change of manuscript "season to season" to "autumn to autumn" (211.32) as well as the editorially rejected first-edition variant of "sunk" for manuscript "sank" (213.18).

Finally, the seemingly authorial "I am" at 232.13 occurs at 269.31, sig. 17_7, in a sheet (Centenary 220.27–234.32) that holds the apparently authoritative addition of first-edition "hard" at 223.33.

This survey indicates that in only one instance (the doubtful punctuation variant at 86.32, in sheet 7) could the first hypothesis be possible, and an uncorrected sheet have been sent to England. We may take it, therefore, that the issue resolves itself to a choice for each sheet between the second and the third hypotheses, that is, further correction (after the proofs for England had been pulled), but made in the one case by a publisher's reader, and in the other by Hawthorne.

The variant "squirrel?" at 59.28 in sheet 5 is much more likely to represent compositorial repair of type than proof-correction; it may prove only that English proof had been pulled from type metal and not from a stereotype plate. On the other hand, if—as is certainly plausible—the agreement between E^1 and manuscript is fortuitous, the result of independent emendation by the English compositor, then sheet 5 has nothing to do with this investigation, and can be forgotten. The spelling variant at 123.31 is in much the same case, very possibly an English compositor's preferential spelling, and thus sheet 10 had better be discarded also. The variant at 86.32 may be thought a standoff, even though the Centenary editors, playing the odds, have adopted it. Although sheet 7 cannot, perhaps, be removed from consideration, no very great weight can be placed on the evidence here.

We are left, then, with a spelling variant at 207.20 (sheet 16) that may well represent the late intervention of a publisher's reader, and with two seemingly authoritative proof-alterations at 74.32 (sheet 6) and at 232.13 (sheet 17). In each of these three sheets one or more earlier proof-alterations appear to have been made. Since in the latter two examples one would wish to reject the hypothesis that anyone but Hawthorne ordered the changes, the case seems to be established for more than one round of proof-correction.

Two possibilities suggest themselves. The changes could have been made, following Hawthorne's instructions (or the proofreader's) in the stereotype plates; hence they could not have appeared in the proofs sent to England from the unaltered original state of the plates. This hypothesis does not seem to be supported by positive evidence. Collation on the Hinman Machine under magnification fails to disclose any anomaly that would suggest reset pages or plates repaired by inserted type metal.

It is much simpler to conjecture that Fields's instructions were not always followed precisely. From the point of view of the printer, whether proofs were pulled from corrected type metal before plating, or from the plates, would seem a trivial detail. To help make up a packet for England the printer may occasionally have included proofs from corrected type-pages not yet stereotyped along with proofs pulled from returned plates. Then, before plating, instructions for further alteration were received from Hawthorne and perhaps from the publisher's reader as well. Such late changes made in unplated type would not be found in the proofs earlier pulled for the English copy.

In this connection the sheets containing these variants offer an interesting study since they tend to run in sequences: the alterations at 59.28, 74.32, and 86.32 occur in sheets 5, 6, and 7 respectively; the suspect alteration at 123.31 in sheet 10; and the alterations at 207.20 and 232.13 in sheets 16 and 17 respectively. If chance is not operating here, the contiguity certainly suggests clusters of type-pages corrected from author's proofs and awaiting delivery to the stereotyper.

While copying the earlier inscription, Hawthorne appears to have made numerous expansions, but no excisions except for three special cases. Two of these deletions contain only a sentence or a clause (10.23–24; 17.15–16), but the third is much more extensive (175.5–27). It would seem to be significant that two are concerned with liquor and one with sexuality. Had other excisions appeared that could be identified as made for purely literary purposes, the argument might be advanced that these three could be included in that category; but under the circumstances they stand out as unique excisions presumably made for other than literary purposes.

Tipped in with the Morgan manuscript is a holograph letter superscribed West Newton, May 2, 1852, and addressed to E. P. Whipple in Boston. In this letter Hawthorne reminds Whipple of his promise to look over the manuscript although he cannot promise to amend any defects that Whipple spies. He particularly requests assistance in titling the romance. He states, "I have put 'Hollingsworth,' on the title-page, but that is not irrevocable; although, I think, the best that has occurred to me—as presenting the original figure about which the rest of the book clustered itself." He lists other possible titles, including "The Blithedale Romance—that would do, in lack of a better."

On the evidence that the stated title "Hollingsworth" has been deleted in the manuscript title page and "The Blithedale Romance" substituted, one may reasonably conjecture that Whipple returned the manuscript to Hawthorne instead of sending it directly on to the publisher. Indeed, the letter urges him to hand it over to Ticknor only if he finds it beyond his powers to read; the implications of Hawthorne's disclaimer of his ability to mend faults, and the instructions that it should be sent to the publisher if Whipple cannot read it, all point to his expectation that the manuscript would be returned to him with Whipple's general criticism.[16]

It is possible that Whipple was responsible for the several necessary pencil corrections in the manuscript (the hand is definitely not that of Sophia Hawthorne), although a press reader may have written them. After Hawthorne's warning, Whipple is most unlikely to have been the source of the usual run of alterations that the author made in the manuscript after initial inscription.

---

[16] If Hawthorne's letter to Whipple and the manuscript had always been associated, a case might be made that Whipple had sent the copy and the letter directly to Ticknor. But the two were brought together at a later time. The letter was sold at auction by Bangs on April 7-8, 1903, as item 103* (bringing $147.50) in the dispersal of Whipple's library.

However, two major alterations do appear in the manuscript that might have been influenced by Whipple. The first is the addition of the final chapter referred to in the *American Notebooks* in an undated entry, "Wrote the last page (199th manuscript) of the Blithedale Romance, April 30th, 1852. Wrote Preface, May 1st. Afterwards modified the conclusion, and lengthened to 201 pages. First proofsheets, May 14th." Since the "afterwards" might chronicle only the order of text, Preface, and added chapter, not much weight can perhaps be given to its phrasing. Nevertheless, the fact that the first two details have dates and the third none may suggest that the conclusion was not appended before the manuscript was sent to Whipple on May 2, the day after completion of the Preface. The case is undemonstrable, but at least some possibility exists that Whipple could have suggested the need for a different ending from Coverdale's reflections at Zenobia's graveside.[17]

Whether the three excisions mentioned above are in the same category with the added conclusion is difficult to determine, and the absence of any reference to them in the Notebook entry need have no significance as bearing on the time at which the deletions were performed. Whipple could have suggested them, just as he could have suggested the altered ending. The most natural candidate, however, is Sophia Peabody Hawthorne, the closest at hand, and certainly the most influential. Before her marriage she had urged on Bronson Alcott censorship of the published version of notes

[17] That the chapter was added before the manuscript was sent to the publisher is indicated by the fact that the new material, Chapter XXIX, was written on folio 199 below the end of Chapter XXVIII, and no evidence exists to suggest that the earlier material on folio 199 had been transcribed from its fair-copy form. Chapter XXIX ends on the verso of folio 200. This final leaf is slightly darker in color than its predecessors, perhaps from exposure as an outside leaf. Thus Whipple could have suggested the change, or Hawthorne could have grown dissatisfied with the conclusion while the manuscript was in Whipple's hands. He could not have kept the copy very long after its return if he received first proof on May 14. All we can conjecture is that the ending very likely was not

she had made on "unpleasant" subjects.[18] In the *American Notebooks*, Randall Stewart calls attention to her omissions of Hawthorne's references to smoking, drinking, and "low company," as well as her firm attitude towards his occasional levity about drunkenness.[19] The long passage in Chapter XX decrying the efforts of temperance workers could not have pleased her. It may be, therefore, that the three manuscript excisions were made in deference to the sensibilities of Hawthorne's wife; but whether wife or Whipple, the reasons could not have been literary. Under these circumstances, the editors have felt justified in restoring the passages in order to present the text of *The Blithedale Romance* in the complete form as Hawthorne wrote it. Although the deletions undoubtedly represent his final intentions, the causes behind these intentions are suspect.

The Centenary text, therefore, is essentially an exact transcript of the Pierpont Morgan Library manuscript in its finally revised state except for the restorations noted above. Substituted for manuscript readings are twenty-eight substantives from the first edition believed to be Hawthorne's revisory proof-corrections, and ten additional readings from

---

present when the copy was sent to Whipple but was added on its return before Hawthorne forwarded the manuscript to the publisher. If only some pattern could be derived from the folds in the manuscript leaves and assumptions made about their physical evidence, one might be able to settle the point. But the pattern of folds defies analysis for the manuscript as a whole. True, the last four folios, 197-200, are creased in an identical manner, vertically 3 15/16 inches from the outer margin. We know, then, that folio 200 had been inscribed before the leaves were creased. Unfortunately, the variety of positions for the creases throughout the manuscript does not encourage the belief that these were made by packing to send to Whipple or in the return. Instead, the very general pattern by which every three or four leaves seem to be similarly creased may perhaps indicate some action in the printing house, or folding to go with proofs. Since the time and the cause of the folding remain obscure, the evidence tells us no more than did the continuation of Chapter XXIX on the same folio as the end of Chapter XXVIII.

18 Edward Mather [Jackson], *Nathaniel Hawthorne* (New York, 1940), pp. 97-98.

19 Randall Stewart (ed.), *The American Notebooks by Nathaniel Hawthorne* (New Haven, 1932), pp. xix, xxi, 5, 66, 258, 274.

the first edition thought to be Hawthorne's corrections of manuscript errors, excluding the obvious dittographic mistakes doubtless corrected by the compositors in the setting. Excluded are eleven first-edition substantive variants thought to represent unauthoritative printer's errors not corrected in the proofreading. For these the manuscript readings have been preferred.

A very few normalizations of spelling forms have been attempted when Hawthorne's own practice was generally different, or when though invariable (as in "cieling") it was well out of step with approved usage of his time. Likewise, critical emendation of the word-division has been undertaken to normalize anomalies according to the form customarily favored by Hawthorne. Some few punctuation emendations have been attempted (a) to normalize anomalies, as above; (b) in smaller part to substitute manifestly superior first-edition punctuation that may possibly have been (but need not be) the result of proof-alteration; (c) in a very few cases to correct manuscript errors reproduced in the print. All of the above have been recorded.

In the apparatus, non-substantive variants between the manuscript and the first edition (I) are ignored when they are not the point that is being recorded; in these circumstances the form of the variant in the MS copy-text is the only one stated. For example, the note in the list of Editorial Emendations at 196.23 reads: Pope ∧]I; ∼ , MS. Here the only pertinent information is that a MS comma has been removed to coincide with the first edition's lack of punctuation. That the MS capitalizes "Pope" accounts for the form of the word itself in the apparatus, reflecting the capital in the text, despite the fact that the first edition reads "pope". This lack of capitalization is unreported: (a) it is not the variant being recorded; (b) the Centenary text is bound to reproduce the manuscript capitalization despite the punctuation variant introduced from the first edition.

The usual silent alterations, in the categories listed in the general discussion of textual procedures appended to this volume, have been made. Also, the differences in the manuscript between such forms as "Mr" and "Mr." have not been reproduced, and Hawthorne's superior "o" without apostrophe (as in "°clock") has been transcribed silently as "o'" as in the first edition. Manuscript and first-edition spacing, like "I 'll" or "had n't", not always constant in the manuscript, has been silently modernized. Dashes that Hawthorne inserted to fill out the manuscript line to the right margin have been ignored unless ambiguous. The editors have had to use their discretion in the transcription of a few words involving a possible a:u confusion. Hawthorne's miniscule "a" is sometimes left open and cannot always be distinguished from his "u". Often the context decides which letter is which, but in some words like "sprang" and "sprung" or "sank" and "sunk" Hawthorne's usage must occasionally be determined from other occurrences in the manuscript and even from other documents. The distinction between "farther" and "further", however, must sometimes remain moot. By the time he wrote *The Blithedale Romance* Hawthorne's strong preference for "farther" was beginning to weaken, and various indubitable "further" forms appear, not always separated from "farther" in respect to usage. The editors have carefully considered each case on its merits and transcribed the form that seemed to be intended in the inscription. But they scarcely dare hope that they have been correct in their estimate on every occasion.[20]

These exceptions apart, the text of *The Blithedale Romance* is established here for the first time in the relative purity of the manuscript form.

F. B.

[20] The first edition is of no assistance since it regularly prints "further", and Hawthorne did not trouble, evidently, to restore "farther" in proof where he wanted it.

THE BLITHEDALE ROMANCE

PREFACE

I N THE 'Blithedale' of this volume, many readers will probably suspect a faint and not very faithful shadowing of Brook Farm, in Roxbury, which (now a little more than ten years ago) was occupied and cultivated by a company of socialists. The Author does not wish to deny, that he had this Community in his mind, and that (having had the good fortune, for a time, to be personally connected with it) he has occasionally availed himself of his actual reminiscences, in the hope of giving a more lifelike tint to the fancy-sketch in the following pages. He begs it to be understood, however, that he has considered the Institution itself as not less fairly the subject of fictitious handling, than the imaginary personages whom he has introduced there. His whole treatment of the affair is altogether incidental to the main purpose of the Romance; nor does he put forward the slightest pretensions to illustrate a theory, or elicit a conclusion, favorable or otherwise, in respect to Socialism.

In short, his present concern with the Socialist Community is merely to establish a theatre, a little removed from the highway of ordinary travel, where the creatures of his brain may play their phantasmagorical antics, without exposing them to too close a comparison with the actual events of real lives. In the old countries, with which Fiction has long been conversant, a certain conventional privilege seems to be awarded to the romancer; his work is not put exactly side by side with nature; and he is allowed a license with regard to every-day Probability, in view of the improved effects which he is bound to produce thereby. Among ourselves, on the contrary, there is as yet no such Faery Land, so like the real world, that, in a suitable remoteness, one cannot well tell the difference, but with an atmosphere of strange enchantment, beheld through which the inhabitants have a propriety of their own. This atmosphere is what the American romancer needs. In its absence, the beings of imagination are compelled to show themselves in the same category as actually living mortals; a necessity that generally renders the paint and pasteboard of their composition but too painfully discernible. With the idea of partially obviating this difficulty, (the sense of which has always pressed very heavily upon him,) the Author has ventured to make free with his old, and affectionately remembered home, at BROOK FARM, as being, certainly, the most romantic episode of his own life—essentially a daydream, and yet a fact—and thus offering an available foothold between fiction and reality. Furthermore, the scene was in good keeping with the personages whom he desired to intro-duce.

These characters, he feels it right to say, are entirely fictitious. It would, indeed, (considering how few amiable qualities he distributes among his imaginary progeny,) be a most grievous wrong to his former excellent associates, were the Auther to allow it to be supposed that he has been sketching any of their likenesses. Had he attempted it, they would at least have recognized the touches of a friendly pencil. But he has done nothing of the kind. The self-concentrated Philanthropist; the high-spirited Woman, bruising herself against the narrow limitations of her sex; the weakly Maiden, whose tremulous nerves endow her with Sibylline attributes; the Minor Poet, beginning life with

strenuous aspirations, which die out with his youthful fervor
—all these might have been looked for, at BROOK FARM, but,
by some accident, never made their appearance there.

The Author cannot close his reference to this subject, without expressing a most earnest wish that some one of the
many cultivated and philosophic minds, which took an
interest in that enterprise, might now give the world its
history. Ripley, with whom rests the honorable paternity of
the Institution, Dana, Dwight, Channing, Burton, Parker,
for instance—with others, whom he dares not name, because
they veil themselves from the public eye—among these is the
ability to convey both the outward narrative and the inner
truth and spirit of the whole affair, together with the lessons
which those years of thought and toil must have elaborated,
for the behoof of future experimentalists. Even the brilliant
Howadji might find as rich a theme in his youthful reminiscences of BROOK FARM, and a more novel one—close at
hand as it lies—than those which he has since made so distant
a pilgrimage to seek, in Syria, and along the current of the
Nile.

CONCORD (Mass.), May, 1852.

THE BLITHEDALE ROMANCE

I

OLD MOODIE

THE EVENING before my departure for Blithedale, I was returning to my bachelor-apartments, after attending the wonderful exhibition of the Veiled Lady, when an elderly-man of rather shabby appearance met me in an obscure part of the street.

"Mr. Coverdale," said he, softly, "can I speak with you a moment?"

As I have casually alluded to the Veiled Lady, it may not be amiss to mention, for the benefit of such of my readers as are unacquainted with her now forgotten celebrity, that she was a phenomenon in the mesmeric line; one of the earliest that had indicated the birth of a new science, or the revival of an old humbug. Since those times, her sisterhood have grown too numerous to attract much individual notice; nor, in fact, has any one of them ever come before the public under such skilfully contrived circumstances of stage-effect, as those which at once mystified and illuminated the remarkable performances of the lady in question. Now-a-days, in the management of his 'subject,' 'clairvoyant,' or 'medium,' the exhibitor affects the simplicity and openness of scientific experiment; and even if he profess to tread a step or two across the boundaries of the spiritual world, yet carries with him the laws of our actual life, and extends them over his preternatural conquests. Twelve or fifteen years ago, on the contrary, all the arts of mysterious arrangement, of picturesque disposition, and artistically contrasted light and shade, were made available in order to set the apparent miracle in the strongest attitude of opposition to ordinary facts. In the case of the Veiled Lady, moreover, the interest of the spectator was further wrought up by the enigma of her identity, and an absurd rumor (probably set afloat by the exhibitor, and at one time very prevalent) that a beautiful young lady, of family and fortune, was enshrouded within the misty drapery of the veil. It was white, with somewhat of a subdued silver sheen, like the sunny side of a cloud; and falling over the wearer, from head to foot, was supposed to insulate her from the material world, from time and space, and to endow her with many of the privileges of a disembodied spirit.

Her pretensions, however, whether miraculous or otherwise, have little to do with the present narrative; except, indeed, that I had propounded, for the Veiled Lady's prophetic solution, a query as to the success of our Blithedale enterprise. The response, by-the-by, was of the true Sibylline stamp, nonsensical in its first aspect, yet, on closer study, unfolding a variety of interpretations, one of which has certainly accorded with the event. I was turning over this riddle in my mind, and trying to catch its slippery purport by the tail, when the old man, above-mentioned, interrupted me.

"Mr. Coverdale!—Mr. Coverdale!" said he, repeating my name twice, in order to make up for the hesitating and ineffectual way in which he uttered it—"I ask your pardon, sir—but I hear you are going to Blithedale tomorrow?"

I knew the pale, elderly face, with the red-tipt nose, and the patch over one eye, and likewise saw something characteristic in the old fellow's way of standing under the arch of a gate, only revealing enough of himself to make me recognize him as an acquaintance. He was a very shy personage, this Mr. Moodie; and the trait was the more singular, as his mode of getting his bread necessarily brought him into the stir and hubbub of the world, more than the generality of men.

"Yes, Mr. Moodie," I answered, wondering what interest he could take in the fact, "it is my intention to go to Blithedale tomorrow. Can I be of any service to you, before my departure?"

"If you pleased, Mr. Coverdale," said he, "you might do me a very great favor."

"A very great one!" repeated I, in a tone that must have expressed but little alacrity of beneficence, although I was ready to do the old man any amount of kindness involving no special trouble to myself. "A very great favor, do you say? My time is brief, Mr. Moodie, and I have a good many preparations to make. But be good enough to tell me what you wish."

"Ah, sir," replied old Moodie, "I don't quite like to do that; and, on further thoughts, Mr. Coverdale, perhaps I had better apply to some older gentleman, or to some lady, if you would have the kindness to make me known to one, who may happen to be going to Blithedale. You are a young man, sir!"

"Does that fact lessen my availability for your purpose?" asked I. "However, if an older man will suit you better, there is Mr. Hollingsworth, who has three or four years the advantage of me in age, and is a much more solid character, and a philanthropist to boot. I am only a poet, and, so the critics tell me, no great affair at that! But what can this business be, Mr. Moodie? It begins to interest me; especially since your hint that a lady's influence might be found desirable. Come; I am really anxious to be of service to you."

But the old fellow, in his civil and demure manner, was both freakish and obstinate; and he had now taken some notion or other into his head that made him hesitate in his former design.

"I wonder, sir," said he, "whether you know a lady whom they call Zenobia?"

"Not personally," I answered, "although I expect that pleasure tomorrow, as she has got the start of the rest of us, and is already a resident at Blithedale. But have you a literary turn, Mr. Moodie?—or have you taken up the advocacy of women's rights?—or what else can have interested you in this lady? Zenobia, by-the-by, as I suppose you know, is merely her public name; a sort of mask in which she comes before the world, retaining all the privileges of privacy—a contrivance, in short, like the white drapery of the Veiled Lady, only a little more transparent. But it is late! Will you tell me what I can do for you?"

"Please to excuse me to-night, Mr. Coverdale," said Moodie. "You are very kind; but I am afraid I have troubled you, when, after all, there may be no need. Perhaps, with your good leave, I will come to your lodgings tomorrow-morning, before you set out for Blithedale. I wish you a good-night, sir, and beg pardon for stopping you."

And so he slipt away; and, as he did not show himself, the next morning, it was only through subsequent events that I ever arrived at a plausible conjecture as to what his business could have been. Arriving at my room, I threw a lump of cannel coal upon the grate, lighted a cigar, and spent an hour in musings of every hue, from the brightest to the most sombre; being, in truth, not so very confident as at some former periods, that this final step, which would mix me up irrevocably with the Blithedale affair, was the wisest that could possibly be taken. It was nothing short of midnight when I went to bed, after drinking a glass of particularly fine Sherry, on which I used to pride myself, in those days. It was the very last bottle; and I finished it, with a friend, the next forenoon, before setting out for Blithedale.

II

BLITHEDALE

THERE can hardly remain for me, (who am really getting to be a frosty bachelor, with another white hair, every week or so, in my moustache,) there can hardly flicker up again so cheery a blaze upon the hearth, as that which I remember, the next day, at Blithedale. It was a wood-fire, in the parlor of an old farm-house, on an April afternoon, but with the fitful gusts of a wintry snow-storm roaring in the chimney. Vividly does that fireside re-create itself, as I rake away the ashes from the embers in my memory, and blow them up with a sigh, for lack of more inspiring breath. Vividly, for an instant, but, anon, with the dimmest gleam, and with just as little fervency for my heart as for my finger-ends! The staunch oaken-logs were long ago burnt out. Their genial glow must be represented, if at all, by the merest phosphoric glimmer, like that which exudes, rather than shines, from damp fragments of decayed trees, deluding the benighted wanderer through a forest. Around such chill mockery of a fire, some few of us might sit on the withered leaves, spreading out each a palm towards the imaginary warmth, and talk over our exploded scheme for beginning the life of Paradise anew.

Paradise, indeed! Nobody else in the world, I am bold to affirm—nobody, at least, in our bleak little world of New

England—had dreamed of Paradise, that day, except as the pole suggests the tropic. Nor, with such materials as were at hand, could the most skilful architect have constructed any better imitation of Eve's bower, than might be seen in the snow-hut of an Esquimaux. But we made a summer of it, in spite of the wild drifts.

It was an April day, as already hinted, and well towards the middle of the month. When morning dawned upon me, in town, its temperature was mild enough to be pronounced even balmy, by a lodger—like myself—in one of the midmost houses of a brick-block; each house partaking of the warmth of all the rest, besides the sultriness of its individual furnace-heat. But, towards noon, there had come snow, driven along the street by a north-easterly blast, and whitening the roofs and sidewalks with a business-like perseverance that would have done credit to our severest January tempest. It set about its task, apparently as much in earnest as if it had been guaranteed from a thaw, for months to come. The greater, surely, was my heroism, when, puffing out a final whiff of cigar-smoke, I quitted my cosey pair of bachelor-rooms—with a good fire burning in the grate, and a closet right at hand, where there was still a bottle or two in the champagne-basket, and a residuum of claret in a box, and somewhat of proof in the concavity of a big demijohn—quitted, I say, these comfortable quarters, and plunged into the heart of the pitiless snow-storm, in quest of a better life.

The better life! Possibly, it would hardly look so, now; it is enough if it looked so, then. The greatest obstacle to being heroic, is the doubt whether one may not be going to prove one's self a fool; the truest heroism is, to resist the doubt—and the profoundest wisdom, to know when it ought to be resisted, and when to be obeyed.

Yet, after all, let us acknowledge it wiser, if not more sagacious, to follow out one's day-dream to its natural consummation, although, if the vision have been worth the having, it is certain never to be consummated otherwise than by a failure. And what of that! Its airiest fragments, impalpable as they may be, will possess a value that lurks not in the most ponderous realities of any practicable scheme. They are not the rubbish of the mind. Whatever else I may repent of, therefore, let it be reckoned neither among my sins nor follies, that I once had faith and force enough to form generous hopes of the world's destiny—yes!—and to do what in me lay for their accomplishment; even to the extent of quitting a warm fireside, flinging away a freshly lighted cigar, and travelling far beyond the strike of city-clocks, through a drifting snow-storm.

There were four of us who rode together through the storm; and Hollingsworth, who had agreed to be of the number, was accidentally delayed, and set forth at a later hour, alone. As we threaded the streets, I remember how the buildings, on either side, seemed to press too closely upon us, insomuch that our mighty hearts found barely room enough to throb between them. The snow-fall, too, looked inexpressibly dreary, (I had almost called it dingy,) coming down through an atmosphere of city-smoke, and alighting on the sidewalk, only to be moulded into the impress of somebody's patched boot or over-shoe. Thus, the track of an old conventionalism was visible on what was freshest from the sky. But—when we left the pavements, and our muffled hoof-tramps beat upon a desolate extent of country-road, and were effaced by the unfettered blast, as soon as stamped—then, there was better air to breathe. Air, that had not been breathed, once and again! Air, that had not been spoken into words of falsehood, formality, and error, like all the air of the dusky city!

"How pleasant it is!" remarked I, while the snow-flakes flew into my mouth, the moment it was opened. "How very mild and balmy is this country-air!"

"Ah, Coverdale, don't laugh at what little enthusiasm you

have left," said one of my companions. "I maintain that this nitrous atmosphere is really exhilarating; and, at any rate, we can never call ourselves regenerated men, till a February north-easter shall be as grateful to us as the softest breeze of June."

So we all of us took courage, riding fleetly and merrily along, by stone-fences that were half-buried in the wave-like drifts; and through patches of woodland, where the tree-trunks opposed a snow-encrusted side towards the north-east; and within ken of deserted villas, with no foot-prints in their avenues; and past scattered dwellings, whence puffed the smoke of country fires, strongly impregnated with the pungent aroma of burning peat. Sometimes, encountering a traveller, we shouted a friendly greeting; and he, unmuffling his ears to the bluster and the snow-spray, and listening eagerly, appeared to think our courtesy worth less than the trouble which it cost him. The churl! He understood the shrill whistle of the blast, but had no intelligence for our blithe tones of brotherhood. This lack of faith in our cordial sympathy, on the traveller's part, was one among the innumerable tokens how difficult a task we had in hand, for the reformation of the world. We rode on, however, with still unflagging spirits, and made such good companionship with the tempest, that, at our journey's end, we professed ourselves almost loth to bid the rude blusterer good bye. But, to own the truth, I was little better than an icicle, and began to be suspicious that I had caught a fearful cold.

And, now, we were seated by the brisk fireside of the old farm-house; the same fire that glimmers so faintly among my reminiscences, at the beginning of this chapter. There we sat, with the snow melting out of our hair and beards, and our faces all a-blaze, what with the past inclemency and present warmth. It was, indeed, a right good fire that we found awaiting us, built up of great, rough logs, and knotty limbs, and splintered fragments of an oak-tree, such as farmers are wont to keep for their own hearths; since these crooked and unmanageable boughs could never be measured into merchantable cords for the market. A family of the old Pilgrims might have swung their kettle over precisely such a fire as this, only, no doubt, a bigger one; and, contrasting it with my coal-grate, I felt, so much the more, that we had transported ourselves a world-wide distance from the system of society that shackled us at breakfast-time.

Good, comfortable Mrs. Foster (the wife of stout Silas Foster, who was to manage the farm, at a fair stipend, and be our tutor in the art of husbandry) bade us a hearty welcome. At her back—a back of generous breadth—appeared two young women, smiling most hospitably, but looking rather awkward withal, as not well knowing what was to be their position in our new arrangement of the world. We shook hands affectionately, all round, and congratulated ourselves that the blessed state of brotherhood and sisterhood, at which we aimed, might fairly be dated from this moment. Our greetings were hardly concluded, when the door opened, and Zenobia—whom I had never before seen, important as was her place in our enterprise—Zenobia entered the parlor.

This (as the reader, if at all acquainted with our literary biography, need scarcely be told) was not her real name. She had assumed it, in the first instance, as her magazine-signature; and as it accorded well with something imperial which her friends attributed to this lady's figure and deportment, they, half-laughingly, adopted it in their familiar intercourse with her. She took the appellation in good part, and even encouraged its constant use, which, in fact, was thus far appropriate, that our Zenobia—however humble looked her new philosophy—had as much native pride as any queen would have known what to do with.

III

A KNOT OF DREAMERS

ZENOBIA bade us welcome, in a fine, frank, mellow voice, and gave each of us her hand, which was very soft and warm. She had something appropriate, I recollect, to say to every individual; and what she said to myself was this:—

"I have long wished to know you, Mr. Coverdale, and to thank you for your beautiful poetry, some of which I have learned by heart;—or, rather, it has stolen into my memory, without my exercising any choice or volition about the matter. Of course—permit me to say—you do not think of relinquishing an occupation in which you have done yourself so much credit. I would almost rather give you up, as an associate, than that the world should lose one of its true poets!"

"Ah, no; there will not be the slightest danger of that, especially after this inestimable praise from Zenobia!" said I, smiling and blushing, no doubt, with excess of pleasure. "I hope, on the contrary, now, to produce something that shall really deserve to be called poetry—true, strong, natural, and sweet, as is the life which we are going to lead—something that shall have the notes of wild-birds twittering through it, or a strain like the wind-anthems in the woods, as the case may be!"

"Is it irksome to you to hear your own verses sung?" asked

Zenobia, with a gracious smile. "If so, I am very sorry; for you will certainly hear me singing them, sometimes, in the summer evenings."

"Of all things," answered I, "that is what will delight me most."

While this passed, and while she spoke to my companions, I was taking note of Zenobia's aspect; and it impressed itself on me so distinctly, that I can now summon her up like a ghost, a little wanner than the life, but otherwise identical with it. She was dressed as simply as possible, in an American print, (I think the dry-goods people call it so,) but with a silken kerchief, between which and her gown there was one glimpse of a white shoulder. It struck me as a great piece of good-fortune that there should be just that glimpse. Her hair —which was dark, glossy, and of singular abundance—was put up rather soberly and primly, without curls, or other ornament, except a single flower. It was an exotic, of rare beauty, and as fresh as if the hot-house gardener had just clipt it from the stem. That flower has struck deep root into my memory. I can both see it and smell it, at this moment. So brilliant, so rare, so costly as it must have been, and yet enduring only for a day, it was more indicative of the pride and pomp, which had a luxuriant growth in Zenobia's character, than if a great diamond had sparkled among her hair.

Her hand, though very soft, was larger than most women would like to have—or than they could afford to have—though not a whit too large in proportion with the spacious plan of Zenobia's entire development. It did one good to see a fine intellect (as hers really was, although its natural tendency lay in another direction than towards literature) so fitly cased. She was, indeed, an admirable figure of a woman, just on the hither verge of her richest maturity, with a combination of features which it is safe to call remarkably beautiful, even if some fastidious persons might pronounce them a little deficient in softness and delicacy. But we find enough of those attributes, everywhere. Preferable—by way of variety, at least —was Zenobia's bloom, health, and vigor, which she possessed in such overflow that a man might well have fallen in love with her for their sake only. In her quiet moods, she seemed rather indolent; but when really in earnest, particularly if there were a spice of bitter feeling, she grew all alive, to her finger-tips.

"I am the first-comer," Zenobia went on to say, while her smile beamed warmth upon us all; "so I take the part of hostess, for to-day, and welcome you as if to my own fireside. You shall be my guests, too, at supper. Tomorrow, if you please, we will be brethren and sisters, and begin our new life from day-break."

"Have we our various parts assigned?" asked some one.

"Oh, we of the softer sex," responded Zenobia, with her mellow, almost broad laugh—most delectable to hear, but not in the least like an ordinary woman's laugh—"we women (there are four of us here, already) will take the domestic and indoor part of the business, as a matter of course. To bake, to boil, to roast, to fry, to stew—to wash, and iron, and scrub, and sweep, and, at our idler intervals, to repose ourselves on knitting and sewing—these, I suppose, must be feminine occupations for the present. By-and-by, perhaps, when our individual adaptations begin to develop themselves, it may be that some of us, who wear the petticoat, will go afield, and leave the weaker brethren to take our places in the kitchen!"

"What a pity," I remarked, "that the kitchen, and the house-work generally, cannot be left out of our system altogether! It is odd enough, that the kind of labor which falls to the lot of women is just that which chiefly distinguishes artificial life—the life of degenerated mortals—from the life of Paradise. Eve had no dinner-pot, and no clothes to mend, and no washing-day."

"I am afraid," said Zenobia, with mirth gleaming out of

her eyes, "we shall find some difficulty in adopting the
Paradisiacal system, for at least a month to come. Look at
that snow-drift sweeping past the window! Are there any figs
ripe, do you think? Have the pine-apples been gathered,
to-day? Would you like a bread-fruit, or a cocoa-nut? Shall
I run out and pluck you some roses? No, no, Mr. Coverdale,
the only flower hereabouts is the one in my hair, which I got
out of a green-house, this morning. As for the garb of Eden,"
added she, shivering playfully, "I shall not assume it till after
May-day!"

Assuredly, Zenobia could not have intended it—the fault
must have been entirely in my imagination—but these last
words, together with something in her manner, irresistibly
brought up a picture of that fine, perfectly developed figure,
in Eve's earliest garment. I almost fancied myself actually
beholding it. Her free, careless, generous modes of expression
often had this effect of creating images which, though pure,
are hardly felt to be quite decorous, when born of a thought
that passes between man and woman. I imputed it, at that
time, to Zenobia's noble courage, conscious of no harm, and
scorning the petty restraints which take the life and color out
of other women's conversation. There was another peculiarity
about her. We seldom meet with women, now-a-days, and in
this country, who impress us as being women at all; their sex
fades away and goes for nothing, in ordinary intercourse.
Not so with Zenobia. One felt an influence breathing out of
her, such as we might suppose to come from Eve, when she
was just made, and her Creator brought her to Adam, saying—
'Behold, here is a woman!' Not that I would convey the idea
of especial gentleness, grace, modesty, and shyness, but of a
certain warm and rich characteristic, which seems, for the
most part, to have been refined away out of the feminine
system.

"And now," continued Zenobia, "I must go and help get
supper. Do you think you can be content—instead of figs,

pine-apples, and all the other delicacies of Adam's supper-table—with tea and toast, and a certain modest supply of ham and tongue, which, with the instinct of a housewife, I brought hither in a basket? And there shall be bread-and-milk, too, if the innocence of your taste demands it."

The whole sisterhood now went about their domestic avocations, utterly declining our offers to assist, farther than by bringing wood, for the kitchen-fire, from a huge pile in the back-yard. After heaping up more than a sufficient quantity, we returned to the sitting-room, drew our chairs closer to the hearth, and began to talk over our prospects. Soon, with a tremendous stamping in the entry, appeared Silas Foster, lank, stalwart, uncouth, and grisly-bearded. He came from foddering the cattle, in the barn, and from the field, where he had been ploughing, until the depth of the snow rendered it impossible to draw a furrow. He greeted us in pretty much the same tone as if he were speaking to his oxen, took a quid from his iron tobacco-box, pulled off his wet cow-hide boots, and sat down before the fire in his stocking-feet. The steam arose from his soaked garments, so that the stout yeoman looked vaporous and spectre-like.

"Well, folks," remarked Silas, "you'll be wishing yourselves back to town again, if this weather holds!"

And, true enough, there was a look of gloom, as the twilight fell silently and sadly out of the sky, its gray or sable flakes intermingling themselves with the fast descending snow. The storm, in its evening aspect, was decidedly dreary. It seemed to have arisen for our especial behoof; a symbol of the cold, desolate, distrustful phantoms that invariably haunt the mind, on the eve of adventurous enterprises, to warn us back within the boundaries of ordinary life.

But our courage did not quail. We would not allow ourselves to be depressed by the snow-drift, trailing past the window, any more than if it had been the sigh of a summer wind among rustling boughs. There have been few brighter seasons for us, than that. If ever men might lawfully dream awake, and give utterance to their wildest visions, without dread of laughter or scorn on the part of the audience—yes, and speak of earthly happiness, for themselves and mankind, as an object to be hopefully striven for, and probably attained —we, who made that little semi-circle round the blazing fire, were those very men. We had left the rusty iron frame-work of society behind us. We had broken through many hindrances that are powerful enough to keep most people on the weary tread-mill of the established system, even while they feel its irksomeness almost as intolerable as we did. We had stept down from the pulpit; we had flung aside the pen; we had shut up the ledger; we had thrown off that sweet, bewitching, enervating indolence, which is better, after all, than most of the enjoyments within mortal grasp. It was our purpose—a generous one, certainly, and absurd, no doubt, in full proportion with its generosity—to give up whatever we had heretofore attained, for the sake of showing mankind the example of a life governed by other than the false and cruel principles, on which human society has all along been based.

And, first of all, we had divorced ourselves from Pride, and were striving to supply its place with familiar love. We meant to lessen the laboring man's great burthen of toil, by performing our due share of it at the cost of our own thews and sinews. We sought our profit by mutual aid, instead of wresting it by the strong hand from an enemy, or filching it craftily from those less shrewd than ourselves, (if, indeed, there were any such, in New England,) or winning it by selfish competition with a neighbor; in one or another of which fashions, every son of woman both perpetrates and suffers his share of the common evil, whether he chooses it or no. And, as the basis of our institution, we purposed to offer up the earnest toil of our bodies, as a prayer, no less than an effort, for the advancement of our race.

Therefore, if we built splendid castles (phalansteries,

perhaps, they might be more fitly called,) and pictured beautiful scenes, among the fervid coals of the hearth around which we were clustering—and if all went to rack with the crumbling embers, and have never since arisen out of the ashes—let us take to ourselves no shame. In my own behalf, I rejoice that I could once think better of the world's improvability than it deserved. It is a mistake into which men seldom fall twice, in a lifetime; or, if so, the rarer and higher is the nature that can thus magnanimously persist in error.

Stout Silas Foster mingled little in our conversation; but when he did speak, it was very much to some practical purpose. For instance:—

"Which man among you," quoth he, "is the best judge of swine? Some of us must go to the next Brighton fair, and buy half-a-dozen pigs!"

Pigs! Good heavens, had we come out from among the swinish multitude, for this? And again, in reference to some discussion about raising early vegetables for the market:—

"We shall never make any hand at market-gardening," said Silas Foster, "unless the women-folks will undertake to do all the weeding. We haven't team enough for that and the regular farm-work, reckoning three of you city-folks as worth one common field-hand. No, no, I tell you, we should have to get up a little too early in the morning, to compete with the market-gardeners round Boston!"

It struck me as rather odd, that one of the first questions raised, after our separation from the greedy, struggling, self-seeking world, should relate to the possibility of getting the advantage over the outside barbarians, in their own field of labor. But, to own the truth, I very soon became sensible, that, as regarded society at large, we stood in a position of new hostility, rather than new brotherhood. Nor could this fail to be the case, in some degree, until the bigger and better half of society should range itself on our side. Constituting so pitiful a minority as now, we were inevitably estranged from the rest of mankind, in pretty fair proportion with the strictness of our mutual bond among ourselves.

This dawning idea, however, was driven back into my inner consciousness by the entrance of Zenobia. She came with the welcome intelligence that supper was on the table. Looking at herself in the glass, and perceiving that her one magnificent flower had grown rather languid, (probably by being exposed to the fervency of the kitchen-fire,) she flung it on the floor, as unconcernedly as a village-girl would throw away a faded violet. The action seemed proper to her character; although, methought, it would still more have befitted the bounteous nature of this beautiful woman to scatter fresh flowers from her hand, and to revive faded ones by her touch. Nevertheless—it was a singular, but irresistible effect—the presence of Zenobia caused our heroic enterprise to show like an illusion, a masquerade, a pastoral, a counterfeit Arcadia, in which we grown-up men and women were making a play-day of the years that were given us to live in. I tried to analyze this impression, but not with much success.

"It really vexes me," observed Zenobia, as we left the room, "that Mr. Hollingsworth should be such a laggard. I should not have thought him at all the sort of person to be turned back by a puff of contrary wind, or a few snow-flakes drifting into his face."

"Do you know Hollingsworth personally?" I inquired.

"No; only as an auditor—auditress, I mean—of some of his lectures," said she. "What a voice he has! And what a man he is! Yet not so much an intellectual man, I should say, as a great heart; at least, he moved me more deeply than I think myself capable of being moved, except by the stroke of a true, strong heart against my own. It is a sad pity that he should have devoted his glorious powers to such a grimy, unbeautiful, and positively hopeless object as this reformation of criminals, about which he makes himself and his wretchedly small audiences so very miserable. To tell you a secret, I never could tolerate a philanthropist, before. Could you?"

"By no means," I answered; "neither can I now!"

"They are, indeed, an odiously disagreeable set of mortals," continued Zenobia. "I should like Mr. Hollingsworth a great deal better, if the philanthropy had been left out. At all events, as a mere matter of taste, I wish he would let the bad people alone, and try to benefit those who are not already past his help. Do you suppose he will be content to spend his life— or even a few months of it—among tolerably virtuous and comfortable individuals, like ourselves?"

"Upon my word, I doubt it," said I. "If we wish to keep him with us, we must systematically commit at least one crime apiece! Mere peccadillos will not satisfy him."

Zenobia turned, sidelong, a strange kind of a glance upon me; but, before I could make out what it meant, we had entered the kitchen, where, in accordance with the rustic simplicity of our new life, the supper-table was spread.

IV

THE SUPPER-TABLE

THE PLEASANT firelight! I must still keep harping on it.

The kitchen-hearth had an old-fashioned breadth, depth, and spaciousness, far within which lay what seemed the butt of a good-sized oak-tree, with the moisture bubbling merrily out of both ends. It was now half-an-hour beyond dusk. The blaze from an armfull of substantial sticks, rendered more combustible by brush-wood and pine, flickered powerfully on the smoke-blackened walls, and so cheered our spirits that we cared not what inclemency might rage and roar, on the other side of our illuminated windows. A yet sultrier warmth was bestowed by a goodly quantity of peat, which was crumbling to white ashes among the burning brands, and incensed the kitchen with its not ungrateful fragrance. The exuberance of this household fire would alone have sufficed to bespeak us no true farmers; for the New England yeoman, if he have the misfortune to dwell within practicable distance of a wood-market, is as niggardly of each stick as if it were a bar of California gold.

But it was fortunate for us, on that wintry eve of our untried life, to enjoy the warm and radiant luxury of a somewhat too abundant fire. If it served no other purpose, it made the men look so full of youth, warm blood, and hope, and the women—

such of them, at least, as were anywise convertible by its magic —so very beautiful, that I would cheerfully have spent my last dollar to prolong the blaze. As for Zenobia, there was a glow in her cheeks that made me think of Pandora, fresh from Vulcan's workshop, and full of the celestial warmth by dint of which he had tempered and moulded her.

"Take your places, my dear friends all," cried she; "seat yourselves without ceremony—and you shall be made happy with such tea as not many of the world's working-people, except yourselves, will find in their cups to-night. After this one supper, you may drink butter-milk, if you please. To-night, we will quaff this nectar, which, I assure you, could not be bought with gold."

We all sat down—grisly Silas Foster, his rotund helpmate, and the two bouncing handmaidens, included—and looked at one another in a friendly, but rather awkward way. It was the first practical trial of our theories of equal brotherhood and sisterhood; and we people of superior cultivation and refinement (for as such, I presume, we unhesitatingly reckoned ourselves) felt as if something were already accomplished towards the millennium of love. The truth is, however, that the laboring oar was with our unpolished companions; it being far easier to condescend, than to accept of condescension. Neither did I refrain from questioning, in secret, whether some of us—and Zenobia among the rest—would so quietly have taken our places among these good people, save for the cherished consciousness that it was not by necessity, but choice. Though we saw fit to drink our tea out of earthen cups to-night, and in earthen company, it was at our own option to use pictured porcelain and handle silver forks again, tomorrow. This same salvo, as to the power of regaining our former position, contributed much, I fear, to the equanimity with which we subsequently bore many of the hardships and humiliations of a life of toil. If ever I have deserved—(which has not often been the case, and, I think, never)—but if ever

I did deserve to be soundly cuffed by a fellow-mortal, for secretly putting weight upon some imaginary social advantage, it must have been while I was striving to prove myself ostentatiously his equal, and no more. It was while I sat beside him on his cobbler's bench, or clinked my hoe against his own, in the cornfield, or broke the same crust of bread, my earth-grimed hand to his, at our noontide lunch. The poor, proud man should look at both sides of sympathy like this.

The silence, which followed upon our sitting down to table, grew rather oppressive; indeed, it was hardly broken by a word, during the first round of Zenobia's fragrant tea.

"I hope," said I, at last, "that our blazing windows will be visible a great way off. There is nothing so pleasant and encouraging to a solitary traveller, on a stormy night, as a flood of firelight, seen amid the gloom. These ruddy window-panes cannot fail to cheer the hearts of all that look at them. Are they not warm and bright with the beacon-fire which we have kindled for humanity?"

"The blaze of that brush-wood will only last a minute or two longer," observed Silas Foster; but whether he meant to insinuate that our moral illumination would have as brief a term, I cannot say.

"Meantime," said Zenobia, "it may serve to guide some wayfarer to a shelter."

And, just as she said this, there came a knock at the house-door.

"There is one of the world's wayfarers!" said I.

"Aye, aye, just so!" quoth Silas Foster. "Our firelight will draw stragglers, just as a candle draws dor-bugs, on a summer night."

Whether to enjoy a dramatic suspense, or that we were selfishly contrasting our own comfort with the chill and dreary situation of the unknown person at the threshold—or that some of us city-folk felt a little startled at the knock which came so unseasonably, through night and storm, to the door of the lonely farm-house—so it happened, that nobody, for an instant or two, arose to answer the summons. Pretty soon, there came another knock. The first had been moderately loud; the second was smitten so forcibly that the knuckles of the applicant must have left their mark in the door-panel.

"He knocks as if he had a right to come in," said Zenobia, laughing. "And what are we thinking of? It must be Mr. Hollingsworth!"

Hereupon, I went to the door, unbolted, and flung it wide open. There, sure enough, stood Hollingsworth, his shaggy great-coat all covered with snow; so that he looked quite as much like a polar bear as a modern philanthropist.

"Sluggish hospitality, this!" said he, in those deep tones of his, which seemed to come out of a chest as capacious as a barrel. "It would have served you right if I had lain down and spent the night on the door-step, just for the sake of putting you to shame. But here is a guest, who will need a warmer and softer bed."

And stepping back to the wagon, in which he had journeyed hither, Hollingsworth received into his arms, and deposited on the door-step, a figure enveloped in a cloak. It was evidently a woman; or rather—judging from the ease with which he lifted her, and the little space which she seemed to fill in his arms—a slim and unsubstantial girl. As she showed some hesitation about entering the door, Hollingsworth, with his usual directness and lack of ceremony, urged her forward, not merely within the entry, but into the warm and strongly lighted kitchen.

"Who is this?" whispered I, remaining behind with him, while he was taking off his great-coat.

"Who? Really, I don't know," answered Hollingsworth, looking at me with some surprise. "It is a young person who belongs here, however; and, no doubt, she has been expected. Zenobia, or some of the women-folks, can tell you all about it."

"I think not," said I, glancing towards the new-comer and

the other occupants of the kitchen. "Nobody seems to welcome her. I should hardly judge that she was an expected guest."

"Well, well," said Hollingsworth, quietly. "We'll make it right."

The stranger, or whatever she were, remained standing precisely on that spot of the kitchen-floor, to which Hollingsworth's kindly hand had impelled her. The cloak falling partly off, she was seen to be a very young woman, dressed in a poor, but decent gown, made high in the neck, and without any regard to fashion or smartness. Her brown hair fell down from beneath a hood, not in curls, but with only a slight wave; her face was of a wan, almost sickly hue, betokening habitual seclusion from the sun and free atmosphere, like a flower-shrub that had done its best to blossom in too scanty light. To complete the pitiableness of her aspect, she shivered either with cold, or fear, or nervous excitement, so that you might have beheld her shadow vibrating on the fire-lighted wall. In short, there has seldom been seen so depressed and sad a figure as this young girl's; and it was hardly possible to help being angry with her, from mere despair of doing anything for her comfort. The fantasy occurred to me, that she was some desolate kind of a creature, doomed to wander about in snow-storms, and that, though the ruddiness of our window-panes had tempted her into a human dwelling, she would not remain long enough to melt the icicles out of her hair.

Another conjecture likewise came into my mind. Recollecting Hollingsworth's sphere of philanthropic action, I deemed it possible that he might have brought one of his guilty patients, to be wrought upon, and restored to spiritual health, by the pure influences which our mode of life would create.

As yet, the girl had not stirred. She stood near the door, fixing a pair of large, brown, melancholy eyes upon Zenobia—only upon Zenobia!—she evidently saw nothing else in the room, save that bright, fair, rosy, beautiful woman. It was the strangest look I ever witnessed; long a mystery to me, and forever a memory. Once, she seemed about to move forward and greet her—I know not with what warmth, or with what words;—but, finally, instead of doing so, she drooped down upon her knees, clasped her hands, and gazed piteously into Zenobia's face. Meeting no kindly reception, her head fell on her bosom.

I never thoroughly forgave Zenobia for her conduct on this occasion. But women are always more cautious, in their casual hospitalities, than men.

"What does the girl mean?" cried she, in rather a sharp tone. "Is she crazy? Has she no tongue?"

And here Hollingsworth stept forward.

"No wonder if the poor child's tongue is frozen in her mouth," said he—and I think he positively frowned at Zenobia —"The very heart will be frozen in her bosom, unless you women can warm it, among you, with the warmth that ought to be in your own!"

Hollingsworth's appearance was very striking, at this moment. He was then about thirty years old, but looked several years older, with his great shaggy head, his heavy brow, his dark complexion, his abundant beard, and the rude strength with which his features seemed to have been hammered out of iron, rather than chiselled or moulded from any finer or softer material. His figure was not tall, but massive and brawny, and well befitting his original occupation, which —as the reader probably knows—was that of a blacksmith. As for external polish, or mere courtesy of manner, he never possessed more than a tolerably educated bear; although, in his gentler moods, there was a tenderness in his voice, eyes, mouth, in his gesture, and in every indescribable manifestation, which few men could resist, and no woman. But he now looked stern and reproachful; and it was with that inauspicious meaning in his glance, that Hollingsworth first met Zenobia's eyes, and began his influence upon her life.

To my surprise, Zenobia—of whose haughty spirit I had been told so many examples—absolutely changed color, and seemed mortified and confused.

"You do not quite do me justice, Mr. Hollingsworth," said she, almost humbly. "I am willing to be kind to the poor girl. Is she a protégée of yours? What can I do for her?"

"Have you anything to ask of this lady?" said Hollingsworth, kindly, to the girl. "I remember you mentioned her name, before we left town."

"Only that she will shelter me," replied the girl, tremulously. "Only that she will let me be always near her!"

"Well, indeed," exclaimed Zenobia, recovering herself, and laughing, "this is an adventure, and well worthy to be the first incident in our life of love and free-heartedness! But I accept it, for the present, without further question—only," added she, "it would be a convenience if we knew your name!"

"Priscilla," said the girl; and it appeared to me that she hesitated whether to add anything more, and decided in the negative. "Pray do not ask me my other name—at least, not yet—if you will be so kind to a forlorn creature."

Priscilla! Priscilla! I repeated the name to myself, three or four times; and, in that little space, this quaint and prim cognomen had so amalgamated itself with my idea of the girl, that it seemed as if no other name could have adhered to her for a moment. Heretofore, the poor thing had not shed any tears; but now that she found herself received, and at least temporarily established, the big drops began to ooze out from beneath her eyelids, as if she were full of them. Perhaps it showed the iron substance of my heart, that I could not help smiling at this odd scene of unknown and unaccountable calamity, into which our cheerful party had been entrapped, without the liberty of choosing whether to sympathize or no.

Hollingsworth's behavior was certainly a great deal more creditable than mine.

"Let us not pry farther into her secrets," he said to Zenobia and the rest of us, apart—and his dark, shaggy face looked really beautiful with its expression of thoughtful benevolence —"Let us conclude that Providence has sent her to us, as the first fruits of the world, which we have undertaken to make happier than we find it. Let us warm her poor, shivering body with this good fire, and her poor, shivering heart with our best kindness. Let us feed her, and make her one of us. As we do by this friendless girl, so shall we prosper! And, in good time, whatever is desirable for us to know will be melted out of her, as inevitably as those tears which we see now."

"At least," remarked I, "you may tell us how and where you met with her."

"An old man brought her to my lodgings," answered Hollingsworth, "and begged me to convey her to Blithedale, where—so I understood him—she had friends. And this is positively all I know about the matter."

Grim Silas Foster, all this while, had been busy at the supper-table, pouring out his own tea, and gulping it down with no more sense of its exquisiteness than if it were a decoction of catnip; helping himself to pieces of dipt toast on the flat of his knife-blade, and dropping half of it on the table-cloth; using the same serviceable implement to cut slice after slice of ham; perpetrating terrible enormities with the butter-plate; and, in all other respects, behaving less like a civilized Christian than the worst kind of an ogre. Being, by this time, fully gorged, he crowned his amiable exploits with a draught from the water-pitcher, and then favored us with his opinion about the business in hand. And, certainly, though they proceeded out of an unwiped mouth, his expressions did him honor.

FANSHAWE,

A TALE.

"Wilt thou go on with me?"—SOUTHEY.

❖

BOSTON:

MARSH & CAPEN, 362 WASHINGTON STREET.

PRESS OF PUTNAM AND HUNT.

1828.

TITLE PAGE OF THE FIRST EDITION OF "FANSHAWE" IN THE OHIO STATE UNIVERSITY LIBRARIES

"Give the girl a hot cup of tea, and a thick slice of this first-rate bacon," said Silas, like a sensible man as he was. "That's what she wants. Let her stay with us as long as she likes, and help in the kitchen, and take the cow-breath at milking-time; and, in a week or two, she'll begin to look like a creature of this world!"

So we sat down again to supper, and Priscilla along with us.

V

UNTIL BEDTIME

S ILAS FOSTER, by the time we concluded our meal, had
  stript off his coat and planted himself on a low chair
  by the kitchen-fire, with a lap-stone, a hammer, a piece
of sole-leather, and some waxed ends, in order to cobble an
old pair of cow-hide boots; he being, in his own phrase,
'something of a dab' (whatever degree of skill that may imply)
at the shoemaking-business. We heard the tap of his hammer,
at intervals, for the rest of the evening. The remainder of the
party adjourned to the sitting-room. Good Mrs. Foster took
her knitting-work, and soon fell fast asleep, still keeping her
needles in brisk movement, and, to the best of my observation,
absolutely footing a stocking out of the texture of a dream.
And a very substantial stocking it seemed to be. One of the
two handmaidens hemmed a towel, and the other appeared
to be making a ruffle, for her Sunday's wear, out of a little
bit of embroidered muslin, which Zenobia had probably
given her.

It was curious to observe how trustingly, and yet how
timidly, our poor Priscilla betook herself into the shadow of
Zenobia's protection. She sat beside her on a stool, looking
up, every now and then, with an expression of humble
delight at her new friend's beauty. A brilliant woman is
often an object of the devoted admiration—it might almost be

termed worship, or idolatry—of some young girl, who perhaps beholds the cynosure only at an awful distance, and has as little hope of personal intercourse as of climbing among the stars of heaven. We men are too gross to comprehend it. Even a woman, of mature age, despises or laughs at such a passion. There occurred to me no mode of accounting for Priscilla's behavior, except by supposing that she had read some of Zenobia's stories, (as such literature goes everywhere,) or her tracts in defence of the sex, and had come hither with the one purpose of being her slave. There is nothing parallel to this, I believe—nothing so foolishly disinterested, and hardly anything so beautiful—in the masculine nature, at whatever epoch of life; or, if there be, a fine and rare development of character might reasonably be looked for, from the youth who should prove himself capable of such self-forgetful affection.

Zenobia happening to change her seat, I took the opportunity, in an under tone, to suggest some such notion as the above.

"Since you see the young woman in so poetical a light," replied she, in the same tone, "you had better turn the affair into a ballad. It is a grand subject, and worthy of supernatural machinery. The storm, the startling knock at the door, the entrance of the sable knight Hollingsworth and this shadowy snow-maiden, who, precisely at the stroke of midnight, shall melt away at my feet, in a pool of ice-cold water, and give me my death with a pair of wet slippers! And when the verses are written, and polished quite to your mind, I will favor you with my idea as to what the girl really is."

"Pray let me have it now," said I. "It shall be woven into the ballad."

"She is neither more nor less," answered Zenobia, "than a seamstress from the city, and she has probably no more transcendental purpose than to do my miscellaneous sewing; for I suppose she will hardly expect to make my dresses."

"How can you decide upon her so easily?" I inquired.

"Oh, we women judge one another by tokens that escape the obtuseness of masculine perceptions," said Zenobia. "There is no proof, which you would be likely to appreciate, except the needle marks on the tip of her forefinger. Then, my supposition perfectly accounts for her paleness, her nervousness, and her wretched fragility. Poor thing! She has been stifled with the heat of a salamander-stove, in a small, close room, and has drunk coffee, and fed upon dough-nuts, raisins, candy, and all such trash, till she is scarcely half-alive; and so, as she has hardly any physique, a poet, like Mr. Miles Coverdale, may be allowed to think her spiritual!"

"Look at her now!" whispered I.

Priscilla was gazing towards us, with an inexpressible sorrow in her wan face, and great tears running down her cheeks. It was difficult to resist the impression, that, cautiously as we had lowered our voices, she must have overheard and been wounded by Zenobia's scornful estimate of her character and purposes.

"What ears the girl must have!" whispered Zenobia, with a look of vexation, partly comic and partly real. "I will confess to you that I cannot quite make her out. However, I am positively not an ill-natured person, unless when very grievously provoked; and as you, and especially Mr. Hollingsworth, take so much interest in this odd creature—and as she knocks, with a very slight tap, against my own heart, likewise—why, I mean to let her in! From this moment, I will be reasonably kind to her. There is no pleasure in tormenting a person of one's own sex, even if she do favor one with a little more love than one can conveniently dispose of;— and that, let me say, Mr. Coverdale, is the most troublesome offence you can offer to a woman."

"Thank you!" said I, smiling. "I don't mean to be guilty of it."

She went towards Priscilla, took her hand, and passed her own rosy finger-tips, with a pretty, caressing movement, over the girl's hair. The touch had a magical effect. So vivid a look of joy flushed up beneath those fingers, that it seemed as if the sad and wan Priscilla had been snatched away, and another kind of creature substituted in her place. This one caress, bestowed voluntarily by Zenobia, was evidently received as a pledge of all that the stranger sought from her, whatever the unuttered boon might be. From that instant, too, she melted in quietly amongst us, and was no longer a foreign element. Though always an object of peculiar interest, a riddle, and a theme of frequent discussion, her tenure at Blithedale was thenceforth fixed; we no more thought of questioning it, than if Priscilla had been recognized as a domestic sprite, who had haunted the rustic fireside, of old, before we had ever been warmed by its blaze.

She now produced, out of a work-bag that she had with her, some little wooden instruments, (what they are called, I never knew,) and proceeded to knit, or net, an article which ultimately took the shape of a silk purse. As the work went on, I remembered to have seen just such purses, before. Indeed, I was the possessor of one. Their peculiar excellence, besides the great delicacy and beauty of the manufacture, lay in the almost impossibility that any uninitiated person should discover the aperture; although, to a practised touch, they would open as wide as charity or prodigality might wish. I wondered if it were not a symbol of Priscilla's own mystery.

Notwithstanding the new confidence with which Zenobia had inspired her, our guest showed herself disquieted by the storm. When the strong puffs of wind spattered the snow against the windows, and made the oaken frame of the farm-house creak, she looked at us apprehensively, as if to inquire whether these tempestuous outbreaks did not betoken some unusual mischief in the shrieking blast. She had been bred up, no doubt, in some close nook, some inauspiciously sheltered court of the city, where the uttermost rage of a tempest, though it might scatter down the slates of the roof into the bricked area, could not shake the casement of her little room. The sense of vast, undefined space, pressing from the outside against the black panes of our uncurtained windows, was fearful to the poor girl, heretofore accustomed to the narrowness of human limits, with the lamps of neighboring tenements glimmering across the street. The house probably seemed to her adrift on the great ocean of the night. A little parallelogram of sky was all that she had hitherto known of nature; so that she felt the awfulness that really exists in its limitless extent. Once, while the blast was bellowing, she caught hold of Zenobia's robe, with precisely the air of one who hears her own name spoken, at a distance, but is unutterably reluctant to obey the call.

We spent rather an incommunicative evening. Hollingsworth hardly said a word, unless when repeatedly and pertinaciously addressed. Then, indeed, he would glare upon us from the thick shrubbery of his meditations, like a tiger out of a jungle, make the briefest reply possible, and betake himself back into the solitude of his heart and mind. The poor fellow had contracted this ungracious habit from the intensity with which he contemplated his own ideas, and the infrequent sympathy which they met with from his auditors; a circumstance that seemed only to strengthen the implicit confidence that he awarded to them. His heart, I imagine, was never really interested in our socialist scheme, but was forever busy with his strange, and, as most people thought it, impracticable plan for the reformation of criminals, through an appeal to their higher instincts. Much as I liked Hollingsworth, it cost me many a groan to tolerate him on this point. He ought to have commenced his investigation of the subject by perpetrating some huge sin, in his proper person, and examining the condition of his higher instincts, afterwards.

The rest of us formed ourselves into a committee for providing our infant Community with an appropriate name; a matter of greatly more difficulty than the uninitiated reader would suppose. Blithedale was neither good nor bad. We should have resumed the old Indian name of the premises, had it possessed the oil-and-honey flow which the aborigines were so often happy in communicating to their local appellations; but it chanced to be a harsh, ill-connected, and interminable word, which seemed to fill the mouth with a mixture of very stiff clay and very crumbly pebbles. Zenobia suggested 'Sunny Glimpse,' as expressive of a vista into a better system of society. This we turned over and over, for awhile, acknowledging its prettiness, but concluded it to be rather too fine and sentimental a name (a fault inevitable by literary ladies, in such attempts) for sun-burnt men to work under. I ventured to whisper 'Utopia,' which, however, was unanimously scouted down, and the proposer very harshly maltreated, as if he had intended a latent satire. Some were for calling our institution 'The Oasis,' in view of its being the one green spot in the moral sand-waste of the world; but others insisted on a proviso for reconsidering the matter, at a twelvemonth's end; when a final decision might be had, whether to name it 'The Oasis,' or 'Saharah.' So, at last, finding it impracticable to hammer out anything better, we resolved that the spot should still be Blithedale, as being of good augury enough.

The evening wore on, and the outer solitude looked in upon us through the windows, gloomy, wild, and vague, like another state of existence, close beside the littler sphere of warmth and light in which we were the prattlers and bustlers of a moment. By-and-by, the door was opened by Silas Foster, with a cotton handkerchief about his head, and a tallow candle in his hand.

"Take my advice, brother-farmers," said he, with a great, broad, bottomless yawn, "and get to bed as soon as you can. I shall sound the horn at day-break; and we've got the cattle to fodder, and nine cows to milk, and a dozen other things to do, before breakfast."

Thus ended the first evening at Blithedale. I went shivering

to my fireless chamber, with the miserable consciousness
(which had been growing upon me for several hours past)
that I had caught a tremendous cold, and should probably
awaken, at the blast of the horn, a fit subject for a hospital.
The night proved a feverish one. During the greater part of
it, I was in that vilest of states when a fixed idea remains
in the mind, like the nail in Sisera's brain, while innumerable
other ideas go and come, and flutter to-and-fro, combining
constant transition with intolerable sameness. Had I made a
record of that night's half-waking dreams, it is my belief that
it would have anticipated several of the chief incidents of
this narrative, including a dim shadow of its catastrophe.
Starting up in bed, at length, I saw that the storm was past,
and the moon was shining on the snowy landscape, which
looked like a lifeless copy of the world in marble.

From the bank of the distant river, which was shimmering
in the moonlight, came the black shadow of the only cloud
in heaven, driven swiftly by the wind, and passing over
meadow and hillock—vanishing amid tufts of leafless trees,
but reappearing on the hither side—until it swept across
our door-step.

How cold an Arcadia was this!

VI

COVERDALE'S SICK-CHAMBER

THE HORN sounded at day-break, as Silas Foster had forewarned us, harsh, uproarious, inexorably drawn out, and as sleep-dispelling as if this hard-hearted old yeoman had got hold of the trump of doom.

On all sides, I could hear the creaking of the bedsteads, as the brethren of Blithedale started from slumber, and thrust themselves into their habiliments, all awry, no doubt, in their haste to begin the reformation of the world. Zenobia put her head into the entry, and besought Silas Foster to cease his clamor, and to be kind enough to leave an armful of firewood and a pail of water at her chamber-door. Of the whole household—unless, indeed, it were Priscilla, for whose habits, in this particular, I cannot vouch—of all our apostolic society, whose mission was to bless mankind, Hollingsworth, I apprehend, was the only one who began the enterprise with prayer. My sleeping-room being but thinly partitioned from his, the solemn murmur of his voice made its way to my ears, compelling me to be an auditor of his awful privacy with the Creator. It affected me with a deep reverence for Hollings-worth, which no familiarity then existing, or that afterwards grew more intimate between us—no, nor my subsequent perception of his own great errors—ever quite effaced. It is so rare, in these times, to meet with a man of prayerful habits,

· 39 ·

(except, of course, in the pulpit,) that such an one is decidedly marked out by a light of transfiguration, shed upon him in the divine interview from which he passes into his daily life.

As for me, I lay abed, and, if I said my prayers, it was backward, cursing my day as bitterly as patient Job himself. The truth was, the hot-house warmth of a town-residence, and the luxurious life in which I indulged myself, had taken much of the pith out of my physical system; and the wintry blast of the preceding day, together with the general chill of our airy old farm-house, had got fairly into my heart and the marrow of my bones. In this predicament, I seriously wished—selfish as it may appear—that the reformation of society had been postponed about half-a-century, or at all events, to such a date as should have put my intermeddling with it entirely out of the question.

What, in the name of common-sense, had I to do with any better society than I had always lived in! It had satisfied me well enough. My pleasant bachelor-parlor, sunny and shadowy, curtained and carpeted, with the bed-chamber adjoining; my centre-table, strewn with books and periodicals; my writing-desk, with a half-finished poem in a stanza of my own contrivance; my morning lounge at the reading-room or picture-gallery; my noontide walk along the cheery pavement, with the suggestive succession of human faces, and the brisk throb of human life, in which I shared; my dinner at the Albion, where I had a hundred dishes at command, and could banquet as delicately as the wizard Michael Scott, when the devil fed him from the King of France's kitchen; my evening at the billiard-club, the concert, the theatre, or at somebody's party, if I pleased:—what could be better than all this? Was it better to hoe, to mow, to toil and moil amidst the accumulations of a barn-yard, to be the chambermaid of two yoke of oxen and a dozen cows, to eat salt-beef and earn it with the sweat of my brow, and thereby take the tough morsel out of some wretch's mouth, into whose vocation I had thrust myself? Above all, was it better to have a fever, and die blaspheming, as I was like to do?

In this wretched plight, with a furnace in my heart, and another in my head, by the heat of which I was kept constantly at the boiling point—yet shivering at the bare idea of extruding so much as a finger into the icy atmosphere of the room—I kept my bed until breakfast-time, when Hollingsworth knocked at the door, and entered.

"Well, Coverdale," cried he, "you bid fair to make an admirable farmer! Don't you mean to get up to-day?"

"Neither to-day nor tomorrow," said I, hopelessly. "I doubt if I ever rise again!"

"What is the matter now?" he asked.

I told him my piteous case, and besought him to send me back to town, in a close carriage.

"No, no!" said Hollingsworth, with kindly seriousness. "If you are really sick, we must take care of you."

Accordingly, he built a fire in my chamber, and having little else to do while the snow lay on the ground, established himself as my nurse. A doctor was sent for, who, being homeopathic, gave me as much medicine, in the course of a fortnight's attendance, as would have lain on the point of a needle. They fed me on water-gruel, and I speedily became a skeleton above ground. But, after all, I have many precious recollections connected with that fit of sickness.

Hollingsworth's more than brotherly attendance gave me inexpressible comfort. Most men—and, certainly, I could not always claim to be one of the exceptions—have a natural indifference, if not an absolutely hostile feeling, towards those whom disease, or weakness, or calamity of any kind, causes to faulter and faint amid the rude jostle of our selfish existence. The education of Christianity, it is true, the sympathy of a like experience, and the example of women, may soften, and possibly subvert, this ugly characteristic of our sex. But it is originally there, and has likewise its analogy in the practice of our brute brethren, who hunt the sick or disabled member of the herd from among them, as an enemy. It is for this reason that the stricken deer goes apart, and the sick lion grimly withdraws himself into his den. Except in love, or the attachments of kindred, or other very long and habitual affection, we really have no tenderness. But there was something of the woman moulded into the great, stalwart frame of Hollingsworth; nor was he ashamed of it, as men often are of what is best in them, nor seemed ever to know that there was such a soft place in his heart. I knew it well, however, at that time; although, afterwards, it came nigh to be forgotten. Methought there could not be two such men alive, as Hollingsworth. There never was any blaze of a fireside that warmed and cheered me, in the down-sinkings and shiverings of my spirit, so effectually as did the light out of those eyes, which lay so deep and dark under his shaggy brows.

Happy the man that has such a friend beside him, when he comes to die! And unless a friend like Hollingsworth be at hand, as most probably there will not, he had better make up his mind to die alone. How many men, I wonder, does one meet with, in a lifetime, whom he would choose for his death-bed companions! At the crisis of my fever, I besought Hollingsworth to let nobody else enter the room, but continually to make me sensible of his own presence by a grasp of the hand, a word—a prayer, if he thought good to utter it—and that then he should be the witness how courageously I would encounter the worst. It still impresses me as almost a matter of regret, that I did not die, then, when I had tolerably made up my mind to it; for Hollingsworth would have gone with me to the hither verge of life, and have sent his friendly and hopeful accents far over on the other side, while I should be treading the unknown path. Now, were I to send for him, he would hardly come to my bedside; nor should I depart the easier, for his presence.

"You are not going to die, this time," said he, gravely smiling. "You know nothing about sickness, and think your case a great deal more desperate than it is."

"Death should take me while I am in the mood," replied I, with a little of my customary levity.

"Have you nothing to do in life," asked Hollingsworth, "that you fancy yourself so ready to leave it?"

"Nothing," answered I—"nothing, that I know of, unless to make pretty verses, and play a part, with Zenobia and the rest of the amateurs, in our pastoral. It seems but an unsubstantial sort of business, as viewed through a mist of fever. But, dear Hollingsworth, your own vocation is evidently to be a priest, and to spend your days and nights in helping your fellow-creatures to draw peaceful dying-breaths."

"And by which of my qualities," inquired he, "can you suppose me fitted for this awful ministry?"

"By your tenderness," I said. "It seems to me the reflection of God's own love."

"And you call me tender!" repeated Hollingsworth, thoughtfully. "I should rather say, that the most marked trait in my character is an inflexible severity of purpose. Mortal man has no right to be so inflexible, as it is my nature and necessity to be!"

"I do not believe it," I replied.

But, in due time, I remembered what he said.

Probably, as Hollingsworth suggested, my disorder was never so serious as, in my ignorance of such matters, I was inclined to consider it. After so much tragical preparation, it was positively rather mortifying to find myself on the mending hand.

All the other members of the Community showed me kindness, according to the full measure of their capacity. Zenobia brought me my gruel, every day, made by her own hands, (not very skilfully, if the truth must be told,) and, whenever I seemed inclined to converse, would sit by my bedside, and talk with so much vivacity as to add several gratuitous throbs to my pulse. Her poor little stories and tracts never half did justice to her intellect; it was only the lack of a fitter avenue that drove her to seek development in literature. She was made (among a thousand other things that she might have been) for a stump-oratress. I recognized no severe culture in Zenobia; her mind was full of weeds. It startled me, sometimes, in my state of moral, as well as bodily faint-heartedness, to observe the hardihood of her philosophy; she made no scruple of oversetting all human institutions, and scattering them as with a breeze from her fan. A female reformer, in her attacks upon society, has an instinctive sense of where the life lies, and is inclined to aim directly at that spot. Especially, the relation between the sexes is naturally among the earliest to attract her notice.

Zenobia was truly a magnificent woman. The homely simplicity of her dress could not conceal, nor scarcely diminish, the queenliness of her presence. The image of her form and face should have been multiplied all over the earth. It was wronging the rest of mankind, to retain her as the spectacle of only a few. The stage would have been her proper sphere. She should have made it a point of duty, moreover, to sit endlessly to painters and sculptors, and preferably to the latter; because the cold decorum of the marble would consist with the utmost scantiness of drapery, so that the eye might chastely be gladdened with her material perfection, in its entirety. I know not well how to express, that the native glow of coloring in her cheeks, and even the flesh-warmth over her round arms, and what was visible of her full bust—in a word, her womanliness incarnated—compelled me sometimes to close my eyes, as if it were not quite the privilege of modesty to gaze at her. Illness and exhaustion, no doubt, had made me morbidly sensitive.

I noticed—and wondered how Zenobia contrived it—that she had always a new flower in her hair. And still it was a hot-house flower—an outlandish flower—a flower of the tropics, such as appeared to have sprung passionately out of a soil, the very weeds of which would be fervid and spicy. Unlike as was the flower of each successive day to the preceding one, it yet so assimilated its richness to the rich beauty of the woman, that I thought it the only flower fit to be worn; so fit, indeed, that Nature had evidently created this floral gem, in a happy exuberance, for the one purpose of worthily adorning Zenobia's head. It might be, that my feverish fantasies clustered themselves about this peculiarity, and caused it to look more gorgeous and wonderful than if beheld with temperate eyes. In the height of my illness, as I well recollect, I went so far as to pronounce it preternatural.

"Zenobia is an enchantress!" whispered I once to Hollingsworth. "She is a sister of the Veiled Lady! That flower in her hair is a talisman. If you were to snatch it away, she would vanish, or be transformed into something else!"

"What does he say?" asked Zenobia.

"Nothing that has an atom of sense in it," answered Hollingsworth. "He is a little beside himself, I believe, and talks about your being a witch, and of some magical property in the flower that you wear in your hair."

"It is an idea worthy of a feverish poet," said she, laughing, rather compassionately, and taking out the flower. "I scorn to owe anything to magic. Here, Mr. Hollingsworth:—you may keep the spell, while it has any virtue in it; but I cannot promise you not to appear with a new one, tomorrow. It is the one relic of my more brilliant, my happier days!"

The most curious part of the matter was, that, long after my slight delirium had passed away—as long, indeed, as I continued to know this remarkable woman—her daily flower affected my imagination, though more slightly, yet in very much the same way. The reason must have been, that, whether intentionally on her part, or not, this favorite ornament was actually a subtile expression of Zenobia's character.

One subject, about which—very impertinently, moreover—
I perplexed myself with a great many conjectures, was,
whether Zenobia had ever been married. The idea, it must
be understood, was unauthorized by any circumstance or
suggestion that had made its way to my ears. So young as
I beheld her, and the freshest and rosiest woman of a
thousand, there was certainly no need of imputing to her a
destiny already accomplished; the probability was far greater,
that her coming years had all life's richest gifts to bring. If
the great event of a woman's existence had been consummated, the world knew nothing of it, although the world
seemed to know Zenobia well. It was a ridiculous piece of
romance, undoubtedly, to imagine that this beautiful personage, wealthy as she was, and holding a position that might
fairly enough be called distinguished, could have given herself
away so privately, but that some whisper and suspicion, and,
by degrees, a full understanding of the fact, would eventually
be blown abroad. But, then, as I failed not to consider, her
original home was at a distance of many hundred miles.
Rumors might fill the social atmosphere, or might once have
filled it, there, which would travel but slowly, against the
wind, towards our north-eastern metropolis, and perhaps melt
into thin air before reaching it.

There was not, and I distinctly repeat it, the slightest
foundation in my knowledge for any surmise of the kind.
But there is a species of intuition—either a spiritual lie, or
the subtle recognition of a fact—which comes to us in a
reduced state of the corporeal system. The soul gets the better
of the body, after wasting illness, or when a vegetable diet
may have mingled too much ether in the blood. Vapors then
rise up to the brain, and take shapes that often image falsehood, but sometimes truth. The spheres of our companions
have, at such periods, a vastly greater influence upon our
own, than when robust health gives us a repellent and self-
defensive energy. Zenobia's sphere, I imagine, impressed itself

powerfully on mine, and transformed me, during this period of my weakness, into something like a mesmerical clairvoyant.

Then, also, as anybody could observe, the freedom of her deportment (though, to some tastes, it might commend itself as the utmost perfection of manner, in a youthful widow, or a blooming matron) was not exactly maidenlike. What girl had ever laughed as Zenobia did! What girl had ever spoken in her mellow tones! Her unconstrained and inevitable manifestation, I said often to myself, was that of a woman to whom wedlock had thrown wide the gates of mystery. Yet, sometimes, I strove to be ashamed of these conjectures. I acknowledged it as a masculine grossness—a sin of wicked interpretation, of which man is often guilty towards the other sex—thus to mistake the sweet, liberal, but womanly frankness of a noble and generous disposition. Still, it was of no avail to reason with myself, nor to upbraid myself. Pertinaciously the thought—'Zenobia is a wife! Zenobia has lived, and loved! There is no folded petal, no latent dew-drop, in this perfectly developed rose!'—irresistibly that thought drove out all other conclusions, as often as my mind reverted to the subject.

Zenobia was conscious of my observation, though not, I presume, of the point to which it led me.

"Mr. Coverdale," said she, one day, as she saw me watching her, while she arranged my gruel on the table, "I have been exposed to a great deal of eye-shot in the few years of my mixing in the world, but never, I think, to precisely such glances as you are in the habit of favoring me with. I seem to interest you very much; and yet—or else a woman's instinct is for once deceived—I cannot reckon you as an admirer. What are you seeking to discover in me?"

"The mystery of your life," answered I, surprised into the truth by the unexpectedness of her attack. "And you will never tell me."

She bent her head towards me, and let me look into her

eyes, as if challenging me to drop a plummet-line down into the depths of her consciousness.

"I see nothing now," said I, closing my own eyes, "unless it be the face of a sprite, laughing at me from the bottom of a deep well."

A bachelor always feels himself defrauded, when he knows, or suspects, that any woman of his acquaintance has given herself away. Otherwise, the matter could have been no concern of mine. It was purely speculative; for I should not, under any circumstances, have fallen in love with Zenobia. The riddle made me so nervous, however, in my sensitive condition of mind and body, that I most ungratefully began to wish that she would let me alone. Then, too, her gruel was very wretched stuff, with almost invariably the smell of pine-smoke upon it, like the evil taste that is said to mix itself up with a witch's best concocted dainties. Why could not she have allowed one of the other women to take the gruel in charge? Whatever else might be her gifts, Nature certainly never intended Zenobia for a cook. Or, if so, she should have meddled only with the richest and spiciest dishes, and such as are to be tasted at banquets, between draughts of intoxicating wine.

VII

THE CONVALESCENT

A S SOON as my incommodities allowed me to think
of past occurrences, I failed not to inquire what had
become of the odd little guest, whom Hollingsworth
had been the medium of introducing among us. It now
appeared, that poor Priscilla had not so literally fallen out of
the clouds, as we were at first inclined to suppose. A letter,
which should have introduced her, had since been received
from one of the city-missionaries, containing a certificate of
character, and an allusion to circumstances which, in the
writer's judgment, made it especially desirable that she should
find shelter in our Community. There was a hint, not very
intelligible, implying either that Priscilla had recently escaped
from some particular peril, or irksomeness of position, or else
that she was still liable to this danger or difficulty, whatever
it might be. We should ill have deserved the reputation of a
benevolent fraternity, had we hesitated to entertain a peti-
tioner in such need, and so strongly recommended to our
kindness; not to mention, moreover, that the strange maiden
had set herself diligently to work, and was doing good service
with her needle. But a slight mist of uncertainty still floated
about Priscilla, and kept her, as yet, from taking a very
decided place among creatures of flesh and blood.

The mysterious attraction, which, from her first entrance

on our scene, she evinced for Zenobia, had lost nothing of its force. I often heard her footsteps, soft and low, accompanying the light, but decided tread of the latter, up the staircase, stealing along the passage-way by her new friend's side, and pausing while Zenobia entered my chamber. Occasionally, Zenobia would be a little annoyed by Priscilla's too close attendance. In an authoritative and not very kindly tone, she would advise her to breathe the pleasant air in a walk, or to go with her work into the barn, holding out half a promise to come and sit on the hay with her, when at leisure. Evidently, Priscilla found but scanty requital for her love. Hollingsworth was likewise a great favorite with her. For several minutes together, sometimes, while my auditory nerves retained the susceptibility of delicate health, I used to hear a low, pleasant murmur, ascending from the room below, and at last ascertained it to be Priscilla's voice, babbling like a little brook to Hollingsworth. She talked more largely and freely with him than with Zenobia, towards whom, indeed, her feelings seemed not so much to be confidence, as involuntary affection. I should have thought all the better of my own qualities, had Priscilla marked me out for the third place in her regards. But, though she appeared to like me tolerably well, I could never flatter myself with being distinguished by her, as Hollingsworth and Zenobia were.

One forenoon, during my convalescence, there came a gentle tap at my chamber-door. I immediately said—"Come in, Priscilla!"—with an acute sense of the applicant's identity. Nor was I deceived. It was really Priscilla, a pale, large-eyed little woman, (for she had gone far enough into her teens to be, at least, on the outer limit of girlhood,) but much less wan than at my previous view of her, and far better conditioned both as to health and spirits. As I first saw her, she had reminded me of plants that one sometimes observes doing their best to vegetate among the bricks of an enclosed court, where there is scanty soil, and never any sunshine. At present, though with no approach to bloom, there were indications that the girl had human blood in her veins.

Priscilla came softly to my bedside, and held out an article of snow-white linen, very carefully and smoothly ironed. She did not seem bashful, nor anywise embarrassed. My weakly condition, I suppose, supplied a medium in which she could approach me.

"Do not you need this?" asked she. "I have made it for you."

It was a night-cap!

"My dear Priscilla," said I, smiling, "I never had on a night-cap in my life! But perhaps it will be better for me to wear one, now that I am a miserable invalid. How admirably you have done it! No, no; I never can think of wearing such an exquisitely wrought night-cap as this, unless it be in the day-time, when I sit up to receive company!"

"It is for use, not beauty," answered Priscilla. "I could have embroidered it and made it much prettier, if I pleased."

While holding up the night-cap, and admiring the fine needle-work, I perceived that Priscilla had a sealed letter, which she was waiting for me to take. It had arrived from the village post-office, that morning. As I did not immediately offer to receive the letter, she drew it back, and held it against her bosom, with both hands clasped over it, in a way that had probably grown habitual to her. Now, on turning my eyes from the night-cap to Priscilla, it forcibly struck me that her air, though not her figure, and the expression of her face, but not its features, had a resemblance to what I had often seen in a friend of mine, one of the most gifted women of the age. I cannot describe it. The points, easiest to convey to the reader, were, a certain curve of the shoulders, and a partial closing of the eyes, which seemed to look more penetratingly into my own eyes, through the narrowed apertures, than if they had been open at full width. It was a singular anomaly of likeness co-existing with perfect dissimilitude.

"Will you give me the letter, Priscilla?" said I.

She started, put the letter into my hand, and quite lost the look that had drawn my notice.

"Priscilla," I inquired, "did you ever see Miss Margaret Fuller?"

"No," she answered.

"Because," said I, "you reminded me of her, just now, and it happens, strangely enough, that this very letter is from her!"

Priscilla, for whatever reason, looked very much discomposed.

"I wish people would not fancy such odd things in me!" she said, rather petulantly. "How could I possibly make myself resemble this lady, merely by holding her letter in my hand?"

"Certainly, Priscilla, it would puzzle me to explain it," I replied. "Nor do I suppose that the letter had anything to do with it. It was just a coincidence—nothing more."

She hastened out of the room; and this was the last that I saw of Priscilla, until I ceased to be an invalid.

Being much alone, during my recovery, I read interminably in Mr. Emerson's Essays, the Dial, Carlyle's works, George Sand's romances, (lent me by Zenobia,) and other books which one or another of the brethren or sisterhood had brought with them. Agreeing in little else, most of these utterances were like the cry of some solitary sentinel, whose station was on the outposts of the advance-guard of human progression; or, sometimes, the voice came sadly from among the shattered ruins of the past, but yet had a hopeful echo in the future. They were well adapted (better, at least, than any other intellectual products, the volatile essence of which had heretofore tinctured a printed page) to pilgrims like ourselves, whose present bivouâc was considerably farther into the waste of chaos than any mortal army of crusaders had ever marched before. Fourier's works, also, in a series of horribly tedious volumes, attracted a good deal of my attention, from the analogy which I could not but recognize between his system and our own. There was far less resemblance, it is true, than the world chose to imagine; inasmuch as the two theories differed, as widely as the zenith from the nadir, in their main principles.

I talked about Fourier to Hollingsworth, and translated, for his benefit, some of the passages that chiefly impressed me.

"When, as a consequence of human improvement," said I, "the globe shall arrive at its final perfection, the great ocean is to be converted into a particular kind of lemonade, such as was fashionable at Paris in Fourier's time. He calls it *limonade à cèdre*. It is positively a fact! Just imagine the city-docks filled, every day, with a flood-tide of this delectable beverage!"

"Why did not the Frenchman make punch of it, at once?" asked Hollingsworth. "The jack-tars would be delighted to go down in ships, and do business in such an element."

I further proceeded to explain, as well as I modestly could, several points of Fourier's system, illustrating them with here and there a page or two, and asking Hollingsworth's opinion as to the expediency of introducing these beautiful peculiarities into our own practice.

"Let me hear no more of it!" cried he, in utter disgust. "I never will forgive this fellow! He has committed the Unpardonable Sin! For what more monstrous iniquity could the Devil himself contrive, than to choose the selfish principle —the principle of all human wrong, the very blackness of man's heart, the portion of ourselves which we shudder at, and which it is the whole aim of spiritual discipline to eradicate—to choose it as the master-workman of his system? To seize upon and foster whatever vile, petty, sordid, filthy, bestial, and abominable corruptions have cankered into our nature, to be the efficient instruments of his infernal regeneration! And his consummated Paradise, as he pictures it, would be worthy of the agency which he counts upon for establishing it. The nauseous villain!"

"Nevertheless," remarked I, "in consideration of the promised delights of his system—so very proper, as they certainly are, to be appreciated by Fourier's countrymen—I cannot but wonder that universal France did not adopt his theory, at a moment's warning. But is there not something very characteristic of his nation in Fourier's manner of putting forth his views? He makes no claim to inspiration. He has not persuaded himself—as Swedenborg did, and as any other than a Frenchman would, with a mission of like importance to communicate—that he speaks with authority from above. He promulgates his system, so far as I can perceive, entirely on his own responsibility. He has searched out and discovered the whole counsel of the Almighty, in respect to mankind, past, present, and for exactly seventy thousand years to come, by the mere force and cunning of his individual intellect!"

"Take the book out of my sight!" said Hollingsworth, with great virulence of expression, "or, I tell you fairly, I shall fling it in the fire! And as for Fourier, let him make a Paradise, if he can, of Gehenna, where, as I conscientiously believe, he is floundering at this moment!"

"And bellowing, I suppose," said I—not that I felt any ill-will towards Fourier, but merely wanted to give the finishing touch to Hollingsworth's image—"bellowing for the least drop of his beloved *limonade à cèdre!*"

There is but little profit to be expected in attempting to argue with a man who allows himself to declaim in this manner; so I dropt the subject, and never took it up again.

But had the system, at which he was so enraged, combined almost any amount of human wisdom, spiritual insight, and imaginative beauty, I question whether Hollingsworth's mind was in a fit condition to receive it. I began to discern that he had come among us, actuated by no real sympathy with our feelings and our hopes, but chiefly because we were estranging ourselves from the world, with which his lonely and exclusive object in life had already put him at odds. Hollingsworth must have been originally endowed with a great spirit of benevolence, deep enough, and warm enough, to be the source of as much disinterested good, as Providence often allows a human being the privilege of conferring upon his fellows. This native instinct yet lived within him. I myself had profited by it, in my necessity. It was seen, too, in his treatment of Priscilla. Such casual circumstances, as were here involved, would quicken his divine power of sympathy, and make him seem, while their influence lasted, the tenderest man and the truest friend on earth. But, by-and-by, you missed the tenderness of yesterday, and grew drearily conscious that Hollingsworth had a closer friend than ever you could be. And this friend was the cold, spectral monster which he had himself conjured up, and on which he was wasting all the warmth of his heart, and of which, at last—as these men of a mighty purpose so invariably do—he had grown to be the bond-slave. It was his philanthropic theory!

This was a result exceedingly sad to contemplate, considering that it had been mainly brought about by the very ardor and exuberance of his philanthropy. Sad, indeed, but by no means unusual. He had taught his benevolence to pour its warm tide exclusively through one channel; so that there was nothing to spare for other great manifestations of love to man, nor scarcely for the nutriment of individual attachments, unless they could minister, in some way, to the terrible egotism which he mistook for an angel of God. Had Hollingsworth's education been more enlarged, he might not so inevitably have stumbled into this pit-fall. But this identical pursuit had educated him. He knew absolutely nothing, except in a single direction, where he had thought so energetically, and felt to such a depth, that, no doubt, the entire reason and justice of the universe appeared to be concentrated thither-ward.

It is my private opinion, that, at this period of his life, Hollingsworth was fast going mad; and, as with other crazy people, (among whom I include humorists of every degree,) it required all the constancy of friendship to restrain his associates from pronouncing him an intolerable bore. Such prolonged fiddling upon one string; such multiform presenta-tion of one idea! His specific object (of which he made the public more than sufficiently aware, through the medium of lectures and pamphlets) was to obtain funds for the con-struction of an edifice, with a sort of collegiate endowment. On this foundation, he purposed to devote himself and a few disciples to the reform and mental culture of our criminal brethren. His visionary edifice was Hollingsworth's one castle in the air; it was the material type, in which his philanthropic dream strove to embody itself; and he made the scheme more definite, and caught hold of it the more strongly, and kept his clutch the more pertinaciously, by rendering it visible to the bodily eye. I have seen him, a hundred times, with a pencil and sheet of paper, sketching the façade, the side-view, or the rear of the structure, or planning the internal arrange-ments, as lovingly as another man might plan those of the projected home, where he meant to be happy with his wife and children. I have known him to begin a model of the building with little stones, gathered at the brookside, whither we had gone to cool ourselves in the sultry noon of haying-time. Unlike all other ghosts, his spirit haunted an edifice which, instead of being time-worn, and full of storied love, and joy, and sorrow, had never yet come into existence.

"Dear friend," said I, once, to Hollingsworth, before leaving my sick-chamber, "I heartily wish that I could make your schemes my schemes, because it would be so great a happiness to find myself treading the same path with you. But I am afraid there is not stuff in me stern enough for a philanthropist

—or not in this peculiar direction—or, at all events, not solely in this. Can you bear with me, if such should prove to be the case?"

"I will, at least, wait awhile," answered Hollingsworth, gazing at me sternly and gloomily. "But how can you be my life-long friend, except you strive with me towards the great object of my life?"

Heaven forgive me! A horrible suspicion crept into my heart, and stung the very core of it as with the fangs of an adder. I wondered whether it were possible that Hollingsworth could have watched by my bedside, with all that devoted care, only for the ulterior purpose of making me a proselyte to his views!

VIII

A MODERN ARCADIA

MAY-DAY—I forget whether by Zenobia's sole decree, or by the unanimous vote of our Community—had been declared a moveable festival. It was deferred until the sun should have had a reasonable time to clear away the snow-drifts, along the lee of the stone-walls, and bring out a few of the readiest wild-flowers. On the forenoon of the substituted day, after admitting some of the balmy air into my chamber, I decided that it was nonsense and effeminacy to keep myself a prisoner any longer. So I descended to the sitting-room, and finding nobody there, proceeded to the barn, whence I had already heard Zenobia's voice, and along with it a girlish laugh, which was not so certainly recognizable. Arriving at the spot, it a little surprised me to discover that these merry outbreaks came from Priscilla.

The two had been a-maying together. They had found anemones in abundance, houstonias by the handfull, some columbines, a few long-stalked violets, and a quantity of white everlasting-flowers, and had filled up their basket with the delicate spray of shrubs and trees. None were prettier than the maple-twigs, the leaf of which looks like a scarlet-bud, in May, and like a plate of vegetable gold in October. Zenobia—who showed no conscience in such matters—had also rifled a cherry-tree of one of its blossomed boughs; and, with all this variety of sylvan ornament, had been decking out Priscilla. Being done with a good deal of taste, it made her look more charming than I should have thought possible, with my recollection of the wan, frost-nipt girl, as heretofore described. Nevertheless, among those fragrant blossoms, and conspicuously, too, had been stuck a weed of evil odor and ugly aspect, which, as soon as I detected it, destroyed the effect of all the rest. There was a gleam of latent mischief— not to call it deviltry—in Zenobia's eye, which seemed to indicate a slightly malicious purpose in the arrangement.

As for herself, she scorned the rural buds and leaflets, and wore nothing but her invariable flower of the tropics.

"What do you think of Priscilla now, Mr. Coverdale?" asked she, surveying her as a child does its doll. "Is not she worth a verse or two?"

"There is only one thing amiss," answered I.

Zenobia laughed, and flung the malignant weed away.

"Yes; she deserves some verses now," said I, "and from a better poet than myself. She is the very picture of the New England spring, subdued in tint, and rather cool, but with a capacity of sunshine, and bringing us a few alpine blossoms, as earnest of something richer, though hardly more beautiful, hereafter. The best type of her is one of those anemones."

"What I find most singular in Priscilla, as her health improves," observed Zenobia, "is her wildness. Such a quiet little body as she seemed, one would not have expected that! Why, as we strolled the woods together, I could hardly keep her from scrambling up the trees like a squirrel! She has never before known what it is to live in the free air, and so it intoxicates her as if she were sipping wine. And she thinks it such a Paradise here, and all of us, particularly Mr. Hollingsworth and myself, such angels! It is quite ridiculous, and provokes one's malice, almost, to see a creature so happy— especially a feminine creature."

"They are always happier than male creatures," said I.

"You must correct that opinion, Mr. Coverdale," replied Zenobia, contemptuously, "or I shall think you lack the poetic insight. Did you ever see a happy woman in your life? Of course, I do not mean a girl—like Priscilla, and a thousand others, for they are all alike, while on the sunny side of experience—but a grown woman. How can she be happy, after discovering that fate has assigned her but one single event, which she must contrive to make the substance of her whole life? A man has his choice of innumerable events."

"A woman, I suppose," answered I, "by constant repetition of her one event, may compensate for the lack of variety."

"Indeed!" said Zenobia.

While we were talking, Priscilla caught sight of Hollingsworth, at a distance, in a blue frock and with a hoe over his shoulder, returning from the field. She immediately set out to meet him, running and skipping, with spirits as light as the breeze of the May-morning, but with limbs too little exercised to be quite responsive; she clapt her hands, too, with great exuberance of gesture, as is the custom of young girls, when their electricity overcharges them. But, all at once, midway to Hollingsworth, she paused, looked round about her, towards the river, the road, the woods, and back towards us, appearing to listen, as if she heard some one calling her name, and knew not precisely in what direction.

"Have you bewitched her?" I exclaimed.

"It is no sorcery of mine," said Zenobia. "But I have seen the girl do that identical thing, once or twice before. Can you imagine what is the matter with her?"

"No; unless," said I, "she has the gift of hearing those 'airy tongues that syllable men's names'—which Milton tells about."

From whatever cause, Priscilla's animation seemed entirely to have deserted her. She seated herself on a rock, and remained there until Hollingsworth came up; and when he took her hand and led her back to us, she rather resembled my original image of the wan and spiritless Priscilla, than the flowery May Queen of a few moments ago. These sudden transformations, only to be accounted for by an extreme nervous susceptibility, always continued to characterize the girl, though with diminished frequency, as her health progressively grew more robust.

I was now on my legs again. My fit of illness had been an avenue between two existences; the low-arched and darksome doorway, through which I crept out of a life of old conventionalisms, on my hands and knees, as it were, and gained admittance into the freer region that lay beyond. In this respect, it was like death. And, as with death, too, it was good to have gone through it. No otherwise could I have rid myself of a thousand follies, fripperies, prejudices, habits, and other such worldly dust as inevitably settles upon the crowd along the broad highway, giving them all one sordid aspect, before noontime, however freshly they may have begun their pilgrimage, in the dewy morning. The very substance upon my bones had not been fit to live with, in any better, truer, or more energetic mode than that to which I was accustomed. So it was taken off me and flung aside, like any other worn out or unseasonable garment; and, after shivering a little while in my skeleton, I began to be clothed anew, and much more satisfactorily than in my previous suit. In literal and physical truth, I was quite another man. I had a lively sense of the exultation with which the spirit will enter on the next stage of its eternal progress, after leaving the heavy burthen of its mortality in an earthly grave, with as little concern for what may become of it, as now affected me for the flesh which I had lost.

Emerging into the genial sunshine, I half fancied that the labors of the brotherhood had already realized some of Fourier's predictions. Their enlightened culture of the soil, and the virtues with which they sanctified their life, had begun to produce an effect upon the material world and its climate. In my new enthusiasm, man looked strong and stately!—and woman, oh, how beautiful!—and the earth, a green garden, blossoming with many-colored delights! Thus Nature, whose laws I had broken in various artificial ways, comported herself towards me as a strict, but loving mother, who uses the rod upon her little boy for his naughtiness, and then gives him a smile, a kiss, and some pretty playthings, to console the urchin for her severity.

In the interval of my seclusion, there had been a number of recruits to our little army of saints and martyrs. They were mostly individuals who had gone through such an experience as to disgust them with ordinary pursuits, but who were not yet so old, nor had suffered so deeply, as to lose their faith in the better time to come. On comparing their minds, one with another, they often discovered that this idea of a Community had been growing up, in silent and unknown sympathy, for years. Thoughtful, strongly-lined faces were among them, sombre brows, but eyes that did not require spectacles, unless prematurely dimmed by the student's lamplight, and hair that seldom showed a thread of silver. Age, wedded to the past, incrusted over with a stony layer of habits, and retaining nothing fluid in its possibilities, would have been absurdly out of place in an enterprise like this. Youth, too, in its early dawn, was hardly more adapted to our purpose; for it would behold the morning radiance of its own spirit beaming over the very same spots of withered grass and barren sand, whence most of us had seen it vanish. We had very young people with us, it is true—downy lads, rosy girls in their first teens, and children of all heights above one's knee;—but these had chiefly been sent hither for education, which it was one of the objects and methods of our institution to supply. Then we had boarders, from town and elsewhere, who lived with us in a familiar way, sympathized more or less in our theories, and sometimes shared in our labors.

On the whole, it was a society such as has seldom met

together; nor, perhaps, could it reasonably be expected to hold together long. Persons of marked individuality—crooked sticks, as some of us might be called—are not exactly the easiest to bind up into a faggot. But, so long as our union should subsist, a man of intellect and feeling, with a free nature in him, might have sought far and near, without finding so many points of attraction as would allure him hitherward. We were of all creeds and opinions, and generally tolerant of all, on every imaginable subject. Our bond, it seems to me, was not affirmative, but negative. We had individually found one thing or another to quarrel with, in our past life, and were pretty well agreed as to the inexpediency of lumbering along with the old system any farther. As to what should be substituted, there was much less unanimity. We did not greatly care—at least, I never did— for the written constitution under which our millennium had commenced. My hope was, that, between theory and practice, a true and available mode of life might be struck out, and that, even should we ultimately fail, the months or years spent in the trial would not have been wasted, either as regarded passing enjoyment, or the experience which makes men wise.

Arcadians though we were, our costume bore no resemblance to the be-ribboned doublets, silk breeches and stockings, and slippers fastened with artificial roses, that distinguish the pastoral people of poetry and the stage. In outward show, I humbly conceive, we looked rather like a gang of beggars or banditti, than either a company of honest laboring men or a conclave of philosophers. Whatever might be our points of difference, we all of us seemed to have come to Blithedale with the one thrifty and laudable idea of wearing out our old clothes. Such garments as had an airing, whenever we strode afield! Coats with high collars, and with no collars, broad-skirted or swallow-tailed, and with the waist at every point between the hip and armpit; pantaloons of a dozen successive epochs, and greatly defaced at the knees by the humiliations of the wearer before his lady-love;—in short, we were a living epitome of defunct fashions, and the very raggedest present-ment of men who had seen better days. It was gentility in tatters. Often retaining a scholarlike or clerical air, you might have taken us for the denizens of Grub-street, intent on getting a comfortable livelihood by agricultural labor; or Coleridge's projected Pantisocracy, in full experiment; or Candide and his motley associates, at work in their cabbage-garden; or anything else that was miserably out at elbows, and most clumsily patched in the rear. We might have been sworn comrades to Falstaff's ragged regiment. Little skill as we boasted in other points of husbandry, every mother's son of us would have served admirably to stick up for a scarecrow. And the worst of the matter was, that the first energetic move-ment, essential to one downright stroke of real labor, was sure to put a finish to these poor habiliments. So we gradually flung them all aside, and took to honest homespun and linsey-woolsey, as preferable, on the whole, to the plan recom-mended, I think, by Virgil—'*Ara nudus; sere nudus*'—which, as Silas Foster remarked when I translated the maxim, would be apt to astonish the women-folks.

After a reasonable training, the yeoman-life throve well with us. Our faces took the sunburn kindly; our chests gained in compass, and our shoulders in breadth and squareness; our great brown fists looked as if they had never been capable of kid gloves. The plough, the hoe, the scythe, and the hay-fork, grew familiar to our grasp. The oxen responded to our voices. We could do almost as fair a day's work as Silas Foster himself, sleep dreamlessly after it, and awake at daybreak with only a little stiffness of the joints, which was usually quite gone by breakfast-time.

To be sure, our next neighbors pretended to be incredulous as to our real proficiency in the business which we had taken in hand. They told slanderous fables about our inability to yoke our own oxen, or to drive them afield, when yoked, or to release the poor brutes from their conjugal bond at nightfall. They had the face to say, too, that the cows laughed at our awkwardness at milking-time, and invariably kicked over the pails; partly in consequence of our putting the stool on the wrong side, and partly because, taking offence at the whisking of their tails, we were in the habit of holding these natural flyflappers with one hand, and milking with the other. They further averred, that we hoed up whole acres of Indian corn and other crops, and drew the earth carefully about the weeds; and that we raised five hundred tufts of burdock, mistaking them for cabbages; and that, by dint of unskilful planting, few of our seeds ever came up at all, or if they did come up, it was stern foremost, and that we spent the better part of the month of June in reversing a field of beans, which had thrust themselves out of the ground in this unseemly way. They quoted it as nothing more than an ordinary occurrence for one or other of us to crop off two or three fingers, of a morning, by our clumsy use of the hay-cutter. Finally, and as an ultimate catastrophe, these mendacious rogues circulated a report that we Communitarians were exterminated, to the last man, by severing ourselves asunder with the sweep of our own scythes!—and that the world had lost nothing by this little accident.

But this was pure envy and malice on the part of the neighboring farmers. The peril of our new way of life was not lest we should fail in becoming practical agriculturalists, but that we should probably cease to be anything else. While our enterprise lay all in theory, we had pleased ourselves with delectable visions of the spiritualization of labor. It was to be our form of prayer, and ceremonial of worship. Each stroke of the hoe was to uncover some aromatic root of wisdom, heretofore hidden from the sun. Pausing in the field, to let the wind exhale the moisture from our foreheads, we were to look upward, and catch glimpses into the far-off soul of truth. In this point of view, matters did not turn out quite so well as we anticipated. It is very true, that, sometimes, gazing casually around me, out of the midst of my toil, I used to discern a richer picturesqueness in the visible scene of earth and sky. There was, at such moments, a novelty, an unwonted aspect on the face of Nature, as if she had been taken by surprise and seen at unawares, with no opportunity to put off her real look, and assume the mask with which she mysteriously hides herself from mortals. But this was all. The clods of earth, which we so constantly belabored and turned over and over, were never etherealized into thought. Our thoughts, on the contrary, were fast becoming cloddish. Our labor symbolized nothing, and left us mentally sluggish in the dusk of the evening. Intellectual activity is incompatible with any large amount of bodily exercise. The yeoman and the scholar— the yeoman and the man of finest moral culture, though not the man of sturdiest sense and integrity—are two distinct individuals, and can never be melted or welded into one substance.

Zenobia soon saw this truth, and gibed me about it, one evening, as Hollingsworth and I lay on the grass, after a hard day's work.

"I am afraid you did not make a song, to-day, while loading the hay-cart," said she, "as Burns did, when he was reaping barley."

"Burns never made a song in haying-time," I answered, very positively. "He was no poet while a farmer, and no farmer while a poet."

"And, on the whole, which of the two characters do you like best?" asked Zenobia. "For I have an idea that you cannot combine them, any better than Burns did. Ah, I see, in my mind's eye, what sort of an individual you are to be, two or three years hence! Grim Silas Foster is your prototype, with his palm of sole-leather, and his joints of rusty iron, (which, all through summer, keep the stiffness of what he calls his winter's rheumatize,) and his brain of—I don't know what his brain is made of, unless it be a Savoy cabbage; but yours may be cauliflower, as a rather more delicate variety. Your physical man will be transmuted into salt-beef and fried pork, at the rate, I should imagine, of a pound and a half a day; that being about the average which we find necessary in the kitchen. You will make your toilet for the day (still like this delightful Silas Foster) by rinsing your fingers and the front part of your face in a little tin-pan of water, at the door-step, and teasing your hair with a wooden pocket-comb, before a seven-by-nine-inch looking-glass. Your only pastime will be, to smoke some very vile tobacco in the black stump of a pipe!"

"Pray spare me!" cried I. "But the pipe is not Silas's only mode of solacing himself with the weed."

"Your literature," continued Zenobia, apparently delighted with her description, "will be the Farmer's Almanac; for, I observe, our friend Foster never gets so far as the newspaper. When you happen to sit down, at odd moments, you will fall asleep, and make nasal proclamation of the fact, as he does; and invariably you must be jogged out of a nap, after supper, by the future Mrs. Coverdale, and persuaded to go regularly to bed. And on Sundays; when you put on a blue coat with brass buttons, you will think of nothing else to do, but to go and lounge over the stone-walls and rail-fences, and stare at the corn growing. And you will look with a knowing eye at oxen, and will have a tendency to clamber over into pig-sties, and feel of the hogs, and give a guess how much they will weigh, after you shall have stuck and dressed them. Already, I have noticed, you begin to speak through your nose, and with a drawl. Pray, if you really did make any poetry to-day, let us hear it in that kind of utterance!"

"Coverdale has given up making verses, now," said Hollingsworth, who never had the slightest appreciation of my poetry. "Just think of him penning a sonnet, with a fist like that! There is at least this good in a life of toil, that it takes the nonsense and fancy-work out of a man, and leaves nothing but what truly belongs to him. If a farmer can make poetry at the plough-tail, it must be because his nature insists on it; and if that be the case, let him make it, in Heaven's name!"

"And how is it with you?" asked Zenobia, in a different voice; for she never laughed at Hollingsworth, as she often did at me.—"You, I think, cannot have ceased to live a life of thought and feeling."

"I have always been in earnest," answered Hollingsworth. "I have hammered thought out of iron, after heating the iron in my heart! It matters little what my outward toil may be. Were I a slave at the bottom of a mine, I should keep the same purpose—the same faith in its ultimate accomplishment—that I do now. Miles Coverdale is not in earnest, either as a poet or a laborer."

"You give me hard measure, Hollingsworth," said I, a little hurt. "I have kept pace with you in the field; and my bones feel as if I had been in earnest, whatever may be the case with my brain!"

"I cannot conceive," observed Zenobia, with great emphasis—and, no doubt, she spoke fairly the feeling of the moment—"I cannot conceive of being, so continually as Mr. Coverdale is, within the sphere of a strong and noble nature, without being strengthened and ennobled by its influence!"

This amiable remark of the fair Zenobia confirmed me in what I had already begun to suspect—that Hollingsworth, like many other illustrious prophets, reformers, and philanthropists, was likely to make at least two proselytes, among the women, to one among the men. Zenobia and Priscilla! These, I believe, (unless my unworthy self might be reckoned for a third,) were the only disciples of his mission; and I spent a great deal of time, uselessly, in trying to conjecture what Hollingsworth meant to do with them—and they with him!

IX

HOLLINGSWORTH, ZENOBIA, PRISCILLA

I T IS not, I apprehend, a healthy kind of mental occupation, to devote ourselves too exclusively to the study of individual men and women. If the person under examination be one's self, the result is pretty certain to be diseased action of the heart, almost before we can snatch a second glance. Or, if we take the freedom to put a friend under our microscope, we thereby insulate him from many of his true relations, magnify his peculiarities, inevitably tear him into parts, and, of course, patch him very clumsily together again. What wonder, then, should we be frightened by the aspect of a monster, which, after all—though we can point to every feature of his deformity in the real personage— may be said to have been created mainly by ourselves!

Thus, as my conscience has often whispered me, I did Hollingsworth a great wrong by prying into his character, and am perhaps doing him as great a one, at this moment, by putting faith in the discoveries which I seemed to make. But I could not help it. Had I loved him less, I might have used him better. He—and Zenobia and Priscilla, both for their own sakes and as connected with him—were separated from the rest of the Community, to my imagination, and stood forth as the indices of a problem which it was my business to solve. Other associates had a portion of my time; other matters amused me; passing occurrences carried me along with them, while they lasted. But here was the vortex of my meditations around which they revolved, and whitherward they too continually tended. In the midst of cheerful society, I had often a feeling of loneliness. For it was impossible not to be sensible, that, while these three characters figured so largely on my private theatre, I—though probably reckoned as a friend by all—was at best but a secondary or tertiary personage with either of them.

I loved Hollingsworth, as has already been enough expressed. But it impressed me, more and more, that there was a stern and dreadful peculiarity in this man, such as could not prove otherwise than pernicious to the happiness of those who should be drawn into too intimate a connection with him. He was not altogether human. There was something else in Hollingsworth, besides flesh and blood, and sympathies and affections, and celestial spirit.

This is always true of those men who have surrendered themselves to an over-ruling purpose. It does not so much impel them from without, nor even operate as a motive power within, but grows incorporate with all that they think and feel, and finally converts them into little else save that one principle. When such begins to be the predicament, it is not cowardice, but wisdom, to avoid these victims. They have no heart, no sympathy, no reason, no conscience. They will keep no friend, unless he make himself the mirror of their purpose; they will smite and slay you, and trample your dead corpse under foot, all the more readily, if you take the first step with them, and cannot take the second, and the third, and every other step of their terribly straight path. They have an idol, to which they consecrate themselves high-priest, and deem it holy work to offer sacrifices of whatever is most precious, and never once seem to suspect—so cunning has the Devil been with them—that this false deity, in whose iron features, immitigable to all the rest of mankind, they see only benignity and love, is but a spectrum of the very priest himself, projected upon the surrounding darkness. And the higher and purer the original object, and the more unselfishly it may have been taken up, the slighter is the probability that they can be led to recognize the process, by which godlike benevolence has been debased into all-devouring egotism.

Of course, I am perfectly aware that the above statement is exaggerated, in the attempt to make it adequate. Professed philanthropists have gone far; but no originally good man, I presume, ever went quite so far as this. Let the reader abate whatever he deems fit. The paragraph may remain, however, both for its truth and its exaggeration, as strongly expressive of the tendencies which were really operative in Hollingsworth, and as exemplifying the kind of error into which my mode of observation was calculated to lead me. The issue was, that, in solitude, I often shuddered at my friend. In my recollection of his dark and impressive countenance, the features grew more sternly prominent than the reality, duskier in their depth and shadow, and more lurid in their light; the frown, that had merely flitted across his brow, seemed to have contorted it with an adamantine wrinkle. On meeting him again, I was often filled with remorse, when his deep eyes beamed kindly upon me, as with the glow of a household fire that was burning in a cave.—"He is a man, after all!" thought I—"his Maker's own truest image, a philanthropic man!—not that steel engine of the Devil's contrivance, a philanthropist!"— But, in my wood-walks, and in my silent chamber, the dark face frowned at me again.

When a young girl comes within the sphere of such a man, she is as perilously situated as the maiden whom, in the old classical myths, the people used to expose to a dragon. If I had any duty whatever, in reference to Hollingsworth, it was, to endeavor to save Priscilla from that kind of personal worship which her sex is generally prone to lavish upon saints and heroes. It often requires but one smile, out of the hero's eyes into the girl's or woman's heart, to transform this devotion, from a sentiment of the highest approval and confidence, into passionate love. Now, Hollingsworth smiled much upon Priscilla; more than upon any other person. If she thought him beautiful, it was no wonder. I often thought him so, with the expression of tender, human care, and gentlest sympathy, which she alone seemed to have power to call out upon his features. Zenobia, I suspect, would have given her eyes, bright as they were, for such a look; it was the least that our poor Priscilla could do, to give her heart for a great many of them. There was the more danger of this, inasmuch as the footing, on which we all associated at Blithedale, was widely different from that of conventional society. While inclining us to the soft affections of the Golden Age, it seemed to authorize any individual, of either sex, to fall in love with any other, regardless of what would elsewhere be judged suitable and prudent. Accordingly, the tender passion was very rife among us, in various degrees of mildness or virulence, but mostly passing away with the state of things that had given it origin. This was all well enough; but, for a girl like Priscilla, and a woman like Zenobia, to jostle one another in their love of a man like Hollingsworth, was likely to be no child's play.

Had I been as cold-hearted as I sometimes thought myself, nothing would have interested me more than to witness the play of passions that must thus have been evolved. But, in honest truth, I would really have gone far to save Priscilla, at least, from the catastrophe in which such a drama would be apt to terminate.

Priscilla had now grown to be a very pretty girl, and still kept budding and blossoming, and daily putting on some new charm, which you no sooner became sensible of, than you thought it worth all that she had previously possessed. So unformed, vague, and without substance, as she had come to us, it seemed as if we could see Nature shaping out a woman before our very eyes, and yet had only a more reverential sense of the mystery of a woman's soul and frame. Yesterday, her cheek was pale; to-day, it had a bloom. Priscilla's smile, like a baby's first one, was a wondrous novelty. Her imperfections and short-comings affected me with a kind of playful pathos, which was as absolutely bewitching a sensation as ever I experienced. After she had been a month or two at Blithedale, her animal spirits waxed high, and kept her pretty constantly in a state of bubble and ferment, impelling her to far more bodily activity than she had yet strength to endure. She was very fond of playing with the other girls, out-of-doors. There is hardly another sight in the world so pretty, as that of a company of young girls, almost women grown, at play, and so giving themselves up to their airy impulse that their tiptoes barely touch the ground.

Girls are incomparably wilder and more effervescent than boys, more untameable, and regardless of rule and limit, with an ever-shifting variety, breaking continually into new modes of fun, yet with a harmonious propriety through all. Their steps, their voices, appear free as the wind, but keep consonance with a strain of music, inaudible to us. Young men and boys, on the other hand, play according to recognized law, old, traditionary games, permitting no caprioles of fancy, but with scope enough for the outbreak of savage instincts. For, young or old, in play or in earnest, man is prone to be a brute.

Especially is it delightful to see a vigorous young girl run a race, with her head thrown back, her limbs moving more friskily than they need, and an air between that of a bird and a young colt. But Priscilla's peculiar charm, in a foot-race, was the weakness and irregularity with which she ran. Growing up without exercise, except to her poor little fingers, she had never yet acquired the perfect use of her legs. Setting buoyantly forth, therefore, as if no rival less swift than Atalanta could compete with her, she ran faulteringly, and often tumbled on the grass. Such an incident—though it seems too slight to think of—was a thing to laugh at, but which brought the water into one's eyes, and lingered in the memory after far greater joys and sorrows were swept out of it, as antiquated trash. Priscilla's life, as I beheld it, was full of trifles that affected me in just this way.

When she had come to be quite at home among us, I used to fancy that Priscilla played more pranks, and perpetrated more mischief, than any other girl in the Community. For example, I once heard Silas Foster, in a very gruff voice, threatening to rivet three horse-shoes round Priscilla's neck and chain her to a post, because she, with some other young people, had clambered upon a load of hay and caused it to slide off the cart. How she made her peace, I never knew; but very soon afterwards, I saw old Silas, with his brawny hands round Priscilla's waist, swinging her to-and-fro and finally depositing her on one of the oxen, to take her first lesson in riding. She met with terrible mishaps in her efforts to milk a cow; she let the poultry into the garden; she generally spoilt whatever part of the dinner she took in charge; she broke crockery; she dropt our biggest pitcher into the well; and—except with her needle, and those little wooden instruments for purse-making—was as unserviceable a member of society as any young lady in the land. There was no other sort of efficiency about her. Yet everybody was kind to Priscilla; everybody loved her, and laughed at her, to her face, and did not laugh, behind her back; everybody would have given her half of his last crust, or the bigger share of his plum-cake. These were pretty certain indications that we were all conscious of a pleasant weakness in the girl, and considered her not quite able to look after her own interests, or fight her battle with the world. And Hollingsworth—perhaps because he had been the means of introducing Priscilla to her new abode—appeared to recognize her as his own especial charge.

Her simple, careless, childish flow of spirits often made me sad. She seemed to me like a butterfly, at play in a flickering bit of sunshine, and mistaking it for a broad and eternal summer. We sometimes hold mirth to a stricter accountability than sorrow; it must show good cause, or the echo of its laughter comes back drearily. Priscilla's gaiety, moreover, was of a nature that showed me how delicate an instrument she was, and what fragile harp-strings were her nerves. As they made sweet music at the airiest touch, it would require but a stronger one to burst them all asunder. Absurd as it might be, I tried to reason with her, and persuade her not to be so joyous, thinking that, if she would draw less lavishly upon her fund of happiness, it would last the longer. I remember doing so, one summer evening, when we tired laborers sat looking on, like Goldsmith's old folks under the village thorn-tree, while the young people were at their sports.

"What is the use or sense of being so very gay?" I said to Priscilla, while she was taking breath after a great frolic. "I love to see a sufficient cause for everything; and I can see none for this. Pray tell me, now, what kind of a world you imagine this to be, which you are so merry in?"

"I never think about it at all," answered Priscilla, laughing. "But this I am sure of—that it is a world where everybody is kind to me, and where I love everybody. My heart keeps dancing within me; and all the foolish things, which you see me do, are only the motions of my heart. How can I be dismal, if my heart will not let me?"

"Have you nothing dismal to remember?" I suggested. "If not, then, indeed, you are very fortunate!"

"Ah!" said Priscilla, slowly.

And then came that unintelligible gesture, when she seemed to be listening to a distant voice.

"For my part," I continued, beneficently seeking to overshadow her with my own sombre humor, "my past life has been a tiresome one enough; yet I would rather look backward ten times, than forward once. For, little as we know of our life to come, we may be very sure, for one thing, that the good we aim at will not be attained. People never do get just the good they seek. If it come at all, it is something else, which they never dreamed of, and did not particularly want. Then, again, we may rest certain that our friends of to-day will not be our friends of a few years hence; but, if we keep one of them, it will be at the expense of the others—and, most probably, we shall keep none. To be sure, there are more to be had! But who cares about making a new set of friends, even should they be better than those around us?"

"Not I!" said Priscilla. "I will live and die with these!"

"Well; but let the future go!" resumed I. "As for the present moment, if we could look into the hearts where we wish to be most valued, what should you expect to see? One's own likeness, in the innermost, holiest niche? Ah, I don't know! It may not be there at all. It may be a dusty image, thrust aside into a corner, and by-and-by to be flung out-of-doors, where any foot may trample upon it. If not to-day, then tomorrow! And so, Priscilla, I do not see much wisdom in being so very merry in this kind of a world!"

It had taken me nearly seven years of worldly life, to hive up the bitter honey which I here offered to Priscilla. And she rejected it!

"I don't believe one word of what you say!" she replied, laughing anew. "You made me sad, for a minute, by talking about the past. But the past never comes back again. Do we dream the same dream twice? There is nothing else that I am afraid of."

So away she ran, and fell down on the green grass, as it was often her luck to do, but got up again without any harm.

"Priscilla, Priscilla!" cried Hollingsworth, who was sitting on the door-step. "You had better not run any more to-night. You will weary yourself too much. And do not sit down out of doors; for there is a heavy dew beginning to fall!"

At his first word, she went and sat down under the porch, at Hollingsworth's feet, entirely contented and happy. What charm was there, in his rude massiveness, that so attracted and soothed this shadowlike girl? It appeared to me—who have always been curious in such matters—that Priscilla's vague and seemingly causeless flow of felicitous feeling was that with which love blesses inexperienced hearts, before they begin to suspect what is going on within them. It transports them to the seventh heaven; and if you ask what brought them thither, they neither can tell nor care to learn, but cherish an ecstatic faith that there they shall abide forever.

Zenobia was in the door-way, not far from Hollingsworth. She gazed at Priscilla, in a very singular way. Indeed, it was a sight worth gazing at, and a beautiful sight too, as the fair girl sat at the feet of that dark, powerful figure. Her air, while perfectly modest, delicate, and virginlike, denoted her as swayed by Hollingsworth, attracted to him, and unconsciously seeking to rest upon his strength. I could not turn away my own eyes, but hoped that nobody, save Zenobia and myself, were witnessing this picture. It is before me now, with the evening twilight a little deepened by the dusk of memory.

"Come hither, Priscilla!" said Zenobia. "I have something to say to you!"

She spoke in little more than a whisper. But it is strange how expressive of moods a whisper may often be. Priscilla felt at once that something had gone wrong.

"Are you angry with me?" she asked, rising slowly and standing before Zenobia in a drooping attitude. "What have I done? I hope you are not angry!"

"No, no, Priscilla!" said Hollingsworth, smiling. "I will answer for it, she is not. You are the one little person in the world, with whom nobody can be angry!"

"Angry with you, child? What a silly idea!" exclaimed Zenobia, laughing. "No, indeed! But, my dear Priscilla, you are getting to be so very pretty that you absolutely need a duenna; and as I am older than you, and have had my own little experience of life, and think myself exceedingly sage, I intend to fill the place of a maiden-aunt. Every day, I shall give you a lecture, a quarter-of-an-hour in length, on the morals, manners, and proprieties of social life. When our pastoral shall be quite played out, Priscilla, my worldly wisdom may stand you in good stead!"

"I am afraid you are angry with me," repeated Priscilla, sadly; for, while she seemed as impressible as wax, the girl often showed a persistency in her own ideas, as stubborn as it was gentle.

"Dear me, what can I say to the child!" cried Zenobia, in a tone of humorous vexation. "Well, well; since you insist on my being angry, come to my room, this moment, and let me beat you!"

Zenobia bade Hollingsworth good night very sweetly, and nodded to me with a smile. But, just as she turned aside with Priscilla into the dimness of the porch, I caught another glance at her countenance. It would have made the fortune of a tragic actress, could she have borrowed it for the moment when she fumbles in her bosom for the concealed dagger, or the exceedingly sharp bodkin, or mingles the ratsbane in her lover's bowl of wine, or her rival's cup of tea. Not that I in the least anticipated any such catastrophe; it being a remarkable truth, that custom has in no one point a greater sway than over our modes of wreaking our wild passions. And, besides, had we been in Italy, instead of New England, it was hardly yet a crisis for the dagger or the bowl.

It often amazed me, however, that Hollingsworth should show himself so recklessly tender towards Priscilla, and never once seem to think of the effect which it might have upon her heart. But the man, as I have endeavored to explain, was thrown completely off his moral balance, and quite bewildered as to his personal relations, by his great excrescence of a philanthropic scheme. I used to see, or fancy, indications that he was not altogether obtuse to Zenobia's influence as a woman. No doubt, however, he had a still more exquisite enjoyment of Priscilla's silent sympathy with his purposes, so unalloyed with criticism, and therefore more grateful than any intellectual approbation, which always involves a possible reserve of latent censure. A man—poet, prophet, or whatever he may be—readily persuades himself of his right to all the worship that is voluntarily tendered. In requital of so rich benefits as he was to confer upon mankind, it would have been hard to deny Hollingsworth the simple solace of a young girl's heart, which he held in his hand, and smelled to, like a rosebud. But what if, while pressing out its fragrance, he should crush the tender rosebud in his grasp!

As for Zenobia, I saw no occasion to give myself any trouble. With her native strength, and her experience of the world, she could not be supposed to need any help of mine. Nevertheless, I was really generous enough to feel some little interest likewise for Zenobia. With all her faults, (which might have been a great many, besides the abundance that I knew of,) she possessed noble traits, and a heart which must at least have been valuable while new. And she seemed ready to fling it away, as uncalculatingly as Priscilla herself. I could not but suspect, that, if merely at play with Hollingsworth, she was sporting with a power which she did not fully estimate. Or, if in earnest, it might chance, between Zenobia's passionate force and his dark, self-delusive egotism, to turn out such earnest as would develop itself in some sufficiently tragic catastrophe, though the dagger and the bowl should go for nothing in it.

Meantime, the gossip of the Community set them down as a pair of lovers. They took walks together, and were not seldom encountered in the wood-paths; Hollingsworth deeply discoursing, in tones solemn and sternly pathetic. Zenobia, with a rich glow on her cheeks, and her eyes softened from their ordinary brightness, looked so beautiful, that, had her companion been ten times a philanthropist, it seemed impossible but that one glance should melt him back into a man. Oftener than anywhere else, they went to a certain point on the slope of a pasture, commanding nearly the whole of our own domain, besides a view of the river and an airy prospect of many distant hills. The bond of our Community was such, that the members had the privilege of building cottages for their own residence, within our precincts, thus laying a hearth-stone and fencing in a home, private and peculiar, to all desirable extent; while yet the inhabitants should continue to share the advantages of an associated life. It was inferred, that Hollingsworth and Zenobia intended to rear their dwelling on this favorite spot.

I mentioned these rumors to Hollingsworth in a playful way.

"Had you consulted me," I went on to observe, "I should have recommended a site further to the left, just a little withdrawn into the wood, with two or three peeps at the prospect, among the trees. You will be in the shady vale of years, long before you can raise any better kind of shade around your cottage, if you build it on this bare slope."

"But I offer my edifice as a spectacle to the world," said Hollingsworth, "that it may take example and build many another like it. Therefore I mean to set it on the open hill-side."

Twist these words how I might, they offered no very satisfactory import. It seemed hardly probable that Hollingsworth should care about educating the public taste in the department of cottage-architecture, desirable as such improvement certainly was.

X

A VISITOR FROM TOWN

HOLLINGSWORTH and I—we had been hoeing potatoes, that forenoon, while the rest of the fraternity were engaged in a distant quarter of the farm —sat under a clump of maples, eating our eleven o'clock lunch, when we saw a stranger approaching along the edge of the field. He had admitted himself from the road-side, through a turnstile, and seemed to have a purpose of speaking with us.

And, by-the-by, we were favored with many visits at Blithedale; especially from people who sympathized with our theories, and perhaps held themselves ready to unite in our actual experiment, as soon as there should appear a reliable promise of its success. It was rather ludicrous, indeed, (to me, at least, whose enthusiasm had insensibly been exhaled, together with the perspiration of many a hard day's toil,) it was absolutely funny, therefore, to observe what a glory was shed about our life and labors, in the imagination of these longing proselytes. In their view, we were as poetical as Arcadians, besides being as practical as the hardest-fisted husbandmen in Massachusetts. We did not, it is true, spend much time in piping to our sheep, or warbling our innocent loves to the sisterhood. But they gave us credit for imbuing the ordinary rustic occupations with a kind of religious poetry,

insomuch .hat our very cow-yards and pig-sties were as de-
lightfully fragrant as a flower-garden. Nothing used to please
me more than to see one of these lay enthusiasts snatch up a
hoe, as they were very prone to do, and set to work with
a vigor that perhaps carried him through about a dozen ill-
directed strokes. Men are wonderfully soon satisfied, in this
day of shameful bodily enervation, when, from one end of
life to the other, such multitudes never taste the sweet weariness that follows accustomed toil. I seldom saw the new
enthusiasm that did not grow as flimsy and flaccid as the
proselyte's moistened shirt-collar, with a quarter-of-an-hour's
active labor, under a July sun.

But the person, now at hand, had not at all the air of one
of these amiable visionaries. He was an elderly man, dressed
rather shabbily, yet decently enough, in a gray frock-coat,
faded towards a brown hue, and wore a broad-brimmed white
hat, of the fashion of several years gone by. His hair was
perfect silver, without a dark thread in the whole of it; his
nose, though it had a scarlet tip, by no means indicated the
jollity of which a red nose is the generally admitted symbol.
He was a subdued, undemonstrative old man, who would
doubtless drink a glass of liquor, now and then, and probably
more than was good for him; not, however, with a purpose
of undue exhilaration, but in the hope of bringing his spirits
up to the ordinary level of the world's cheerfulness. Drawing
nearer, there was a shy look about him, as if he were ashamed
of his poverty, or, at any rate, for some reason or other, would
rather have us glance at him sidelong than take a full-front
view. He had a queer appearance of hiding himself behind
the patch on his left eye.

"I know this old gentleman," said I to Hollingsworth, as
we sat observing him—"that is, I have met him a hundred
times, in town, and have often amused my fancy with wondering what he was, before he came to be what he is. He
haunts restaurants and such places, and has an odd way of

lurking in corners or getting behind a door, whenever practicable, and holding out his hand, with some little article in
it, which he wishes you to buy. The eye of the world seems
to trouble him, although he necessarily lives so much in it. I
never expected to see him in an open field."

"Have you learned anything of his history?" asked Hollingsworth.

"Not a circumstance," I answered. "But there must be
something curious in it. I take him to be a harmless sort of a
person, and a tolerably honest one; but his manners, being
so furtive, remind me of those of a rat—a rat without the
mischief, the fierce eye, the teeth to bite with, or the desire
to bite. See, now! He means to skulk along that fringe of
bushes, and approach us on the other side of our clump of
maples."

We soon heard the old man's velvet tread on the grass,
indicating that he had arrived within a few feet of where
we sat.

"Good morning, Mr. Moodie," said Hollingsworth, addressing the stranger as an acquaintance. "You must have had a
hot and tiresome walk from the city. Sit down, and take a
morsel of our bread and cheese!"

The visitor made a grateful little murmur of acquiescence,
and sat down in a spot somewhat removed; so that, glancing
round, I could see his gray pantaloons and dusty shoes, while
his upper part was mostly hidden behind the shrubbery. Nor
did he come forth from this retirement during the whole of
the interview that followed. We handed him such food as
we had, together with a brown jug of molasses-and-water,
(would that it had been brandy, or something better, for the
sake of his chill old heart!) like priests offering dainty sacrifice
to an enshrined and invisible idol. I have no idea that he
really lacked sustenance; but it was quite touching, nevertheless, to hear him nibbling away at our crusts.

"Mr. Moodie," said I, "do you remember selling me one

of those very pretty little silk purses, of which you seem to have a monopoly in the market? I keep it, to this day, I can assure you."

"Ah, thank you!" said our guest. "Yes, Mr. Coverdale, I used to sell a good many of those little purses."

He spoke languidly, and only those few words, like a watch with an inelastic spring, that just ticks, a moment or two, and stops again. He seemed a very forlorn old man. In the wantonness of youth, strength, and comfortable condition—making my prey of people's individualities, as my custom was—I tried to identify my mind with the old fellow's, and take his view of the world, as if looking through a smoke-blackened glass at the sun. It robbed the landscape of all its life. Those pleasantly swelling slopes of our farm, descending towards the wide meadows, through which sluggishly circled the brimfull tide of the Charles, bathing the long sedges on its hither and farther shores; the broad, sunny gleam over the winding water; that peculiar picturesqueness of the scene, where capes and headlands put themselves boldly forth upon the perfect level of the meadow, as into a green lake, with inlets between the promontories; the shadowy woodland, with twinkling showers of light falling into its depths; the sultry heat-vapor, which rose everywhere like incense, and in which my soul delighted, as indicating so rich a fervor in the passionate day, and in the earth that was burning with its love:—I beheld all these things as through old Moodie's eyes. When my eyes are dimmer than they have yet come to be, I will go thither again, and see if I did not catch the tone of his mind aright, and if the cold and lifeless tint of his perceptions be not then repeated in my own.

Yet it was unaccountable to myself, the interest that I felt in him.

"Have you any objection," said I, "to telling me who made those little purses?"

"Gentlemen have often asked me that," said Moodie,

slowly; "but I shake my head, and say little or nothing, and creep out of the way, as well as I can. I am a man of few words; and if gentlemen were to be told one thing, they would be very apt, I suppose, to ask me another. But it happens, just now, Mr. Coverdale, that you can tell me more about the maker of those little purses, than I can tell you."

"Why do you trouble him with needless questions, Coverdale?" interrupted Hollingsworth. "You must have known, long ago, that it was Priscilla. And so, my good friend, you have come to see her? Well, I am glad of it. You will find her altered very much for the better, since that wintry evening when you put her into my charge. Why, Priscilla has a bloom in her cheeks, now!"

"Has my pale little girl a bloom?" repeated Moodie, with a kind of slow wonder. "Priscilla with a bloom in her cheeks! Ah, I am afraid I shall not know my little girl. And is she happy?"

"Just as happy as a bird," answered Hollingsworth.

"Then, gentlemen," said our guest, apprehensively, "I don't think it well for me to go any further. I crept hitherward only to ask about Priscilla; and now that you have told me such good news, perhaps I can do no better than to creep back again. If she were to see this old face of mine, the child would remember some very sad times which we have spent together. Some very sad times indeed! She has forgotten them, I know—them and me—else she could not be so happy, nor have a bloom in her cheeks. Yes—yes—yes," continued he, still with the same torpid utterance; "with many thanks to you, Mr. Hollingsworth, I will creep back to town again."

"You shall do no such thing, Mr. Moodie!" said Hollingsworth, bluffly. "Priscilla often speaks of you; and if there lacks anything to make her cheeks bloom like two damask roses, I'll venture to say, it is just the sight of your face. Come; we will go and find her."

"Mr. Hollingsworth!" said the old man, in his hesitating way.

"Well!" answered Hollingsworth.

"Has there been any call for Priscilla?" asked Moodie; and though his face was hidden from us, his tone gave a sure indication of the mysterious nod and wink with which he put the question. "You know, I think, sir, what I mean."

"I have not the remotest suspicion what you mean, Mr. Moodie," replied Hollingsworth. "Nobody, to my knowledge, has called for Priscilla, except yourself. But, come; we are losing time, and I have several things to say to you, by the way."

"And, Mr. Hollingsworth!" repeated Moodie.

"Well, again!" cried my friend, rather impatiently. "What now?"

"There is a lady here," said the old man; and his voice lost some of its wearisome hesitation. "You will account it a very strange matter for me to talk about; but I chanced to know this lady, when she was but a little child. If I am rightly informed, she has grown to be a very fine woman, and makes a brilliant figure in the world, with her beauty, and her talents, and her noble way of spending her riches. I should recognize this lady, so people tell me, by a magnificent flower in her hair!"

"What a rich tinge it gives to his colorless ideas, when he speaks of Zenobia!" I whispered to Hollingsworth. "But how can there possibly be any interest or connecting link between him and her?"

"The old man, for years past," whispered Hollingsworth, "has been a little out of his right mind, as you probably see."

"What I would inquire," resumed Moodie, "is, whether this beautiful lady is kind to my poor Priscilla."

"Very kind," said Hollingsworth.

"Does she love her?" asked Moodie.

"It should seem so," answered my friend. "They are always together."

"Like a gentlewoman and her maid servant, I fancy?" suggested the old man.

There was something so singular in his way of saying this, that I could not resist the impulse to turn quite round, so as to catch a glimpse of his face; almost imagining that I should see another person than old Moodie. But there he sat, with the patched side of his face towards me.

"Like an elder and younger sister, rather," replied Hollingsworth.

"Ah," said Moodie, more complaisantly—for his latter tones had harshness and acidity in them—"it would gladden my old heart to witness that. If one thing would make me happier than another, Mr. Hollingsworth, it would be, to see that beautiful lady holding my little girl by the hand."

"Come along," said Hollingsworth, "and perhaps you may."

After a little more delay on the part of our freakish visitor, they set forth together; old Moodie keeping a step or two behind Hollingsworth, so that the latter could not very conveniently look him in the face. I remained under the tuft of maples, doing my utmost to draw an inference from the scene that had just passed. In spite of Hollingsworth's off-hand explanation, it did not strike me that our strange guest was really beside himself, but only that his mind needed screwing up, like an instrument long out of tune, the strings of which have ceased to vibrate smartly and sharply. Methought it would be profitable for us, projectors of a happy life, to welcome this old gray shadow, and cherish him as one of us, and let him creep about our domain, in order that he might be a little merrier for our sakes, and we, sometimes, a little sadder for his. Human destinies look ominous, without some perceptible intermixture of the sable or the gray. And then, too, should any of our fraternity grow feverish with an over-exulting sense of prosperity, it would be a sort of cooling regimen to slink off into the woods, and spend an hour, or a day, or as many days as might be requisite to the cure, in uninterrupted communion with this deplorable old Moodie!

Going homeward to dinner, I had a glimpse of him behind the trunk of a tree, gazing earnestly towards a particular window of the farm-house. And, by-and-by, Priscilla appeared at this window, playfully drawing along Zenobia, who looked as bright as the very day that was blazing down upon us, only not, by many degrees, so well advanced towards her noon. I was convinced that this pretty sight must have been purposely arranged by Priscilla, for the old man to see. But either the girl held her too long, or her fondness was resented as too great a freedom; for Zenobia suddenly put Priscilla decidedly away, and gave her a haughty look, as from a mistress to a dependant. Old Moodie shook his head—and again, and again, I saw him shake it, as he withdrew along the road—and, at the last point whence the farm-house was visible, he turned, and shook his uplifted staff.

XI

THE WOOD-PATH

NOT LONG after the preceding incident, in order to get the ache of too constant labor out of my bones, and to relieve my spirit of the irksomeness of a settled routine, I took a holiday. It was my purpose to spend it, all alone, from breakfast-time till twilight, in the deepest wood-seclusion that lay anywhere around us. Though fond of society, I was so constituted as to need these occasional retirements, even in a life like that of Blithedale, which was itself characterized by a remoteness from the world. Unless renewed by a yet farther withdrawal towards the inner circle of self-communion, I lost the better part of my individuality. My thoughts became of little worth, and my sensibilities grew as arid as a tuft of moss, (a thing whose life is in the shade, the rain, or the noontide dew,) crumbling in the sunshine, after long expectance of a shower. So, with my heart full of a drowsy pleasure, and cautious not to dissipate my mood by previous intercourse with any one, I hurried away, and was soon pacing a wood-path, arched overhead with boughs, and dusky brown beneath my feet.

At first, I walked very swiftly, as if the heavy floodtide of social life were roaring at my heels, and would outstrip and overwhelm me, without all the better diligence in my escape. But, threading the more distant windings of the track, I abated my pace and looked about me for some side-aisle, that should admit me into the innermost sanctuary of this green cathedral; just as, in human acquaintanceship, a casual opening sometimes lets us, all of a sudden, into the long-sought intimacy of a mysterious heart. So much was I absorbed in my reflections—or rather, in my mood, the substance of which was as yet too shapeless to be called thought—that footsteps rustled on the leaves, and a figure passed me by, almost without impressing either the sound or sight upon my consciousness.

A moment afterwards, I heard a voice at a little distance behind me, speaking so sharply and impertinently that it made a complete discord with my spiritual state, and caused the latter to vanish, as abruptly as when you thrust a finger into a soap-bubble.

"Halloo, friend!" cried this most unseasonable voice. "Stop a moment, I say! I must have a word with you!"

I turned about, in a humor ludicrously irate. In the first place, the interruption, at any rate, was a grievous injury; then, the tone displeased me. And, finally, unless there be real affection in his heart, a man cannot—such is the bad state to which the world has brought itself—cannot more effectually show his contempt for a brother-mortal, nor more gallingly assume a position of superiority, than by addressing him as 'friend.' Especially does the misapplication of this phrase bring out that latent hostility, which is sure to animate peculiar sects, and those who, with however generous a purpose, have sequestered themselves from the crowd; a feeling, it is true, which may be hidden in some dog-kennel of the heart, grumbling there in the darkness, but is never quite extinct, until the dissenting party have gained power and scope enough to treat the world generously. For my part, I should have taken it as far less an insult to be styled 'fellow,' 'clown,' or 'bumpkin.' To either of these appellations, my rustic garb (it was a linen blouse, with checked shirt and striped pantaloons, a chip-hat on my head, and a rough hickory-stick in my hand) very fairly entitled me. As the case stood, my temper darted at once to the opposite pole; not friend, but enemy!

"What do you want with me?" said I, facing about.

"Come a little nearer, friend!" said the stranger, beckoning.

"No," answered I. "If I can do anything for you, without too much trouble to myself, say so. But recollect, if you please, that you are not speaking to an acquaintance, much less a friend!"

"Upon my word, I believe not!" retorted he, looking at me with some curiosity; and lifting his hat, he made me a salute, which had enough of sarcasm to be offensive, and just enough of doubtful courtesy to render any resentment of it absurd.— "But I ask your pardon! I recognize a little mistake. If I may take the liberty to suppose it, you, sir, are probably one of the Æsthetic—or shall I rather say ecstatic?—laborers, who have planted themselves hereabouts. This is your forest of Arden; and you are either the banished Duke, in person, or one of the chief nobles in his train. The melancholy Jacques, perhaps? Be it so! In that case, you can probably do me a favor."

I never, in my life, felt less inclined to confer a favor on any man.

"I am busy!" said I.

So unexpectedly had the stranger made me sensible of his presence, that he had almost the effect of an apparition, and certainly a less appropriate one (taking into view the dim woodland solitude about us) than if the salvage man of antiquity, hirsute and cinctured with a leafy girdle, had started out of a thicket. He was still young, seemingly a little under thirty, of a tall and well-developed figure, and as handsome a man as ever I beheld. The style of his beauty, however, though a masculine style, did not at all commend itself to my taste. His countenance—I hardly know how to describe the peculiarity—had an indecorum in it, a kind of rudeness, a hard, coarse, forth-putting freedom of expression, which no degree of external polish could have abated, one single jot. Not that it was vulgar. But he had no fineness of nature; there was in his eyes (although they might have artifice enough of another sort) the naked exposure of something that ought not to be left prominent. With these vague allusions to what I have seen in other faces, as well as his, I leave the quality to be comprehended best—because with an intuitive repugnance—by those who possess least of it.

His hair, as well as his beard and moustache, was coal-black; his eyes, too, were black and sparkling, and his teeth remarkably brilliant. He was rather carelessly, but well and fashionably dressed, in a summer-morning costume. There was a gold chain, exquisitely wrought, across his vest. I never saw a smoother or whiter gloss than that upon his shirt-bosom, which had a pin in it, set with a gem that glimmered, in the leafy shadow where he stood, like a living tip of fire. He carried a stick with a wooden head, carved in vivid imitation of that of a serpent. I hated him, partly, I do believe, from a comparison of my own homely garb with his well-ordered foppishness.

"Well, sir," said I, a little ashamed of my first irritation, but still with no waste of civility, "be pleased to speak at once, as I have my own business in hand."

"I regret that my mode of addressing you was a little unfortunate," said the stranger, smiling; for he seemed a very acute sort of person, and saw, in some degree, how I stood affected towards him. "I intended no offence, and shall certainly comport myself with due ceremony hereafter. I merely wish to make a few inquiries respecting a lady, formerly of my acquaintance, who is now resident in your Community, and, I believe, largely concerned in your social enterprise. You call her, I think, Zenobia."

"That is her name in literature," observed I—"a name, too, which possibly she may permit her private friends to know and address her by;—but not one which they feel at liberty to recognize, when used of her, personally, by a stranger or casual acquaintance."

"Indeed!" answered this disagreeable person; and he turned aside his face, for an instant, with a brief laugh, which struck me as a noteworthy expression of his character. "Perhaps I might put forward a claim, on your own grounds, to call the lady by a name so appropriate to her splendid qualities. But I am willing to know her by any cognomen that you may suggest."

Heartily wishing that he would be either a little more offensive, or a good deal less so, or break off our intercourse altogether, I mentioned Zenobia's real name.

"True," said he; "and, in general society, I have never heard her called otherwise. And, after all, our discussion of the point has been gratuitous. My object is only to inquire when, where, and how, this lady may most conveniently be seen?"

"At her present residence, of course," I replied. "You have but to go thither and ask for her. This very path will lead you within sight of the house;—so I wish you good morning."

"One moment, if you please," said the stranger. "The course you indicate would certainly be the proper one, in an ordinary morning-call. But my business is private, personal, and somewhat peculiar. Now, in a Community like this, I should judge that any little occurrence is likely to be discussed rather more minutely than would quite suit my views. I refer solely to myself, you understand, and without intimating that it would be other than a matter of entire indifference to the lady. In short, I especially desire to see her in private. If her habits are such as I have known them, she is probably often to be met with in the woods, or by the river-side; and I think you could do me the favor to point out some favorite walk, where, about this hour, I might be fortunate enough to gain an interview."

I reflected, that it would be quite a super-erogatory piece of quixotism, in me, to undertake the guardianship of Zenobia, who, for my pains, would only make me the butt of endless ridicule, should the fact ever come to her knowledge. I therefore described a spot which, as often as any other, was Zenobia's resort, at this period of the day; nor was it so remote from the farm-house as to leave her in much peril, whatever might be the stranger's character.

"A single word more!" said he; and his black eyes sparkled at me, whether with fun or malice I knew not, but certainly as if the Devil were peeping out of them. "Among your fraternity, I understand, there is a certain holy and benevolent blacksmith; a man of iron, in more senses than one; a rough, cross-grained, well-meaning individual, rather boorish in his manners—as might be expected—and by no means of the highest intellectual cultivation. He is a philanthropical lecturer, with two or three disciples, and a scheme of his own, the preliminary step in which involves a large purchase of land, and the erection of a spacious edifice, at an expense considerably beyond his means; inasmuch as these are to be reckoned in copper or old iron, much more conveniently than in gold or silver. He hammers away upon his one topic, as lustily as ever he did upon a horse-shoe! Do you know such a person?"

I shook my head, and was turning away.

"Our friend," he continued, "is described to me as a brawny, shaggy, grim, and ill-favored personage, not particularly well-calculated, one would say, to insinuate himself with the softer sex. Yet, so far has this honest fellow succeeded with one lady, whom we wot of, that he anticipates, from her abundant resources, the necessary funds for realizing his plan in brick and mortar!"

Here the stranger seemed to be so much amused with his sketch of Hollingsworth's character and purposes, that he burst into a fit of merriment, of the same nature as the brief, metallic laugh already alluded to, but immensely prolonged and enlarged. In the excess of his delight, he opened his mouth wide, and disclosed a gold band around the upper part of his teeth; thereby making it apparent that every one of his brilliant grinders and incisors was a sham. This discovery affected me very oddly. I felt as if the whole man were a moral and physical humbug; his wonderful beauty of face, for aught I knew, might be removeable like a mask; and, tall and comely as his figure looked, he was perhaps but a wizened little elf, gray and decrepit, with nothing genuine about him, save the wicked expression of his grin. The fantasy of his spectral character so wrought upon me, together with the contagion of his strange mirth on my sympathies, that I soon began to laugh as loudly as himself.

By-and-by, he paused, all at once; so suddenly, indeed, that my own cachinnation lasted a moment longer.

"Ah, excuse me!" said he. "Our interview seems to proceed more merrily than it began."

"It ends here," answered I. "And I take shame to myself, that my folly has lost me the right of resenting your ridicule of a friend."

"Pray allow me," said the stranger, approaching a step nearer, and laying his gloved hand on my sleeve. "One other favor I must ask of you. You have a young person, here at Blithedale, of whom I have heard—whom, perhaps, I have known—and in whom, at all events, I take a peculiar interest. She is one of those delicate, nervous young creatures, not uncommon in New England, and whom I suppose to have become what we find them by the gradual refining away of the physical system, among your women. Some philosophers choose to glorify this habit of body by terming it spiritual; but, in my opinion, it is rather the effect of unwholesome food, bad air, lack of out-door exercise, and neglect of bathing, on the part of these damsels and their female progenitors; all resulting in a kind of hereditary dyspepsia. Zenobia, even with her uncomfortable surplus of vitality, is far the better model of womanhood. But—to revert again to this young person—she goes among you by the name of Priscilla. Could you possibly afford me the means of speaking with her?"

"You have made so many inquiries of me," I observed, "that I may at least trouble you with one. What is your name?"

He offered me a card, with 'Professor Westervelt' engraved on it. At the same time, as if to vindicate his claim to the professorial dignity, so often assumed on very questionable grounds, he put on a pair of spectacles, which so altered the character of his face that I hardly knew him again. But I liked the present aspect no better than the former one.

"I must decline any further connection with your affairs," said I, drawing back. "I have told you where to find Zenobia. As for Priscilla, she has closer friends than myself, through whom, if they see fit, you can gain access to her."

"In that case," returned the Professor, ceremoniously raising his hat, "good morning to you."

He took his departure, and was soon out of sight among the windings of the wood-path. But, after a little reflection, I could not help regretting that I had so peremptorily broken off the interview, while the stranger seemed inclined to continue it. His evident knowledge of matters, affecting my three friends, might have led to disclosures, or inferences, that would perhaps have been serviceable. I was particularly struck with the fact, that, ever since the appearance of Priscilla, it had been the tendency of events to suggest and establish a connection between Zenobia and her. She had come, in the first instance, as if with the sole purpose of claiming Zenobia's protection. Old Moodie's visit, it appeared, was chiefly to ascertain whether this object had been accomplished. And here, to-day, was the questionable Professor, linking one with the other in his inquiries, and seeking communication with both.

Meanwhile, my inclination for a ramble having been baulked, I lingered in the vicinity of the farm, with perhaps a vague idea that some new event would grow out of Westervelt's proposed interview with Zenobia. My own part, in these transactions, was singularly subordinate. It resembled that of the Chorus in a classic play, which seems to be set aloof from the possibility of personal concernment, and bestows the whole measure of its hope or fear, its exultation or sorrow, on the fortunes of others, between whom and itself this sympathy is the only bond. Destiny, it may be—the most skilful of stage-managers—seldom chooses to arrange its scenes, and carry forward its drama, without securing the presence of at least one calm observer. It is his office to give applause, when due, and sometimes an inevitable tear, to detect the final fitness of incident to character, and distil, in his long-brooding thought, the whole morality of the performance.

Not to be out of the way, in case there were need of me in my vocation, and, at the same time, to avoid thrusting myself where neither Destiny nor mortals might desire my presence, I remained pretty near the verge of the woodlands. My position was off the track of Zenobia's customary walk, yet not so remote but that a recognized occasion might speedily have brought me thither.

XII

COVERDALE'S HERMITAGE

L
ONG since, in this part of our circumjacent wood, I had found out for myself a little hermitage. It was a kind of leafy cave, high upward into the air, among the midmost branches of a white-pine tree. A wild grape-vine, of unusual size and luxuriance, had twined and twisted itself up into the tree, and, after wreathing the entanglement of its tendrils around almost every bough, had caught hold of three or four neighboring trees, and married the whole clump with a perfectly inextricable knot of polygamy. Once, while sheltering myself from a summer shower, the fancy had taken me to clamber up into this seemingly impervious mass of foliage. The branches yielded me a passage, and closed again, beneath, as if only a squirrel or a bird had passed. Far aloft, around the stem of the central pine, behold, a perfect nest for Robinson Crusoe or King Charles! A hollow chamber, of rare seclusion, had been formed by the decay of some of the pine-branches, which the vine had lovingly strangled with its embrace, burying them from the light of day in an aerial sepulchre of its own leaves. It cost me but little ingenuity to enlarge the interior, and open loop-holes through the verdant walls. Had it ever been my fortune to spend a honey-moon, I should have thought seriously of

• 98 •

inviting my bride up thither, where our next neighbors would have been two orioles in another part of the clump.

It was an admirable place to make verses, tuning the rhythm to the breezy symphony that so often stirred among the vine-leaves; or to meditate an essay for the Dial, in which the many tongues of Nature whispered mysteries, and seemed to ask only a little stronger puff of wind, to speak out the solution of its riddle. Being so pervious to air-currents, it was just the nook, too, for the enjoyment of a cigar. This hermitage was my one exclusive possession, while I counted myself a brother of the socialists. It symbolized my individuality, and aided me in keeping it inviolate. None ever found me out in it, except, once, a squirrel. I brought thither no guest, because, after Hollingsworth failed me, there was no longer the man alive with whom I could think of sharing all. So there I used to sit, owl-like, yet not without liberal and hospitable thoughts. I counted the innumerable clusters of my vine, and forereckoned the abundance of my vintage. It gladdened me to anticipate the surprise of the Community, when, like an allegorical figure of rich October, I should make my appearance, with shoulders bent beneath the burthen of ripe grapes, and some of the crushed ones crimsoning my brow as with a blood-stain.

Ascending into this natural turret, I peeped, in turn, out of several of its small windows. The pine-tree, being ancient, rose high above the rest of the wood, which was of comparatively recent growth. Even where I sat, about midway between the root and the topmost bough, my position was lofty enough to serve as an observatory, not for starry investigations, but for those sublunary matters in which lay a lore as infinite as that of the planets. Through one loop-hole, I saw the river lapsing calmly onward, while, in the meadow near its brink, a few of the brethren were digging peat for our winter's fuel. On the interior cart-road of our farm, I discerned Hollingsworth, with a yoke of oxen hitched to a drag of stones, that were to be piled into a fence, on which we employed ourselves at the odd intervals of other labor. The harsh tones of his voice, shouting to the sluggish steers, made me sensible, even at such a distance, that he was ill at ease, and that the baulked philanthropist had the battle-spirit in his heart.

"Haw Buck!" quoth he. "Come along there, ye lazy ones! What are ye about now? Gee!"

"Mankind, in Hollingsworth's opinion," thought I, "is but another yoke of oxen, as stubborn, stupid, and sluggish, as our old Brown and Bright. He vituperates us aloud, and curses us in his heart, and will begin to prick us with the goad stick, by-and-by. But, are we his oxen? And what right has he to be the driver? And why, when there is enough else to do, should we waste our strength in dragging home the ponderous load of his philanthropic absurdities? At my height above the earth, the whole matter looks ridiculous!"

Turning towards the farm-house, I saw Priscilla (for, though a great way off, the eye of faith assured me that it was she) sitting at Zenobia's window, and making little purses, I suppose, or perhaps mending the Community's old linen. A bird flew past my tree; and as it clove its way onward into the sunny atmosphere, I flung it a message for Priscilla.

"Tell her," said I, "that her fragile thread of life has in-extricably knotted itself with other and tougher threads, and most likely it will be broken. Tell her that Zenobia will not be long her friend. Say that Hollingsworth's heart is on fire with his own purpose, but icy for all human affection, and that, if she has given him her love, it is like casting a flower into a sepulchre. And say, that, if any mortal really cares for her, it is myself, and not even I, for her realities—poor little seamstress, as Zenobia rightly called her!—but for the fancy-work with which I have idly decked her out!"

The pleasant scent of the wood, evolved by the hot sun, stole up to my nostrils, as if I had been an idol in its niche. Many trees mingled their fragrance into a thousand-fold odor. Possibly, there was a sensual influence in the broad light of noon that lay beneath me. It may have been the cause, in part, that I suddenly found myself possessed by a mood of disbelief in moral beauty or heroism, and a conviction of the folly of attempting to benefit the world. Our especial scheme of reform, which, from my observatory, I could take in with the bodily eye, looked so ridiculous that it was impossible not to laugh aloud.

"But the joke is a little too heavy," thought I. "If I were wise, I should get out of the scrape, with all diligence, and then laugh at my companions for remaining in it!"

While thus musing, I heard, with perfect distinctness, somewhere in the wood beneath, the peculiar laugh, which I have described as one of the disagreeable characteristics of Professor Westervelt. It brought my thoughts back to our recent interview. I recognized, as chiefly due to this man's influence, the sceptical and sneering view which, just now, had filled my mental vision in regard to all life's better purposes. And it was through his eyes, more than my own, that I was looking at Hollingsworth, with his glorious, if impracticable dream, and at the noble earthliness of Zenobia's character, and even at Priscilla, whose impalpable grace lay so singularly between disease and beauty. The essential charm of each had vanished. There are some spheres, the contact with which inevitably degrades the high, debases the pure, deforms the beautiful. It must be a mind of uncommon strength, and little impressibility, that can permit itself the habit of such intercourse, and not be permanently deterio-rated; and yet the Professor's tone represented that of worldly society at large, where a cold scepticism smothers what it can of our spiritual aspirations, and makes the rest ridiculous.

I detested this kind of man, and all the more, because a part of my own nature showed itself responsive to him.

Voices were now approaching, through the region of the wood which lay in the vicinity of my tree. Soon, I caught glimpses of two figures—a woman and a man—Zenobia and the stranger—earnestly talking together as they advanced.

Zenobia had a rich, though varying color. It was, most of the while, a flame, and anon a sudden paleness. Her eyes glowed, so that their light sometimes flashed upward to me, as when the sun throws a dazzle from some bright object on the ground. Her gestures were free, and strikingly impressive. The whole woman was alive with a passionate intensity, which I now perceived to be the phase in which her beauty culminated. Any passion would have become her well, and passionate love, perhaps, the best of all. This was not love, but anger, largely intermixed with scorn. Yet the idea strangely forced itself upon me, that there was a sort of familiarity between these two companions, necessarily the result of an intimate love—on Zenobia's part, at least—in days gone by, but which had prolonged itself into as intimate a hatred, for all futurity. As they passed among the trees, reckless as her movement was, she took good heed that even the hem of her garment should not brush against the stranger's person. I wondered whether there had always been a chasm, guarded so religiously, betwixt these two.

As for Westervelt, he was not a whit more warmed by Zenobia's passion, than a salamander by the heat of its native furnace. He would have been absolutely statuesque, save for a look of slight perplexity tinctured strongly with derision. It was a crisis in which his intellectual perceptions could not altogether help him out. He failed to comprehend, and cared but little for comprehending, why Zenobia should put herself into such a fume; but satisfied his mind that it was all folly, and only another shape of a woman's manifold absurdity, which men can never understand. How many a woman's evil fate has yoked her with a man like this! Nature thrusts some of us into the world miserably incomplete, on the emotional side, with hardly any sensibilities except what pertain to us as animals. No passion, save of the senses; no holy tenderness, nor the delicacy that results from this. Externally, they bear a close resemblance to other men, and have perhaps all save the finest grace; but when a woman wrecks herself on such a being, she ultimately finds that the real womanhood, within her, has no corresponding part in him. Her deepest voice lacks a response; the deeper her cry, the more dead his silence. The fault may be none of his; he cannot give her what never lived within his soul. But the wretchedness, on her side, and the moral deterioration attendant on a false and shallow life, without strength enough to keep itself sweet, are among the most pitiable wrongs that mortals suffer.

Now, as I looked down from my upper region at this man and woman—outwardly so fair a sight, and wandering like two lovers in the wood—I imagined that Zenobia, at an earlier period of youth, might have fallen into the misfortune above indicated. And when her passionate womanhood, as was inevitable, had discovered its mistake, there had ensued the character of eccentricity and defiance, which distinguished the more public portion of her life.

Seeing how aptly matters had chanced, thus far, I began to think it the design of fate to let me into all Zenobia's secrets, and that therefore the couple would sit down beneath my tree, and carry on a conversation which would leave me nothing to inquire. No doubt, however, had it so happened, I should have deemed myself honorably bound to warn them of a listener's presence by flinging down a handful of unripe grapes; or by sending an unearthly groan out of my hiding-place, as if this were one of the trees of Dante's ghostly forest.

But real life never arranges itself exactly like a romance. In the first place, they did not sit down at all. Secondly, even while they passed beneath the tree, Zenobia's utterance was so hasty and broken, and Westervelt's so cool and low, that I hardly could make out an intelligible sentence, on either side. What I seem to remember, I yet suspect may have been patched together by my fancy, in brooding over the matter, afterwards.

"Why not fling the girl off," said Westervelt, "and let her go?"

"She clung to me from the first," replied Zenobia. "I neither know nor care what it is in me that so attaches her. But she loves me, and I will not fail her."

"She will plague you, then," said he, "in more ways than one."

"The poor child!" exclaimed Zenobia. "She can do me neither good nor harm. How should she?"

I know not what reply Westervelt whispered; nor did Zenobia's subsequent exclamation give me any clue, except that it evidently inspired her with horror and disgust.

"With what kind of a being am I linked!" cried she. "If my Creator cares aught for my soul, let him release me from this miserable bond!"

"I did not think it weighed so heavily," said her companion.

"Nevertheless," answered Zenobia, "it will strangle me at last!"

And then I heard her utter a helpless sort of moan; a sound which, struggling out of the heart of a person of her pride and strength, affected me more than if she had made the wood dolorously vocal with a thousand shrieks and wails.

Other mysterious words, besides what are above-written, they spoke together; but I understood no more, and even question whether I fairly understood so much as this. By long brooding over our recollections, we subtilize them into something akin to imaginary stuff, and hardly capable of being distinguished from it. In a few moments, they were completely beyond ear-shot. A breeze stirred after them, and awoke the leafy tongues of the surrounding trees, which forthwith began to babble, as if innumerable gossips had all at once got wind of Zenobia's secret. But, as the breeze grew stronger, its voice among the branches was as if it said—'Hush! Hush!'—and I resolved that to no mortal would I disclose what I had heard. And, though there might be room for casuistry, such, I conceive, is the most equitable rule in all similar conjunctures.

XIII

ZENOBIA'S LEGEND

THE illustrious Society of Blithedale, though it toiled in downright earnest for the good of mankind, yet not unfrequently illuminated its laborious life with an afternoon or evening of pastime. Pic-nics under the trees were considerably in vogue; and, within doors, fragmentary bits of theatrical performance, such as single acts of tragedy or comedy, or dramatic proverbs and charades. Zenobia, besides, was fond of giving us readings from Shakspeare, and often with a depth of tragic power, or breadth of comic effect, that made one feel it an intolerable wrong to the world, that she did not at once go upon the stage. *Tableaux vivants* were another of our occasional modes of amusement, in which scarlet shawls, old silken robes, ruffs, velvets, furs, and all kinds of miscellaneous trumpery, converted our familiar companions into the people of a pictorial world. We had been thus engaged, on the evening after the incident narrated in the last chapter. Several splendid works of art—either arranged after engravings from the Old Masters, or original illustrations of scenes in history or romance—had been presented, and we were earnestly entreating Zenobia for more.

She stood, with a meditative air, holding a large piece of gauze, or some such ethereal stuff, as if considering what picture should next occupy the frame; while at her feet lay a heap of many-colored garments, which her quick fancy and magic skill could so easily convert into gorgeous draperies for heroes and princesses.

"I am getting weary of this," said she, after a moment's thought. "Our own features, and our own figures and airs, show a little too intrusively through all the characters we assume. We have so much familiarity with one another's realities, that we cannot remove ourselves, at pleasure, into an imaginary sphere. Let us have no more pictures, to-night; but, to make you what poor amends I can, how would you like to have me trump up a wild, spectral legend, on the spur of the moment?"

Zenobia had the gift of telling a fanciful little story, off hand, in a way that made it greatly more effective, than it was usually found to be, when she afterwards elaborated the same production with her pen. Her proposal, therefore, was greeted with acclamation.

"Oh, a story, a story, by all means!" cried the young girls. "No matter how marvellous, we will believe it, every word! And let it be a ghost-story, if you please!"

"No; not exactly a ghost-story," answered Zenobia; "but something so nearly like it that you shall hardly tell the difference. And, Priscilla, stand you before me, where I may look at you, and get my inspiration out of your eyes. They are very deep and dreamy, to-night!"

I know not whether the following version of her story will retain any portion of its pristine character. But, as Zenobia told it, wildly and rapidly, hesitating at no extravagance, and dashing at absurdities which I am too timorous to repeat—giving it the varied emphasis of her inimitable voice, and the pictorial illustration of her mobile face, while, through it all, we caught the freshest aroma of the thoughts, as they came bubbling out of her mind—thus narrated, and thus heard, the legend seemed quite a remarkable affair. I scarcely knew, at the time, whether she intended us to laugh, or be more seriously impressed. From beginning to end it was undeniable nonsense, but not necessarily the worse for that.

THE SILVERY VEIL

You have heard, my dear friends, of the Veiled Lady, who grew suddenly so very famous, a few months ago. And have you never thought how remarkable it was, that this marvellous creature should vanish, all at once, while her renown was on the increase, before the public had grown weary of her, and when the enigma of her character, instead of being solved, presented itself more mystically at every exhibition? Her last appearance, as you know, was before a crowded audience. The next evening—although the bills had announced her, at the corner of every street, in red letters of a gigantic size—there was no Veiled Lady to be seen! Now, listen to my simple little tale; and you shall hear the very latest incident in the known life—(if life it may be called, which seemed to have no more reality than the candlelight image of one's self, which peeps at us outside of a dark window-pane)—the life of this shadowy phenomenon.

A party of young gentlemen, you are to understand, were enjoying themselves, one afternoon, as young gentlemen are sometimes fond of doing, over a bottle or two of champagne; and—among other ladies less mysterious—the subject of the Veiled Lady, as was very natural, happened to come up before them for discussion. She rose, as it were, with the sparkling effervescence of their wine, and appeared in a more airy and fantastic light, on account of the medium through which they saw her. They repeated to one another, between jest and earnest, all the wild stories that were in vogue; nor, I presume, did they hesitate to add any small circumstance that the inventive whim of the moment might suggest, to heighten the marvellousness of their theme.

"But what an audacious report was that," observed one, "which pretended to assert the identity of this strange creature with a young lady"—and here he mentioned her name—"the daughter of one of our most distinguished families!"

"Ah, there is more in that story than can well be accounted for!" remarked another. "I have it on good authority, that the young lady in question is invariably out of sight, and not to be traced, even by her own family, at the hours when the Veiled Lady is before the public; nor can any satisfactory explanation be given of her disappearance. And just look at the thing! Her brother is a young fellow of spirit. He cannot but be aware of these rumors in reference to his sister. Why, then, does he not come forward to defend her character, unless he is conscious that an investigation would only make the matter worse?"

It is essential to the purposes of my legend to distinguish one of these young gentlemen from his companions; so, for the sake of a soft and pretty name, (such as we, of the literary sisterhood, invariably bestow upon our heroes,) I deem it fit to call him 'Theodore.'

"Pshaw!" exclaimed Theodore. "Her brother is no such fool! Nobody, unless his brain be as full of bubbles as this wine, can seriously think of crediting that ridiculous rumor. Why, if my senses did not play me false, (which never was the case yet,) I affirm that I saw that very lady, last evening, at the exhibition, while this veiled phenomenon was playing off her juggling tricks! What can you say to that?"

"Oh, it was a spectral illusion that you saw!" replied his friends, with a general laugh. "The Veiled Lady is quite up to such a thing."

However, as the above-mentioned fable could not hold its ground against Theodore's downright refutation, they went on to speak of other stories, which the wild babble of the town had set afloat. Some upheld, that the veil covered the most beautiful countenance in the world; others—and certainly with more reason, considering the sex of the Veiled

Lady—that the face was the most hideous and horrible, and that this was her sole motive for hiding it. It was the face of a corpse; it was the head of a skeleton; it was a monstrous visage, with snaky locks, like Medusa's, and one great red eye in the centre of the forehead. Again, it was affirmed, that there was no single and unchangeable set of features, beneath the veil, but that whosoever should be bold enough to lift it, would behold the features of that person, in all the world, who was destined to be his fate; perhaps he would be greeted by the tender smile of the woman whom he loved; or, quite as probably, the deadly scowl of his bitterest enemy would throw a blight over his life. They quoted, moreover, this startling explanation of the whole affair:—that the Magician (who exhibited the Veiled Lady, and who, by-the-by, was the handsomest man in the whole world) had bartered his own soul for seven years' possession of a familiar fiend, and that the last year of the contract was wearing towards its close.

If it were worth our while, I could keep you till an hour beyond midnight, listening to a thousand such absurdities as these. But, finally, our friend Theodore, who prided himself upon his common-sense, found the matter getting quite beyond his patience.

"I offer any wager you like," cried he, setting down his glass so forcibly as to break the stem of it, "that, this very evening, I find out the mystery of the Veiled Lady!"

Young men, I am told, boggle at nothing, over their wine. So, after a little more talk, a wager of considerable amount was actually laid, the money staked, and Theodore left to choose his own method of settling the dispute.

How he managed it, I know not, nor is it of any great importance to this veracious legend; the most natural way, to be sure, was by bribing the door-keeper, or, possibly, he preferred clambering in at the window. But, at any rate, that very evening, while the exhibition was going forward in the hall, Theodore contrived to gain admittance into the private withdrawing-room, whither the Veiled Lady was accustomed to retire, at the close of her performances. There he waited, listening, I suppose, to the stifled hum of the great audience; and, no doubt, he could distinguish the deep tones of the Magician, causing the wonders that he wrought to appear more dark and intricate, by his mystic pretence of an explanation; perhaps, too, in the intervals of the wild, breezy music which accompanied the exhibition, he might hear the low voice of the Veiled Lady, conveying her Sibylline responses. Firm as Theodore's nerves might be, and much as he prided himself on his sturdy perception of realities, I should not be surprised if his heart throbbed at a little more than its ordinary rate!

Theodore concealed himself behind a screen. In due time, the performance was brought to a close; and whether the door was softly opened, or whether her bodiless presence came through the wall, is more than I can say; but, all at once, without the young man's knowing how it happened, a veiled figure stood in the centre of the room. It was one thing to be in presence of this mystery, in the hall of exhibition, where the warm, dense life of hundreds of other mortals kept up the beholder's courage, and distributed her influence among so many; it was another thing to be quite alone with her, and that, too, with a hostile, or, at least, an unauthorized and unjustifiable purpose. I rather imagine that Theodore now began to be sensible of something more serious in his enterprise than he had been quite aware of, while he sat with his boon-companions over their sparkling wine.

Very strange, it must be confessed, was the movement with which the figure floated to-and-fro over the carpet, with the silvery veil covering her from head to foot; so impalpable, so ethereal, so without substance, as the texture seemed, yet hiding her every outline in an impenetrability like that of midnight. Surely, she did not walk! She floated, and flitted, and hovered about the room;—no sound of a footstep, no perceptible motion of a limb;—it was as if a wandering breeze wafted her before it, at its own wild and gentle pleasure. But, by-and-by, a purpose began to be discernible, throughout the seeming vagueness of her unrest. She was in quest of something! Could it be, that a subtile presentiment had informed her of the young man's presence? And, if so, did the Veiled Lady seek, or did she shun him? The doubt in Theodore's mind was speedily resolved; for, after a moment or two of these erratic flutterings, she advanced, more decidedly, and stood motionless before the screen.

"Thou art here!" said a soft, low voice. "Come forth, Theodore!"

Thus summoned by his name, Theodore, as a man of courage, had no choice. He emerged from his concealment, and presented himself before the Veiled Lady, with the wine-flush, it may be, quite gone out of his cheeks.

"What wouldst thou with me?" she inquired, with the same gentle composure that was in her former utterance.

"Mysterious creature," replied Theodore, "I would know who and what you are!"

"My lips are forbidden to betray the secret!" said the Veiled Lady.

"At whatever risk, I must discover it!" rejoined Theodore.

"Then," said the Mystery, "there is no way, save to lift my veil!"

And Theodore, partly recovering his audacity, stept forward, on the instant, to do as the Veiled Lady had suggested. But she floated backward to the opposite side of the room, as if the young man's breath had possessed power enough to waft her away.

"Pause, one little instant," said the soft, low voice, "and learn the conditions of what thou art so bold to undertake! Thou canst go hence, and think of me no more; or, at thy option, thou canst lift this mysterious veil, beneath which I am a sad and lonely prisoner, in a bondage which is worse to me than death. But, before raising it, I entreat thee, in all maiden modesty, to bend forward, and impress a kiss, where my breath stirs the veil; and my virgin lips shall come forward to meet thy lips; and from that instant, Theodore, thou shalt be mine, and I thine, with never more a veil between us! And all the felicity of earth and of the future world shall be thine and mine together. So much may a maiden say behind the veil! If thou shrinkest from this, there is yet another way."

"And what is that?" asked Theodore.

"Dost thou hesitate," said the Veiled Lady, "to pledge thyself to me, by meeting these lips of mine, while the veil yet hides my face? Has not thy heart recognized me? Dost thou come hither, not in holy faith, nor with a pure and generous purpose, but in scornful scepticism and idle curiosity? Still, thou mayst lift the veil! But from that instant, Theodore, I am doomed to be thy evil fate; nor wilt thou ever taste another breath of happiness!"

There was a shade of inexpressible sadness in the utterance of these last words. But Theodore, whose natural tendency was towards scepticism, felt himself almost injured and insulted by the Veiled Lady's proposal that he should pledge himself, for life and eternity, to so questionable a creature as herself; or even that she should suggest an inconsequential kiss, taking into view the probability that her face was none of the most bewitching. A delightful idea, truly, that he should salute the lips of a dead girl, or the jaws of a skeleton, or the grinning cavity of a monster's mouth! Even should she prove a comely maiden enough, in other respects, the odds were ten to one that her teeth were defective; a terrible drawback on the delectableness of a kiss!

"Excuse me, fair lady," said Theodore—and I think he nearly burst into a laugh—"if I prefer to lift the veil first; and for this affair of the kiss, we may decide upon it, afterwards!"

"Thou hast made thy choice," said the sweet, sad voice, behind the veil; and there seemed a tender, but unresentful sense of wrong done to womanhood by the young man's contemptuous interpretation of her offer. "I must not counsel thee to pause; although thy fate is still in thine own hand!"

Grasping at the veil, he flung it upward, and caught a glimpse of a pale, lovely face, beneath; just one momentary glimpse; and then the apparition vanished, and the silvery veil fluttered slowly down, and lay upon the floor. Theodore was alone. Our legend leaves him there. His retribution was, to pine, forever and ever, for another sight of that dim, mournful face—which might have been his life-long, household, fireside joy—to desire, and waste life in a feverish quest, and never meet it more!

But what, in good sooth, had become of the Veiled Lady? Had all her existence been comprehended within that mysterious veil, and was she now annihilated? Or was she a spirit, with a heavenly essence, but which might have been tamed down to human bliss, had Theodore been brave and true enough to claim her? Hearken, my sweet friends—and hearken, dear Priscilla—and you shall learn the little more that Zenobia can tell you!

Just at the moment, so far as can be ascertained, when the Veiled Lady vanished, a maiden, pale and shadowy, rose up amid a knot of visionary people, who were seeking for the better life. She was so gentle and so sad—a nameless melancholy gave her such hold upon their sympathies—that they never thought of questioning whence she came. She might have heretofore existed; or her thin substance might have been moulded out of air, at the very instant when they first beheld her. It was all one to them; they took her to their hearts. Among them was a lady, to whom, more than to all the rest, this pale, mysterious girl attached herself.

But, one morning, the lady was wandering in the woods, and there met her a figure in an Oriental robe, with a dark

ZENOBIA'S LEGEND

beard, and holding in his hand a silvery veil. He motioned
her to stay. Being a woman of some nerve, she did not shriek,
nor run away, nor faint, as many ladies would have been
apt to do, but stood quietly, and bade him speak. The truth
was, she had seen his face before, but had never feared it,
although she knew him to be a terrible magician.

"Lady," said he, with a warning gesture, "you are in peril!"

"Peril!" she exclaimed. "And of what nature?"

"There is a certain maiden," replied the Magician, "who
has come out of the realm of Mystery, and made herself
your most intimate companion. Now, the fates have so
ordained it, that, whether by her own will, or no, this
stranger is your deadliest enemy. In love, in worldly fortune,
in all your pursuit of happiness, she is doomed to fling a
blight over your prospects. There is but one possibility of
thwarting her disastrous influence."

"Then, tell me that one method," said the lady.

"Take this veil!" he answered, holding forth the silvery
texture. "It is a spell; it is a powerful enchantment, which
I wrought for her sake, and beneath which she was once my
prisoner. Throw it, at unawares, over the head of this secret
foe, stamp your foot, and cry—'Arise, Magician, here is the
Veiled Lady'—and immediately I will rise up through the
earth, and seize her. And from that moment, you are safe!"

So the lady took the silvery veil, which was like woven air,
or like some substance airier than nothing, and that would
float upward and be lost among the clouds, were she once
to let it go. Returning homeward, she found the shadowy
girl, amid the knot of visionary transcendentalists, who were
still seeking for the better life. She was joyous, now, and had
a rose-bloom in her cheeks, and was one of the prettiest
creatures, and seemed one of the happiest, that the world
could show. But the lady stole noiselessly behind her, and
threw the veil over her head. As the slight, ethereal texture
sank inevitably down over her figure, the poor girl strove to

raise it, and met her dear friend's eyes with one glance of mortal terror, and deep, deep reproach. It could not change her purpose.

"Arise, Magician!" she exclaimed, stamping her foot upon the earth. "Here is the Veiled Lady!"

At the word, uprose the bearded man in the Oriental robes—the beautiful!—the dark Magician, who had bartered away his soul! He threw his arms around the Veiled Lady; and she was his bond-slave, forever more!

Zenobia, all this while, had been holding the piece of gauze, and so managed it as greatly to increase the dramatic effect of the legend, at those points where the magic veil was to be described. Arriving at the catastrophe, and uttering the fatal words, she flung the gauze over Priscilla's head; and, for an instant, her auditors held their breath, half expecting, I verily believe, that the Magician would start up through the floor, and carry off our poor little friend, before our eyes.

As for Priscilla, she stood, droopingly, in the midst of us, making no attempt to remove the veil.

"How do you find yourself, my love?" said Zenobia, lifting a corner of the gauze, and peeping beneath it, with a mischievous smile. "Ah, the dear little soul! Why, she is really going to faint! Mr. Coverdale, Mr. Coverdale, pray bring a glass of water!"

Her nerves being none of the strongest, Priscilla hardly recovered her equanimity during the rest of the evening. This, to be sure, was a great pity; but, nevertheless, we thought it a very bright idea of Zenobia's, to bring her legend to so effective a conclusion.

XIV

ELIOT'S PULPIT

O UR SUNDAYS, at Blithedale, were not ordinarily
kept with such rigid observance as might have befitted
the descendants of the Pilgrims, whose high enterprise, as we sometimes flattered ourselves, we had taken up,
and were carrying it onward and aloft, to a point which they
never dreamed of attaining.

On that hallowed day, it is true, we rested from our labors.
Our oxen, relieved from their week-day yoke, roamed at large
through the pasture; each yoke-fellow, however, keeping close
beside his mate, and continuing to acknowledge, from the
force of habit and sluggish sympathy, the union which the
taskmaster had imposed for his own hard ends. As for us,
human yoke-fellows, chosen companions of toil, whose hoes
had clinked together throughout the week, we wandered off,
in various directions, to enjoy our interval of repose. Some, I
believe, went devoutly to the village-church. Others, it may
be, ascended a city or a country-pulpit, wearing the clerical
robe with so much dignity that you would scarcely have suspected the yeoman's frock to have been flung off, only since
milking-time. Others took long rambles among the rustic
lanes and by-paths, pausing to look at black, old farm-houses,
with their sloping roofs; and at the modern cottage, so like
a plaything that it seemed as if real joy or sorrow could have

no scope within; and at the more pretending villa, with its range of wooden columns, supporting the needless insolence of a great portico. Some betook themselves into the wide, dusky barn, and lay there, for hours together, on the odorous hay; while the sunstreaks and the shadows strove together— these to make the barn solemn, those to make it cheerful—and both were conquerors; and the swallows twittered a cheery anthem, flashing into sight, or vanishing, as they darted to-and-fro among the golden rules of sunshine. And others went a little way into the woods, and threw themselves on Mother Earth, pillowing their heads on a heap of moss, the green decay of an old log; and dropping asleep, the humble-bees and musquitoes sung and buzzed about their ears, causing the slumberers to twitch and start, without awakening.

With Hollingsworth, Zenobia, Priscilla, and myself, it grew to be a custom to spend the Sabbath-afternoon at a certain rock. It was known to us under the name of Eliot's pulpit, from a tradition that the venerable Apostle Eliot had preached there, two centuries gone by, to an Indian auditory. The old pine-forest, through which the Apostle's voice was wont to sound, had fallen, an immemorial time ago. But the soil, being of the rudest and most broken surface, had apparently never been brought under tillage; other growths, maple, and beech, and birch, had succeeded to the primeval trees; so that it was still as wild a tract of woodland as the great-great-great-great grandson of one of Eliot's Indians (had any such posterity been in existence) could have desired, for the site and shelter of his wigwam. These after-growths, indeed, lose the stately solemnity of the original forest. If left in due neglect, however, they run into an entanglement of softer wildness, among the rustling leaves of which the sun can scatter cheerfulness, as it never could among the dark-browed pines.

The rock itself rose some twenty or thirty feet, a shattered granite boulder, or heap of boulders, with an irregular outline and many fissures, out of which sprang shrubs, bushes, and even trees; as if the scanty soil, within those crevices, were sweeter to their roots than any other earth. At the base of the pulpit, the broken boulders inclined towards each other, so as to form a shallow cave, within which our little party had sometimes found protection from a summer shower. On the threshold, or just across it, grew a tuft of pale columbines, in their season, and violets, sad and shadowy recluses, such as Priscilla was, when we first knew her; children of the sun, who had never seen their father, but dwelt among damp mosses, though not akin to them. At the summit, the rock was overshadowed by the canopy of a birch-tree, which served as a sounding-board for the pulpit. Beneath this shade, (with my eyes of sense half shut, and those of the imagination widely opened,) I used to see the holy Apostle of the Indians, with the sunlight flickering down upon him through the leaves, and glorifying his figure as with the half-perceptible glow of a transfiguration.

I the more minutely describe the rock, and this little Sabbath solitude, because Hollingsworth, at our solicitation, often ascended Eliot's pulpit, and—not exactly preached—but talked to us, his few disciples, in a strain that rose and fell as naturally as the wind's breath among the leaves of the birch-tree. No other speech of man has ever moved me like some of those discourses. It seemed most pitiful—a positive calamity to the world—that a treasury of golden thoughts should thus be scattered, by the liberal handful, down among us three, when a thousand hearers might have been the richer for them; and Hollingsworth the richer, likewise, by the sympathy of multitudes. After speaking much or little, as might happen, he would descend from his gray pulpit, and generally fling himself at full length on the ground, face downward. Meanwhile, we talked around him, on such topics as were suggested by the discourse.

Since her interview with Westervelt, Zenobia's continual

inequalities of temper had been rather difficult for her friends to bear. On the first Sunday after that incident, when Hollingsworth had clambered down from Eliot's pulpit, she declaimed with great earnestness and passion, nothing short of anger, on the injustice which the world did to women, and equally to itself, by not allowing them, in freedom and honor, and with the fullest welcome, their natural utterance in public.

"It shall not always be so!" cried she. "If I live another year, I will lift up my own voice, in behalf of woman's wider liberty."

She, perhaps, saw me smile.

"What matter of ridicule do you find in this, Miles Coverdale?" exclaimed Zenobia, with a flash of anger in her eyes. "That smile, permit me to say, makes me suspicious of a low tone of feeling, and shallow thought. It is my belief—yes, and my prophecy, should I die before it happens—that, when my sex shall achieve its rights, there will be ten eloquent women, where there is now one eloquent man. Thus far, no woman in the world has ever once spoken out her whole heart and her whole mind. The mistrust and disapproval of the vast bulk of society throttles us, as with two gigantic hands at our throats! We mumble a few weak words, and leave a thousand better ones unsaid. You let us write a little, it is true, on a limited range of subjects. But the pen is not for woman. Her power is too natural and immediate. It is with the living voice, alone, that she can compel the world to recognize the light of her intellect and the depth of her heart!"

Now—though I could not well say so to Zenobia—I had not smiled from any unworthy estimate of woman, or in denial of the claims which she is beginning to put forth. What amused and puzzled me, was the fact, that women, however intellectually superior, so seldom disquiet themselves about the rights or wrongs of their sex, unless their own individual affections chance to lie in idleness, or to be ill at ease. They are not natural reformers, but become such by the pressure of exceptional misfortune. I could measure Zenobia's inward trouble, by the animosity with which she now took up the general quarrel of woman against man.

"I will give you leave, Zenobia," replied I, "to fling your utmost scorn upon me, if you ever hear me utter a sentiment unfavorable to the widest liberty which woman has yet dreamed of. I would give her all she asks, and add a great deal more, which she will not be the party to demand, but which men, if they were generous and wise, would grant of their own free motion. For instance, I should love dearly—for the next thousand years, at least—to have all government devolve into the hands of women. I hate to be ruled by my own sex; it excites my jealousy and wounds my pride. It is the iron sway of bodily force, which abases us, in our com- pelled submission. But, how sweet the free, generous courtesy, with which I would kneel before a woman-ruler!"

"Yes; if she were young and beautiful," said Zenobia, laughing. "But how if she were sixty, and a fright?"

"Ah; it is you that rate womanhood low," said I. "But let me go on. I have never found it possible to suffer a bearded priest so near my heart and conscience, as to do me any spiritual good. I blush at the very thought! Oh, in the better order of things, Heaven grant that the ministry of souls may be left in charge of women! The gates of the Blessed City will be thronged with the multitude that enter in, when that day comes! The task belongs to woman. God meant it for her. He has endowed her with the religious sentiment in its utmost depth and purity, refined from that gross, intel- lectual alloy, with which every masculine theologist—save only One, who merely veiled Himself in mortal and masculine shape, but was, in truth, divine—has been prone to mingle it. I have always envied the Catholics their faith in that sweet, sacred Virgin Mother, who stands between them and the Deity, intercepting somewhat of His awful splendor, but permitting His love to stream upon the worshipper, more intelligibly to human comprehension, through the medium of a woman's tenderness. Have I not said enough, Zenobia?"

"I cannot think that this is true," observed Priscilla, who had been gazing at me with great, disapproving eyes. "And I am sure I do not wish it to be true!"

"Poor child!" exclaimed Zenobia, rather contemptuously. "She is the type of womanhood, such as man has spent centuries in making it. He is never content, unless he can degrade himself by stooping towards what he loves. In denying us our rights, he betrays even more blindness to his own interests, than profligate disregard of ours!"

"Is this true?" asked Priscilla, with simplicity, turning to Hollingsworth. "Is it all true that Mr. Coverdale and Zenobia have been saying?"

"No, Priscilla," answered Hollingsworth, with his customary bluntness. "They have neither of them spoken one true word yet."

"Do you despise woman?" said Zenobia. "Ah, Hollingsworth, that would be most ungrateful!"

"Despise her?—No!" cried Hollingsworth, lifting his great shaggy head and shaking it at us, while his eyes glowed almost fiercely. "She is the most admirable handiwork of God, in her true place and character. Her place is at man's side. Her office, that of the Sympathizer; the unreserved, unquestioning Believer; the Recognition, withheld in every other manner, but given, in pity, through woman's heart, lest man should utterly lose faith in himself; the Echo of God's own voice, pronouncing—'It is well done!' All the separate action of woman is, and ever has been, and always shall be, false, foolish, vain, destructive of her own best and holiest qualities, void of every good effect, and productive of intolerable mischiefs! Man is a wretch without woman; but woman is a monster—and, thank Heaven, an almost impossible and

hitherto imaginary monster—without man, as her acknowledged principal! As true as I had once a mother, whom I
loved, were there any possible prospect of woman's taking
the social stand which some of them—poor, miserable, abortive
creatures, who only dream of such things because they have
missed woman's peculiar happiness, or because Nature made
them really neither man nor woman!—if there were a chance
of their attaining the end which these petticoated monstrosities
have in view, I would call upon my own sex to use its physical
force, that unmistakeable evidence of sovereignty, to scourge
them back within their proper bounds! But it will not be
needful. The heart of true womanhood knows where its own
sphere is, and never seeks to stray beyond it!"

Never was mortal blessed—if blessing it were—with a glance
of such entire acquiescence and unquestioning faith, happy
in its completeness, as our little Priscilla unconsciously bestowed on Hollingsworth. She seemed to take the sentiment
from his lips into her heart, and brood over it in perfect
content. The very woman whom he pictured—the gentle
parasite, the soft reflection of a more powerful existence—sat
there at his feet.

I looked at Zenobia, however, fully expecting her to resent
—as I felt, by the indignant ebullition of my own blood, that
she ought—this outrageous affirmation of what struck me as
the intensity of masculine egotism. It centred everything in
itself, and deprived woman of her very soul, her inexpressible
and unfathomable all, to make it a mere incident in the great
sum of man. Hollingsworth had boldly uttered what he, and
millions of despots like him, really felt. Without intending
it, he had disclosed the well-spring of all these troubled
waters. Now, if ever, it surely behoved Zenobia to be the
champion of her sex.

But, to my surprise, and indignation too, she only looked
humbled. Some tears sparkled in her eyes, but they were
wholly of grief, not anger.

"Well; be it so," was all she said. "I, at least, have deep cause to think you right. Let man be but manly and godlike, and woman is only too ready to become to him what you say!"

I smiled—somewhat bitterly, it is true—in contemplation of my own ill-luck. How little did these two women care for me, who had freely conceded all their claims, and a great deal more, out of the fulness of my heart; while Hollingsworth, by some necromancy of his horrible injustice, seemed to have brought them both to his feet!

"Women almost invariably behave thus!" thought I. "What does the fact mean? Is it their nature? Or is it, at last, the result of ages of compelled degradation? And, in either case, will it be possible ever to redeem them?"

An intuition now appeared to possess all the party, that, for this time, at least, there was no more to be said. With one accord, we arose from the ground, and made our way through the tangled undergrowth towards one of those pleasant wood-paths, that wound among the over-arching trees. Some of the branches hung so low as partly to conceal the figures that went before, from those who followed. Priscilla had leaped up more lightly than the rest of us, and ran along in advance, with as much airy activity of spirit as was typified in the motion of a bird, which chanced to be flitting from tree to tree, in the same direction as herself. Never did she seem so happy as that afternoon. She skipt, and could not help it, from very playfulness of heart.

Zenobia and Hollingsworth went next, in close contiguity, but not with arm in arm. Now, just when they had passed the impending bough of a birch-tree, I plainly saw Zenobia take the hand of Hollingsworth in both her own, press it to her bosom, and let it fall again!

The gesture was sudden and full of passion; the impulse had evidently taken her by surprise; it expressed all! Had Zenobia knelt before him, or flung herself upon his breast, and gasped out—'I love you, Hollingsworth!'—I could not have been more certain of what it meant. They then walked onward, as before. But, methought, as the declining sun threw Zenobia's magnified shadow along the path, I beheld it tremulous; and the delicate stem of the flower, which she wore in her hair, was likewise responsive to her agitation.

Priscilla—through the medium of her eyes, at least—could not possibly have been aware of the gesture above-described. Yet, at that instant, I saw her droop. The buoyancy, which just before had been so birdlike, was utterly departed; the life seemed to pass out of her, and even the substance of her figure to grow thin and gray. I almost imagined her a shadow, fading gradually into the dimness of the wood. Her pace became so slow, that Hollingsworth and Zenobia passed by, and I, without hastening my footsteps, overtook her.

"Come, Priscilla," said I, looking her intently in the face, which was very pale and sorrowful, "we must make haste after our friends. Do you feel suddenly ill? A moment ago, you flitted along so lightly that I was comparing you to a bird. Now, on the contrary, it is as if you had a heavy heart, and very little strength to bear it with. Pray take my arm!"

"No," said Priscilla, "I do not think it would help me. It is my heart, as you say, that makes me heavy; and I know not why. Just now, I felt very happy."

No doubt, it was a kind of sacrilege in me to attempt to come within her maidenly mystery. But as she appeared to be tossed aside by her other friends, or carelessly let fall, like a flower which they had done with, I could not resist the impulse to take just one peep beneath her folded petals.

"Zenobia and yourself are dear friends, of late," I remarked. "At first—that first evening when you came to us—she did not receive you quite so warmly as might have been wished."

"I remember it," said Priscilla. "No wonder she hesitated to love me, who was then a stranger to her, and a girl of no grace or beauty; she being herself so beautiful!"

"But she loves you now, of course," suggested I. "And, at this very instant, you feel her to be your dearest friend?"

"Why do you ask me that question?" exclaimed Priscilla, as if frightened at the scrutiny into her feelings which I compelled her to make. "It somehow puts strange thoughts into my mind. But I do love Zenobia dearly! If she only loves me half as well, I shall be happy!"

"How is it possible to doubt that, Priscilla?" I rejoined. "But, observe how pleasantly and happily Zenobia and Hollingsworth are walking together! I call it a delightful spectacle. It truly rejoices me that Hollingsworth has found so fit and affectionate a friend! So many people in the world mistrust him—so many disbelieve and ridicule, while hardly any do him justice, or acknowledge him for the wonderful man he is—that it is really a blessed thing for him to have won the sympathy of such a woman as Zenobia. Any man might be proud of that. Any man, even if he be as great as Hollingsworth, might love so magnificent a woman. How very beautiful Zenobia is! And Hollingsworth knows it, too!"

There may have been some petty malice in what I said. Generosity is a very fine thing, at a proper time, and within due limits. But it is an insufferable bore, to see one man engrossing every thought of all the women, and leaving his friend to shiver in outer seclusion, without even the alternative of solacing himself with what the more fortunate individual has rejected. Yes; it was out of a foolish bitterness of heart that I had spoken.

"Go on before!" said Priscilla, abruptly, and with true feminine imperiousness, which heretofore I had never seen her exercise. "It pleases me best to loiter along by myself. I do not walk so fast as you."

With her hand, she made a little gesture of dismissal. It provoked me, yet, on the whole, was the most bewitching thing that Priscilla had ever done. I obeyed her, and strolled moodily homeward, wondering—as I had wondered a thousand times, already—how Hollingsworth meant to dispose of these two hearts, which (plainly to my perception, and, as I could not but now suppose, to his) he had engrossed into his own huge egotism.

There was likewise another subject, hardly less fruitful of speculation. In what attitude did Zenobia present herself to Hollingsworth? Was it in that of a free woman, with no mortgage on her affections nor claimant to her hand, but fully at liberty to surrender both, in exchange for the heart and hand which she apparently expected to receive? But, was it a vision that I had witnessed in the wood? Was Westervelt a goblin? Were those words of passion and agony, which Zenobia had uttered in my hearing, a mere stage-declamation? Were they formed of a material lighter than common air? Or, supposing them to bear sterling weight, was it not a perilous and dreadful wrong, which she was meditating towards herself and Hollingsworth?

Arriving nearly at the farm-house, I looked back over the long slope of pasture-land, and beheld them standing together, in the light of sunset, just on the spot where, according to the gossip of the Community, they meant to build their cottage. Priscilla, alone and forgotten, was lingering in the shadow of the wood.

XV

A CRISIS

THUS the summer was passing away; a summer of toil, of interest, of something that was not pleasure, but which went deep into my heart, and there became a rich experience. I found myself looking forward to years, if not to a lifetime, to be spent on the same system. The Community were now beginning to form their permanent plans. One of our purposes was to erect a Phalanstery (as I think we called it, after Fourier; but the phraseology of those days is not very fresh in my remembrance) where the great and general family should have its abiding-place. Individual members, too, who made it a point of religion to preserve the sanctity of an exclusive home, were selecting sites for their cottages, by the wood-side, or on the breezy swells, or in the sheltered nook of some little valley, according as their taste might lean towards snugness or the picturesque. Altogether, by projecting our minds outward, we had imparted a show of novelty to existence, and contemplated it as hopefully as if the soil, beneath our feet, had not been fathom-deep with the dust of deluded generations, on every one of which, as on ourselves, the world had imposed itself as a hitherto unwedded bride.

Hollingsworth and myself had often discussed these prospects. It was easy to perceive, however, that he spoke with little or no fervor, but either as questioning the fulfilment of our anticipations, or, at any rate, with a quiet consciousness that it was no personal concern of his. Shortly after the scene at Eliot's pulpit, while he and I were repairing an old stone-fence, I amused myself with sallying forward into the future time.

"When we come to be old men," I said, "they will call us Uncles, or Fathers—Father Hollingsworth and Uncle Coverdale—and we will look back cheerfully to these early days, and make a romantic story for the young people (and if a little more romantic than truth may warrant, it will be no harm) out of our severe trials and hardships. In a century or two, we shall every one of us be mythical personages, or exceedingly picturesque and poetical ones, at all events. They will have a great public hall, in which your portrait, and mine, and twenty other faces that are living now, shall be hung up; and as for me, I will be painted in my shirt-sleeves, and with the sleeves rolled up, to show my muscular development. What stories will be rife among them about our mighty strength," continued I, lifting a big stone and putting it into its place; "though our posterity will really be far stronger than ourselves, after several generations of a simple, natural, and active life! What legends of Zenobia's beauty, and Priscilla's slender and shadowy grace, and those mysterious qualities which make her seem diaphanous with spiritual light! In due course of ages, we must all figure heroically in an Epic Poem; and we will ourselves—at least, I will—bend unseen over the future poet, and lend him inspiration, while he writes it."

"You seem," said Hollingsworth, "to be trying how much nonsense you can pour out in a breath."

"I wish you would see fit to comprehend," retorted I, "that the profoundest wisdom must be mingled with nine-tenths of nonsense; else it is not worth the breath that utters it. But I do long for the cottages to be built, that the creeping plants may begin to run over them, and the moss to gather on the walls, and the trees—which we will set out—to cover them with a breadth of shadow. This spick-and-span novelty does not quite suit my taste. It is time, too, for children to be born among us. The first-born child is still to come! And I shall never feel as if this were a real, practical, as well as poetical, system of human life, until somebody has sanctified it by death."

"A pretty occasion for martyrdom, truly!" said Hollings-worth.

"As good as any other!" I replied. "I wonder, Hollings-worth, who, of all these strong men, and fair women and maidens, is doomed the first to die. Would it not be well, even before we have absolute need of it, to fix upon a spot for a cemetery? Let us choose the rudest, roughest, most uncultivable spot, for Death's garden-ground; and Death shall teach us to beautify it, grave by grave. By our sweet, calm way of dying, and the airy elegance out of which we will shape our funeral rites, and the cheerful allegories which we will model into tombstones, the final scene shall lose its terrors; so that, hereafter, it may be happiness to live, and bliss to die. None of us must die young. Yet, should Providence ordain it so, the event shall not be sorrowful, but affect us with a tender, delicious, only half-melancholy, and almost smiling pathos!"

"That is to say," muttered Hollingsworth, "you will die like a Heathen, as you certainly live like one! But, listen to me, Coverdale. Your fantastic anticipations make me discern, all the more forcibly, what a wretched, unsubstantial scheme is this, on which we have wasted a precious summer of our lives. Do you seriously imagine that any such realities as you, and many others here, have dreamed of, will ever be brought to pass?"

"Certainly, I do," said I. "Of course, when the reality comes, it will wear the every-day, common-place, dusty, and rather homely garb, that reality always does put on. But, setting aside the ideal charm, I hold, that our highest antici- pations have a solid footing on common-sense."

"You only half believe what you say," rejoined Hollings- worth; "and as for me, I neither have faith in your dream, nor would care the value of this pebble for its realization, were that possible. And what more do you want of it? It has given you a theme for poetry. Let that content you. But, now, I ask you to be, at last, a man of sobriety and earnestness, and aid me in an enterprise which is worth all our strength, and the strength of a thousand mightier than we!"

There can be no need of giving, in detail, the conversation that ensued. It is enough to say, that Hollingsworth once more brought forward his rigid and unconquerable idea; a scheme for the reformation of the wicked by methods moral, intellectual, and industrial, by the sympathy of pure, humble, and yet exalted minds, and by opening to his pupils the possibility of a worthier life than that which had become their fate. It appeared, unless he over-estimated his own means, that Hollingsworth held it at his choice (and he did so choose) to obtain possession of the very ground on which we had planted our Community, and which had not yet been made irrevocably ours, by purchase. It was just the founda- tion that he desired. Our beginnings might readily be adapted to his great end. The arrangements, already completed, would work quietly into his system. So plausible looked his theory, and, more than that, so practical; such an air of reasonable- ness had he, by patient thought, thrown over it; each segment of it was contrived to dove-tail into all the rest, with such a complicated applicability; and so ready was he with a response for every objection—that, really, so far as logic and argument went, he had the matter all his own way.

"But," said I, "whence can you, having no means of your own, derive the enormous capital which is essential to this experiment? State-street, I imagine, would not draw its purse-strings very liberally, in aid of such a speculation."

"I have the funds—as much, at least, as is needed for a commencement—at command," he answered. "They can be produced within a month, if necessary."

My thoughts reverted to Zenobia. It could only be her wealth which Hollingsworth was appropriating so lavishly. And on what conditions was it to be had? Did she fling it into the scheme, with the uncalculating generosity that characterizes a woman, when it is her impulse to be generous at all? And did she fling herself along with it? But Hollingsworth did not volunteer an explanation.

"And have you no regrets," I inquired, "in overthrowing this fair system of our new life, which has been planned so deeply, and is now beginning to flourish so hopefully around us? How beautiful it is, and, so far as we can yet see, how practicable! The Ages have waited for us, and here we are—the very first that have essayed to carry on our mortal existence, in love, and mutual help! Hollingsworth, I would be loth to take the ruin of this enterprise upon my conscience!"

"Then let it rest wholly upon mine!" he answered, knitting his black brows. "I see through the system. It is full of defects—irremediable and damning ones!—from first to last, there is nothing else! I grasp it in my hand, and find no substance whatever. There is not human nature in it!"

"Why are you so secret in your operations?" I asked. "God forbid that I should accuse you of intentional wrong; but the besetting sin of a philanthropist, it appears to me, is apt to be a moral obliquity. His sense of honor ceases to be the sense of other honorable men. At some point of his course—I know not exactly when nor where—he is tempted to palter with the right, and can scarcely forbear persuading himself that the importance of his public ends renders it allowable to throw aside his private conscience. Oh, my dear friend, beware this error! If you meditate the overthrow of this establishment, call together our companions, state your design, support it with all your eloquence, but allow them an opportunity of defending themselves!"

"It does not suit me," said Hollingsworth. "Nor is it my duty to do so."

"I think it is!" replied I.

Hollingsworth frowned; not in passion, but like Fate, inexorably.

"I will not argue the point," said he. "What I desire to know of you is—and you can tell me in one word—whether I am to look for your co-operation in this great scheme of good. Take it up with me! Be my brother in it! It offers you (what you have told me, over and over again, that you most need) a purpose in life, worthy of the extremest self-devotion —worthy of martyrdom, should God so order it! In this view, I present it to you. You can greatly benefit mankind. Your peculiar faculties, as I shall direct them, are capable of being so wrought into this enterprise, that not one of them need lie idle. Strike hands with me; and, from this moment, you shall never again feel the languor and vague wretchedness of an indolent or half-occupied man! There may be no more aimless beauty in your life; but, in its stead, there shall be strength, courage, immitigable will—everything that a manly and generous nature should desire! We shall succeed! We shall have done our best for this miserable world; and happiness (which never comes but incidentally) will come to us unawares!"

It seemed his intention to say no more. But, after he had quite broken off, his deep eyes filled with tears, and he held out both his hands to me.

"Coverdale," he murmured, "there is not the man in this wide world, whom I can love as I could you. Do not forsake me!"

As I look back upon this scene, through the coldness and dimness of so many years, there is still a sensation as if

Hollingsworth had caught hold of my heart, and were pulling it towards him with an almost irresistible force. It is a mystery to me, how I withstood it. But, in truth, I saw in his scheme of philanthropy nothing but what was odious. A loathsomeness that was to be forever in my daily work! A great, black ugliness of sin, which he proposed to collect out of a thousand human hearts, and that we should spend our lives in an experiment of transmuting it into virtue! Had I but touched his extended hand, Hollingsworth's magnetism would perhaps have penetrated me with his own conception of all these matters. But I stood aloof. I fortified myself with doubts whether his strength of purpose had not been too gigantic for his integrity, impelling him to trample on considerations that should have been paramount to every other.

"Is Zenobia to take a part in your enterprise?" I asked.

"She is," said Hollingsworth.

"She!—the beautiful!—the gorgeous!" I exclaimed. "And how have you prevailed with such a woman to work in this squalid element?"

"Through no base methods, as you seem to suspect," he answered, "but by addressing whatever is best and noblest in her."

Hollingsworth was looking on the ground. But, as he often did so—generally, indeed, in his habitual moods of thought—I could not judge whether it was from any special unwillingness now to meet my eyes. What it was that dictated my next question, I cannot precisely say. Nevertheless, it rose so inevitably into my mouth, and, as it were, asked itself, so involuntarily, that there must needs have been an aptness in it.

"What is to become of Priscilla?"

Hollingsworth looked at me fiercely, and with glowing eyes. He could not have shown any other kind of expression than that, had he meant to strike me with a sword.

"Why do you bring in the names of these women?" said he, after a moment of pregnant silence. "What have they to do with the proposal which I make you? I must have your answer! Will you devote yourself, and sacrifice all to this great end, and be my friend of friends, forever?"

"In Heaven's name, Hollingsworth," cried I, getting angry, and glad to be angry, because so only was it possible to oppose his tremendous concentrativeness and indomitable will, "cannot you conceive that a man may wish well to the world, and struggle for its good, on some other plan than precisely that which you have laid down? And will you cast off a friend, for no unworthiness, but merely because he stands upon his right, as an individual being, and looks at matters through his own optics, instead of yours?"

"Be with me," said Hollingsworth, "or be against me! There is no third choice for you."

"Take this, then, as my decision," I answered. "I doubt the wisdom of your scheme. Furthermore, I greatly fear that the methods, by which you allow yourself to pursue it, are such as cannot stand the scrutiny of an unbiassed conscience."

"And you will not join me?"

"No!"

I never said the word—and certainly can never have it to say, hereafter—that cost me a thousandth part so hard an effort as did that one syllable. The heart-pang was not merely figurative, but an absolute torture of the breast. I was gazing steadfastly at Hollingsworth. It seemed to me that it struck him, too, like a bullet. A ghastly paleness—always so terrific on a swarthy face—overspread his features. There was a convulsive movement of his throat, as if he were forcing down some words that struggled and fought for utterance. Whether words of anger, or words of grief, I cannot tell; although, many and many a time, I have vainly tormented myself with conjecturing which of the two they were. One other appeal to my friendship—such as once, already, Hollingsworth had made—taking me in the revulsion that followed a strenuous exercise of opposing will, would completely have subdued me. But he left the matter there.

"Well!" said he.

And that was all! I should have been thankful for one word more, even had it shot me through the heart, as mine did him. But he did not speak it; and, after a few moments, with one accord, we set to work again, repairing the stone-fence. Hollingsworth, I observed, wrought like a Titan; and, for my own part, I lifted stones which, at this day—or, in a calmer mood, at that one—I should no more have thought it possible to stir, than to carry off the gates of Gaza on my back.

XVI

LEAVE-TAKINGS

A FEW DAYS after the tragic passage-at-arms between Hollingsworth and me, I appeared at the dinner-table, actually dressed in a coat, instead of my customary blouse; with a satin cravat, too, a white vest, and several other things that made me seem strange and outlandish to myself. As for my companions, this unwonted spectacle caused a great stir upon the wooden benches, that bordered either side of our homely board.

"What's in the wind now, Miles?" asked one of them. "Are you deserting us?"

"Yes, for a week or two," said I. "It strikes me that my health demands a little relaxation of labor, and a short visit to the seaside, during the dog-days."

"You look like it!" grumbled Silas Foster, not greatly pleased with the idea of losing an efficient laborer, before the stress of the season was well over. "Now, here's a pretty fellow! His shoulders have broadened, a matter of six inches, since he came among us; he can do his day's work, if he likes, with any man or ox on the farm;—and yet he talks about going to the seashore for his health! Well, well, old woman," added he to his wife, "let me have a platefull of that pork and cabbage! I begin to feel in a very weakly way. When the others have had their turn, you and I will take a jaunt to Newport or Saratoga!"

"Well, but, Mr. Foster," said I, "you must allow me to take a little breath."

"Breath!" retorted the old yeoman. "Your lungs have the play of a pair of blacksmith's bellows, already. What on earth do you want more? But go along! I understand the business. We shall never see your face here again. Here ends the reformation of the world, so far as Miles Coverdale has a hand in it!"

"By no means," I replied. "I am resolute to die in the last ditch, for the good of the cause."

"Die in a ditch!" muttered gruff Silas, with genuine Yankee intolerance of any intermission of toil, except on Sunday, the Fourth of July, the autumnal Cattle-show, Thanksgiving, or the annual Fast. "Die in a ditch! I believe in my conscience you would, if there were no steadier means than your own labor to keep you out of it!"

The truth was, that an intolerable discontent and irksomeness had come over me. Blithedale was no longer what it had been. Everything was suddenly faded. The sun-burnt and arid aspect of our woods and pastures, beneath the August sky, did but imperfectly symbolize the lack of dew and moisture that, since yesterday, as it were, had blighted my fields of thought, and penetrated to the innermost and shadiest of my contemplative recesses. The change will be recognized by many, who, after a period of happiness, have endeavored to go on with the same kind of life, in the same scene, in spite of the alteration or withdrawal of some principal circumstance. They discover (what heretofore, perhaps, they had not known) that it was this which gave the bright color and vivid reality to the whole affair.

I stood on other terms than before, not only with Hollingsworth, but with Zenobia and Priscilla. As regarded the two latter, it was that dreamlike and miserable sort of change that

denies you the privilege to complain, because you can assert
no positive injury, nor lay your finger on anything tangible.
It is a matter which you do not see, but feel, and which, when
you try to analyze it, seems to lose its very existence, and
resolve itself into a sickly humor of your own. Your understanding, possibly, may put faith in this denial. But your
heart will not so easily rest satisfied. It incessantly remon-
strates, though, most of the time, in a bass-note, which you do
not separately distinguish; but, now-and-then, with a sharp
cry, importunate to be heard, and resolute to claim belief.
'Things are not as they were!'—it keeps saying—'You shall not
impose on me! I will never be quiet! I will throb painfully!
I will be heavy, and desolate, and shiver with cold! For I, your
deep heart, know when to be miserable, as once I knew when
to be happy! All is changed for us! You are beloved no more!'
And, were my life to be spent over again, I would invariably
lend my ear to this Cassandra of the inward depths, however
clamorous the music and the merriment of a more superficial region.

My outbreak with Hollingsworth, though never definitely
known to our associates, had really an effect upon the moral
atmosphere of the Community. It was incidental to the closeness of relationship, into which we had brought ourselves,
that an unfriendly state of feeling could not occur between
any two members, without the whole society being more or
less commoted and made uncomfortable thereby. This species
of nervous sympathy (though a pretty characteristic enough,
sentimentally considered, and apparently betokening an actual
bond of love among us) was yet found rather inconvenient in
its practical operation; mortal tempers being so infirm and
variable as they are. If one of us happened to give his neighbor a box on the ear, the tingle was immediately felt, on the
same side of everybody's head. Thus, even on the supposition
that we were far less quarrelsome than the rest of the world,
a great deal of time was necessarily wasted in rubbing our ears.

Musing on all these matters, I felt an inexpressible longing
for at least a temporary novelty. I thought of going across the
Rocky Mountains, or to Europe, or up the Nile—of offering
myself a volunteer on the Exploring Expedition—of taking a
ramble of years, no matter in what direction, and coming back
on the other side of the world. Then, should the colonists of
Blithedale have established their enterprise on a permanent
basis, I might fling aside my pilgrim-staff and dusty shoon, and
rest as peacefully here as elsewhere. Or, in case Hollingsworth should occupy the ground with his School of Reform,
as he now purposed, I might plead earthly guilt enough, by
that time, to give me what I was inclined to think the only
trustworthy hold on his affections. Meanwhile, before deciding on any ultimate plan, I determined to remove myself to
a little distance, and take an exterior view of what we had
all been about.

In truth, it was dizzy work, amid such fermentation of
opinions as was going on in the general brain of the Community. It was a kind of Bedlam, for the time being; although,
out of the very thoughts that were wildest and most destructive, might grow a wisdom, holy, calm, and pure, and that
should incarnate itself with the substance of a noble and
happy life. But, as matters now were, I felt myself (and
having a decided tendency towards the actual, I never liked to
feel it) getting quite out of my reckoning, with regard to the
existing state of the world. I was beginning to lose the sense
of what kind of a world it was, among innumerable schemes
of what it might or ought to be. It was impossible, situated
as we were, not to imbibe the idea that everything in nature
and human existence was fluid, or fast becoming so; that the
crust of the Earth, in many places, was broken, and its whole
surface portentously upheaving; that it was a day of crisis, and
that we ourselves were in the critical vortex. Our great globe
floated in the atmosphere of infinite space like an unsubstantial bubble. No sagacious man will long retain his sagacity,

if he live exclusively among reformers and progressive people, without periodically returning into the settled system of things, to correct himself by a new observation from that old stand-point.

It was now time for me, therefore, to go and hold a little talk with the conservatives, the writers of the North American Review, the merchants, the politicians, the Cambridge men, and all those respectable old blockheads, who still, in this intangibility and mistiness of affairs, kept a death-grip on one or two ideas which had not come into vogue since yesterday-morning.

The brethren took leave of me with cordial kindness; and as for the sisterhood, I had serious thoughts of kissing them all round, but forbore to do so, because, in all such general salutations, the penance is fully equal to the pleasure. So I kissed none of them, and nobody, to say the truth, seemed to expect it.

"Do you wish me," I said to Zenobia, "to announce, in town, and at the watering-places, your purpose to deliver a course of lectures on the rights of women?"

"Women possess no rights," said Zenobia, with a half-melancholy smile; "or, at all events, only little girls and grandmothers would have the force to exercise them."

She gave me her hand, freely and kindly, and looked at me, I thought, with a pitying expression in her eyes; nor was there any settled light of joy in them, on her own behalf, but a troubled and passionate flame, flickering and fitful.

"I regret, on the whole, that you are leaving us," she said; "and all the more, since I feel that this phase of our life is finished, and can never be lived over again. Do you know, Mr. Coverdale, that I have been several times on the point of making you my confidant, for lack of a better and wiser one? But you are too young to be my Father Confessor; and you would not thank me for treating you like one of those

good little handmaidens, who share the bosom-secrets of a
tragedy-queen!"

"I would at least be loyal and faithful," answered I, "and
would counsel you with an honest purpose, if not wisely."

"Yes," said Zenobia, "you would be only too wise—too
honest. Honesty and wisdom are such a delightful pastime,
at another person's expense!"

"Ah, Zenobia," I exclaimed, "if you would but let me
speak!"

"By no means," she replied; "especially when you have
just resumed the whole series of social conventionalisms, together with that straight-bodied coat. I would as lief open
my heart to a lawyer or a clergyman! No, no, Mr. Coverdale;
if I choose a counsellor, in the present aspect of my affairs,
it must be either an angel or a madman; and I rather apprehend that the latter would be likeliest of the two to speak
the fitting word. It needs a wild steersman when we voyage
through Chaos! The anchor is up! Farewell!"

Priscilla, as soon as dinner was over, had betaken herself
into a corner, and set to work on a little purse. As I approached her, she let her eyes rest on me, with a calm, serious
look; for, with all her delicacy of nerves, there was a singular
self-possession in Priscilla, and her sensibilities seemed to lie
sheltered from ordinary commotion, like the water in a
deep well.

"Will you give me that purse, Priscilla," said I, "as a
parting keepsake?"

"Yes," she answered; "if you will wait till it is finished."

"I must not wait, even for that," I replied. "Shall I find
you here, on my return?"

"I never wish to go away," said she.

"I have sometimes thought," observed I, smiling, "that
you, Priscilla, are a little prophetess; or, at least, that you have
spiritual intimations respecting matters which are dark to us
grosser people. If that be the case, I should like to ask you

what is about to happen. For I am tormented with a strong foreboding, that, were I to return even so soon as tomorrow morning, I should find everything changed. Have you any impressions of this nature?"

"Ah, no!" said Priscilla, looking at me apprehensively. "If any such misfortune is coming, the shadow has not reached me yet. Heaven forbid! I should be glad if there might never be any change, but one summer follow another, and all just like this!"

"No summer ever came back, and no two summers ever were alike," said I, with a degree of Orphic wisdom that astonished myself. "Times change, and people change; and if our hearts do not change as readily, so much the worse for us! Good bye, Priscilla!"

I gave her hand a pressure, which, I think, she neither resisted nor returned. Priscilla's heart was deep, but of small compass; it had room but for a very few dearest ones, among whom she never reckoned me.

On the door-step, I met Hollingsworth. I had a momentary impulse to hold out my hand, or, at least, to give a parting nod, but resisted both. When a real and strong affection has come to an end, it is not well to mock the sacred past with any show of those common-place civilities that belong to ordinary intercourse. Being dead henceforth to him, and he to me, there could be no propriety in our chilling one another with the touch of two corpse-like hands, or playing at looks of courtesy with eyes that were impenetrable beneath the glaze and the film. We passed, therefore, as if mutually invisible.

I can nowise explain what sort of whim, prank, or perversity it was, that, after all these leave-takings, induced me to go to the pig-stye and take leave of the swine! There they lay, buried as deeply among the straw as they could burrow, four huge black grunters, the very symbols of slothful ease and sensual comfort. They were asleep, drawing short and heavy breaths, which heaved their big sides up and down. Unclosing their eyes, however, at my approach, they looked dimly forth at the outer world, and simultaneously uttered a gentle grunt; not putting themselves to the trouble of an additional breath for that particular purpose, but grunting with their ordinary inhalation. They were involved, and almost stifled, and buried alive, in their own corporeal substance. The very unreadiness and oppression, wherewith these greasy citizens gained breath enough to keep their life-machinery in sluggish movement, appeared to make them only the more sensible of the ponderous and fat satisfaction of their existence. Peeping at me, an instant, out of their small, red, hardly perceptible eyes, they dropt asleep again; yet not so far asleep but that their unctuous bliss was still present to them, betwixt dream and reality.

"You must come back in season to eat part of a spare-rib," said Silas Foster, giving my hand a mighty squeeze. "I shall have these fat fellows hanging up by the heels, heads downward, pretty soon, I tell you!"

"Oh, cruel Silas, what a horrible idea!" cried I. "All the rest of us, men, women, and live-stock, save only these four porkers, are bedevilled with one grief or another; they alone are happy—and you mean to cut their throats, and eat them! It would be more for the general comfort to let them eat us; and bitter and sour morsels we should be!"

XVII

THE HOTEL

ARRIVING in town, (where my bachelor-rooms, long
before this time, had received some other occupant,)
I established myself, for a day or two, in a certain
respectable hotel. It was situated somewhat aloof from my
former track in life; my present mood inclining me to avoid
most of my old companions, from whom I was now sundered
by other interests, and who would have been likely enough
to amuse themselves at the expense of the amateur working-
man. The hotel-keeper put me into a back-room of the third
story of his spacious establishment. The day was lowering,
with occasional gusts of rain, and an ugly-tempered east-wind,
which seemed to come right off the chill and melancholy sea,
hardly mitigated by sweeping over the roofs, and amalga-
mating itself with the dusky element of city-smoke. All the
effeminacy of past days had returned upon me at once. Summer as it still was, I ordered a coal-fire in the rusty grate, and
was glad to find myself growing a little too warm with an
artificial temperature.

My sensations were those of a traveller, long sojourning in
remote regions, and at length sitting down again amid cus-
toms once familiar. There was a newness and an oldness,
oddly combining themselves into one impression. It made me
acutely sensible how strange a piece of mosaic-work had lately

been wrought into my life. True; if you look at it in one way, it had been only a summer in the country. But, considered in a profounder relation, it was part of another age, a different state of society, a segment of an existence peculiar in its aims and methods, a leaf of some mysterious volume, interpolated into the current history which Time was writing off. At one moment, the very circumstances now surrounding me—my coal-fire, and the dingy room in the bustling hotel—appeared far off and intangible. The next instant, Blithedale looked vague, as if it were at a distance both in time and space, and so shadowy, that a question might be raised whether the whole affair had been anything more than the thoughts of a speculative man. I had never before experienced a mood that so robbed the actual world of its solidity. It nevertheless involved a charm, on which—a devoted epicure of my own emotions—I resolved to pause, and enjoy the moral sillabub until quite dissolved away.

Whatever had been my taste for solitude and natural scenery, yet the thick, foggy, stifled element of cities, the entangled life of many men together, sordid as it was, and empty of the beautiful, took quite as strenuous a hold upon my mind. I felt as if there could never be enough of it. Each characteristic sound was too suggestive to be passed over, unnoticed. Beneath and around me, I heard the stir of the hotel; the loud voices of guests, landlord, or barkeeper; steps echoing on the staircase; the ringing of a bell, announcing arrivals or departures; the porter lumbering past my door with baggage, which he thumped down upon the floors of neighboring chambers; the lighter feet of chamber-maids scudding along the passages;—it is ridiculous to think what an interest they had for me. From the street, came the tumult of the pavements, pervading the whole house with a continual uproar, so broad and deep that only an unaccustomed ear would dwell upon it. A company of the city-soldiery, with a full military band, marched in front of the hotel, invisible to me, but stirringly

audible both by its foot-tramp and the clangor of its instruments. Once or twice, all the city-bells jangled together,
announcing a fire, which brought out the engine-men and
their machines, like an army with its artillery rushing to
battle. Hour by hour, the clocks in many steeples responded
one to another. In some public hall, not a great way off, there
seemed to be an exhibition of a mechanical diorama; for, three
times during the day, occurred a repetition of obstreperous
music, winding up with the rattle of imitative cannon and
musketry, and a huge final explosion. Then ensued the
applause of the spectators, with clap of hands, and thump of
sticks, and the energetic pounding of their heels. All this
was just as valuable, in its way, as the sighing of the breeze
among the birch-trees, that overshadowed Eliot's pulpit.

Yet I felt a hesitation about plunging into this muddy tide
of human activity and pastime. It suited me better, for the
present, to linger on the brink, or hover in the air above it.
So I spent the first day, and the greater part of the second,
in the laziest manner possible, in a rocking-chair, inhaling
the fragrance of a series of cigars, with my legs and slippered
feet horizontally disposed, and in my hand a novel, purchased
of a railroad bibliopolist. The gradual waste of my cigar
accomplished itself with an easy and gentle expenditure of
breath. My book was of the dullest, yet had a sort of sluggish
flow, like that of a stream in which your boat is as often
aground as afloat. Had there been a more impetuous rush, a
more absorbing passion of the narrative, I should the sooner
have struggled out of its uneasy current, and have given myself up to the swell and subsidence of my thoughts. But, as
it was, the torpid life of the book served as an unobtrusive
accompaniment to the life within me and about me. At intervals, however, when its effect grew a little too soporific—not
for my patience, but for the possibility of keeping my eyes
open—I bestirred myself, started from the rocking-chair, and
looked out of the window.

A gray sky; the weathercock of a steeple, that rose beyond the opposite range of buildings, pointing from the eastward; a sprinkle of small, spiteful-looking raindrops on the window-pane! In that ebb-tide of my energies, had I thought of venturing abroad, these tokens would have checked the abortive purpose.

After several such visits to the window, I found myself getting pretty well acquainted with that little portion of the backside of the universe which it presented to my view. Over against the hotel and its adjacent houses, at the distance of forty or fifty yards, was the rear of a range of buildings, which appeared to be spacious, modern, and calculated for fashionable residences. The interval between was apportioned into grass-plots, and here and there an apology for a garden, pertaining severally to these dwellings. There were apple-trees, and pear and peach-trees, too, the fruit on which looked singularly large, luxuriant, and abundant; as well it might, in a situation so warm and sheltered, and where the soil had doubtless been enriched to a more than natural fertility. In two or three places, grape-vines clambered upon trellises, and bore clusters already purple, and promising the richness of Malta or Madeira in their ripened juice. The blighting winds of our rigid climate could not molest these trees and vines; the sunshine, though descending late into this area, and too early intercepted by the height of the surrounding houses, yet lay tropically there, even when less than temperate in every other region. Dreary as was the day, the scene was illuminated by not a few sparrows and other birds, which spread their wings, and flitted and fluttered, and alighted now here, now there, and busily scratched their food out of the wormy earth. Most of these winged people seemed to have their domicile in a robust and healthy buttonwood-tree. It aspired upward, high above the roof of the houses, and spread a dense head of foliage half across the area.

There was a cat—as there invariably is, in such places—who evidently thought herself entitled to all the privileges of forest-life, in this close heart of city-conventionalisms. I watched her creeping along the low, flat roofs of the offices, descending a flight of wooden steps, gliding among the grass, and besieging the buttonwood-tree, with murderous purpose against its feathered citizens. But, after all, they were birds of city-breeding, and doubtless knew how to guard themselves against the peculiar perils of their position.

Bewitching to my fancy are all those nooks and crannies, where Nature, like a stray partridge, hides her head among the long-established haunts of men! It is likewise to be remarked, as a general rule, that there is far more of the picturesque, more truth to native and characteristic tendencies, and vastly greater suggestiveness, in the back view of a residence, whether in town or country, than in its front. The latter is always artificial; it is meant for the world's eye, and is therefore a veil and a concealment. Realities keep in the rear, and put forward an advance-guard of show and humbug. The posterior aspect of any old farm-house, behind which a railroad has unexpectedly been opened, is so different from that looking upon the immemorial highway, that the spectator gets new ideas of rural life and individuality, in the puff or two of steam-breath which shoots him past the premises. In a city, the distinction between what is offered to the public, and what is kept for the family, is certainly not less striking.

But, to return to my window, at the back of the hotel. Together with a due contemplation of the fruit-trees, the grape-vines, the buttonwood-tree, the cat, the birds, and many other particulars, I failed not to study the row of fashionable dwellings to which all these appertained. Here, it must be confessed, there was a general sameness. From the upper-story to the first floor, they were so much alike that I could only conceive of the inhabitants as cut out on one identical pattern, like little wooden toy-people of German manufacture.

One long, united roof, with its thousands of slates glittering in the rain, extended over the whole. After the distinctness of separate characters, to which I had recently been accustomed, it perplexed and annoyed me not to be able to resolve this combination of human interests into well-defined elements. It seemed hardly worth while for more than one of those families to be in existence; since they all had the same glimpse of the sky, all looked into the same area, all received just their equal share of sunshine through the front windows, and all listened to precisely the same noises of the street on which they bordered. Men are so much alike, in their nature, that they grow intolerable unless varied by their circumstances.

Just about this time, a waiter entered my room. The truth was, I had rung the bell and ordered a sherry-cobbler.

"Can you tell me," I inquired, "what families reside in any of those houses opposite?"

"The one right opposite is a rather stylish boarding-house," said the waiter. "Two of the gentlemen-boarders keep horses at the stable of our establishment. They do things in very good style, sir, the people that live there."

I might have found out nearly as much for myself, on examining the house a little more closely. In one of the upper chambers, I saw a young man in a dressing-gown, standing before the glass and brushing his hair, for a quarter-of-an-hour together. He then spent an equal space of time in the elaborate arrangement of his cravat, and finally made his appearance in a dress-coat, which I suspected to be newly come from the tailor's, and now first put on for a dinner-party. At a window of the next story below, two children, prettily dressed, were looking out. By-and-by, a middle-aged gentleman came softly behind them, kissed the little girl, and playfully pulled the little boy's ear. It was a papa, no doubt, just come in from his counting-room or office; and anon appeared mamma, stealing as softly behind papa, as he had stolen behind the children, and laying her hand on his shoulder to surprise him. Then followed a kiss between papa and mamma, but a noiseless one; for the children did not turn their heads.

"I bless God for these good folks!" thought I to myself. "I have not seen a prettier bit of nature, in all my summer in the country, than they have shown me here in a rather stylish boarding-house. I will pay them a little more attention, by-and-by."

On the first floor, an iron balustrade ran along in front of the tall, and spacious windows, evidently belonging to a back drawing-room; and, far into the interior, through the arch of the sliding-doors, I could discern a gleam from the windows of the front apartment. There were no signs of present occupancy in this suite of rooms; the curtains being enveloped in a protective covering, which allowed but a small portion of their crimson material to be seen. But two housemaids were industriously at work; so that there was good prospect that the boarding-house might not long suffer from the absence of its most expensive and profitable guests. Meanwhile, until they should appear, I cast my eyes downward to the lower regions. There, in the dusk that so early settles into such places, I saw the red glow of the kitchen-range; the hot cook, or one of her subordinates, with a ladle in her hand, came to draw a cool breath at the back-door; as soon as she disappeared, an Irish man-servant, in a white jacket, crept slily forth and threw away the fragments of a china-dish, which unquestionably he had just broken. Soon afterwards, a lady, showily dressed, with a curling front of what must have been false hair, and reddish brown, I suppose, in hue—though my remoteness allowed me only to guess at such particulars—this respectable mistress of the boarding-house made a momentary transit across the kitchen-window, and appeared no more. It was her final, comprehensive glance, in order to make sure that soup, fish, and flesh, were in a proper state of readiness, before the serving up of dinner.

There was nothing else worth noticing about the house; unless it be, that, on the peak of one of the dormer-windows, which opened out of the roof, sat a dove, looking very dreary and forlorn; insomuch that I wondered why she chose to sit there, in the chilly rain, while her kindred were doubtless nestling in a warm and comfortable dove-cote. All at once, this dove spread her wings, and launching herself in the air, came flying so straight across the intervening space, that I fully expected her to alight directly on my window-sill. In the latter part of her course, however, she swerved aside, flew upward, and vanished, as did likewise the slight, fantastic pathos with which I had invested her.

XVIII

THE BOARDING-HOUSE

THE NEXT day, as soon as I thought of looking again towards the opposite house, there sat the dove again, on the peak of the same dormer-window!

It was by no means an early hour; for, the preceding evening, I had ultimately mustered enterprise enough to visit the theatre, had gone late to bed, and slept beyond all limit, in my remoteness from Silas Foster's awakening horn. Dreams had tormented me, throughout the night. The train of thoughts which, for months past, had worn a track through my mind, and to escape which was one of my chief objects in leaving Blithedale, kept treading remorselessly to-and-fro, in their old footsteps, while slumber left me impotent to regulate them. It was not till I had quitted my three friends that they first began to encroach upon my dreams. In those of the last night, Hollingsworth and Zenobia, standing on either side of my bed, had bent across it to exchange a kiss of passion. Priscilla, beholding this—for she seemed to be peeping in at the chamber-window—had melted gradually away, and left only the sadness of her expression in my heart. There it still lingered, after I awoke; one of those unreasonable sadnesses that you know not how to deal with, because it involves nothing for common-sense to clutch.

It was a gray and dripping forenoon; gloomy enough in town, and still gloomier in the haunts to which my recollec-

tions persisted in transporting me. For, in spite of my efforts
to think of something else, I thought how the gusty rain was
drifting over the slopes and valleys of our farm; how wet must
be the foliage that overshadowed the pulpit-rock; how cheerless, in such a day, my hermitage—the tree-solitude of my
owl-like humors—in the vine-encircled heart of the tall pine!
It was a phase of home-sickness. I had wrenched myself too
suddenly out of an accustomed sphere. There was no choice
now, but to bear the pang of whatever heart-strings were
snapt asunder, and that illusive torment (like the ache of a
limb long ago cut off) by which a past mode of life prolongs
itself into the succeeding one. I was full of idle and shapeless
regrets. The thought impressed itself upon me, that I had left
duties unperformed. With the power, perhaps, to act in the
place of destiny, and avert misfortune from my friends, I had
resigned them to their fate. That cold tendency, between
instinct and intellect, which made me pry with a speculative
interest into people's passions and impulses, appeared to have
gone far towards unhumanizing my heart.

But a man cannot always decide for himself whether his
own heart is cold or warm. It now impresses me, that, if I
erred at all, in regard to Hollingsworth, Zenobia, and Priscilla,
it was through too much sympathy, rather than too little.

To escape the irksomeness of these meditations, I resumed
my post at the window. At first sight, there was nothing new
to be noticed. The general aspect of affairs was the same as
yesterday, except that the more decided inclemency of to-day
had driven the sparrows to shelter, and kept the cat within
doors, whence, however, she soon emerged, pursued by the
cook, and with what looked like the better half of a roast
chicken in her mouth. The young man in the dress-coat was
invisible; the two children, in the story below, seemed to be
romping about the room, under the superintendence of a
nursery-maid. The damask curtains of the drawing-room, on

the first floor, were now fully displayed, festooned gracefully from top to bottom of the windows, which extended from the ceiling to the carpet. A narrower window, at the left of the drawing-room, gave light to what was probably a small boudoir, within which I caught the faintest imaginable glimpse of a girl's figure, in airy drapery. Her arm was in regular movement, as if she were busy with her German worsted, or some other such pretty and unprofitable handiwork.

While intent upon making out this girlish shape, I became sensible that a figure had appeared at one of the windows of the drawing-room. There was a presentiment in my mind; or perhaps my first glance, imperfect and sidelong as it was, had sufficed to convey subtle information of the truth. At any rate, it was with no positive surprise, but as if I had all along expected the incident, that, directing my eyes thitherward, I beheld—like a full-length picture, in the space between the heavy festoons of the window-curtains—no other than Zenobia! At the same instant, my thoughts made sure of the identity of the figure in the boudoir. It could only be Priscilla.

Zenobia was attired, not in the almost rustic costume which she had heretofore worn, but in a fashionable morning-dress. There was, nevertheless, one familiar point. She had, as usual, a flower in her hair, brilliant, and of a rare variety, else it had not been Zenobia. After a brief pause at the window, she turned away, exemplifying, in the few steps that removed her out of sight, that noble and beautiful motion which character-ized her as much as any other personal charm. Not one woman in a thousand could move so admirably as Zenobia. Many women can sit gracefully; some can stand gracefully; and a few, perhaps, can assume a series of graceful positions. But natural movement is the result and expression of the whole being, and cannot be well and nobly performed, unless responsive to something in the character. I often used to think that music—light and airy, wild and passionate, or the full harmony of stately marches, in accordance with her varying mood—should have attended Zenobia's footsteps.

I waited for her re-appearance. It was one peculiarity, distinguishing Zenobia from most of her sex, that she needed for her moral well-being, and never would forego, a large amount of physical exercise. At Blithedale, no inclemency of sky or muddiness of earth had ever impeded her daily walks. Here, in town, she probably preferred to tread the extent of the two drawing-rooms, and measure out the miles by spaces of forty feet, rather than bedraggle her skirts over the sloppy pavements. Accordingly, in about the time requisite to pass through the arch of the sliding-doors to the front window, and to return upon her steps, there she stood again, between the festoons of the crimson curtains. But another personage was now added to the scene. Behind Zenobia appeared that face which I had first encountered in the wood-path; the man who had passed, side by side with her, in such mysterious familiarity and estrangement, beneath my vine-curtained hermitage in the tall pine-tree. It was Westervelt. And though he was looking closely over her shoulder, it still seemed to me, as on the former occasion, that Zenobia repelled him—that, perchance, they mutually repelled each other—by some incompatibility of their spheres.

This impression, however, might have been altogether the result of fancy and prejudice, in me. The distance was so great as to obliterate any play of feature, by which I might otherwise have been made a partaker of their counsels.

There now needed only Hollingsworth and old Moodie to complete the knot of characters, whom a real intricacy of events, greatly assisted by my method of insulating them from other relations, had kept so long upon my mental stage, as actors in a drama. In itself, perhaps, it was no very remarkable event, that they should thus come across me, at the moment when I imagined myself free. Zenobia, as I well knew, had retained an establishment in town, and had not unfrequently withdrawn herself from Blithedale, during brief intervals, on one of which occasions she had taken Priscilla along with her. Nevertheless, there seemed something fatal in the coincidence that had borne me to this one spot, of all others in a great city, and transfixed me there, and compelled me again to waste my already wearied sympathies on affairs which were none of mine, and persons who cared little for me. It irritated my nerves; it affected me with a kind of heart-sickness. After the effort which it cost me to fling them off—after consummating my escape, as I thought, from these goblins of flesh and blood, and pausing to revive myself with a breath or two of an atmosphere in which they should have no share—it was a positive despair, to find the same figures arraying themselves before me, and presenting their old problem in a shape that made it more insoluble than ever.

I began to long for a catastrophe. If the noble temper of Hollingsworth's soul were doomed to be utterly corrupted by the too powerful purpose, which had grown out of what was noblest in him; if the rich and generous qualities of Zenobia's womanhood might not save her; if Priscilla must perish by her tenderness and faith, so simple and so devout;—then be it so! Let it all come! As for me, I would look on, as it seemed my part to do, understandingly, if my intellect could fathom the meaning and the moral, and, at all events, reverently and sadly. The curtain fallen, I would pass onward with my poor individual life, which was now attenuated of much of its proper substance, and diffused among many alien interests.

Meanwhile, Zenobia and her companion had retreated from the window. Then followed an interval, during which I directed my eyes towards the figure in the boudoir. Most certainly it was Priscilla, although dressed with a novel and fanciful elegance. The vague perception of it, as viewed so far off, impressed me as if she had suddenly passed out of a

chrysalis state and put forth wings. Her hands were not now
in motion. She had dropt her work, and sat with her head
thrown back, in the same attitude that I had seen several
times before, when she seemed to be listening to an imperfectly distinguished sound.

Again the two figures in the drawing-room became visible.
They were now a little withdrawn from the window, face to
face, and, as I could see by Zenobia's emphatic gestures, were
discussing some subject in which she, at least, felt a passionate
concern. By-and-by, she broke away, and vanished beyond
my ken. Westervelt approached the window, and leaned his
forehead against a pane of glass, displaying the sort of smile
on his handsome features which, when I before met him, had
let me into the secret of his gold-bordered teeth. Every human
being, when given over to the Devil, is sure to have the
wizard mark upon him, in one form or another. I fancied
that this smile, with its peculiar revelation, was the Devil's
signet on the Professor.

This man, as I had soon reason to know, was endowed
with a cat-like circumspection; and though precisely the most
unspiritual quality in the world, it was almost as effective
as spiritual insight, in making him acquainted with whatever
it suited him to discover. He now proved it, considerably to
my discomfiture, by detecting and recognizing me, at my post
of observation. Perhaps I ought to have blushed at being
caught in such an evident scrutiny of Professor Westervelt
and his affairs. Perhaps I did blush. Be that as it might, I
retained presence of mind enough not to make my position
yet more irksome, by the poltroonery of drawing back.

Westervelt looked into the depths of the drawing-room,
and beckoned. Immediately afterwards, Zenobia appeared at
the window, with color much heightened, and eyes which, as
my conscience whispered me, were shooting bright arrows,
barbed with scorn, across the intervening space, directed full
at my sensibilities as a gentleman. If the truth must be told,

far as her flight-shot was, those arrows hit the mark. She signified her recognition of me by a gesture with her head and hand, comprising at once a salutation and dismissal. The next moment, she administered one of those pitiless rebukes which a woman always has at hand, ready for an offence, (and which she so seldom spares, on due occasion,) by letting down a white linen curtain between the festoons of the damask ones. It fell like the drop-curtain of a theatre, in the interval between the acts.

Priscilla had disappeared from the boudoir. But the dove still kept her desolate perch, on the peak of the attic-window.

XIX

ZENOBIA'S DRAWING-ROOM

THE REMAINDER of the day, so far as I was concerned, was spent in meditating on these recent incidents. I contrived, and alternately rejected, innumerable methods of accounting for the presence of Zenobia and Priscilla, and the connection of Westervelt with both. It must be owned, too, that I had a keen, revengeful sense of the insult inflicted by Zenobia's scornful recognition, and more particularly by her letting down the curtain; as if such were the proper barrier to be interposed between a character like hers, and a perceptive faculty like mine. For, was mine a mere vulgar curiosity? Zenobia should have known me better than to suppose it. She should have been able to appreciate that quality of the intellect and the heart, which impelled me (often against my own will, and to the detriment of my own comfort) to live in other lives, and to endeavor—by generous sympathies, by delicate intuitions, by taking note of things too slight for record, and by bringing my human spirit into manifold accordance with the companions whom God assigned me—to learn the secret which was hidden even from themselves.

Of all possible observers, methought, a woman, like Zenobia, and a man, like Hollingsworth, should have selected me. And, now, when the event has long been past, I retain the same opinion of my fitness for the office. True; I might have condemned them. Had I been judge, as well as witness, my sentence might have been stern as that of Destiny itself. But, still, no trait of original nobility of character; no struggle against temptation; no iron necessity of will, on the one hand, nor extenuating circumstance to be derived from passion and despair, on the other; no remorse that might co-exist with error, even if powerless to prevent it; no proud repentance, that should claim retribution as a meed—would go unappreciated. True, again, I might give my full assent to the punishment which was sure to follow. But it would be given mournfully, and with undiminished love. And, after all was finished, I would come, as if to gather up the white ashes of those who had perished at the stake, and to tell the world— the wrong being now atoned for—how much had perished there, which it had never yet known how to praise.

I sat in my rocking-chair, too far withdrawn from the window to expose myself to another rebuke, like that already inflicted. My eyes still wandered towards the opposite house, but without effecting any new discoveries. Late in the afternoon, the weathercock on the church-spire indicated a change of wind; the sun shone dimly out, as if the golden wine of its beams were mingled half-and-half with water. Nevertheless, they kindled up the whole range of edifices, threw a glow over the windows, glistened on the wet roofs, and, slowly withdrawing upward, perched upon the chimney-tops; thence they took a higher flight, and lingered an instant on the tip of the spire, making it the final point of more cheerful light in the whole sombre scene. The next moment, it was all gone. The twilight fell into the area like a shower of dusky snow; and before it was quite dark, the gong of the hotel summoned me to tea.

When I returned to my chamber, the glow of an astral lamp was penetrating mistily through the white curtain of Zenobia's drawing-room. The shadow of a passing figure was now-and-then cast upon this medium, but with too vague an outline for even my adventurous conjectures to read the hieroglyphic that it presented.

All at once, it occurred to me how very absurd was my behavior, in thus tormenting myself with crazy hypotheses as to what was going on within that drawing-room, when it was at my option to be personally present there. My relations with Zenobia, as yet unchanged—as a familiar friend, and associated in the same life-long enterprise—gave me the right, and made it no more than kindly courtesy demanded, to call on her. Nothing, except our habitual independence of conventional rules, at Blithedale, could have kept me from sooner recognizing this duty. At all events, it should now be performed.

In compliance with this sudden impulse, I soon found myself actually within the house, the rear of which, for two days past, I had been so sedulously watching. A servant took my card, and immediately returning, ushered me up-stairs. On the way, I heard a rich, and, as it were, triumphant burst of music from a piano, in which I felt Zenobia's character, although heretofore I had known nothing of her skill upon the instrument. Two or three canary-birds, excited by this gush of sound, sang piercingly, and did their utmost to produce a kindred melody. A bright illumination streamed through the door of the front drawing-room; and I had barely stept across the threshold before Zenobia came forward to meet me, laughing, and with an extended hand.

"Ah, Mr. Coverdale," said she, still smiling, but, as I thought, with a good deal of scornful anger underneath, "it has gratified me to see the interest which you continue to take in my affairs! I have long recognized you as a sort of transcendental Yankee, with all the native propensity of your countrymen to investigate matters that come within their range, but rendered almost poetical, in your case, by the refined methods which you adopt for its gratification. After

all, it was an unjustifiable stroke, on my part—was it not?—
to let down the window-curtain!"

"I cannot call it a very wise one," returned I, with a secret
bitterness which, no doubt, Zenobia appreciated. "It is really
impossible to hide anything, in this world, to say nothing of
the next. All that we ought to ask, therefore, is, that the witnesses of our conduct, and the speculators on our motives,
should be capable of taking the highest view which the circumstances of the case may admit. So much being secured, I,
for one, would be most happy in feeling myself followed,
everywhere, by an indefatigable human sympathy."

"We must trust for intelligent sympathy to our guardian
angels, if any there be," said Zenobia. "As long as the only
spectator of my poor tragedy is a young man, at the window
of his hotel, I must still claim the liberty to drop the curtain."

While this passed, as Zenobia's hand was extended, I had
applied the very slightest touch of my fingers to her own. In
spite of an external freedom, her manner made me sensible
that we stood upon no real terms of confidence. The thought
came sadly across me, how great was the contrast betwixt this
interview and our first meeting. Then, in the warm light of
the country fireside, Zenobia had greeted me cheerily and
hopefully, with a full sisterly grasp of the hand, conveying
as much kindness in it as other women could have evinced by
the pressure of both arms around my neck, or by yielding a
cheek to the brotherly salute. The difference was as complete
as between her appearance, at that time—so simply attired,
and with only the one superb flower in her hair—and now,
when her beauty was set off by all that dress and ornament
could do for it. And they did much. Not, indeed, that they
created, or added anything to what Nature had lavishly done
for Zenobia. But, those costly robes which she had on, those
flaming jewels on her neck, served as lamps to display the
personal advantages which required nothing less than such
an illumination, to be fully seen. Even her characteristic

flower, though it seemed to be still there, had undergone a cold and bright transfiguration; it was a flower exquisitely imitated in jeweller's work, and imparting the last touch that transformed Zenobia into a work of art.

"I scarcely feel," I could not forbear saying, "as if we had ever met before. How many years ago it seems, since we last sat beneath Eliot's pulpit, with Hollingsworth extended on the fallen leaves, and Priscilla at his feet! Can it be, Zenobia, that you ever really numbered yourself with our little band of earnest, thoughtful, philanthropic laborers?"

"Those ideas have their time and place," she answered, coldly. "But, I fancy, it must be a very circumscribed mind that can find room for no others."

Her manner bewildered me. Literally, moreover, I was dazzled by the brilliancy of the room. A chandelier hung down in the centre, glowing with I know not how many lights; there were separate lamps, also, on two or three tables, and on marble brackets, adding their white radiance to that of the chandelier. The furniture was exceedingly rich. Fresh from our old farm-house, with its homely board and benches in the dining-room, and a few wicker-chairs in the best parlor, it struck me that here was the fulfilment of every fantasy of an imagination, revelling in various methods of costly self-indulgence and splendid ease. Pictures, marbles, vases; in brief, more shapes of luxury than there could be any object in enumerating, except for an auctioneer's advertisement— and the whole repeated and doubled by the reflection of a great mirror, which showed me Zenobia's proud figure, likewise, and my own. It cost me, I acknowledge, a bitter sense of shame, to perceive in myself a positive effort to bear up against the effect which Zenobia sought to impose on me. I reasoned against her, in my secret mind, and strove so to keep my footing. In the gorgeousness with which she had surrounded herself—in the redundance of personal ornament, which the largeness of her physical nature and the rich type

of her beauty caused to seem so suitable—I malevolently
beheld the true character of the woman, passionate, luxurious,
lacking simplicity, not deeply refined, incapable of pure
and perfect taste.

But, the next instant, she was too powerful for all my
opposing struggles. I saw how fit it was that she should make
herself as gorgeous as she pleased, and should do a thousand
things that would have been ridiculous in the poor, thin,
weakly characters of other women. To this day, however, I
hardly know whether I then beheld Zenobia in her truest
attitude, or whether that were the truer one in which she
had presented herself at Blithedale. In both, there was something like the illusion which a great actress flings around her.

"Have you given up Blithedale forever?" I inquired.

"Why should you think so?" asked she.

"I cannot tell," answered I; "except that it appears all like
a dream that we were ever there together."

"It is not so to me," said Zenobia. "I should think it a
poor and meagre nature, that is capable of but one set of
forms, and must convert all the past into a dream, merely
because the present happens to be unlike it. Why should we
be content with our homely life of a few months past, to the
exclusion of all other modes? It was good; but there are other
lives as good or better. Not, you will understand, that I
condemn those who give themselves up to it more entirely
than I, for myself, should deem it wise to do."

It irritated me, this self-complacent, condescending, quali-
fied approval and criticism of a system to which many
individuals—perhaps as highly endowed as our gorgeous
Zenobia—had contributed their all of earthly endeavor, and
their loftiest aspirations. I determined to make proof if there
were any spell that would exorcise her out of the part which
she seemed to be acting. She should be compelled to give
me a glimpse of something true; some nature, some passion,
no matter whether right or wrong, provided it were real.

"Your allusion to that class of circumscribed characters, who can live only in one mode of life," remarked I, coolly, "reminds me of our poor friend Hollingsworth. Possibly, he was in your thoughts, when you spoke thus. Poor fellow! It is a pity that, by the fault of a narrow education, he should have so completely immolated himself to that one idea of his; especially as the slightest modicum of common-sense would teach him its utter impracticability. Now that I have returned into the world, and can look at his project from a distance, it requires quite all my real regard for this respectable and well-intentioned man to prevent me laughing at him—as, I find, society at large does!"

Zenobia's eyes darted lightning; her cheeks flushed; the vividness of her expression was like the effect of a powerful light, flaming up suddenly within her. My experiment had fully succeeded. She had shown me the true flesh and blood of her heart, by thus involuntarily resenting my slight, pitying, half-kind, half-scornful mention of the man who was all in all with her. She herself, probably, felt this; for it was hardly a moment before she tranquillized her uneven breath, and seemed as proud and self-possessed as ever.

"I rather imagine," said she, quietly, "that your appreciation falls short of Mr. Hollingsworth's just claims. Blind enthusiasm, absorption in one idea, I grant, is generally ridiculous, and must be fatal to the respectability of an ordinary man; it requires a very high and powerful character, to make it otherwise. But a great man—as, perhaps, you do not know—attains his normal condition only through the inspiration of one great idea. As a friend of Mr. Hollingsworth, and, at the same time, a calm observer, I must tell you that he seems to me such a man. But you are very pardonable for fancying him ridiculous. Doubtless, he is so—to you! There can be no truer test of the noble and heroic, in any individual, than the degree in which he possesses the faculty of distinguishing heroism from absurdity."

I dared make no retort to Zenobia's concluding apothegm. In truth, I admired her fidelity. It gave me a new sense of Hollingsworth's native power, to discover that his influence was no less potent with this beautiful woman, here, in the midst of artificial life, than it had been, at the foot of the gray rock, and among the wild birch-trees of the wood-path, when she so passionately pressed his hand against her heart. The great, rude, shaggy, swarthy man! And Zenobia loved him!

"Did you bring Priscilla with you?" I resumed. "Do you know, I have sometimes fancied it not quite safe, considering the susceptibility of her temperament, that she should be so constantly within the sphere of a man like Hollingsworth? Such tender and delicate natures, among your sex, have often, I believe, a very adequate appreciation of the heroic element in men. But, then, again, I should suppose them as likely as any other women to make a reciprocal impression. Hollingsworth could hardly give his affections to a person capable of taking an independent stand, but only to one whom he might absorb into himself. He has certainly shown great tenderness for Priscilla."

Zenobia had turned aside. But I caught the reflection of her face in the mirror, and saw that it was very pale;—as pale, in her rich attire, as if a shroud were round her.

"Priscilla is here," said she, her voice a little lower than usual. "Have not you learnt as much, from your chamber-window? Would you like to see her?"

She made a step or two into the back drawing-room, and called:—

"Priscilla! Dear Priscilla!"

XX

THEY VANISH

PRISCILLA immediately answered the summons, and made her appearance through the door of the boudoir.

I had conceived the idea—which I now recognized as a very foolish one—that Zenobia would have taken measures to debar me from an interview with this girl, between whom and herself there was so utter an opposition of their dearest interests, that, on one part or the other, a great grief, if not likewise a great wrong, seemed a matter of necessity. But, as Priscilla was only a leaf, floating on the dark current of events, without influencing them by her own choice or plan—as she probably guessed not whither the stream was bearing her, nor perhaps even felt its inevitable movement—there could be no peril of her communicating to me any intelligence with regard to Zenobia's purposes.

On perceiving me, she came forward with great quietude of manner; and when I held out my hand, her own moved slightly towards it, as if attracted by a feeble degree of magnetism.

"I am glad to see you, my dear Priscilla," said I, still holding her hand. "But everything that I meet with, now-a-days, makes me wonder whether I am awake. You, especially, have always seemed like a figure in a dream—and now more than ever."

"Oh, there is substance in these fingers of mine!" she answered, giving my hand the faintest possible pressure, and then taking away her own. "Why do you call me a dream? Zenobia is much more like one than I; she is so very, very beautiful! And, I suppose," added Priscilla, as if thinking aloud, "everybody sees it, as I do."

But, for my part, it was Priscilla's beauty, not Zenobia's, of which I was thinking, at that moment. She was a person who could be quite obliterated, so far as beauty went, by anything unsuitable in her attire; her charm was not positive and material enough to bear up against a mistaken choice of color, for instance, or fashion. It was safest, in her case, to attempt no art of dress; for it demanded the most perfect taste, or else the happiest accident in the world, to give her precisely the adornment which she needed. She was now dressed in pure white, set off with some kind of a gauzy fabric, which—as I bring up her figure in my memory, with a faint gleam on her shadowy hair, and her dark eyes bent shyly on mine, through all the vanished years—seems to be floating about her like a mist. I wondered what Zenobia meant by evolving so much loveliness out of this poor girl. It was what few women could afford to do; for, as I looked from one to the other, the sheen and splendor of Zenobia's presence took nothing from Priscilla's softer spell, if it might not rather be thought to add to it.

"What do you think of her?" asked Zenobia.

I could not understand the look of melancholy kindness with which Zenobia regarded her. She advanced a step, and beckoning Priscilla near her, kissed her cheek; then, with a slight gesture of repulse, she moved to the other side of the room. I followed.

"She is a wonderful creature," I said. "Ever since she came among us, I have been dimly sensible of just this charm which you have brought out. But it was never absolutely visible till now. She is as lovely as a flower!"

"Well; say so, if you like," answered Zenobia. "You are a poet—at least, as poets go, now-a-days—and must be allowed to make an opera-glass of your imagination, when you look at women. I wonder, in such Arcadian freedom of falling in love as we have lately enjoyed, it never occurred to you to fall in love with Priscilla! In society, indeed, a genuine American never dreams of stepping across the inappreciable air-line which separates one class from another. But what was rank to the colonists of Blithedale?"

"There were other reasons," I replied, "why I should have demonstrated myself an ass, had I fallen in love with Priscilla. By-the-by, has Hollingsworth ever seen her in this dress?"

"Why do you bring up his name, at every turn?" asked Zenobia, in an undertone, and with a malign look which wandered from my face to Priscilla's. "You know not what you do! It is dangerous, sir, believe me, to tamper thus with earnest human passions, out of your own mere idleness, and for your sport. I will endure it no longer! Take care that it does not happen again! I warn you!"

"You partly wrong me, if not wholly," I responded. "It is an uncertain sense of some duty to perform, that brings my thoughts, and therefore my words, continually to that one point."

"Oh, this stale excuse of duty!" said Zenobia, in a whisper so full of scorn that it penetrated me like the hiss of a serpent. "I have often heard it before, from those who sought to interfere with me, and I know precisely what it signifies. Bigotry; self-conceit; an insolent curiosity; a meddlesome temper; a cold-blooded criticism, founded on a shallow interpretation of half-perceptions; a monstrous scepticism in regard to any conscience or any wisdom, except one's own; a most irreverent propensity to thrust Providence aside, and substitute one's self in its awful place—out of these, and other motives as miserable as these, comes your idea of duty!

But beware, sir! With all your fancied acuteness, you step blindfold into these affairs. For any mischief that may follow your interference, I hold you responsible!"

It was evident, that, with but a little further provocation, the lioness would turn to bay; if, indeed, such were not her attitude, already. I bowed, and, not very well knowing what else to do, was about to withdraw. But, glancing again towards Priscilla, who had retreated into a corner, there fell upon my heart an intolerable burthen of despondency, the purport of which I could not tell, but only felt it to bear reference to her. I approached her, and held out my hand; a gesture, however, to which she made no response. It was always one of her peculiarities that she seemed to shrink from even the most friendly touch, unless it were Zenobia's or Hollingsworth's. Zenobia, all this while, stood watching us, but with a careless expression, as if it mattered very little what might pass.

"Priscilla," I inquired, lowering my voice, "when do you go back to Blithedale?"

"Whenever they please to take me," said she.

"Did you come away of your own free-will?" I asked.

"I am blown about like a leaf," she replied. "I never have any free-will."

"Does Hollingsworth know that you are here?" said I.

"He bade me come," answered Priscilla.

She looked at me, I thought, with an air of surprise, as if the idea were incomprehensible, that she should have taken this step without his agency.

"What a gripe this man has laid upon her whole being!" muttered I, between my teeth. "Well; as Zenobia so kindly intimates, I have no more business here. I wash my hands of it all. On Hollingsworth's head be the consequences! Priscilla," I added, aloud, "I know not that ever we may meet again. Farewell!"

As I spoke the word, a carriage had rumbled along the street, and stopt before the house. The door-bell rang, and steps were immediately afterwards heard on the staircase. Zenobia had thrown a shawl over her dress.

"Mr. Coverdale," said she, with cool courtesy, "you will perhaps excuse us. We have an engagement, and are going out."

"Whither?" I demanded.

"Is not that a little more than you are entitled to inquire?" said she, with a smile. "At all events, it does not suit me to tell you."

The door of the drawing-room opened, and Westervelt appeared. I observed that he was elaborately dressed, as if for some grand entertainment. My dislike for this man was infinite. At that moment, it amounted to nothing less than a creeping of the flesh, as when, feeling about in a dark place, one touches something cold and slimy, and questions what the secret hatefulness may be. And, still, I could not but acknowledge, that, for personal beauty, for polish of manner, for all that externally befits a gentleman, there was hardly another like him. After bowing to Zenobia, and graciously saluting Priscilla in her corner, he recognized me by a slight, but courteous inclination.

"Come, Priscilla," said Zenobia, "it is time. Mr. Coverdale, good evening!"

As Priscilla moved slowly forward, I met her in the middle of the drawing-room.

"Priscilla," said I, in the hearing of them all, "do you know whither you are going?"

"I do not know," she answered.

"Is it wise to go?—and is it your choice to go?" I asked. "If not—I am your friend, and Hollingsworth's friend—tell me so, at once!"

"Possibly," observed Westervelt, smiling, "Priscilla sees in me an older friend than either Mr. Coverdale or Mr. Hollingsworth. I shall willingly leave the matter at her option."

While thus speaking, he made a gesture of kindly invitation; and Priscilla passed me, with the gliding movement of a sprite, and took his offered arm. He offered the other to Zenobia. But she turned her proud and beautiful face upon him, with a look which—judging from what I caught of it in profile—would undoubtedly have smitten the man dead, had he possessed any heart, or had this glance attained to it. It seemed to rebound, however, from his courteous visage, like an arrow from polished steel. They all three descended the stairs; and when I likewise reached the street-door, the carriage was already rolling away.

XXI

AN OLD ACQUAINTANCE

THUS excluded from everybody's confidence, and attaining no further, by my most earnest study, than to an uncertain sense of something hidden from me, it would appear reasonable that I should have flung off all these alien perplexities. Obviously, my best course was, to betake myself to new scenes. Here, I was only an intruder. Elsewhere, there might be circumstances in which I could establish a personal interest, and people who would respond, with a portion of their sympathies, for so much as I should bestow of mine.

Nevertheless, there occurred to me one other thing to be done. Remembering old Moodie, and his relationship with Priscilla, I determined to seek an interview, for the purpose of ascertaining whether the knot of affairs was as inextricable, on that side, as I found it on all others. Being tolerably well acquainted with the old man's haunts, I went, the next day, to the saloon of a certain establishment about which he often lurked. It was a reputable place enough, affording good entertainment in the way of meat, drink, and fumigation; and there, in my young and idle days and nights, when I was neither nice nor wise, I had often amused myself with watching the staid humors and sober jollities of the thirsty souls around me.

At my first entrance, old Moodie was not there. The more patiently to await him, I lighted a cigar, and establishing myself in a corner, took a quiet, and, by sympathy, a boozy kind of pleasure in the customary life that was going forward. Human nature, in my opinion, has a naughty instinct that approves of wine, at least, if not of stronger liquor. The temperance-men may preach till doom's day; and still this cold and barren world will look warmer, kindlier, mellower, through the medium of a toper's glass; nor can they, with all their efforts, really spill his draught upon the floor, until some hitherto unthought-of discovery shall supply him with a truer element of joy. The general atmosphere of life must first be rendered so inspiriting that he will not need his delirious solace. The custom of tippling has its defensible side, as well as any other question. But these good people snatch at the old, time-honored demijohn, and offer nothing—either sensual or moral—nothing whatever to supply its place; and human life, as it goes with a multitude of men, will not endure so great a vacuum as would be left by the withdrawal of that big-bellied convexity. The space, which it now occupies, must somehow or other be filled up. As for the rich, it would be little matter if a blight fell upon their vineyards; but the poor man—whose only glimpse of a better state is through the muddy medium of his liquor—what is to be done for him? The reformers should make their efforts positive, instead of negative; they must do away with evil by substituting good.

The saloon was fitted up with a good deal of taste. There were pictures on the walls, and among them an oil-painting of a beef-steak, with such an admirable show of juicy tenderness, that the beholder sighed to think it merely visionary, and incapable of ever being put upon a gridiron. Another work of high art was the lifelike representation of a noble sirloin; another, the hind-quarters of a deer, retaining the hoofs and tawny fur; another, the head and shoulders of a salmon; and, still more exquisitely finished, a brace of canvass-back ducks, in which the mottled feathers were depicted with the accuracy of a daguerreotype. Some very hungry painter, I suppose, had wrought these subjects of still life, heightening his imagination with his appetite, and earning, it is to be hoped, the privilege of a daily dinner off whichever of his pictorial viands he liked best. Then there was a fine old cheese, in which you could almost discern the mites; and some sardines, on a small plate, very richly done, and looking as if oozy with the oil in which they had been smothered. All these things were so perfectly imitated, that you seemed to have the genuine article before you, and yet with an indescribable, ideal charm; it took away the grossness from what was fleshiest and fattest, and thus helped the life of man, even in its earthliest relations, to appear rich and noble, as well as warm, cheerful, and substantial. There were pictures, too, of gallant revellers, those of the old time, Flemish, apparently, with doublets and slashed sleeves, drinking their wine out of fantastic, long-stemmed glasses; quaffing joyously, quaffing forever, with inaudible laughter and song; while the champagne bubbled immortally against their moustaches, or the purple tide of Burgundy ran inexhaustibly down their throats.

But, in an obscure corner of the saloon, there was a little picture—excellently done, moreover—of a ragged, bloated, New England toper, stretched out on a bench, in the heavy, apoplectic sleep of drunkenness. The death-in-life was too well portrayed. You smelt the fumy liquor that had brought on this syncope. Your only comfort lay in the forced reflection, that, real as he looked, the poor caitiff was but imaginary, a bit of painted canvass, whom no delirium tremens, nor so much as a retributive headache, awaited, on the morrow.

By this time, it being past eleven o'clock, the two bar-keepers of the saloon were in pretty constant activity. One of these young men had a rare faculty in the concoction of gin-cocktails. It was a spectacle to behold, how, with a tumbler in each hand, he tossed the contents from one to the other. Never conveying it awry, nor spilling the least drop, he compelled the frothy liquor, as it seemed to me, to spout forth from one glass and descend into the other, in a great parabolic curve, as well-defined and calculable as a planet's orbit. He had a good forehead, with a particularly large development just above the eyebrows; fine intellectual gifts, no doubt, which he had educated to this profitable end; being famous for nothing but gin-cocktails, and commanding a fair salary by his one accomplishment. These cocktails, and other artificial combinations of liquor, (of which there were at least a score, though mostly, I suspect, fantastic in their differences,) were much in favor with the younger class of customers, who, at farthest, had only reached the second stage of potatory life. The staunch, old soakers, on the other hand—men who, if put on tap, would have yielded a red alcoholic liquor, by way of blood—usually confined themselves to plain brandy-and-water, gin, or West India rum; and, oftentimes, they prefaced their dram with some medicinal remark as to the wholesomeness and stomachic qualities of that particular drink. Two or three appeared to have bottles of their own, behind the counter; and winking one red eye to the bar-keeper, he forthwith produced these choicest and peculiar cordials, which it was a matter of great interest and favor, among their acquaintances, to obtain a sip of.

Agreeably to the Yankee habit, under whatever circumstances, the deportment of all these good fellows, old or young, was decorous and thoroughly correct. They grew only the more sober in their cups; there was no confused babble, nor boisterous laughter. They sucked in the joyous fire of the decanters, and kept it smouldering in their inmost recesses, with a bliss known only to the heart which it warmed and comforted. Their eyes twinkled a little, to be sure; they hemmed vigorously, after each glass, and laid a hand upon the pit of the stomach, as if the pleasant titillation, there, was what constituted the tangible part of their enjoyment. In that spot, unquestionably, and not in the brain, was the acme of the whole affair. But the true purpose of their drinking— and one that will induce men to drink, or do something equivalent, as long as this weary world shall endure—was the renewed youth and vigor, the brisk, cheerful sense of things present and to come, with which, for about a quarter-of-an-hour, the dram permeated their systems. And when such quarters-of-an-hour can be obtained in some mode less baneful to the great sum of a man's life—but, nevertheless, with a little spice of impropriety, to give it a wild flavor—we temperance-people may ring out our bells for victory!

The prettiest object in the saloon was a tiny fountain, which threw up its feathery jet, through the counter, and sparkled down again into an oval basin, or lakelet, con-taining several gold-fishes. There was a bed of bright sand, at the bottom, strewn with coral and rock-work; and the fishes went gleaming about, now turning up the sheen of a golden side, and now vanishing into the shadows of the water, like the fanciful thoughts that coquet with a poet in his dream. Never before, I imagine, did a company of water-drinkers remain so entirely uncontaminated by the bad ex-ample around them; nor could I help wondering that it had not occurred to any freakish inebriate, to empty a glass of liquor into their lakelet. What a delightful idea! Who would not be a fish, if he could inhale jollity with the essential element of his existence!

I had begun to despair of meeting old Moodie, when, all at once, I recognized his hand and arm, protruding from behind a screen that was set up for the accommodation of bashful topers. As a matter of course, he had one of Priscilla's little purses, and was quietly insinuating it under the notice of a person who stood near. This was always old Moodie's way. You hardly ever saw him advancing towards you, but became aware of his proximity without being able to guess how he had come thither. He glided about like a spirit, assuming visibility close to your elbow, offering his petty trifles of merchandise, remaining long enough for you to purchase, if so disposed, and then taking himself off, between two breaths, while you happened to be thinking of something else.

By a sort of sympathetic impulse that often controlled me, in those more impressible days of my life, I was induced to approach this old man in a mode as undemonstrative as his own. Thus, when, according to his custom, he was probably just about to vanish, he found me at his elbow.

"Ah!" said he, with more emphasis than was usual with him. "It is Mr. Coverdale!"

"Yes, Mr. Moodie, your old acquaintance," answered I. "It is some time now since we ate our luncheon together, at Blithedale, and a good deal longer since our little talk together, at the street-corner."

"That was a good while ago," said the old man.

And he seemed inclined to say not a word more. His existence looked so colorless and torpid—so very faintly shadowed on the canvass of reality—that I was half afraid lest he should altogether disappear, even while my eyes were fixed full upon his figure. He was certainly the wretchedest old ghost in the world, with his crazy hat, the dingy handkerchief about his throat, his suit of threadbare gray, and especially that patch over his right eye, behind which he always seemed to be hiding himself. There was one method, however, of bringing him out into somewhat stronger relief. A glass of brandy would effect it. Perhaps the gentler influence of a bottle of claret might do the same. Nor could I think it a matter for the recording angel to write down against me, if—with my painful consciousness of the frost in this old man's blood, and the positive ice that had congealed about his heart—I should thaw him out, were it only for an hour, with the summer warmth of a little wine. What else could possibly be done for him? How else could he be imbued with energy enough to hope for a happier state, hereafter? How else be inspirited to say his prayers? For there are states of our spiritual system, when the throb of the soul's life is too faint and weak to render us capable of religious aspiration.

"Mr. Moodie," said I, "shall we lunch together? And would you like to drink a glass of wine?"

His one eye gleamed. He bowed; and it impressed me that he grew to be more of a man at once, either in anticipation of the wine, or as a grateful response to my goodfellowship in offering it.

"With pleasure," he replied.

The barkeeper, at my request, showed us into a private room, and, soon afterwards, set some fried oysters and a bottle of claret on the table; and I saw the old man glance curiously at the label of the bottle, as if to learn the brand.

"It should be good wine," I remarked, "if it have any right to its label."

"You cannot suppose, sir," said Moodie, with a sigh, "that a poor old fellow, like me, knows any difference in wines."

And yet, in his way of handling the glass, in his preliminary snuff at the aroma, in his first cautious sip of the wine, and the gustatory skill with which he gave his palate the full advantage of it, it was impossible not to recognize the connoisseur.

"I fancy, Mr. Moodie," said I, "you are a much better judge of wines than I have yet learned to be. Tell me fairly— did you never drink it where the grape grows?"

"How should that have been, Mr. Coverdale?" answered old Moodie, shyly; but then he took courage, as it were, and uttered a feeble little laugh. "The flavor of this wine," added he, "and its perfume, still more than its taste, makes me remember that I was once a young man!"

"I wish, Mr. Moodie," suggested I—not that I greatly cared about it, however, but was only anxious to draw him into some talk about Priscilla and Zenobia—"I wish, while we sit over our wine, you would favor me with a few of those youthful reminiscences."

"Ah," said he, shaking his head, "they might interest you more than you suppose. But I had better be silent, Mr. Coverdale. If this good wine—though claret, I suppose, is not apt to play such a trick—but if it should make my tongue run too freely, I could never look you in the face again."

"You never did look me in the face, Mr. Moodie," I replied, "until this very moment."

"Ah!" sighed old Moodie.

It was wonderful, however, what an effect the mild grape-juice wrought upon him. It was not in the wine, but in the associations which it seemed to bring up. Instead of the mean, slouching, furtive, painfully depressed air of an old city-vagabond, more like a gray kennel-rat than any other living thing, he began to take the aspect of a decayed gentleman. Even his garments—especially after I had myself quaffed a glass or two—looked less shabby than when we first sat down. There was, by-and-by, a certain exuberance and elaborateness of gesture, and manner, oddly in contrast with all that I had hitherto seen of him. Anon, with hardly any impulse from me, old Moodie began to talk. His communications referred exclusively to a long past and more fortunate period of his life, with only a few unavoidable allusions to the circumstances that had reduced him to his present state. But, having once got the clue, my subsequent researches acquainted me with the main facts of the following narrative; although, in writing it out, my pen has perhaps allowed itself a trifle of romantic and legendary license, worthier of a small poet than of a grave biographer.

XXII

FAUNTLEROY

FIVE-AND-TWENTY years ago, at the epoch of this
story, there dwelt, in one of the middle states, a man
whom we shall call Fauntleroy; a man of wealth, and
magnificent tastes, and prodigal expenditure. His home
might almost be styled a palace; his habits, in the ordinary
sense, princely. His whole being seemed to have crystallized
itself into an external splendor, wherewith he glittered in
the eyes of the world, and had no other life than upon this
gaudy surface. He had married a lovely woman, whose
nature was deeper than his own. But his affection for her,
though it showed largely, was superficial, like all his other
manifestations and developments; he did not so truly keep
this noble creature in his heart, as wear her beauty for the
most brilliant ornament of his outward state. And there was
born to him a child, a beautiful daughter, whom he took
from the beneficent hand of God with no just sense of her
immortal value, but as a man, already rich in gems, would
receive another jewel. If he loved her, it was because she
shone.

After Fauntleroy had thus spent a few empty years, cor-
ruscating continually an unnatural light, the source of it—
which was merely his gold—began to grow more shallow, and
finally became exhausted. He saw himself in imminent peril

of losing all that had heretofore distinguished him; and, conscious of no innate worth to fall back upon, he recoiled from this calamity, with the instinct of a soul shrinking from annihilation. To avoid it—wretched man!—or, rather, to defer it, if but for a month, a day, or only to procure himself the life of a few breaths more, amid the false glitter which was now less his own than ever—he made himself guilty of a crime. It was just the sort of crime, growing out of its artificial state, which society (unless it should change its entire constitution for this man's unworthy sake) neither could nor ought to pardon. More safely might it pardon murder. Fauntleroy's guilt was discovered. He fled; his wife perished by the necessity of her innate nobleness, in its alliance with a being so ignoble; and betwixt her mother's death and her father's ignominy, his daughter was left worse than orphaned.

There was no pursuit after Fauntleroy. His family-connections, who had great wealth, made such arrangements with those whom he had attempted to wrong, as secured him from the retribution that would have overtaken an unfriended criminal. The wreck of his estate was divided among his creditors. His name, in a very brief space, was forgotten by the multitude who had passed it so diligently from mouth to mouth. Seldom, indeed, was it recalled, even by his closest former intimates. Nor could it have been otherwise. The man had laid no real touch on any mortal's heart. Being a mere image, an optical delusion, created by the sunshine of prosperity, it was his law to vanish into the shadow of the first intervening cloud. He seemed to leave no vacancy; a phenomenon which, like many others that attended his brief career, went far to prove the illusiveness of his existence.

Not, however, that the physical substance of Fauntleroy had literally melted into vapor. He had fled northward, to the New England metropolis, and had taken up his abode, under another name, in a squalid street, or court, of the older portion of the city. There he dwelt among poverty-stricken wretches, sinners, and forlorn, good people, Irish, and whomsoever else were neediest. Many families were clustered in each house together, above stairs and below, in the little peaked garrets, and even in the dusky cellars. The house, where Fauntleroy paid weekly rent for a chamber and a closet, had been a stately habitation, in its day. An old colonial Governor had built it, and lived there, long ago, and held his levees in a great room where now slept twenty Irish bedfellows, and died in Fauntleroy's chamber, which his embroidered and white-wigged ghost still haunted. Tattered hangings, a marble hearth, traversed with many cracks and fissures, a richly-carved oaken mantel-piece, partly hacked-away for kindling-stuff, a stuccoed ceiling, defaced with great, unsightly patches of the naked laths;—such was the chamber's aspect, as if, with its splinters and rags of dirty splendor, it were a kind of practical gibe at this poor, ruined man of show.

At first, and at irregular intervals, his relatives allowed Fauntleroy a little pittance to sustain life; not from any love, perhaps, but lest poverty should compel him, by new offences, to add more shame to that with which he had already stained them. But he showed no tendency to further guilt. His character appeared to have been radically changed (as, indeed, from its shallowness, it well might) by his miserable fate; or, it may be, the traits now seen in him were portions of the same character, presenting itself in another phase. Instead of any longer seeking to live in the sight of the world, his impulse was to shrink into the nearest obscurity, and to be unseen of men, were it possible, even while standing before their eyes. He had no pride; it was all trodden in the dust. No ostentation; for how could it survive, when there was nothing left of Fauntleroy, save penury and shame! His very gait demonstrated that he would gladly have faded out of view, and have crept about invisibly, for the sake of sheltering himself from the irksomeness of a human glance. Hardly, it was averred, within the memory of those who knew him now, had he the hardihood to show his full front to the world. He skulked in corners, and crept about in a sort of noonday twilight, making himself gray and misty, at all hours, with his morbid intolerance of sunshine.

In his torpid despair, however, he had done an act which that condition of the spirit seems to prompt, almost as often as prosperity and hope. Fauntleroy was again married. He had taken to wife a forlorn, meek-spirited, feeble young woman, a seamstress, whom he found dwelling with her mother in a contiguous chamber of the old gubernatorial residence. This poor phantom—as the beautiful and noble companion of his former life had done—brought him a daughter. And sometimes, as from one dream into another, Fauntleroy looked forth out of his present grimy environment, into that past magnificence, and wondered whether the grandee of yesterday or the pauper of to-day were real. But, in my mind, the one and the other were alike impalpable. In truth, it was Fauntleroy's fatality to behold whatever he touched dissolve. After a few years, his second wife (dim shadow that she had always been) faded finally out of the world, and left Fauntleroy to deal as he might with their pale and nervous child. And, by this time, among his distant relatives—with whom he had grown a weary thought, linked with contagious infamy, and which they were only too willing to get rid of—he was himself supposed to be no more.

The younger child, like his elder one, might be considered as the true offspring of both parents, and as the reflection of their state. She was a tremulous little creature, shrinking involuntarily from all mankind, but in timidity, and no sour repugnance. There was a lack of human substance in her; it seemed as if, were she to stand up in a sunbeam, it would pass right through her figure, and trace out the cracked and dusty window-panes upon the naked floor. But, nevertheless, the poor child had a heart; and from her mother's gentle character, she had inherited a profound and still capacity of affection. And so her life was one of love. She bestowed it partly on her father, but, in greater part, on an idea.

For Fauntleroy, as they sat by their cheerless fireside—which was no fireside, in truth, but only a rusty stove—had often talked to the little girl about his former wealth, the noble loveliness of his first wife, and the beautiful child whom she had given him. Instead of the fairy tales, which other parents tell, he told Priscilla this. And, out of the loneliness of her sad little existence, Priscilla's love grew, and tended upward, and twined itself perseveringly around this unseen sister; as a grape-vine might strive to clamber out of a gloomy hollow among the rocks, and embrace a young tree, standing in the sunny warmth above. It was almost like worship, both in its earnestness and its humility; nor was it the less humble, though the more earnest, because Priscilla could claim human kindred with the being whom she so devoutly loved. As with worship, too, it gave her soul the refreshment of a purer atmosphere. Save for this singular, this melancholy, and yet beautiful affection, the child could hardly have lived; or, had she lived, with a heart shrunken for lack of any sentiment to fill it, she must have yielded to the barren miseries of her position, and have grown to womanhood, characterless and worthless. But, now, amid all the sombre coarseness of her father's outward life, and of her own, Priscilla had a higher and imaginative life within. Some faint gleam thereof was often visible upon her face. It was as if, in her spiritual visits to her brilliant sister, a portion of the latter's brightness had permeated our dim Priscilla, and still lingered, shedding a faint illumination through the cheerless chamber, after she came back.

As the child grew up, so pallid and so slender, and with much unaccountable nervousness, and all the weaknesses of neglected infancy still haunting her, the gross and simple neighbors whispered strange things about Priscilla. The big, red, Irish matrons, whose innumerable progeny swarmed out of the adjacent doors, used to mock at the pale Western child. They fancied—or, at least, affirmed it, between jest and earnest—that she was not so solid flesh and blood as other children, but mixed largely with a thinner element. They called her ghost-child, and said that she could indeed vanish, when she pleased, but could never, in her densest moments, make herself quite visible. The sun, at mid-day, would shine through her; in the first gray of the twilight, she lost all the distinctness of her outline; and, if you followed the dim thing into a dark corner, behold! she was not there. And it was true, that Priscilla had strange ways; strange ways, and stranger words, when she uttered any words at all. Never stirring out of the old Governor's dusky house, she sometimes talked of distant places and splendid rooms, as if she had just left them. Hidden things were visible to her, (at least, so the people inferred from obscure hints, escaping unawares out of her mouth,) and silence was audible. And, in all the world, there was nothing so difficult to be endured, by those who had any dark secret to conceal, as the glance of Priscilla's timid and melancholy eyes.

Her peculiarities were the theme of continual gossip among the other inhabitants of the gubernatorial mansion. The rumor spread thence into a wider circle. Those who knew old Moodie—as he was now called—used often to jeer him, at the very street-corners, about his daughter's gift of second-sight and prophecy. It was a period when science (though mostly through its empirical professors) was bringing forward, anew, a hoard of facts and imperfect theories, that had partially won credence, in elder times, but which modern scepticism had swept away as rubbish. These things were now tossed up again, out of the surging ocean of human thought and experience. The story of Priscilla's preternatural manifestations, therefore, attracted a kind of notice of which it would have been deemed wholly unworthy, a few years earlier. One day, a gentleman ascended the creaking staircase, and inquired which was old Moodie's chamber-door. And, several times, he came again. He was a marvellously handsome man, still youthful, too, and fashionably dressed. Except that Priscilla, in those days, had no beauty, and, in the languor of her existence, had not yet blossomed into womanhood, there would have been rich food for scandal in these visits; for the girl was unquestionably their sole object, although her father was supposed always to be present. But, it must likewise be added, there was something about Priscilla that calumny could not meddle with; and thus far was she privileged, either by the preponderance of what was spiritual, or the thin and watery blood that left her cheek so pallid.

Yet, if the busy tongues of the neighborhood spared Priscilla, in one way, they made themselves amends by renewed and wilder babble, on another score. They averred that the strange gentleman was a wizard, and that he had taken advantage of Priscilla's lack of earthly substance to subject her to himself, as his familiar spirit, through whose medium he gained cognizance of whatever happened, in regions near or remote. The boundaries of his power were defined by the verge of the pit of Tartarus, on the one hand, and the third sphere of the celestial world, on the other. Again, they declared their suspicion that the wizard, with all his show of manly beauty, was really an aged and wizened figure, or else that his semblance of a human body was only a necromantic, or perhaps a mechanical contrivance, in which a demon walked about. In proof of it, however, they could merely instance a gold band around his upper teeth, which had once been visible to several old women, when he smiled at them from the top of the Governor's staircase. Of course, this was all absurdity, or mostly so. But, after every possible deduction, there remained certain very mysterious points about the stranger's character, as well as the connection that he established with Priscilla. Its nature, at that period, was even less understood than now, when miracles of this kind have grown so absolutely stale, that I would gladly, if the truth allowed, dismiss the whole matter from my narrative.

We must now glance backward, in quest of the beautiful daughter of Fauntleroy's prosperity. What had become of her? Fauntleroy's only brother, a bachelor, and with no other relative so near, had adopted the forsaken child. She grew up in affluence, with native graces clustering luxuriantly about her. In her triumphant progress towards womanhood, she was adorned with every variety of feminine accomplishment. But she lacked a mother's care. With no adequate control, on any hand, (for a man, however stern, however wise, can never sway and guide a female child,) her character was left to shape itself. There was good in it, and evil. Passionate, self-willed, and imperious, she had a warm and generous nature; showing the richness of the soil, however, chiefly by the weeds that flourished in it, and choked up the herbs of grace. In her girlhood, her uncle died. As Fauntleroy was supposed to be likewise dead, and no other heir was known to exist, his wealth devolved on her, although, dying suddenly, the uncle left no will. After his death, there were obscure passages in Zenobia's history. There were whispers of an attachment, and even a secret marriage, with a fascinating and accomplished, but unprincipled young man. The incidents and appearances, however, which led to this surmise, soon passed away and were forgotten.

Nor was her reputation seriously affected by the report. In fact, so great was her native power and influence, and such seemed the careless purity of her nature, that whatever Zenobia did was generally acknowledged as right for her to do. The world never criticised her so harshly as it does most women who transcend its rules. It almost yielded its assent, when it beheld her stepping out of the common path, and asserting the more extensive privileges of her sex, both theoretically and by her practice. The sphere of ordinary womanhood was felt to be narrower than her development required.

A portion of Zenobia's more recent life is told in the fore-going pages. Partly in earnest—and, I imagine, as was her disposition, half in a proud jest, or in a kind of recklessness that had grown upon her, out of some hidden grief—she had given her countenance, and promised liberal pecuniary aid, to our experiment of a better social state. And Priscilla followed her to Blithedale. The sole bliss of her life had been a dream of this beautiful sister, who had never so much as known of her existence. By this time, too, the poor girl was enthralled in an intolerable bondage, from which she must either free herself or perish. She deemed herself safest near Zenobia, into whose large heart she hoped to nestle.

One evening, months after Priscilla's departure, when Moodie (or shall we call him Fauntleroy?) was sitting alone in the state-chamber of the old Governor, there came foot-steps up the staircase. There was a pause on the landing-place. A lady's musical, yet haughty accents were heard making an inquiry from some denizen of the house, who had thrust a head out of a contiguous chamber. There was then a knock at Moodie's door.

"Come in!" said he.

And Zenobia entered. The details of the interview that followed, being unknown to me—while, notwithstanding, it would be a pity quite to lose the picturesqueness of the situation—I shall attempt to sketch it, mainly from fancy, although with some general grounds of surmise in regard to the old man's feelings.

She gazed, wonderingly, at the dismal chamber. Dismal
to her, who beheld it only for an instant, and how much
more so to him, into whose brain each bare spot on the
ceiling, every tatter of the paper-hangings, and all the splintered carvings of the mantel-piece, seen wearily through long
years, had worn their several prints! Inexpressibly miserable
is this familiarity with objects that have been, from the first,
disgustful.

"I have received a strange message," said Zenobia, after
a moment's silence, "requesting, or rather enjoining it upon
me, to come hither. Rather from curiosity than any other
motive—and because, though a woman, I have not all the
timidity of one—I have complied. Can it be you, sir, who
thus summoned me?"

"It was," answered Moodie.

"And what was your purpose?" she continued. "You require
charity, perhaps? In that case, the message might have been
more fitly worded. But you are old and poor; and age and
poverty should be allowed their privileges. Tell me, therefore,
to what extent you need my aid."

"Put up your purse," said the supposed mendicant, with
an inexplicable smile. "Keep it—keep all your wealth—until
I demand it all, or none! My message had no such end in
view. You are beautiful, they tell me; and I desired to
look at you!"

He took the one lamp that showed the discomfort and
sordidness of his abode, and approaching Zenobia, held it
up, so as to gain the more perfect view of her, from top to
toe. So obscure was the chamber, that you could see the
reflection of her diamonds thrown upon the dingy wall, and
flickering with the rise and fall of Zenobia's breath. It was
the splendor of those jewels on her neck, like lamps that burn
before some fair temple, and the jewelled flower in her hair,
more than the murky yellow light, that helped him to see
her beauty. But he beheld it, and grew proud at heart; his

own figure, in spite of his mean habiliments, assumed an air of state and grandeur.

"It is well!" cried old Moodie. "Keep your wealth. You are right worthy of it. Keep it, therefore, but with one condition, only!"

Zenobia thought the old man beside himself, and was moved with pity.

"Have you none to care for you?" asked she. "No daughter? —no kind-hearted neighbor?—no means of procuring the attendance which you need? Tell me, once again, can I do nothing for you?"

"Nothing," he replied. "I have beheld what I wished. Now, leave me! Linger not a moment longer; or I may be tempted to say what would bring a cloud over that queenly brow. Keep all your wealth, but with only this one condition. Be kind—be no less kind than sisters are—to my poor Priscilla!"

And, it may be, after Zenobia withdrew, Fauntleroy paced his gloomy chamber, and communed with himself, as follows: —or, at all events, it is the only solution, which I can offer, of the enigma presented in his character.

"I am unchanged—the same man as of yore!" said he. "True; my brother's wealth, he dying intestate, is legally my own. I know it; yet, of my own choice, I live a beggar, and go meanly clad, and hide myself behind a forgotten ignominy. Looks this like ostentation? Ah, but, in Zenobia, I live again! Beholding her so beautiful—so fit to be adorned with all imaginable splendor of outward state—the cursed vanity, which, half-a-lifetime since, dropt off like tatters of once gaudy apparel from my debased and ruined person, is all renewed for her sake! Were I to re-appear, my shame would go with me from darkness into daylight. Zenobia has the splendor, and not the shame. Let the world admire her, and be dazzled by her, the brilliant child of my prosperity! It is Fauntleroy that still shines through her!"

But, then, perhaps, another thought occurred to him.

"My poor Priscilla! And am I just, to her, in surrendering all to this beautiful Zenobia? Priscilla! I love her best—I love her only!—but with shame, not pride. So dim, so pallid, so shrinking—the daughter of my long calamity! Wealth were but a mockery in Priscilla's hands. What is its use, except to fling a golden radiance around those who grasp it? Yet, let Zenobia take heed! Priscilla shall have no wrong!"

But, while the man of show thus meditated—that very evening, so far as I can adjust the dates of these strange incidents—Priscilla—poor, pallid flower!—was either snatched from Zenobia's hand, or flung wilfully away!

XXIII

A VILLAGE-HALL

WELL! I betook myself away, and wandered up and down, like an exorcised spirit that had been driven from its old haunts, after a mighty struggle. It takes down the solitary pride of man, beyond most other things, to find the impracticability of flinging aside affections that have grown irksome. The bands, that were silken once, are apt to become iron fetters, when we desire to shake them off. Our souls, after all, are not our own. We convey a property in them to those with whom we associate, but to what extent can never be known, until we feel the tug, the agony, of our abortive effort to resume an exclusive sway over ourselves. Thus, in all the weeks of my absence, my thoughts continually reverted back, brooding over the by-gone months, and bringing up incidents that seemed hardly to have left a trace of themselves, in their passage. I spent painful hours in recalling these trifles, and rendering them more misty and unsubstantial than at first, by the quantity of speculative musing, thus kneaded in with them. Hollingsworth, Zenobia, Priscilla! These three had absorbed my life into themselves. Together with an inexpressible longing to know their fortunes, there was likewise a morbid resentment of my own pain, and a stubborn reluctance to come again within their sphere.

All that I learned of them, therefore, was comprised in a few brief and pungent squibs, such as the newspapers were then in the habit of bestowing on our socialist enterprise. There was one paragraph which, if I rightly guessed its purport, bore reference to Zenobia, but was too darkly hinted to convey even thus much of certainty. Hollingsworth, too, with his philanthropic project, afforded the penny-a-liners a theme for some savage and bloody-minded jokes; and, considerably to my surprise, they affected me with as much indignation as if we had still been friends.

Thus passed several weeks; time long enough for my brown and toil-hardened hands to re-accustom themselves to gloves. Old habits, such as were merely external, returned upon me with wonderful promptitude. My superficial talk, too, assumed altogether a worldly tone. Meeting former acquaintances, who showed themselves inclined to ridicule my heroic devotion to the cause of human welfare, I spoke of the recent phase of my life as indeed fair matter for a jest. But I also gave them to understand that it was, at most, only an experiment, on which I had staked no valuable amount of hope or fear; it had enabled me to pass the summer in a novel and agreeable way, had afforded me some grotesque specimens of artificial simplicity, and could not, therefore, so far as I was concerned, be reckoned a failure. In no one instance, however, did I voluntarily speak of my three friends. They dwelt in a profounder region. The more I consider myself, as I then was, the more do I recognize how deeply my connection with those three had affected all my being.

As it was already the epoch of annihilated space, I might, in the time I was away from Blithedale, have snatched a glimpse at England, and been back again. But my wanderings were confined within a very limited sphere. I hopped and fluttered, like a bird with a string about its leg, gyrating round a small circumference, and keeping up a restless activity to no purpose. Thus, it was still in our familiar Massachusetts—

in one of its white country-villages—that I must next particularize an incident.

The scene was one of those Lyceum-halls, of which almost every village has now its own, dedicated to that sober and pallid, or, rather, drab-colored, mode of winter-evening entertainment, the Lecture. Of late years, this has come strangely into vogue, when the natural tendency of things would seem to be, to substitute lettered for oral methods of addressing the public. But, in halls like this, besides the winter course of lectures, there is a rich and varied series of other exhibitions. Hither comes the ventriloquist, with all his mysterious tongues; the thaumaturgist, too, with his miraculous transformations of plates, doves, and rings, his pancakes smoking in your hat, and his cellar of choice liquors, represented in one small bottle. Here, also, the itinerant professor instructs separate classes of ladies and gentlemen in physiology, and demonstrates his lessons by the aid of real skeletons, and mannikins in wax, from Paris. Here is to be heard the choir of Ethiopian melodists, and to be seen, the diorama of Moscow or Bunker Hill, or the moving panorama of the Chinese wall. Here is displayed the museum of wax figures, illustrating the wide catholicism of earthly renown by mixing up heroes and statesmen, the Pope and the Mormon Prophet, kings, queens, murderers, and beautiful ladies; every sort of person, in short, except authors, of whom I never beheld even the most famous, done in wax. And here, in this many-purposed hall, (unless the selectmen of the village chance to have more than their share of the puritanism, which, however diversified with later patchwork, still gives its prevailing tint to New England character,) here the company of strolling players sets up its little stage, and claims patronage for the legitimate drama.

But, on the autumnal evening which I speak of, a number of printed handbills—stuck up in the bar-room and on the sign-post of the hotel, and on the meeting-house porch, and distributed largely through the village—had promised the inhabitants an interview with that celebrated and hitherto inexplicable phenomenon, the Veiled Lady!

The hall was fitted up with an amphitheatrical descent of seats towards a platform, on which stood a desk, two lights, a stool, and a capacious, antique chair. The audience was of a generally decent and respectable character; old farmers, in their Sunday black coats, with shrewd, hard, sun-dried faces, and a cynical humor, oftener than any other expression, in their eyes; pretty girls, in many-colored attire; pretty young men—the schoolmaster, the lawyer, or student-at-law, the shopkeeper—all looking rather suburban than rural. In these days, there is absolutely no rusticity, except when the actual labor of the soil leaves its earth-mould on the person. There was likewise a considerable proportion of young and middle-aged women, many of them stern in feature, with marked foreheads, and a very definite line of eyebrow; a type of womanhood in which a bold intellectual development seems to be keeping pace with the progressive delicacy of the physical constitution. Of all these people I took note, at first, according to my custom. But I ceased to do so, the moment that my eyes fell on an individual who sat two or three seats below me, immoveable, apparently deep in thought, with his back, of course, towards me, and his face turned stead-fastly upon the platform.

After sitting awhile, in contemplation of this person's familiar contour, I was irresistibly moved to step over the intervening benches, lay my hand on his shoulder, put my mouth close to his ear, and address him in a sepulchral, melo-dramatic whisper:—

"Hollingsworth! Where have you left Zenobia!"

His nerves, however, were proof against my attack. He turned half around, and looked me in the face, with great, sad eyes, in which there was neither kindness nor resentment, nor any perceptible surprise.

• 197 •

"Zenobia, when I last saw her," he answered, "was at Blithedale."

He said no more. But there was a great deal of talk going on, near me, among a knot of people who might be considered as representing the mysticism, or, rather, the mystic sensuality, of this singular age. The nature of the exhibition, that was about to take place, had probably given the turn to their conversation.

I heard, from a pale man in blue spectacles, some stranger stories than ever were written in a romance; told, too, with a simple, unimaginative steadfastness, which was terribly efficacious in compelling the auditor to receive them into the category of established facts. He cited instances of the miraculous power of one human being over the will and passions of another; insomuch that settled grief was but a shadow, beneath the influence of a man possessing this potency, and the strong love of years melted away like a vapor. At the bidding of one of these wizards, the maiden, with her lover's kiss still burning on her lips, would turn from him with icy indifference; the newly made widow would dig up her buried heart out of her young husband's grave, before the sods had taken root upon it; a mother, with her babe's milk in her bosom, would thrust away her child. Human character was but soft wax in his hands; and guilt, or virtue, only the forms into which he should see fit to mould it. The religious sentiment was a flame which he could blow up with his breath, or a spark that he could utterly extinguish. It is unutterable, the horror and disgust with which I listened, and saw, that, if these things were to be believed, the individual soul was virtually annihilated, and all that is sweet and pure, in our present life, debased, and that the idea of man's eternal responsibility was made ridiculous, and immortality rendered, at once, impossible, and not worth acceptance. But I would have perished on the spot, sooner than believe it.

The epoch of rapping spirits, and all the wonders that

have followed in their train—such as tables, upset by invisible agencies, bells, self-tolled at funerals, and ghostly music, performed on jewsharps—had not yet arrived. Alas, my countrymen, methinks we have fallen on an evil age! If these phenomena have not humbug at the bottom, so much the worse for us. What can they indicate, in a spiritual way, except that the soul of man is descending to a lower point than it has ever before reached, while incarnate? We are pursuing a downward course, in the eternal march, and thus bring ourselves into the same range with beings whom death, in requital of their gross and evil lives, has degraded below humanity. To hold intercourse with spirits of this order, we must stoop, and grovel in some element more vile than earthly dust. These goblins, if they exist at all, are but the shadows of past mortality, outcasts, mere refuse-stuff, adjudged unworthy of the eternal world, and, on the most favorable supposition, dwindling gradually into nothingness. The less we have to say to them, the better; lest we share their fate!

The audience now began to be impatient; they signified their desire for the entertainment to commence, by thump of sticks and stamp of boot-heels. Nor was it a great while longer, before, in response to their call, there appeared a bearded personage in Oriental robes, looking like one of the enchanters of the Arabian Nights. He came upon the platform from a side-door—saluted the spectators, not with a salaam, but a bow—took his station at the desk—and first blowing his nose with a white handkerchief, prepared to speak. The environment of the homely village-hall, and the absence of many ingenious contrivances of stage-effect, with which the exhibition had heretofore been set off, seemed to bring the artifice of this character more openly upon the surface. No sooner did I behold the bearded enchanter, than laying my hand again on Hollingsworth's shoulder, I whispered in his ear:—

"Do you know him?"

"I never saw the man before," he muttered, without turning his head.

But I had seen him, three times, already. Once, on occasion of my first visit to the Veiled Lady; a second time, in the wood-path at Blithedale; and, lastly, in Zenobia's drawing-room. It was Westervelt. A quick association of ideas made me shudder, from head to foot; and, again, like an evil spirit, bringing up reminiscences of a man's sins, I whispered a question in Hollingsworth's ear.

"What have you done with Priscilla?"

He gave a convulsive start, as if I had thrust a knife into him, writhed himself round on his seat, glared fiercely into my eyes, but answered not a word.

The Professor began his discourse, explanatory of the psychological phenomena, as he termed them, which it was his purpose to exhibit to the spectators. There remains no very distinct impression of it on my memory. It was eloquent, ingenious, plausible, with a delusive show of spirituality, yet really imbued throughout with a cold and dead materialism. I shivered, as at a current of chill air, issuing out of a sepulchral vault and bringing the smell of corruption along with it. He spoke of a new era that was dawning upon the world; an era that would link soul to soul, and the present life to what we call futurity, with a closeness that should finally convert both worlds into one great, mutually conscious brotherhood. He described (in a strange, philosophical guise, with terms of art, as if it were a matter of chemical discovery) the agency by which this mighty result was to be effected; nor would it have surprised me, had he pretended to hold up a portion of his universally pervasive fluid, as he affirmed it to be, in a glass phial.

At the close of his exordium, the Professor beckoned with his hand—one, twice, thrice—and a figure came gliding upon the platform, enveloped in a long veil of silvery whiteness. It fell about her, like the texture of a summer cloud, with a kind of vagueness, so that the outline of the form, beneath it, could not be accurately discerned. But the movement of the Veiled Lady was graceful, free, and unembarrassed, like that of a person accustomed to be the spectacle of thousands. Or, possibly, a blindfold prisoner within the sphere with which this dark, earthly magician had surrounded her, she was wholly unconscious of being the central object to all those straining eyes.

Pliant to his gesture, (which had even an obsequious courtesy, but, at the same time, a remarkable decisiveness,) the figure placed itself in the great chair. Sitting there, in such visible obscurity, it was perhaps as much like the actual presence of a disembodied spirit as anything that stage-trickery could devise. The hushed breathing of the spectators proved how high-wrought were their anticipations of the wonders to be performed, through the medium of this incomprehensible creature. I, too, was in breathless suspense, but with a far different presentiment of some strange event at hand.

"You see before you the Veiled Lady," said the bearded Professor, advancing to the verge of the platform. "By the agency of which I have just spoken, she is, at this moment, in communion with the spiritual world. That silvery veil is, in one sense, an enchantment, having been dipt, as it were, and essentially imbued, through the potency of my art, with the fluid medium of spirits. Slight and ethereal as it seems, the limitations of time and space have no existence within its folds. This hall—these hundreds of faces, encompassing her within so narrow an amphitheatre—are of thinner substance, in her view, than the airiest vapor that the clouds are made of. She beholds the Absolute!"

As preliminary to other, and far more wonderful psychological experiments, the exhibitor suggested that some of his auditors should endeavor to make the Veiled Lady sensible of their presence by such methods—provided, only, no touch were laid upon her person—as they might deem best adapted to that end. Accordingly, several deep-lunged country-fellows, who looked as if they might have blown the apparition away with a breath, ascended the platform. Mutually encouraging one another, they shouted so close to her ear, that the veil stirred like a wreath of vanishing mist; they smote upon the floor with bludgeons; they perpetrated so hideous a clamor, that methought it might have reached, at least a little way, into the eternal sphere. Finally, with the assent of the Professor, they laid hold of the great chair, and were startled, apparently, to find it soar upward, as if lighter than the air through which it rose. But the Veiled Lady remained seated and motionless, with a composure that was hardly less than awful, because implying so immeasurable a distance betwixt her and these rude persecutors.

"These efforts are wholly without avail," observed the Professor, who had been looking on with an aspect of serene indifference. "The roar of a battery of cannon would be inaudible to the Veiled Lady. And yet, were I to will it, sitting in this very hall, she could hear the desert-wind sweeping over the sands, as far off as Arabia; the ice-bergs grinding one against the other, in the polar seas; the rustle of a leaf in an East Indian forest; the lowest whispered breath of the bashfullest maiden in the world, uttering the first confession of her love! Nor does there exist the moral inducement, apart from my own behest, that could persuade her to lift the silvery veil, or arise out of that chair!"

Greatly to the Professor's discomposure, however, just as he spoke these words, the Veiled Lady arose. There was a mysterious tremor that shook the magic veil. The spectators, it may be, imagined that she was about to take flight into that invisible sphere, and to the society of those purely spiritual beings, with whom they reckoned her so near akin. Hollingsworth, a moment ago, had mounted the platform, and now stood gazing at the figure, with a sad intentness that brought the whole power of his great, stern, yet tender soul, into his glance.

"Come!" said he, waving his hand towards her. "You are safe!"

She threw off the veil, and stood before that multitude of people, pale, tremulous, shrinking, as if only then had she discovered that a thousand eyes were gazing at her. Poor maiden! How strangely had she been betrayed! Blazoned abroad as a wonder of the world, and performing what were adjudged as miracles—in the faith of many, a seeress and a prophetess—in the harsher judgment of others, a mountebank —she had kept, as I religiously believe, her virgin reserve and sanctity of soul, throughout it all. Within that encircling veil, though an evil hand had flung it over her, there was as deep a seclusion as if this forsaken girl had, all the while, been sitting under the shadow of Eliot's pulpit, in the Blithedale woods, at the feet of him who now summoned her to the shelter of his arms. And the true heart-throb of a woman's affection was too powerful for the jugglery that had hitherto environed her. She uttered a shriek and fled to Hollingsworth, like one escaping from her deadliest enemy, and was safe forever!

XXIV

THE MASQUERADERS

TWO NIGHTS had passed since the foregoing occurrences, when, in a breezy September forenoon, I set forth from town, on foot, towards Blithedale.

It was the most delightful of all days for a walk, with a dash of invigorating ice-temper in the air, but a coolness that soon gave place to the brisk glow of exercise, while the vigor remained as elastic as before. The atmosphere had a spirit and sparkle in it. Each breath was like a sip of ethereal wine, tempered, as I said, with a crystal lump of ice. I had started on this expedition in an exceedingly sombre mood, as well befitted one who found himself tending towards home, but was conscious that nobody would be quite overjoyed to greet him there. My feet were hardly off the pavement, however, when this morbid sensation began to yield to the lively influences of air and motion. Nor had I gone far, with fields yet green on either side, before my step became as swift and light as if Hollingsworth were waiting to exchange a friendly hand-grip, and Zenobia's and Priscilla's open arms would welcome the wanderer's re-appearance. It has happened to me, on other occasions, as well as this, to prove how a state of physical well-being can create a kind of joy, in spite of the profoundest anxiety of mind.

The pathway of that walk still runs along, with sunny freshness, through my memory. I know not why it should be so. But my mental eye can even now discern the September grass, bordering the pleasant roadside with a brighter verdure than while the summer-heats were scorching it; the trees, too, mostly green, although, here and there, a branch or shrub has donned its vesture of crimson and gold, a week or two before its fellows. I see the tufted barberry bushes, with their small clusters of scarlet fruit; the toadstools, likewise, some spotlessly white, others yellow or red—mysterious growths, springing suddenly from no root or seed, and growing nobody can tell how or wherefore. In this respect, they resembled many of the emotions in my breast. And I still see the little rivulets, chill, clear, and bright, that murmured beneath the road, through subterranean rocks, and deepened into mossy pools where tiny fish were darting to-and-fro, and within which lurked the hermit-frog. But, no—I never can account for it—that, with a yearning interest to learn the upshot of all my story, and returning to Blithedale for that sole purpose, I should examine these things so like a peaceful-bosomed naturalist. Nor why, amid all my sympathies and fears, there shot, at times, a wild exhilaration through my frame!

Thus I pursued my way, along the line of the ancient stone-wall that Paul Dudley built, and through white villages, and past orchards of ruddy apples, and fields of ripening maize, and patches of woodland, and all such sweet rural scenery as looks the fairest, a little beyond the suburbs of a town. Hollingsworth, Zenobia, Priscilla! They glided mistily before me, as I walked. Sometimes, in my solitude, I laughed with the bitterness of self-scorn, remembering how unreservedly I had given up my heart and soul to interests that were not mine. What had I ever had to do with them? And why, being now free, should I take this thraldom on me, once again? It was both sad and dangerous, I whispered to myself, to be in too close affinity with the passions, the errors, and the misfortunes, of individuals who stood within a circle of their own, into which, if I stept at all, it must be as an intruder, and at a peril that I could not estimate.

Drawing nearer to Blithedale, a sickness of the spirits kept alternating with my flights of causeless buoyancy. I indulged in a hundred odd and extravagant conjectures. Either there was no such place as Blithedale, nor ever had been, nor any brotherhood of thoughtful laborers, like what I seemed to recollect there; or else it was all changed, during my absence. It had been nothing but dream-work and enchantment. I should seek in vain for the old farm-house, and for the greensward, the potatoe-fields, the root-crops, and acres of Indian corn, and for all that configuration of the land which I had imagined. It would be another spot, and an utter strangeness.

These vagaries were of the spectral throng, so apt to steal out of an unquiet heart. They partly ceased to haunt me, on my arriving at a point whence, through the trees, I began to catch glimpses of the Blithedale farm. That, surely, was something real. There was hardly a square foot of all those acres, on which I had not trodden heavily in one or another kind of toil. The curse of Adam's posterity—and, curse or blessing be it, it gives substance to the life around us—had first come upon me there. In the sweat of my brow, I had there earned bread and eaten it, and so established my claim to be on earth, and my fellowship with all the sons of labor. I could have knelt down, and have laid my breast against that soil. The red clay, of which my frame was moulded, seemed nearer akin to those crumbling furrows than to any other portion of the world's dust. There was my home; and there might be my grave.

I felt an invincible reluctance, nevertheless, at the idea of presenting myself before my old associates, without first ascertaining the state in which they were. A nameless fore-boding weighed upon me. Perhaps, should I know all the circumstances that had occurred, I might find it my wisest course to turn back, unrecognized, unseen, and never look at Blithedale more. Had it been evening, I would have stolen softly to some lighted window of the old farm-house, and peeped darkling in, to see all their well-known faces round the supper-board. Then, were there a vacant seat, I might noiselessly unclose the door, glide in, and take my place among them, without a word. My entrance might be so quiet, my aspect so familiar, that they would forget how long I had been away, and suffer me to melt into the scene, as a wreath of vapor melts into a larger cloud. I dreaded a boisterous greeting. Beholding me at table, Zenobia, as a matter of course, would send me a cup of tea, and Hollingsworth fill my plate from the great dish of pan-dowdy, and Priscilla, in her quiet way, would hand the cream, and others help me to the bread and butter. Being one of them again, the knowledge of what had happened would come to me, without a shock. For, still, at every turn of my shifting fantasies, the thought stared me in the face, that some evil thing had befallen us, or was ready to befall.

Yielding to this ominous impression, I now turned aside into the woods, resolving to spy out the posture of the Community, as craftily as the wild Indian before he makes his onset. I would go wandering about the outskirts of the farm, and, perhaps catching sight of a solitary acquaintance, would approach him amid the brown shadows of the trees, (a kind of medium fit for spirits departed and revisitant, like myself,) and entreat him to tell me how all things were.

The first living creature that I met, was a partridge, which sprung up beneath my feet, and whirred away; the next was a squirrel, who chattered angrily at me, from an overhanging bough. I trod along by the dark, sluggish river, and remember pausing on the bank, above one of its blackest and most placid pools—(the very spot, with the barkless stump of a tree aslantwise over the water, is depicting itself to my fancy, at this

instant)—and wondering how deep it was, and if any over-
laden soul had ever flung its weight of mortality in thither,
and if it thus escaped the burthen, or only made it heavier.
And perhaps the skeleton of the drowned wretch still lay
beneath the inscrutable depth, clinging to some sunken log
at the bottom with the gripe of its old despair. So slight,
however, was the track of these gloomy ideas, that I soon
forgot them in the contemplation of a brood of wild ducks,
which were floating on the river, and anon took flight, leaving
each a bright streak over the black surface. By-and-by, I came
to my hermitage, in the heart of the white-pine tree, and
clambering up into it, sat down to rest. The grapes, which I
had watched throughout the summer, now dangled around
me in abundant clusters of the deepest purple, deliciously
sweet to the taste, and though wild, yet free from that un-
gentle flavor which distinguishes nearly all our native and
uncultivated grapes. Methought a wine might be pressed out
of them, possessing a passionate zest, and endowed with a
new kind of intoxicating quality, attended with such bac-
chanalian ecstasies as the tamer grapes of Madeira, France,
and the Rhine, are inadequate to produce. And I longed to
quaff a great goblet of it, at that moment!

While devouring the grapes, I looked on all sides out of
the peep-holes of my hermitage, and saw the farm-house, the
fields, and almost every part of our domain, but not a single
human figure in the landscape. Some of the windows of the
house were open, but with no more signs of life than in a
dead man's unshut eyes. The barn-door was ajar, and swinging in the breeze. The big, old dog—he was a relic of the
former dynasty of the farm—that hardly ever stirred out of
the yard, was nowhere to be seen. What, then, had become
of all the fraternity and sisterhood? Curious to ascertain this
point, I let myself down out of the tree, and going to the
edge of the wood, was glad to perceive our herd of cows,
chewing the cud, or grazing, not far off. I fancied, by their

manner, that two or three of them recognized me, (as, indeed, they ought, for I had milked them, and been their chamberlain, times without number;) but, after staring me in the face, a little while, they phlegmatically began grazing and chewing their cuds again. Then I grew foolishly angry at so cold a reception, and flung some rotten fragments of an old stump at these unsentimental cows.

Skirting farther round the pasture, I heard voices and much laughter proceeding from the interior of the wood. Voices, male and feminine; laughter, not only of fresh young throats, but the bass of grown people, as if solemn organ-pipes should pour out airs of merriment. Not a voice spoke, but I knew it better than my own; not a laugh, but its cadences were familiar. The wood, in this portion of it, seemed as full of jollity as if Comus and his crew were holding their revels, in one of its usually lonesome glades. Stealing onward as far as I durst, without hazard of discovery, I saw a concourse of strange figures beneath the overshadowing branches; they appeared, and vanished, and came again, confusedly, with the streaks of sunlight glimmering down upon them.

Among them was an Indian chief, with blanket, feathers and war-paint, and uplifted tomahawk; and near him, looking fit to be his woodland-bride, the goddess Diana, with the crescent on her head, and attended by our big, lazy dog, in lack of any fleeter hound. Drawing an arrow from her quiver, she let it fly, at a venture, and hit the very tree behind which I happened to be lurking. Another group consisted of a Bavarian broom-girl, a negro of the Jim Crow order, one or two foresters of the middle-ages, a Kentucky woodsman in his trimmed hunting-shirt and deerskin leggings, and a Shaker elder, quaint, demure, broad-brimmed, and square-skirted. Shepherds of Arcadia, and allegoric figures from the Faerie Queen, were oddly mixed up with these. Arm in arm, or otherwise huddled together, in strange discrepancy, stood grim Puritans, gay Cavaliers, and Revolutionary officers, with three-cornered cocked-hats, and queues longer than their swords. A bright-complexioned, dark-haired, vivacious little gipsy, with a red shawl over her head, went from one group to another, telling fortunes by palmistry; and Moll Pitcher, the renowned old witch of Lynn, broomstick in hand, showed herself prominently in the midst, as if announcing all these apparitions to be the offspring of her necromantic art. But Silas Foster, who leaned against a tree near by, in his customary blue frock, and smoking a short pipe, did more to disenchant the scene, with his look of shrewd, acrid, Yankee observation, than twenty witches and necromancers could have done, in the way of rendering it weird and fantastic.

A little further off, some old-fashioned skinkers and drawers, all with portentously red noses, were spreading a banquet on the leaf-strewn earth; while a horned and long-tailed gentleman (in whom I recognized the fiendish musician, erst seen by Tam O'Shanter) tuned his fiddle, and summoned the whole motley rout to a dance, before partaking of the festal cheer. So they joined hands in a circle, whirling round so swiftly, so madly, and so merrily, in time and tune with the Satanic music, that their separate incongruities were blended all together; and they became a kind of entanglement that went nigh to turn one's brain, with merely looking at it. Anon, they stopt, all of a sudden, and staring at one another's figures, set up a roar of laughter; whereat, a shower of the September leaves (which, all day long, had been hesitating whether to fall or no) were shaken off by the movement of the air, and came eddying down upon the revellers.

Then, for lack of breath, ensued a silence; at the deepest point of which, tickled by the oddity of surprising my grave associates in this masquerading trim, I could not possibly refrain from a burst of laughter, on my own separate account.

"Hush!" I heard the pretty gipsy fortuneteller say. "Who is that laughing?"

"Some profane intruder!" said the goddess Diana. "I shall send an arrow through his heart, or change him into a stag, as I did Actaeon, if he peeps from behind the trees!"

"Me take his scalp!" cried the Indian chief, brandishing his tomahawk, and cutting a great caper in the air.

"I'll root him in the earth, with a spell that I have at my tongue's end!" squeaked Moll Pitcher. "And the green moss shall grow all over him, before he gets free again!"

"The voice was Miles Coverdale's," said the fiendish fiddler, with a whisk of his tail and a toss of his horns. "My music has brought him hither. He is always ready to dance to the devil's tune!"

Thus put on the right track, they all recognized the voice at once, and set up a simultaneous shout.

"Miles! Miles! Miles Coverdale, where are you?" they cried. "Zenobia! Queen Zenobia! Here is one of your vassals lurking in the wood. Command him to approach, and pay his duty!"

The whole fantastic rabble forthwith streamed off in pursuit of me, so that I was like a mad poet hunted by chimaeras. Having fairly the start of them, however, I succeeded in making my escape, and soon left their merriment and riot at a good distance in the rear. Its fainter tones assumed a kind of mournfulness, and were finally lost in the hush and solemnity of the wood. In my haste, I stumbled over a heap of logs and sticks that had been cut for firewood, a great while ago, by some former possessor of the soil, and piled up square, in order to be carted or sledded away to the farm-house. But, being forgotten, they had lain there, perhaps fifty years, and possibly much longer; until, by the accumulation of moss, and the leaves falling over them and decaying there, from autumn to autumn, a green mound was formed, in which the softened outline of the wood-pile was still perceptible. In the fitful mood that then swayed my mind, I found something strangely affecting in this simple circumstance. I imagined the long-dead woodman, and his long-dead wife and children, coming out of their chill graves, and essaying to make a fire with this heap of mossy fuel!

From this spot I strayed onward, quite lost in reverie, and neither knew nor cared whither I was going, until a low, soft, well-remembered voice spoke, at a little distance.

"There is Mr. Coverdale!"

"Miles Coverdale!" said another voice—and its tones were very stern—"Let him come forward, then!"

"Yes, Mr. Coverdale," cried a woman's voice—clear and melodious, but, just then, with something unnatural in its chord—"You are welcome! But you come half-an-hour too late, and have missed a scene which you would have enjoyed!"

I looked up, and found myself nigh Eliot's pulpit, at the base of which sat Hollingsworth, with Priscilla at his feet, and Zenobia standing before them.

XXV

THE THREE TOGETHER

HOLLINGSWORTH was in his ordinary working-dress. Priscilla wore a pretty and simple gown, with a kerchief about her neck, and a calash, which she had flung back from her head, leaving it suspended by the strings. But Zenobia (whose part among the masquers, as may be supposed, was no inferior one) appeared in a costume of fanciful magnificence, with her jewelled flower as the central ornament of what resembled a leafy crown, or coronet. She represented the Oriental princess, by whose name we were accustomed to know her. Her attitude was free and noble, yet, if a queen's, it was not that of a queen triumphant, but dethroned, on trial for her life, or perchance condemned, already. The spirit of the conflict seemed, nevertheless, to be alive in her. Her eyes were on fire; her cheeks had each a crimson spot, so exceedingly vivid, and marked with so definite an outline, that I at first doubted whether it were not artificial. In a very brief space, however, this idea was shamed by the paleness that ensued, as the blood sank suddenly away. Zenobia now looked like marble.

One always feels the fact, in an instant, when he has intruded on those who love, or those who hate, at some acme of their passion that puts them into a sphere of their own, where no other spirit can pretend to stand on equal ground

• 213 •

with them. I was confused—affected even with a species of terror—and wished myself away. The intentness of their feelings gave them the exclusive property of the soil and atmosphere, and left me no right to be or breathe there.

"'Hollingsworth—Zenobia—I have just returned to Blithe-dale," said I, "and had no thought of finding you here. We shall meet again at the house. I will retire."

"This place is free to you," answered Hollingsworth.

"As free as to ourselves," added Zenobia. "This long while past, you have been following up your game, groping for human emotions in the dark corners of the heart. Had you been here a little sooner, you might have seen them dragged into the daylight. I could even wish to have my trial over again, with you standing by, to see fair-play! Do you know, Mr. Coverdale, I have been on trial for my life?"

She laughed, while speaking thus. But, in truth, as my eyes wandered from one of the group to another, I saw in Hollingsworth all that an artist could desire for the grim portrait of a Puritan magistrate, holding inquest of life and death in a case of witchcraft;—in Zenobia, the sorceress her-self, not aged, wrinkled, and decrepit, but fair enough to tempt Satan with a force reciprocal to his own;—and, in Priscilla, the pale victim, whose soul and body had been wasted by her spells. Had a pile of faggots been heaped against the rock, this hint of impending doom would have completed the suggestive picture.

"It was too hard upon me," continued Zenobia, addressing Hollingsworth, "that judge, jury, and accuser, should all be comprehended in one man! I demur, as I think the lawyers say, to the jurisdiction. But let the learned Judge Coverdale seat himself on the top of the rock, and you and me stand at its base, side by side, pleading our cause before him! There might, at least, be two criminals, instead of one."

"You forced this on me," replied Hollingsworth, looking her sternly in the face. "Did I call you hither from among the masqueraders yonder? Do I assume to be your judge? No; except so far as I have an unquestionable right of judgment, in order to settle my own line of behavior towards those, with whom the events of life bring me in contact. True; I have already judged you, but not on the world's part—neither do I pretend to pass a sentence!"

"Ah, this is very good!" said Zenobia, with a smile. "What strange beings you men are, Mr. Coverdale!—is it not so? It is the simplest thing in the world, with you, to bring a woman before your secret tribunals, and judge and condemn her, unheard, and then tell her to go free without a sentence. The misfortune is, that this same secret tribunal chances to be the only judgment-seat that a true woman stands in awe of, and that any verdict short of acquittal is equivalent to a death-sentence!"

The more I looked at them, and the more I heard, the stronger grew my impression that a crisis had just come and gone. On Hollingsworth's brow, it had left a stamp like that of irrevocable doom, of which his own will was the instrument. In Zenobia's whole person, beholding her more closely, I saw a riotous agitation; the almost delirious disquietude of a great struggle, at the close of which, the vanquished one felt her strength and courage still mighty within her, and longed to renew the contest. My sensations were as if I had come upon a battle-field, before the smoke was as yet cleared away.

And what subjects had been discussed here? All, no doubt, that, for so many months past, had kept my heart and my imagination idly feverish. Zenobia's whole character and history; the true nature of her mysterious connection with Westervelt; her later purposes towards Hollingsworth, and, reciprocally, his in reference to her; and, finally, the degree in which Zenobia had been cognizant of the plot against Priscilla, and what, at last, had been the real object of that scheme. On these points, as before, I was left to my own conjectures. One thing, only, was certain. Zenobia and Hollingsworth were friends no longer. If their heart-strings were ever intertwined, the knot had been adjudged an entanglement, and was now violently broken.

But Zenobia seemed unable to rest content with the matter, in the posture which it had assumed.

"Ah! Do we part so?" exclaimed she, seeing Hollingsworth about to retire.

"And why not?" said he, with almost rude abruptness. "What is there further to be said between us?"

"Well; perhaps nothing!" answered Zenobia, looking him in the face, and smiling. "But we have come, many times before, to this gray rock, and we have talked very softly, among the whisperings of the birch-trees. They were pleasant hours! I love to make the latest of them, though not altogether so delightful, loiter away as slowly as may be. And, besides, you have put many queries to me, at this, which you design to be our last interview; and being driven, as I must acknowledge, into a corner, I have responded with reasonable frankness. But, now, with your free consent, I desire the privilege of asking a few questions in my turn."

"I have no concealments," said Hollingsworth.

"We shall see!" answered Zenobia. "I would first inquire, whether you have supposed me to be wealthy?"

"On that point," observed Hollingsworth, "I have had the opinion which the world holds."

"And I held it, likewise," said Zenobia. "Had I not, Heaven is my witness, the knowledge should have been as free to you as me. It is only three days since I knew the strange fact that threatens to make me poor; and your own acquaintance with it, I suspect, is of at least as old a date. I fancied myself affluent. You are aware, too, of the disposition which I purposed making of the larger portion of my imaginary opulence;—nay, were it all, I had not hesitated. Let me ask you further, did

I ever propose or intimate any terms of compact, on which depended this—as the world would consider it—so important sacrifice?"

"You certainly spoke of none," said Hollingsworth.

"Nor meant any," she responded. "I was willing to realize your dream, freely—generously, as some might think—but, at all events, fully—and heedless though it should prove the ruin of my fortune. If, in your own thoughts, you have imposed any conditions of this expenditure, it is you that must be held responsible for whatever is sordid and unworthy in them. And, now, one other question! Do you love this girl?"

"Oh, Zenobia!" exclaimed Priscilla, shrinking back, as if longing for the rock to topple over, and hide her.

"Do you love her?" repeated Zenobia.

"Had you asked me that question, a short time since," replied Hollingsworth, after a pause, during which, it seemed to me, even the birch-trees held their whispering breath, "I should have told you—'No!' My feelings for Priscilla differed little from those of an elder brother, watching tenderly over the gentle sister whom God has given him to protect."

"And what is your answer, now?" persisted Zenobia.

"I do love her!" said Hollingsworth, uttering the words with a deep, inward breath, instead of speaking them outright. "As well declare it thus, as in any other way. I do love her!"

"Now, God be judge between us," cried Zenobia, breaking into sudden passion, "which of us two has most mortally offended Him! At least, I am a woman—with every fault, it may be, that a woman ever had, weak, vain, unprincipled, (like most of my sex; for our virtues, when we have any, are merely impulsive and intuitive,) passionate, too, and pursuing my foolish and unattainable ends, by indirect and cunning, though absurdly chosen means, as an hereditary bond-slave must—false, moreover, to the whole circle of good, in my reckless truth to the little good I saw before me—but still a woman! A creature, whom only a little change of earthly fortune, a little kinder smile of Him who sent me hither, and one true heart to encourage and direct me, might have made all that a woman can be! But how is it with you? Are you a man? No; but a monster! A cold, heartless, self-beginning and self-ending piece of mechanism!"

"With what, then, do you charge me?" asked Hollingsworth, aghast, and greatly disturbed at this attack. "Show me one selfish end in all I ever aimed at, and you may cut it out of my bosom with a knife!"

"It is all self!" answered Zenobia, with still intenser bitterness. "Nothing else; nothing but self, self, self! The fiend, I doubt not, has made his choicest mirth of you, these seven years past, and especially in the mad summer which we have spent together. I see it now! I am awake, disenchanted, disenthralled! Self, self, self! You have embodied yourself in a project. You are a better masquerader than the witches and gipsies yonder; for your disguise is a self-deception. See whither it has brought you! First, you aimed a death-blow, and a treacherous one, at this scheme of a purer and higher life, which so many noble spirits had wrought out. Then, because Coverdale could not be quite your slave, you threw him ruthlessly away. And you took me, too, into your plan, as long as there was hope of my being available, and now fling me aside again, a broken tool! But, foremost, and blackest of your sins, you stifled down your inmost consciousness!— you did a deadly wrong to your own heart!—you were ready to sacrifice this girl, whom, if God ever visibly showed a purpose, He put into your charge, and through whom He was striving to redeem you!"

"This is a woman's view," said Hollingsworth, growing deadly pale—"a woman's, whose whole sphere of action is in the heart, and who can conceive of no higher nor wider one!"

"Be silent!" cried Zenobia, imperiously. "You know neither man nor woman! The utmost that can be said in your behalf— and because I would not be wholly despicable in my own eyes, but would fain excuse my wasted feelings, nor own it wholly a delusion, therefore I say it—is, that a great and rich heart has been ruined in your breast. Leave me, now! You have done with me, and I with you. Farewell!"

"Priscilla," said Hollingsworth, "come!"

Zenobia smiled; possibly, I did so too. Not often, in human life, has a gnawing sense of injury found a sweeter morsel of revenge, than was conveyed in the tone with which Hollingsworth spoke those two words. It was the abased and tremulous tone of a man, whose faith in himself was shaken, and who sought, at last, to lean on an affection. Yes; the strong man bowed himself, and rested on this poor Priscilla. Oh, could she have failed him, what a triumph for the lookers-on!

And, at first, I half imagined that she was about to fail him. She rose up, stood shivering, like the birch-leaves that trembled over her head, and then slowly tottered, rather than walked, towards Zenobia. Arriving at her feet, she sank down there, in the very same attitude which she had assumed on their first meeting, in the kitchen of the old farm-house. Zenobia remembered it.

"Ah, Priscilla," said she, shaking her head, "how much is changed since then! You kneel to a dethroned princess. You, the victorious one! But he is waiting for you. Say what you wish, and leave me."

"We are sisters!" gasped Priscilla.

I fancied that I understood the word and action; it meant the offering of herself, and all she had, to be at Zenobia's disposal. But the latter would not take it thus.

"True; we are sisters!" she replied; and, moved by the sweet word, she stooped down and kissed Priscilla—but not lovingly;

for a sense of fatal harm, received through her, seemed to be lurking in Zenobia's heart—"We had one father! You knew it from the first; I, but a little while—else some things, that have chanced, might have been spared you. But I never wished you harm. You stood between me and an end which I desired. I wanted a clear path. No matter what I meant. It is over now. Do you forgive me?"

"Oh, Zenobia," sobbed Priscilla, "it is I that feel like the guilty one!"

"No, no, poor little thing!" said Zenobia, with a sort of contempt. "You have been my evil fate; but there never was a babe with less strength or will to do an injury. Poor child! Methinks you have but a melancholy lot before you, sitting all alone in that wide, cheerless heart, where, for aught you know—and as I, alas! believe—the fire which you have kindled may soon go out. Ah, the thought makes me shiver for you! What will you do, Priscilla, when you find no spark among the ashes?"

"Die!" she answered.

"That was well said!" responded Zenobia, with an approving smile. "There is all a woman in your little compass, my poor sister. Meanwhile, go with him, and live!"

She waved her away, with a queenly gesture, and turned her own face to the rock. I watched Priscilla, wondering what judgment she would pass, between Zenobia and Hollingsworth; how interpret his behavior, so as to reconcile it with true faith both towards her sister and herself; how compel her love for him to keep any terms whatever with her sisterly affection! But, in truth, there was no such difficulty as I imagined. Her engrossing love made it all clear. Hollingsworth could have no fault. That was the one principle at the centre of the universe. And the doubtful guilt or possible integrity of other people, appearances, self-evident facts, the testimony of her own senses—even Hollingsworth's self-accusation, had he volunteered it—would have weighed not the value of a mote of thistle-down, on the other side. So secure was she of his right, that she never thought of comparing it with another's wrong, but left the latter to itself.

Hollingsworth drew her arm within his, and soon disappeared with her among the trees. I cannot imagine how Zenobia knew when they were out of sight; she never glanced again towards them. But, retaining a proud attitude, so long as they might have thrown back a retiring look, they were no sooner departed—utterly departed—than she began slowly to sink down. It was as if a great, invisible, irresistible weight were pressing her to the earth. Settling upon her knees, she leaned her forehead against the rock, and sobbed convulsively; dry sobs, they seemed to be, such as have nothing to do with tears.

XXVI

ZENOBIA AND COVERDALE

ZENOBIA had entirely forgotten me. She fancied her-self alone with her great grief. And had it been only a common pity that I felt for her—the pity that her proud nature would have repelled, as the one worst wrong which the world yet held in reserve—the sacredness and awful-ness of the crisis might have impelled me to steal away, silently, so that not a dry leaf should rustle under my feet. I would have left her to struggle, in that solitude, with only the eye of God upon her. But, so it happened, I never once dreamed of questioning my right to be there, now, as I had questioned it, just before, when I came so suddenly upon Hollingsworth and herself, in the passion of their recent debate. It suits me not to explain what was the analogy that I saw, or imagined, between Zenobia's situation and mine; nor, I believe, will the reader detect this one secret, hidden beneath many a revelation which perhaps concerned me less. In simple truth, however, as Zenobia leaned her forehead against the rock, shaken with that tearless agony, it seemed to me that the self-same pang, with hardly mitigated torment, leaped thrilling from her heart-strings to my own. Was it wrong, therefore, if I felt myself consecrated to the priest-hood, by sympathy like this, and called upon to minister to this woman's affliction, so far as mortal could?

But, indeed, what could mortal do for her? Nothing! The attempt would be a mockery and an anguish. Time, it is true, would steal away her grief, and bury it, and the best of her heart in the same grave. But Destiny itself, methought, in its kindliest mood, could do no better for Zenobia, in the way of quick relief, than to cause the impending rock to impend a little further, and fall upon her head. So I leaned against a tree, and listened to her sobs, in unbroken silence. She was half prostrate, half kneeling, with her forehead still pressed against the rock. Her sobs were the only sound; she did not groan, nor give any other utterance to her distress. It was all involuntary.

At length, she sat up, put back her hair, and stared about her with a bewildered aspect, as if not distinctly recollecting the scene through which she had passed, nor cognizant of the situation in which it left her. Her face and brow were almost purple with the rush of blood. They whitened, however, by-and-by, and, for some time, retained this deathlike hue. She put her hand to her forehead, with a gesture that made me forcibly conscious of an intense and living pain there.

Her glance, wandering wildly to-and-fro, passed over me, several times, without appearing to inform her of my presence. But, finally, a look of recognition gleamed from her eyes into mine.

"Is it you, Miles Coverdale?" said she, smiling. "Ah, I perceive what you are about! You are turning this whole affair into a ballad. Pray let me hear as many stanzas as you happen to have ready!"

"Oh, hush, Zenobia!" I answered. "Heaven knows what an ache is in my soul!"

"It is genuine tragedy, is it not?" rejoined Zenobia, with a sharp, light laugh. "And you are willing to allow, perhaps, that I have had hard measure. But it is a woman's doom, and I have deserved it like a woman; so let there be no pity, as, on my part, there shall be no complaint. It is all right now, or will shortly be so. But, Mr. Coverdale, by all means, write this ballad, and put your soul's ache into it, and turn your sympathy to good account, as other poets do, and as poets must, unless they choose to give us glittering icicles instead of lines of fire. As for the moral, it shall be distilled into the final stanza, in a drop of bitter honey."

"What shall it be, Zenobia?" I inquired, endeavoring to fall in with her mood.

"Oh, a very old one will serve the purpose," she replied. "There are no new truths, much as we have prided ourselves on finding some. A moral? Why, this:—that, in the battle-field of life, the downright stroke, that would fall only on a man's steel head-piece, is sure to light on a woman's heart, over which she wears no breastplate, and whose wisdom it is, therefore, to keep out of the conflict. Or this:—that the whole universe, her own sex and yours, and Providence, or Destiny, to boot, make common cause against the woman who swerves one hair's breadth out of the beaten track. Yes; and add, (for I may as well own it, now,) that, with that one hair's breadth, she goes all astray, and never sees the world in its true aspect, afterwards!"

"This last is too stern a moral," I observed. "Cannot we soften it a little?"

"Do it, if you like, at your own peril, not on my responsi-bility," she answered; then, with a sudden change of subject, she went on:—"After all, he has flung away what would have served him better than the poor, pale flower he kept. What can Priscilla do for him? Put passionate warmth into his heart, when it shall be chilled with frozen hopes? Strengthen his hands, when they are weary with much doing and no per-formance? No; but only tend towards him with a blind, instinctive love, and hang her little, puny weakness for a clog upon his arm! She cannot even give him such sympathy as is worth the name. For will he never, in many an hour of darkness, need that proud, intellectual sympathy which he might have had from me?—the sympathy that would flash light along his course, and guide as well as cheer him? Poor Hollingsworth! Where will he find it now?"

"Hollingsworth has a heart of ice!" said I, bitterly. "He is a wretch!"

"Do him no wrong!" interrupted Zenobia, turning haughtily upon me. "Presume not to estimate a man like Hollingsworth! It was my fault, all along, and none of his. I see it now! He never sought me. Why should he seek me? What had I to offer him? A miserable, bruised, and battered heart, spoilt long before he met me! A life, too, hopelessly entangled with a villain's! He did well to cast me off. God be praised, he did it! And yet, had he trusted me, and borne with me a little longer, I would have saved him all this trouble."

She was silent, for a time, and stood with her eyes fixed on the ground. Again raising them, her look was more mild and calm.

"Miles Coverdale!" said she.

"Well, Zenobia!" I responded. "Can I do you any service?"

"Very little," she replied. "But it is my purpose, as you may well imagine, to remove from Blithedale; and, most likely, I may not see Hollingsworth again. A woman in my position, you understand, feels scarcely at her ease among former friends. New faces—unaccustomed looks—those only can she tolerate. She would pine, among familiar scenes; she would be apt to blush, too, under the eyes that knew her secret; her heart might throb uncomfortably; she would mortify herself, I suppose, with foolish notions of having sacrificed the honor of her sex, at the foot of proud, contumacious man. Poor womanhood, with its rights and wrongs! Here will be new matter for my course of lectures, at the idea of which you smiled, Mr. Coverdale, a month or two ago. But, as you have really a heart and sympathies, as far as they go, and as I shall depart without seeing Hollingsworth, I must entreat you to be a messenger between him and me."

"Willingly," said I, wondering at the strange way in which her mind seemed to vibrate from the deepest earnest to mere levity. "What is the message?"

"True;—what is it?" exclaimed Zenobia. "After all, I hardly know. On better consideration, I have no message. Tell him—tell him something pretty and pathetic, that will come nicely and sweetly into your ballad—anything you please, so it be tender and submissive enough. Tell him he has murdered me! Tell him that I'll haunt him!"—she spoke these words with the wildest energy—"And give him—no, give Priscilla—this!"

Thus saying, she took the jewelled flower out of her hair; and it struck me as the act of a queen, when worsted in a combat, discrowning herself, as if she found a sort of relief in abasing all her pride.

"Bid her wear this for Zenobia's sake," she continued. "She is a pretty little creature, and will make as soft and gentle a wife as the veriest Bluebeard could desire. Pity that she must fade so soon! These delicate and puny maidens always do. Ten years hence, let Hollingsworth look at my face and Priscilla's, and then choose betwixt them. Or, if he pleases, let him do it now!"

How magnificently Zenobia looked, as she said this! The effect of her beauty was even heightened by the over-consciousness and self-recognition of it, into which, I suppose, Hollingsworth's scorn had driven her. She understood the look of admiration in my face; and—Zenobia to the last—it gave her pleasure.

"It is an endless pity," said she, "that I had not bethought myself of winning your heart, Mr. Coverdale, instead of Hollingsworth's. I think I should have succeeded; and many women would have deemed you the worthier conquest of the two. You are certainly much the handsomest man. But there is a fate in these things. And beauty, in a man, has been of little account with me, since my earliest girlhood, when, for once, it turned my head. Now, farewell!"

"Zenobia, whither are you going?" I asked.

"No matter where," said she. "But I am weary of this place, and sick to death of playing at philanthropy and progress. Of all varieties of mock-life, we have surely blundered into the very emptiest mockery, in our effort to establish the one true system. I have done with it; and Blithedale must find another woman to superintend the laundry, and you, Mr. Coverdale, another nurse to make your gruel, the next time you fall ill. It was, indeed, a foolish dream! Yet it gave us some pleasant summer days, and bright hopes, while they lasted. It can do no more; nor will it avail us to shed tears over a broken bubble. Here is my hand! Adieu!"

She gave me her hand, with the same free, whole-souled gesture as on the first afternoon of our acquaintance; and being greatly moved, I bethought me of no better method of expressing my deep sympathy than to carry it to my lips. In so doing, I perceived that this white hand—so hospitably warm when I first touched it, five months since—was now cold as a veritable piece of snow.

"How very cold!" I exclaimed, holding it between both my own, with the vain idea of warming it. "What can be the reason? It is really deathlike!"

"The extremities die first, they say," answered Zenobia, laughing. "And so you kiss this poor, despised, rejected hand! Well, my dear friend, I thank you! You have reserved your homage for the fallen. Lip of man will never touch my hand again. I intend to become a Catholic, for the sake of going into a nunnery. When you next hear of Zenobia, her face

will be behind the black-veil; so look your last at it now—
for all is over! Once more, farewell!"

She withdrew her hand, yet left a lingering pressure, which
I felt long afterwards. So intimately connected, as I had
been, with perhaps the only man in whom she was ever truly
interested, Zenobia looked on me as the representative of all
the past, and was conscious that, in bidding me adieu, she
likewise took final leave of Hollingsworth, and of this whole
epoch of her life. Never did her beauty shine out more lus-
trously, than in the last glimpse that I had of her. She
departed, and was soon hidden among the trees.

But, whether it was the strong impression of the foregoing
scene, or whatever else the cause, I was affected with a fantasy
that Zenobia had not actually gone, but was still hovering
about the spot, and haunting it. I seemed to feel her eyes
upon me. It was as if the vivid coloring of her character had
left a brilliant stain upon the air. By degrees, however, the
impression grew less distinct. I flung myself upon the fallen
leaves, at the base of Eliot's pulpit. The sunshine withdrew
up the tree-trunks, and flickered on the topmost boughs; gray
twilight made the wood obscure; the stars brightened out; the
pendent boughs became wet with chill autumnal dews. But
I was listless, worn-out with emotion on my own behalf, and
sympathy for others, and had no heart to leave my comfortless
lair, beneath the rock.

I must have fallen asleep, and had a dream, all the circumstances of which utterly vanished at the moment when they
converged to some tragical catastrophe, and thus grew too
powerful for the thin sphere of slumber that enveloped them.
Starting from the ground, I found the risen moon shining
upon the rugged face of the rock, and myself all in a tremble.

XXVII

MIDNIGHT

I T COULD not have been far from midnight, when I
came beneath Hollingsworth's window, and finding it
open, flung in a tuft of grass, with earth at the roots, and
heard it fall upon the floor. He was either awake, or sleeping
very lightly; for scarcely a moment had gone by, before he
looked out and discerned me standing in the moonlight.

"Is it you, Coverdale?" he asked. "What is the matter?"

"Come down to me, Hollingsworth!" I answered. "I am
anxious to speak with you."

The strange tone of my own voice startled me, and him,
probably, no less. He lost no time, and soon issued from the
house-door, with his dress half-arranged.

"Again, what is the matter?" he asked, impatiently.

"Have you seen Zenobia," said I, "since you parted from
her, at Eliot's pulpit?"

"No," answered Hollingsworth; "nor did I expect it."

His voice was deep, but had a tremor in it. Hardly had he
spoken, when Silas Foster thrust his head, done up in a
cotton handkerchief, out of another window, and took what
he called—as it literally was—a squint at us.

"Well, folks, what are ye about here?" he demanded. "Aha,
are you there, Miles Coverdale? You have been turning night
into day, since you left us, I reckon; and so you find it quite

natural to come prowling about the house, at this time o' night, frightening my old woman out of her wits, and making her disturb a tired man out of his best nap. In with you, you vagabond, and to bed!"

"Dress yourself quietly, Foster," said I. "We want your assistance."

I could not, for the life of me, keep that strange tone out of my voice. Silas Foster, obtuse as were his sensibilities, seemed to feel the ghastly earnestness that was conveyed in it, as well as Hollingsworth did. He immediately withdrew his head, and I heard him yawning, muttering to his wife, and again yawning heavily, while he hurried on his clothes. Meanwhile, I showed Hollingsworth a delicate handkerchief, marked with a well-known cypher, and told where I had found it, and other circumstances which had filled me with a suspicion so terrible, that I left him, if he dared, to shape it out for himself. By the time my brief explanation was finished, we were joined by Silas Foster, in his blue woollen frock.

"Well, boys," cried he, peevishly, "what is to pay now?"

"Tell him, Hollingsworth!" said I.

Hollingsworth shivered, perceptibly, and drew in a hard breath betwixt his teeth. He steadied himself, however, and looking the matter more firmly in the face than I had done, explained to Foster my suspicions and the grounds of them, with a distinctness from which, in spite of my utmost efforts, my words had swerved aside. The tough-nerved yeoman, in his comment, put a finish on the business, and brought out the hideous idea in its full terror, as if he were removing the napkin from the face of a corpse.

"And so you think she's drowned herself!" he cried.

I turned away my face.

"What on earth should the young woman do that for?" exclaimed Silas, his eyes half out of his head with mere surprise. "Why, she has more means than she can use or waste, and lacks nothing to make her comfortable, but a husband—and that's an article she could have, any day! There's some mistake about this, I tell you!"

"Come," said I, shuddering. "Let us go and ascertain the truth."

"Well, well," answered Silas Foster, "just as you say. We'll take the long pole, with the hook at the end, that serves to get the bucket out of the draw-well, when the rope is broken. With that, and a couple of long-handled hay-rakes, I'll answer for finding her, if she's anywhere to be found. Strange enough! Zenobia drown herself! No, no, I don't believe it. She had too much sense, and too much means, and enjoyed life a great deal too well."

When our few preparations were completed, we hastened, by a shorter than the customary route, through fields and pastures, and across a portion of the meadow, to the particular spot, on the river-bank, which I had paused to contemplate, in the course of my afternoon's ramble. A nameless presentiment had again drawn me thither, after leaving Eliot's pulpit. I showed my companions where I had found the handkerchief, and pointed to two or three footsteps, impressed into the clayey margin, and tending towards the water. Beneath its shallow verge, among the water-weeds, there were further traces, as yet unobliterated by the sluggish current, which was there almost at a stand-still. Silas Foster thrust his face down close to these footsteps, and picked up a shoe, that had escaped my observation, being half imbedded in the mud.

"There's a kid-shoe that never was made on a Yankee last," observed he. "I know enough of shoemaker's craft to tell that. French manufacture; and see what a high instep!— and how evenly she trod in it! There never was a woman that stept handsomer in her shoes than Zenobia did. Here," he added, addressing Hollingsworth, "would you like to keep the shoe?"

Hollingsworth started back.

"Give it to me, Foster," said I.

I dabbled it in the water, to rinse off the mud, and have
kept it ever since. Not far from this spot, lay an old, leaky
punt, drawn up on the oozy river-side, and generally half-full
of water. It served the angler to go in quest of pickerel, or
the sportsman to pick up his wild-ducks. Setting this crazy
barque afloat, I seated myself in the stern, with the paddle,
while Hollingsworth sat in the bows, with the hooked pole,
and Silas Foster amidships, with a hay-rake.

"It puts me in mind of my young days," remarked Silas,
"when I used to steal out of bed to go bobbing for horn-pouts
and eels. Heigh-ho!—well!—life and death together make sad
work for us all. Then, I was a boy, bobbing for fish; and now
I am getting to be an old fellow, and here I be, groping for
a dead body! I tell you what, lads, if I thought anything had
really happened to Zenobia, I should feel kind o' sorrowful."

"I wish, at least, you would hold your tongue!" muttered I.

The moon, that night, though past the full, was still large
and oval, and having risen between eight and nine o'clock,
now shone aslantwise over the river, throwing the high, opposite bank, with its woods, into deep shadow, but lighting up
the hither shore pretty effectually. Not a ray appeared to fall
on the river itself. It lapsed imperceptibly away, a broad,
black, inscrutable depth, keeping its own secrets from the
eye of man, as impenetrably as mid-ocean could.

"Well, Miles Coverdale," said Foster, "you are the helms-
man. How do you mean to manage this business?"

"I shall let the boat drift, broadside foremost, past that
stump," I replied. "I know the bottom, having sounded it in
fishing. The shore, on this side, after the first step or two,
goes off very abruptly; and there is a pool, just by the stump,
twelve or fifteen feet deep. The current could not have force
enough to sweep any sunken object—even if partially buoyant
—out of that hollow."

"Come, then," said Silas. "But I doubt whether I can
touch bottom with this hay-rake, if it's as deep as you say.

Mr. Hollingsworth, I think you'll be the lucky man, to-night, such luck as it is!"

We floated past the stump. Silas Foster plied his rake manfully, poking it as far as he could into the water, and immersing the whole length of his arm besides. Hollingsworth at first sat motionless, with the hooked-pole elevated in the air. But, by-and-by, with a nervous and jerky movement, he began to plunge it into the blackness that upbore us, setting his teeth, and making precisely such thrusts, methought, as if he were stabbing at a deadly enemy. I bent over the side of the boat. So obscure, however, so awfully mysterious, was that dark stream, that—and the thought made me shiver like a leaf—I might as well have tried to look into the enigma of the eternal world, to discover what had become of Zenobia's soul, as into the river's depths, to find her body. And there, perhaps, she lay, with her face upward, while the shadow of the boat, and my own pale face peering downward, passed slowly betwixt her and the sky.

Once, twice, thrice, I paddled the boat up stream, and again suffered it to glide, with the river's slow, funereal motion, downward. Silas Foster had raked up a large mass of stuff, which, as it came towards the surface, looked somewhat like a flowing garment, but proved to be a monstrous tuft of water-weeds. Hollingsworth, with a gigantic effort, upheaved a sunken log. When once free of the bottom, it rose partly out of water—all weedy and slimy, a devilish-looking object, which the moon had not shone upon for half a hundred years —then plunged again, and sullenly returned to its old resting-place, for the remnant of the century.

"That looked ugly!" quoth Silas. "I half thought it was the Evil One on the same errand as ourselves—searching for Zenobia!"

"He shall never get her!" said I, giving the boat a strong impulse.

"That's not for you to say, my boy!" retorted the yeoman. "Pray God he never has, and never may! Slow work this, however! I should really be glad to find something. Pshaw! What a notion that is, when the only good-luck would be, to paddle, and drift and poke, and grope, hereabouts, till morning, and have our labor for our pains! For my part, I shouldn't wonder if the creature had only lost her shoe in the mud, and saved her soul alive, after all. My stars, how she will laugh at us, tomorrow morning!"

It is indescribable what an image of Zenobia—at the breakfast-table, full of warm and mirthful life—this surmise of Silas Foster's brought before my mind. The terrible phantasm of her death was thrown by it into the remotest and dimmest back-ground, where it seemed to grow as improbable as a myth.

"Yes, Silas; it may be as you say!" cried I.

The drift of the stream had again borne us a little below the stump, when I felt—yes, felt, for it was as if the iron hook had smote my breast—felt Hollingsworth's pole strike some object at the bottom of the river. He started up, and almost overset the boat.

"Hold on!" cried Foster. "You have her!"

Putting a fury of strength into the effort, Hollingsworth heaved amain, and up came a white swash to the surface of the river. It was the flow of a woman's garments. A little higher, and we saw her dark hair, streaming down the current. Black River of Death, thou hadst yielded up thy victim! Zenobia was found!

Silas Foster laid hold of the body—Hollingsworth, likewise, grappled with it—and I steered towards the bank, gazing, all the while, at Zenobia, whose limbs were swaying in the current, close at the boat's side. Arriving near the shore, we all three stept into the water, bore her out, and laid her on the ground, beneath a tree.

"Poor child!" said Foster—and his dry old heart, I verily believe, vouchsafed a tear—"I'm sorry for her!"

Were I to describe the perfect horror of the spectacle, the reader might justly reckon it to me for a sin and shame. For more than twelve long years I have borne it in my memory, and could now reproduce it as freshly as if it were still before my eyes. Of all modes of death, methinks it is the ugliest. Her wet garments swathed limbs of terrible inflexibility. She was the marble image of a death-agony. Her arms had grown rigid in the act of struggling, and were bent before her, with clenched hands; her knees, too, were bent, and—thank God for it!—in the attitude of prayer. Ah, that rigidity! It is impossible to bear the terror of it. It seemed—I must needs impart so much of my own miserable idea—it seemed as if her body must keep the same position in the coffin, and that her skeleton would keep it in the grave, and that when Zenobia rose, at the Day of Judgment, it would be in just the same attitude as now!

One hope I had; and that, too, was mingled half with fear. She knelt, as if in prayer. With the last, choking consciousness, her soul, bubbling out through her lips, it may be, had given itself up to the Father, reconciled and penitent. But her arms! They were bent before her, as if she struggled against Providence in never-ending hostility. Her hands! They were clenched in immitigable defiance. Away with the hideous thought! The flitting moment, after Zenobia sank into the dark pool—when her breath was gone, and her soul at her lips—was as long, in its capacity of God's infinite forgiveness, as the lifetime of the world.

Foster bent over the body, and carefully examined it.

"You have wounded the poor thing's breast," said he to Hollingsworth. "Close by her heart, too!"

"Ha!" cried Hollingsworth, with a start.

And so he had, indeed, both before and after death.

"See!" said Foster. "That's the place where the iron struck her. It looks cruelly, but she never felt it!"

He endeavored to arrange the arms of the corpse decently by its side. His utmost strength, however, scarcely sufficed to bring them down; and rising again, the next instant, they bade him defiance, exactly as before. He made another effort, with the same result.

"In God's name, Silas Foster," cried I, with bitter indignation, "let that dead woman alone!"

"Why, man, it's not decent!" answered he, staring at me in amazement. "I can't bear to see her looking so! Well, well," added he, after a third effort, "'tis of no use, sure enough; and we must leave the women to do their best with her, after we get to the house. The sooner that's done, the better."

We took two rails from a neighboring fence, and formed a bier by laying across some boards from the bottom of the boat. And thus we bore Zenobia homeward. Six hours before, how beautiful! At midnight, what a horror! A reflection occurs to me, that will show ludicrously, I doubt not, on my page, but must come in, for its sterling truth. Being the woman that she was, could Zenobia have foreseen all these ugly circumstances of death, how ill it would become her, the altogether unseemly aspect which she must put on, and, especially, old Silas Foster's efforts to improve the matter, she would no more have committed the dreadful act, than have exhibited herself to a public assembly in a badly-fitting garment! Zenobia, I have often thought, was not quite simple in her death. She had seen pictures, I suppose, of drowned persons, in lithe and graceful attitudes. And she deemed it well and decorous to die as so many village-maidens have, wronged in their first-love, and seeking peace in the bosom of the old, familiar stream—so familiar that they could not dread it—where, in childhood, they used to bathe their little feet, wading mid-leg deep, unmindful of wet skirts. But, in Zenobia's case, there was some tint of the Arcadian affectation that had been visible enough in all our lives, for a few months past.

This, however, to my conception, takes nothing from the tragedy. For, has not the world come to an awfully sophisticated pass, when, after a certain degree of acquaintance with it, we cannot even put ourselves to death in whole-hearted simplicity?

Slowly, slowly, with many a dreary pause—resting the bier often on some rock, or balancing it across a mossy log, to take fresh hold—we bore our burthen onward, through the moonlight, and, at last, laid Zenobia on the floor of the old farm-house. By-and-by, came three or four withered women, and stood whispering around the corpse, peering at it through their spectacles, holding up their skinny hands, shaking their night-capt heads, and taking counsel of one another's experience what was to be done.

With those tire-women, we left Zenobia!

XXVIII

BLITHEDALE-PASTURE

LITHEDALE, thus far in its progress, had never found
the necessity of a burial-ground. There was some con-
sultation among us, in what spot Zenobia might most
fitly be laid. It was my own wish, that she should sleep at
the base of Eliot's pulpit, and that, on the rugged front of
the rock, the name by which we familiarly knew her—
ZENOBIA—and not another word, should be deeply cut, and
left for the moss and lichens to fill up, at their long leisure.
But Hollingsworth (to whose ideas, on this point, great
deference was due) made it his request that her grave might
be dug on the gently sloping hill-side, in the wide pasture,
where, as we once supposed, Zenobia and he had planned
to build their cottage. And thus it was done, accordingly.

She was buried very much as other people have been,
for hundreds of years gone by. In anticipation of a death,
we Blithedale colonists had sometimes set our fancies at work
to arrange a funereal ceremony, which should be the proper
symbolic expression of our spiritual faith and eternal hopes;
and this we meant to substitute for those customary rites,
which were moulded originally out of the Gothic gloom, and,
by long use, like an old velvet-pall, have so much more than
their first death-smell in them. But, when the occasion came,
we found it the simplest and truest thing, after all, to content

ourselves with the old fashion, taking away what we could, but interpolating no novelties, and particularly avoiding all frippery of flowers and cheerful emblems. The procession moved from the farm-house. Nearest the dead walked an old man in deep mourning, his face mostly concealed in a white handkerchief, and with Priscilla leaning on his arm. Hollingsworth and myself came next. We all stood around the narrow niche in the cold earth; all saw the coffin lowered in; all heard the rattle of the crumbly soil upon its lid—that final sound, which mortality awakens on the utmost verge of sense, as if in the vain hope of bringing an echo from the spiritual world.

I noticed a stranger—a stranger to most of those present, though known to me—who, after the coffin had descended, took up a handful of earth, and flung it first into the grave. I had given up Hollingsworth's arm, and now found myself near this man.

"It was an idle thing—a foolish thing—for Zenobia to do!" said he. "She was the last woman in the world to whom death could have been necessary. It was too absurd! I have no patience with her."

"Why so?" I inquired, smothering my horror at his cold comment in my eager curiosity to discover some tangible truth, as to his relation with Zenobia. "If any crisis could justify the sad wrong she offered to herself, it was surely that in which she stood. Everything had failed her—prosperity, in the world's sense, for her opulence was gone—the heart's prosperity, in love. And there was a secret burthen on her, the nature of which is best known to you. Young as she was, she had tried life fully, had no more to hope, and something, perhaps, to fear. Had Providence taken her away in its own holy hand, I should have thought it the kindest dispensation that could be awarded to one so wrecked."

"You mistake the matter completely," rejoined Westervelt.

"What, then, is your own view of it?" I asked.

"Her mind was active, and various in its powers," said he; "her heart had a manifold adaptation; her constitution an infinite buoyancy, which (had she possessed only a little patience to await the reflux of her troubles) would have borne her upward, triumphantly, for twenty years to come. Her beauty would not have waned—or scarcely so, and surely not beyond the reach of art to restore it—in all that time. She had life's summer all before her, and a hundred varieties of brilliant success. What an actress Zenobia might have been! It was one of her least valuable capabilities. How forcibly she might have wrought upon the world, either directly in her own person, or by her influence upon some man, or a series of men, of controlling genius! Every prize that could be worth a woman's having—and many prizes which other women are too timid to desire—lay within Zenobia's reach."

"In all this," I observed, "there would have been nothing to satisfy her heart."

"Her heart!" answered Westervelt, contemptuously. "That troublesome organ (as she had hitherto found it) would have been kept in its due place and degree, and have had all the gratification it could fairly claim. She would soon have established a control over it. Love had failed her, you say! Had it never failed her before? Yet she survived it, and loved again—possibly, not once alone, nor twice either. And now to drown herself for yonder dreamy philanthropist!"

"Who are you," I exclaimed, indignantly, "that dare to speak thus of the dead? You seem to intend a eulogy, yet leave out whatever was noblest in her, and blacken, while you mean to praise. I have long considered you as Zenobia's evil fate. Your sentiments confirm me in the idea, but leave me still ignorant as to the mode in which you have influenced her life. The connection may have been indissoluble, except by death. Then, indeed—always in the hope of God's infinite mercy—I cannot deem it a misfortune that she sleeps in yonder grave!"

"No matter what I was to her," he answered, gloomily, yet without actual emotion. "She is now beyond my reach. Had she lived, and hearkened to my counsels, we might have served each other well. But there Zenobia lies, in yonder pit, with the dull earth over her. Twenty years of a brilliant lifetime thrown away for a mere woman's whim!"

Heaven deal with Westervelt according to his nature and deserts!—that is to say, annihilate him. He was altogether earthy, worldly, made for time and its gross objects, and incapable—except by a sort of dim reflection, caught from other minds—of so much as one spiritual idea. Whatever stain Zenobia had, was caught from him; nor does it seldom happen that a character of admirable qualities loses its better life, because the atmosphere, that should sustain it, is rendered poisonous by such breath as this man mingled with Zenobia's. Yet his reflections possessed their share of truth. It was a woful thought, that a woman of Zenobia's diversified capacity should have fancied herself irretrievably defeated on the broad battle-field of life, and with no refuge, save to fall on her own sword, merely because Love had gone against her. It is nonsense, and a miserable wrong—the result, like so many others, of masculine egotism—that the success or failure of woman's existence should be made to depend wholly on the affections, and on one species of affection; while man has such a multitude of other chances, that this seems but an incident. For its own sake, if it will do no more, the world should throw open all its avenues to the passport of a woman's bleeding heart.

As we stood around the grave, I looked often towards Priscilla, dreading to see her wholly overcome with grief. And deeply grieved, in truth, she was. But a character, so simply constituted as hers, has room only for a single predominant affection. No other feeling can touch the heart's inmost core, nor do it any deadly mischief. Thus, while we see that such a being responds to every breeze, with tremulous vibration, and imagine that she must be shattered by the first rude blast, we find her retaining her equilibrium amid shocks that might have overthrown many a sturdier frame. So with Priscilla! Her one possible misfortune was Hollingsworth's unkindness; and that was destined never to befall her—never yet, at least—for Priscilla has not died.

But, Hollingsworth! After all the evil that he did, are we to leave him thus, blest with the entire devotion of this one true heart, and with wealth at his disposal, to execute the long contemplated project that had led him so far astray? What retribution is there here? My mind being vexed with precisely this query, I made a journey, some years since, for the sole purpose of catching a last glimpse at Hollingsworth, and judging for myself whether he were a happy man or no. I learned that he inhabited a small cottage, that his way of life was exceedingly retired, and that my only chance of encountering him or Priscilla was, to meet them in a secluded lane, where, in the latter part of the afternoon, they were accustomed to walk. I did meet them, accordingly. As they approached me, I observed in Hollingsworth's face a depressed and melancholy look, that seemed habitual; the powerfully built man showed a self-distrustful weakness, and a childlike, or childish, tendency to press close, and closer still, to the side of the slender woman whose arm was within his. In Priscilla's manner, there was a protective and watchful quality, as if she felt herself the guardian of her companion, but, likewise, a deep, submissive, unquestioning reverence, and also a veiled happiness in her fair and quiet countenance.

Drawing nearer, Priscilla recognized me, and gave me a kind and friendly smile, but with a slight gesture which I could not help interpreting as an entreaty not to make myself known to Hollingsworth. Nevertheless, an impulse took possession of me, and compelled me to address him.

"I have come, Hollingsworth," said I, "to view your grand edifice for the reformation of criminals. Is it finished yet?"

"No—nor begun!" answered he, without raising his eyes. "A very small one answers all my purposes."

Priscilla threw me an upbraiding glance. But I spoke again, with a bitter and revengeful emotion, as if flinging a poisoned arrow at Hollingsworth's heart.

"Up to this moment," I inquired, "how many criminals have you reformed?"

"Not one!" said Hollingsworth, with his eyes still fixed on the ground. "Ever since we parted, I have been busy with a single murderer!"

Then the tears gushed into my eyes, and I forgave him. For I remembered the wild energy, the passionate shriek, with which Zenobia had spoken those words—'Tell him he has murdered me! Tell him that I'll haunt him!'—and I knew what murderer he meant, and whose vindictive shadow dogged the side where Priscilla was not.

The moral which presents itself to my reflections, as drawn from Hollingsworth's character and errors, is simply this:—that, admitting what is called Philanthropy, when adopted as a profession, to be often useful by its energetic impulse to society at large, it is perilous to the individual, whose ruling passion, in one exclusive channel, it thus becomes. It ruins, or is fearfully apt to ruin, the heart; the rich juices of which God never meant should be pressed violently out, and distilled into alcoholic liquor, by an unnatural process; but should render life sweet, bland, and gently beneficent, and insensibly influence other hearts and other lives to the same blessed end. I see in Hollingsworth an exemplification of the most awful truth in Bunyan's book of such;—from the very gate of Heaven, there is a by-way to the pit!

But, all this while, we have been standing by Zenobia's grave. I have never since beheld it, but make no question that the grass grew all the better, on that little parallelogram of pasture-land, for the decay of the beautiful woman who slept beneath. How much Nature seems to love us! And how readily, nevertheless, without a sigh or a complaint, she converts us to a meaner purpose, when her highest one—that of conscious, intellectual life, and sensibility—has been untimely baulked! While Zenobia lived, Nature was proud of her, and directed all eyes upon that radiant presence, as her fairest handiwork. Zenobia perished. Will not Nature shed a tear? Ah, no! She adopts the calamity at once into her system, and is just as well pleased, for aught we can see, with the tuft of ranker vegetation that grew out of Zenobia's heart, as with all the beauty which has bequeathed us no earthly representative, except in this crop of weeds. It is because the spirit is inestimable, that the lifeless body is so little valued.

XXIX

MILES COVERDALE'S CONFESSION

I T REMAINS only to say a few words about myself. Not improbably, the reader might be willing to spare me the trouble; for I have made but a poor and dim figure in my own narrative, establishing no separate interest, and suffering my colorless life to take its hue from other lives. But one still retains some little consideration for one's self; so I keep these last two or three pages for my individual and sole behoof.

But what, after all, have I to tell? Nothing, nothing, nothing! I left Blithedale within the week after Zenobia's death, and went back thither no more. The whole soil of our farm, for a long time afterwards, seemed but the sodded earth over her grave. I could not toil there, nor live upon its products. Often, however, in these years that are darkening around me, I remember our beautiful scheme of a noble and unselfish life, and how fair, in that first summer, appeared the prospect that it might endure for generations, and be perfected, as the ages rolled away, into the system of a people, and a world. Were my former associates now there— were there only three or four of those true-hearted men, still laboring in the sun—I sometimes fancy that I should direct my world-weary footsteps thitherward, and entreat them to receive me, for old friendship's sake. More and more, I feel that we had struck upon what ought to be a truth. Posterity may dig it up, and profit by it. The experiment, so far as its original projectors were concerned, proved long ago a failure, first lapsing into Fourierism, and dying, as it well deserved, for this infidelity to its own higher spirit. Where once we toiled with our whole hopeful hearts, the town-paupers, aged, nerveless, and disconsolate, creep sluggishly a-field. Alas, what faith is requisite to bear up against such results of generous effort!

My subsequent life has passed—I was going to say, happily —but, at all events, tolerably enough. I am now at middle-age—well, well, a step or two beyond the midmost point, and I care not a fig who knows it!—a bachelor, with no very decided purpose of ever being otherwise. I have been twice to Europe, and spent a year or two, rather agreeably, at each visit. Being well to do in the world, and having nobody but myself to care for, I live very much at my ease, and fare sumptuously every day. As for poetry, I have given it up, notwithstanding that Doctor Griswold—as the reader, of course, knows—has placed me at a fair elevation among our minor minstrelsy, on the strength of my pretty little volume, published ten years ago. As regards human progress, (in spite of my irrepressible yearnings over the Blithedale reminiscences,) let them believe in it who can, and aid in it who choose! If I could earnestly do either, it might be all the better for my comfort. As Hollingsworth once told me, I lack a purpose. How strange! He was ruined, morally, by an overplus of the very same ingredient, the want of which, I occasionally suspect, has rendered my own life all an emptiness. I by no means wish to die. Yet, were there any cause, in this whole chaos of human struggle, worth a sane man's dying for, and which my death would benefit, then—provided, however, the effort did not involve an unreasonable amount of trouble—methinks I might be bold to offer up my life. If Kossuth, for example, would pitch the battle-field of Hungarian rights within an easy ride of my abode, and choose a mild, sunny morning, after breakfast, for the conflict, Miles Coverdale would gladly be his man, for one brave rush upon the levelled bayonets. Farther than that, I should be loth to pledge myself.

I exaggerate my own defects. The reader must not take my own word for it, nor believe me altogether changed from the young man, who once hoped strenuously, and struggled, not so much amiss. Frostier heads than mine have gained honor in the world; frostier hearts have imbibed new warmth, and been newly happy. Life, however, it must be owned, has come to rather an idle pass with me. Would my friends like to know what brought it thither? There is one secret—I have concealed it all along, and never meant to let the least whisper of it escape—one foolish little secret, which possibly may have had something to do with these inactive years of meridian manhood, with my bachelorship, with the unsatisfied retrospect that I fling back on life, and my listless glance towards the future. Shall I reveal it? It is an absurd thing for a man in his afternoon—a man of the world, moreover, with these three white hairs in his brown moustache, and that deepening track of a crow's foot on each temple—an absurd thing ever to have happened, and quite the absurdest for an old bachelor, like me, to talk about. But it rises in my throat; so let it come.

I perceive, moreover, that the confession, brief as it shall be, will throw a gleam of light over my behavior throughout the foregoing incidents, and is, indeed, essential to the full understanding of my story. The reader, therefore, since I have disclosed so much, is entitled to this one word more. As I write it, he will charitably suppose me to blush, and turn away my face:—

I—I myself—was in love—with—PRISCILLA!

THE END.

TEXTUAL NOTES

18.10 closer] The final "r" is not formed very prominently in MS and might have been overlooked by Fox, the compositor, who set "close" in 1852. The comparative seems to refer to the episode in the preceding chapter, 12.28, "And, now, we were seated by the brisk fireside of the old farm-house". We learn at 9.6 and again at 13.21 that this fire was laid in the "parlor", which must have been the same as the "sitting-room" of 18.10. In 12.33 the fire was spoken of as a "right good fire", composed of great logs and limbs; and as the travelers sit before it, the snow melts from their hair and beards, and their faces are ablaze. Hence it would appear that Zenobia's greeting and the subsequent conversation, followed by a trip to the woodpile to restock the kitchen fire, had given the opportunity for the sitting-room fire to die down slightly so that on their return the brethren would pull their chairs *closer* than before. If Hawthorne is here exhibiting the same scrupulous concern that he seems to have given to a minor change at 169.29 (see textual note below), it might be argued that never having specified previously that the chairs had been close to the hearth, he is here removing the comparative "closer"; but the circumstances would seem to differ sufficiently to negate this line of argument. Finally, it may be thought that the apparent difficulty with a final "r" shown at 37.25 (although by another compositor) would support the misreading hypothesis somewhat more strongly than a revision theory in both words.

37.25 littler] The final "r" is not prominently formed in MS and is very slightly smudged, though clear enough. Yet Munn, the compositor, may have overlooked the letter or thought that the little smudge was intended to delete it. The meaning is relatively indifferent, but the contrast of the gloomy outdoors with the warmth and light within would seem to make the comparative somewhat more appropriate, as found in MS, than the reading "little" in the first edition.

85.11 wintry] The reading "winter" in 1852 for MS "wintry" clearly represents a compositorial error by Munn. The evening mentioned was in April, in the spring, and only its characteristics are referred to as "wintry" here, as earlier (9.7, 23.20, 40.8).

86.32 Priscilla.]The MS question mark, instead of the 1852 period, would ordinarily appear to be the preferred reading were it not for the odd fact that E^1 and MS agree here against the first American edition. This concurrence raises the question whether the query had not been set originally in 1852 (thence transferred to E^1) but subsequently altered at a later stage of the proofing. Actually, all depends upon one's guess whether the E^1 compositor, faced with copy showing a period, would feel the interrogative sense so strongly that he altered the punctuation independently. If he did so, it is curious, perhaps, that the American compositor in the same circumstances reduced a manuscript question mark to a period. Any decision can be only speculative, but it may be thought that the odds just slightly favor the hypothesis that the period was a proof-alteration, in which case it must represent Hawthorne's final intention. For evidence concerning the late stage of proof-alteration in some sheets, see the Textual Introduction.

87.12 complaisantly] MS and first edition read "complacently", which by the dictionary definitions of the time is quite possible for "soft, agreeable, courteous". Hence no cause would exist to alter the authoritative spelling were it not that at 165.27 (see textual note) Hawthorne in the MS writes "self-complaisant" when he means "in a self-satisfied manner," a sense that is not found in the OED or in American dictionaries contemporary with Hawthorne. (Here, too, 1852 reads "-complacent".) In view of the practically identical meaning of the two words, except for the special sense in which "complacent" can be read, it seems probable that Hawthorne confused them and used in these two cases the word diametrically opposite to his intention. It may be remarked that Hawthorne's spelling was sometimes a little erratic, and his French often needs emendation.

97.8 exultation] This is the reading of 1852 and, seemingly, of the MS. Hawthorne frequently failed to close his "a's" and only the context can determine whether such letters represent "a" or "u". In this word the "u" is open; but so, for instance, is the "a" of "fear" two words before. Hence despite the first-edition reading, MS "exaltation" might be thought to be at least a possibility. But "exultation" seems to be a better antonym to "sorrow" than "exaltation", and one would need better evidence than is available in the MS inscription to go against the first-edition reading in this case, especially in view of the phrase "the loftiest exultation of the melody" in MS and first edition of *The House of the Seven Gables*, 254.10.

110.27 of considerable] One of the easiest errors to make in copying is to omit the article "a", as seems to have happened in MS at 19.33, 128.31, 150.17, 203.10, all repaired in the first edition. If so, presumably a compositor can make the same mistake and omit the word when setting type. On the other hand, in reading proof Hawthorne may have been conscious of the repetition of "a" in MS "So, after a little more talk, a wager of a considerable amount" and preferred the terser expression.

111.9 Sibylline] Both MS and 1852 read "sibylline", but in the other appearances at 3.1 and 6.20, MS capitals occur.

116.6 uprose] MS "uprose" is clearly one word, and this form was faithfully transferred to 1852 and repeated in all American editions collated. The reading "up rose" as in E$^{1-2}$ might be thought more suitable, but on the evidence Hawthorne intended "uprose".

123.31 behoved] MS and E^1 join in "behoved" against 1852 "behooved". If E^1 derived its spelling from the American sheets, then the present form in 1852 represents a later stage of proof-correction. Any tinkering with MS spelling of this word would appear to be non-authorial since "behove" was much the commoner form. Because E^1 may have adopted the customary spelling without regard for the form in the American sheets, one cannot positively identify "behoove" as a late proof-correction. Even if it were, however, one might assign it to some agency other than Hawthorne, such as the proofreader who pestered him in *The Scarlet Letter,* and thus in either case refuse to modify conventional spelling of the MS form.

132.31 nor] That first-edition "or" is a compositorial sophistication is indicated by the prior use of the same construction in *The House of the Seven Gables,* 25.10, "it was never acted upon, nor openly expressed."

148.33 roof] The first-edition singular, replacing MS "roofs", is an example of scrupulous correction in proof. At 148.11 the buildings are called a "range", although they are also referred to in the plural as "residences" (148.13) or "dwellings" (149.31) or "houses" (150.16). But in 150.1 we learn that "one long, united roof . . . extended over the whole" of this range. This must be the "roof of the houses" (1852) that the buttonwood-tree aspires to top. When in 149.4 the cat is described as "creeping along the low, flat roofs", the plural roofs are specified as those "of the offices", which are apparently the low, flat roofs of humble buildings like tool-houses or of rear projections from the range, individual with each house. These cannot be the "roof(s)" that concerned the buttonwood-tree. In an almost identical passage in *The American Notebooks,* pp. 248-49, from which the present description was drawn, the singular "roof" is used for the range of houses and "roofs" for the offices, as in the first edition.

150.11 bordered] This seems to be the most difficult crux in the romance. No sense of "board" (as in the first edition) is found in Hawthorne's *Pronouncing Dictionary* or in contemporary Webster's except to board a ship or to take rooms and meals in a house. The *OED* cites a very rare meaning "to border on" from the sixteenth and seventeenth centuries but no later except for one use as a noun in the nineteenth century in the phrase "sea board". Three possibilities may be advanced. (1) Although the *OED* lists only a few examples, Hawthorne was familiar with a rare meaning of two centuries before, and deliberately in proof substituted "boarded" for "bordered" intending the same sense. (2) Although Hawthorne wrote "bordered" in MS, when he came to the proofs he changed the meaning to the usual sense of "boarded" intending to indicate that the people lived along this street in boarding-houses. (3) The compositor set "boarded" in error for "bordered" and the change was not detected in proof. In favor of the first possibility is the fact that accepted authorial proof-corrections outnumber undetected printer's errors three to one in this text. Against it is the absence of any reason to change an acceptable word to a quite obsolete form that in context would almost inevitably be misunderstood by the reader as intended in another sense. In favor of the second is, again, the proportion of proof-correction to undetected printer's error. As for the reason, a possible one is advanced by M. A. Crane in his unpublished University of Illinois dissertation, "A Textual and Critical Edition of Hawthorne's *Blithedale Romance*" (1953), p. xxxii. "It seems plausible that in copying out the text, Hawthorne lost track of the subject of his sentence, and, assuming it to be *dwellings* or some such word, misread *boarded* (which makes no sense referring to *buildings*) as *bordered* (which makes no sense referring to people). Fortunately, the typesetter caught this error and called it to attention." Against this view is the difficulty that other examples of Hawthorne misreading his own writing and allowing it to stand are wanting. (Dr. Crane's examples on pp. xxxi-xxxii are more convincing as authentic revisions than as misread words.) That the typesetter would catch an error like this is a pretty fiction, of course, with no substantiating evidence. Moreover, it is perhaps a trifle strong to assert that "bordered" makes no sense as applied to people. The subject word, actually, is the collective "family", and if in this passage "families" can "glimpse", and have "looked" into the area and "received just their equal share of sunshine", it may be allowable for them to "border" on the street. The question also arises whether to "board on" a street is actually an acceptable idiom. But the case need not rest on such if's and and's. Below, in 150.17, the waiter informs Coverdale that "the one right opposite is a rather stylish boarding-house"; but it is clear that this is only one house in the series of "residences" that make up the range, with the added inference that it is the only boarding-house. Moreover, at this point in his scrutiny when Coverdale is speculating about the families who all listened to precisely the same noises from the street on which they bordered or boarded, he has no means of knowing that this or any other of the houses is a boarding-house (since the waiter has not yet informed him of the fact); and, finally, he has not at that time singled out the one house in question and its first floor which will soon be occupied by Zenobia. Instead, he is looking at all the houses, as a group, and thinking of the various families that live in the buildings of the range, all of whom border but do not board on the street. It is quite certain that not all the houses in the range are boarding-houses; but the point is of little consequence since at the time Coverdale does not even know that one of the residences is a boarding-house and so he could not have used the word, especially to describe the lives of families in the other houses. One is left, then, with the third hypothesis as the most plausible. It would seem that "boarded" for MS "bordered" is the compositor Fox's anticipatory memorial error. If he were reading ahead in his copy before he set it, as compositors setting by hand and styling copy are advised to do, he would have very shortly come to the boarding-house, which he then proceeded in his typesetting to confuse with another word of similar sound.

165.27 self-complacent] This is compositor Henderson's normalization or correction of MS "self-complaisant". The dictionary that Hawthorne used, *The New Critical Pronouncing Dictionary* (1813), defines "complaisant" as "civil, affable, soft". Webster's of 1828 defines it as "civil, courteous, obliging, kind", and "complacent" as "cheerful, civil, affable, soft, kind". Although the two words are interchangeable in most circumstances, according to these definitions which do not mention the modern pejorative sense, it is evident in context that Hawthorne is approaching very close to the idea of undue self-satisfaction, being over-pleased with oneself, which according to the *OED* had begun to tinge "complacent" (but not "complaisant") in the eighteenth century. If this is so, and the context admits no doubt, the MS spelling "complaisant" is wrong, and the first-edition "complacent" is right. One may well believe, however, that Hawthorne had mistaken these two words and precisely reversed their meanings. At 87.12 (see textual note) he had used the spelling "complacently" in contrasting Moodie's softer tones with the "harshness and acidity" that had preceded them. If Hawthorne ever intended to distinguish the two words, then "complaisantly" would have been the necessary spelling there (in contrast to 165.27 and its sense). It follows that either he used the two words without distinction, and was thus unaware that "complacent" but not "complaisant" had developed a pejorative sense of undue self-satisfaction, or else he was aware of the distinction but confused the two words. The latter may seem the more likely; and this hypothesis has governed the editorial treatment at 87.12 and 165.27.

169.29 near her] Although the first edition's "near her" is dangerously close in sound to MS "nearer", and thus for Munn may represent something like the memorial error of "boarded" for "bordered", the first-edition variant more probably results from the same sort of careful proofreading that at 148.33 had changed "roofs" to "roof". Coverdale has shaken hands with Priscilla, and she seems still to be standing before him, "her dark eyes bent shyly on mine", as he looks from her to Zenobia. To be scrupulous, there is no indication that Priscilla has moved *near* Zenobia, after greeting Coverdale, in a manner that would make it appropriate for her to be beckoned *nearer*. Thus it is likely that Hawthorne made the change in proof in order to be consistent in the details of his account.

170.15 undertone] MS may read "under tone" as in the first edition; but the odds are that a single word was intended. For instance, in *The House of the Seven Gables* although two words seem to be written at 103.3 in the MS, there can be no question of the reading "undertone" at 139.9.

177.15. farthest] Even though the "a" is open and the word could be read as "furthest" as in the first edition, a slight loop in the first upward stroke, present in many closed Hawthorne "a's" but not observed in his "u's", betrays the correct reading.

178.29 had begun] This is the reading of MS, whereas the first edition's "had began" is country speech although appropriate enough in the eighteenth century. That Hawthorne would alter "begun" to "began" in proof seems difficult to credit. Thus "began" is likely a compositorial slip. It would be idle speculation, of course, to suggest that Hawthorne in proof could have attempted to change "had begun" to the simple preterit "began" and his proof-markings were misunderstood.

180.4 inspirited] First edition's "inspired" is clearly Henderson's memorial vulgarization of a characteristic Hawthorne word that had appeared earlier at 175.13.

207.20 befall] The agreement of MS and E[1] in "befal" against first-edition "befall" suggests that the spelling change was made in an advanced state of the proof. If so, the alteration could have been made by the publisher's reader, encouraged by "befallen" in the line above. On the evidence of the change of MS "arches" to first-edition "rocks" (205.15) in the same sheet, Hawthorne had already passed "befal" once in proof. However, Hawthorne's own practice was not consistent. In *The House of the Seven Gables*, for instance, the MS reads "befall", retained by the first edition, at Centenary 113.21. And "befalls" is found in both texts, at Centenary 161.10. On the other hand, "befell" may be "befel" or "befell" in the same manuscript. On the whole, the reading "befall" in the first edition, whatever its source, seems to represent Hawthorne's customary spelling more faithfully than MS "befal", although "befal" can scarcely be called wrong.

EDITORIAL EMENDATIONS IN THE COPY-TEXT

(NOTE: Except for such silent typographical alterations as are remarked in the appendix on general textual procedures as applying to all Centenary texts, supplemented by the statement at the end of the Textual Introduction, every editorial change made from the final inscription of the printer's copy manuscript of *The Blithedale Romance* is listed here. Only the immediate source of the emendation is noticed; the Historical Collation may be con sulted for the complete history, within the editions collated, of any substantive readings that qualify for inclusion in that listing. An alteration assigned to CENTENARY is made for the first time in the present edition if by "the first time" is understood "the first time in respect to the editions chosen for collation." Asterisked readings are discussed in the Textual Notes. The following texts are referred to: MS (the Pierpont Morgan Library manuscript), I (1852 first American edition), II (1876 Little Classics Edition), III (1883 Riverside Edition), IV (1900 Autograph Edition), E¹ (1852 first English edition), E² (1854 second English edition). The wavy dash ∼ represents the same word that appears before the bracket and is used in recording punctuation variants. A caret ∧ indicates the absence of a punctuation mark.)

3.22	CONCORD (Mass.), May,] I; ∼ . (∼ .) ∧ ∼ ∧ MS
7.23	availability] I; availibility MS
7.30	influence] I; agency MS
9.3	moustache,)∧] CENTENARY; ∼ ∧) ∧ MS; ∼ ∧), I–IV, E¹⁻²

10.23–24	and somewhat . . . demijohn] MS (*deleted*); *omit* I–IV, E¹⁻²
12.25	good bye] CENTENARY; good-bye MS; good-by I, III–IV, E¹⁻²; good︿by II
13.11	husbandry︿)] I; ~ ,) MS
15.30	lay] I; was MS
17.15–16	I almost . . . beholding it.] MS (*deleted*); *omit* I–IV, E¹⁻²
*18.10	closer] *stet* MS
18.30	of] I; of of MS
19.11	intolerable] I; intolerably MS
19.33	than an effort] I; than effort MS
25.15	brush-wood] I; brushwood MS
29.8	protégée] IV; protegée MS, I–III, E¹⁻²
30.2	creditable ︿] I; to his credit, MS
30.18	she] I; he MS
30.30	from] I; out of MS
32.3	kitchen-fire] CENTENARY; ~ ︿ ~ MS, I–IV, E¹⁻²
32.4	sole-leather] I; ~ ︿ ~ MS
36.34	Community] CENTENARY (E¹); community MS, I–IV
37.20	'Saharah.'] CENTENARY; ︿ ~ . ︿ MS; ︿Sahara.︿ I, II, E¹⁻²; "Sahara." III–IV
*37.25	littler] *stet* MS
38.21	door-step] I; doorstep MS
39.11	chamber-door] I; ~ ︿ ~ MS
40.21	with a] I; with the MS
53.13	à] II (E¹); a MS, I
54.26	à] II (E¹); a MS, I
54.26	cèdre!"] I; ~ ! ︿ MS
57.6	life-long] I; ~ ︿ ~ MS
58.1	MAY-DAY] i.e. May-day
58.16	houstonias] III; housatonias MS, I–II, E¹⁻²
58.16	handfull] CENTENARY; handful MS, I–IV
60.29	unless,] I; ~ ︿ MS
63.13	farther] CENTENARY; longer MS; further I–IV, E¹⁻²
64.6	Grub-street] I; Grubb-street MS
64.12	to] I; of MS

65.18   other] I; another MS
66.23   to-day] I; today MS
68.5   it,] I; ~ ∧ MS
68.25   ennobled] I; enobled MS
71.24–26 "He . . . all!" . . . "his . . . philanthropist!"]
         I; ' ~ . . . ~ ! ' . . . ' ~ . . . ~ ! ' MS
73.4   short-comings] I; ~ ∧ ~ MS
73.30   to] I; of MS
74.16   lesson] *stet* MS
74.20   and ∧] I; ~ , MS
74.32   recognize her as his] I; consider her his MS, E¹
76.15   out-of-doors] CENTENARY; ~ ∧ ~ ∧ ~ MS,
         I–IV, E¹⁻²
77.1   girl?] I; ~ . MS
77.27   Hollingsworth,] I; ~ ∧ MS
78.1,   quarter-of-an-hour] CENTENARY; ~ ∧ ~ ∧ ~
  82.11,   ∧ ~ MS, I–IV, E¹⁻²
  150.24–25
79.24   develop] I; develope MS
*85.11   wintry] *stet* MS
*86.32   Priscilla.] I; ~ ? MS, E¹
*87.12   complaisantly] CENTENARY; complacently MS,
         I–IV, E¹⁻²
91.4   I,] I; ~ ∧ MS
92.34   too,] I; ~ ∧ MS
93.25   Community] CENTENARY (E¹); community MS,
         I–IV
94.11   Devil] II; devil MS, I, E¹⁻²
*97.8   exultation] *stet* MS
98.4,   white-pine tree] I; white pine-tree MS
  208.11
98.7   around almost] *stet* MS
100.19   Priscilla ∧] I; ~ , MS
100.33   her!] I; ~ ∧ MS
101.4   was] I; is MS
101.20   sceptical] I; skeptical MS
105.8   stronger,] I; ~ ∧ MS
106.11   *vivants*] I; *vivantes* MS
*110.27 of considerable] I; of a considerable MS
*111.9   Sibylline] CENTENARY (E¹); sibylline MS, I–IV

113.4	lips] I; kiss MS
*116.6	uprose] *stet* MS
119.15	opened,)] CENTENARY; ~) MS, I–IV, E¹⁻²
120.23	weak] I; *omit* MS
121.31	Himself] CENTENARY; himself MS, I–IV, E¹⁻²
121.35	His] CENTENARY; his MS, I–IV, E¹⁻²
122.1	His] CENTENARY; his MS, I–IV, E¹⁻²
123.7	woman!—] I; ~ — MS
123.19–20	pictured— . . . existence—] I; ~ , . . . ~ , MS
*123.31	behoved] *stet* MS (E¹)
125.27	carelessly] I; carlessly MS
128.21	a] I; *omit* MS
129.25	diaphanous] I; diaphonous MS
130.3	spick-and-span] I; ~ - ~ ~ MS
131.29	rest,] CENTENARY; ~ ; MS; ~ I–IV, E¹⁻²
132.11	all?] I; ~ . MS
*132.31	nor] *stet* MS
133.17	faculties] I; facuties MS
133.22	aimless] I; useless MS
135.8	cannot] I; can | not MS
141.22	and] I; or MS
144.18	hanging up by] I; hanging by MS
145.2	occupant,)] CENTENARY; ~) MS; ~), I–IV, E¹⁻²
146.10	were] I; *omit* MS
146.12	thoughts] I; thought MS
146.25	barkeeper] CENTENARY (E¹); bar-keeper MS, I–IV
148.20	trellises] I; trellices MS
148.32	buttonwood-tree] I; ~ ~ MS
*148.33	roof] I; roofs MS
*150.11	bordered] *stet* MS
150.17	a] I; *omit* MS
151.11	sliding-doors] I; ~ ~ MS
154.3	valleys] I; vallies MS
154.15	of] I; of | of MS
155.3, 184.15, 191.4	ceiling] I; cieling MS
155.16	thitherward,] I; ~ ; MS

156.7	amount of] I; amount of of MS
158.10	By-and-by] CENTENARY (E¹); $\sim_\wedge\sim_\wedge\sim$ MS, I–IV
158.15	Devil] II (E¹); devil MS, I, E²
158.17	Devil's] II (E¹); devil's MS, I, E²
163.17	her own] I; my own MS
164.6	$_\wedge$ How] I; " $\sim$ MS
*165.27	self-complacent] I; self-complaisant MS
*169.29	near her] I; nearer MS
*170.15	undertone] stet MS
175.5–27	Human nature . . . substituting good.] MS (deleted); omit I–IV, E¹⁻²
175.15	as well as] CENTENARY; as well | as well as MS
176.11	imitated,] I; $\sim_\wedge$ MS
176.26	New England] I; $\sim$ - $\sim$ MS
177.2	hand,] I; $\sim_\wedge$ MS
*177.15	farthest] stet MS
178.5	one] I; omit MS
*178.29	begun] stet MS
178.33	it] I; itself MS
179.2	spirit,] I; $\sim_\wedge$ MS
179.16	some time] I; sometime MS
*180.4	inspirited] stet MS
182.20–21	corruscating] stet MS, I
183.25	Nor could it] I; Nor it could it MS
186.28	life $_\wedge$] I; $\sim$, MS
187.6	earnest–] I; $\sim$, MS
188.7	Except] I; Only MS
192.18	follows:] possibly $\sim$; as in I
193.4	shrinking–] CENTENARY (E¹); $\sim$, $_\wedge$ MS; $\sim$,– I–IV
193.10	Priscilla–poor, pallid flower!–] I; $\sim$, $\sim$, $\sim$ $\sim$, $_\wedge$ MS
193.11	away!] I; $\sim$. MS
194.7	shake] I; fling MS
196.23	Pope $_\wedge$] I; $\sim$, MS
196.29	its] I; it MS
196.30	character,)$_\wedge$] CENTENARY; $\sim_\wedge$) $_\wedge$ MS; $\sim_\wedge$), I–IV, E¹⁻²
198.20	the newly] I; the | the newly MS

198.26	flame ∧] I; ～ , MS
199.2	agencies] I; agency MS
200.28	effected] *just possibly* MS *may read* affected
203.10	and a] I; a *omit* MS
203.11	prophetess] I; propetess MS
205.15	rocks] I; arches MS
*207.20	befall] I; befal MS, E¹
208.6	its] *just possibly mended in* MS *from* its *to* Its
208.20	ecstasies] II (E¹); ectasies MS; ecstacies I
210.17	O'Shanter] I; °Shanter MS
211.32	autumn to autumn] I; season to season MS
212.4	fuel!] I; ～ . MS
213.18	sank] *stet* MS
217.17	breath,] I; ～ . MS
217.27	Him] III (E¹); him MS, I–II
218.9	at] *stet* MS
218.30	He put] IV (E¹); he put MS, I–III
223.13	back] I; back back MS
223.33	hard] I; *omit* MS
224.12	this:] I; ～ ; MS
226.14	this!] I; ～ . MS
231.9	anywhere] *just possibly* MS *reads* any where
232.13	I am] I; I'm MS, E¹
234.10–11	breakfast-table] I; ～ ∧	～ MS
241.19	battle-field] I; battlefield MS
247.25	come. ∧] I; ～ :– MS
247.26–32	I perceive . . . my face:–] I; *omit* MS

REJECTED FIRST-EDITION
SUBSTANTIVE READINGS

(NOTE: Although the readings below are listed in the Historical Collation, they are given separately here since the information is of critical importance. An asterisk indicates that a Textual Note discusses the reading.)

10.23–24	and somewhat . . . demijohn] MS (*deleted*); *omit* I
17.15–16	I almost . . . beholding it.] MS (*deleted*); *omit* I
*18.10	closer] MS; close I
*37.25	littler] MS; little I
74.16	lesson] MS; lessons I
*85.11	wintry] MS; winter I
98.7	around almost] MS; almost around I
*132.31	nor] MS; or I
*150.11	bordered] MS; boarded I
175.5–27	Human nature . . . substituting good.] MS (*deleted*); *omit* I
*178.29	begun] MS; began I
*180.4	inspirited] MS; inspired I
213.18	sank] MS; sunk I
218.9	at] MS; by I

WORD-DIVISION

1. *End-of-the-Line Hyphenation in the Centenary Edition*

(NOTE: No hyphenation of a possible compound at the end of a line in the Centenary text is present in the manuscript except for the following readings, which are hyphenated within the line in the manuscript. Hyphenated compounds in which both elements are capitalized are not included.)

11.25	hoof-|tramps
12.8	tree-|trunks
18.1	supper-|table
20.27	self-|seeking
21.17	play-|day
25.6	earth-|grimed
27.18	fire-|lighted
35.29	farm-|house
54.23	ill-|will
56.27	haying-|time
64.18	linsey-|woolsey
64.27	hay-|fork
75.12	thorn-|tree
80.5	hearth-|stone
82.5	ill-|directed
87.23	off-|hand
97.15	long-|brooding

98.4	grape-|vine
99.17	fore-|reckoned
100.6	battle-|spirit
100.33	fancy-|work
103.33	hiding-|place
112.15	wine-|flush
136.9	stone-|fence
141.10	yesterday-|morning
144.9	life-|machinery
148.3	window-|pane
149.32	upper-|story
156.17	wood-|path
156.19	vine-|curtained
157.9	heart-|sickness
164.23	self-|indulgence
167.26	chamber-|window
176.1	canvass-|back
176.35	gin-|cocktails
178.22	water-|drinkers
180.12	good-|fellowship
184.2	poverty-|stricken
187.28	second-|sight
197.15	middle-|aged
200.5	drawing-|room
201.13	stage-|trickery
208.1	over-|laden
213.1	working-|dress
215.14	death-|sentence
220.34	self-|accusation
224.12	battle-|field
226.27	over-|consciousness
233.28	resting-|place
246.11	middle-|age

2. *End-of-the-Line Hyphenation in the Manuscript*

(NOTE: The following compounds, or possible compounds, are hyphenated at the end of the line in the manuscript copy-text. The form in which they have been transcribed in the Centenary Edition, as listed below, represents the practice of the manuscript as ascertained by other appearances or by parallels within the manuscript. Other Hawthorne manuscripts of the period have been consulted when evidence was not available in *The Blithedale Romance* manuscript.)

1.9	fancy-sketch
2.20	foothold
8.29	midnight
9.6	farm-house
9.8	fireside
10.15	sidewalks
11.12	snow-storm
12.4	north-easter
13.7	world-wide
20.22	farm-work
23.18	wood-market
25.24	wayfarer
25.26	house-door
30.21	supper-table
30.30	water-pitcher
31.4	milking-time
33.15	self-forgetful
35.31	outbreaks
37.17	sand-waste
39.16	sleeping-room
40.14	intermeddling
44.9	faint-heartedness
51.1	sunshine
58.18	everlasting
64.2	lady-love
64.32	breakfast-time
67.10	door-step
68.4	plough-tail
81.2	forenoon
81.6	road-side
91.28	woodland
92.1	forth-putting

94.7	farm-house
105.4	ear-shot
106.2	downright
119.12	birch-tree
128.13	wood-side
130.5	first-born
130.20	tombstones
132.1	purse-strings
142.17	steersman
146.26	staircase
148.9	backside
148.14	grass-plots
151.23	back-door
153.18	chamber-window
154.6	owl-like
175.30	beef-steak
178.17	gold-fishes
184.12	white-wigged
187.8	ghost-child
188.34	staircase
200.5	wood-path
201.15	high-wrought
202.2	country-fellows
205.24	stone-wall
206.12	greensward
207.4	farm-house
221.1	thistle-down
231.16	river-bank

3. Special Cases

(NOTE: In the following list the compound, or possible compound, is hyphenated at the end of the line in the manuscript and in the Centenary Edition.)

2.19	day-|dream] day-|dream (i.e. day-dream)
31.1	first-|rate] first-|rate (i.e. first-rate)

63.33   broad-|skirted] broad-|skirted
         (i.e. broad-skirted)
64.9   cabbage-|garden] cabbage-|garden
         (i.e. cabbage-garden)
89.5   wood-|seclusion] wood-|seclusion
         (i.e. wood-seclusion)
124.17   wood-|paths] wood-|paths (i.e. wood-paths)
129.4   stone-|fence] stone-|fence (i.e. stone-fence)
149.20   rail-|road] rail-|road (i.e. railroad)
181.14   grape-|juice] grape-|juice (i.e. grape-juice)

HISTORICAL COLLATION

The following editions have been collated and their variants recorded: I, 1852 first edition; II, 1876 Little Classics Edition; III, 1883 Riverside Edition; IV, 1900 Autograph Edition; and the English editions E^1 of 1852 (see Textual Introduction) and E^2 of 1854.

Machine collations of the plates of editions I, II, and III show variants between the first and last printings of these plates, but the provenience of intermediate variants is not further specified in this listing. The superior letter *a* indicates first printing, *z* last printing. Plates of I were used for 1852 and subsequent printings as a single volume, and for the collected Hawthorne editions of 1865 (untitled), 1876 Illustrated Library, 1879 Fireside, 1880 Globe, 1884 Globe (Crowell), and 1886 New Fireside. Plates of II include the 1876 Little Classics, 1891 Popular, 1894 Salem, and 1899 Concord. The 1883 Riverside plates, III, were used for 1884 Wayside, 1884–85 Complete Works (London), 1891 Standard Library, 1902 New Wayside, and 1909 Fireside. No printings of IV, subsequent to 1900 Autograph, have been collated. Typographical errors not forming accepted words have not been recorded in editions after the first unless they are plate-changes.

5.15	them ever come] them come III–IV
7.30	influence] agency MS
10.23–24	and somewhat . . . demijohn] MS (*deleted*); *omit* I–IV, E$^{1-2}$
12.11	past] passed III–IV
15.30	lay] was MS

15.35	find] found E²
17.15–16	I almost . . . beholding it.] MS (*deleted*); *omit* I–IV, E¹⁻²
18.10	closer] close I–IV, E¹⁻²
18.30	of] of of MS
19.11	intolerable] intolerably MS
19.33	than an effort] than effort MS
20.22	you] your III–IV
20.31	at] as III
23.6	of] at III–IV
25.17	warm and bright with] warm with III–IV
26.33	has] had IV
28.5	drooped] dropped III–IV
30.2	creditable] to his credit MS
30.18	she] he MS
30.30	from] out of MS
30.31	about] of E²
37.18	twelvemonth's] twelvemonths' IV
37.25	littler] little I–IV, E¹⁻²
40.1	an] a E¹⁻²
40.2	a] the IV
40.7	I indulged] I had indulged E²
40.21	with a] with the MS
40.25	I shared] I had shared E²
41.22	lain] laid III–IV
46.27	subtle] subtile II–IV
47.16	nor] not E¹⁻²
50.3	tread] dread E¹
55.16	could] can E²
58.16	houstonias] housatonias I–II, E¹⁻²
59.9	deviltry] devilry E¹⁻²
59.28	squirrel!] ∼ ? I; ∼ . II–IV
61.28	earthly] early III–IV
63.13	farther] longer MS; further I–IV, E¹⁻²
64.12	to] of MS
65.8	with] in E²
65.18	other] another MS
65.27	agriculturalists] agriculturists, I–IV, E¹⁻²
70.22	one] once II^a
70.30	straight] strait II–IV
72.27	which such a] which a E¹

73.9–10	was very fond] was fond E[1-2]
73.22	caprioles] caprices E[1-2]
73.30	to] of MS
74.2	swept] wept II–IV
74.16	lesson] lessons I–IV, E[1-2]
74.19	biggest pitcher] biggest water pitcher IV
74.32	recognize her as his] consider her his MS, E[1-2]
75.18	which you are so merry in] in which you appear to be so merry E[1-2]
77.7	nor] or E[2]
77.17	were] was IV
79.8	smelled to] smelled too II[a], IV
80.9	rear] raise E[1-2]
80.11	these] those III–IV
80.14	further] farther II–IV
81.1	been] beeen III[a]
81.17	imagination] imaginations IV
82.13	not at all] not all III[a]
84.17	farther] further I, E[1-2]
85.11	wintry]winter I–IV, E[1-2]
85.20	further] farther II–IV
86.32	Priscilla.] ~ ? E[1-2]
87.12	complaisantly] complacently MS, I–IV, E[1-2]
90.4	lets] let E[1-2]
90.13	a] your E[2]
90.30	until] untill I[1865]
91.9	less a] less to a E[1-2]
91.11	with some curiosity] with curiosity E[1-2]
98.7	around almost] almost around I–III, E[1-2]
101.4	was] is MS
103.23	there] here II–IV
109.14	purposes] purpose E[1-2]
110.27	of considerable] of a considerable MS
113.4	lips] kiss MS
116.6	uprose] up rose E[1-2]
118.14	awakening] awaking III–IV
120.23	weak] *omit* MS
123.31	behoved] behooved I–IV
125.21	and very] and a very IV
127.15	it not a] it a III–IV
128.21	a] *omit* MS

132.31	nor] or I–IV, E[1-2]
133.22	aimless] useless MS
134.15	your] our E[1-2]
141.22	and] or MS
142.12	straight-bodied] strait-bodied II–IV
144.18	hanging up by] hanging by MS
144.18	heads] head E[1-2]
146.10	were] *omit* MS
146.12	thoughts] thought MS
148.33	roof] roofs MS, IV
149.2	to all the] to the III–IV
150.3	accustomed] acccustomed III[a]
150.11	bordered] boarded I–IV, E[1-2]
150.17	a] *omit* MS
154.15	of] of of MS
156.7	amount of] amount of of MS
156.28	been made a] been a E[1-2]
159.5	an] any II[z]–IV
163.17	her own] my own MS
164.13	others] other II–IV
165.27	self-complacent] self-complaisant MS
165.32	part] path E[2]
166.33	individual] indi_Aidual I[1871]
168.19	I, still holding] I, holding E[1-2]
169.29	near her] nearer MS
171.11	approached her, and] approached and III–IV
175.5–27	Human nature . . . substituting good.] MS (*deleted*); *omit* I–IV, E[1-2]
175.15	as well as] as well as well as MS; *omit* I–IV, E[1-2]
177.15	farthest] furthest I–IV, E[1-2]
178.5	one] *omit* MS
178.29	begun] began I, E[1-2]
178.33	it] itself MS
179.16	ate our luncheon] ate luncheon III–IV
180.4	inspirited] inspired I–IV, E[1-2]
187.30	empirical] empiracle III[a]
188.7	Except] Only MS
194.7	shake] fling MS
196.27	selectmen] select men E[1-2]
196.29	its] it MS
198.20	the] the the MS

199.2	agencies] agency MS
201.4	that of a] that of of a III[a]
202.6	a wreath of vanishing] a vanishing E[1-2]
203.10	and a] and MS
205.15	rocks] arches MS
207.20	befall] befal E[1-2]
208.22	it at that] it that III–IV
209.8	farther] further I, E[1-2]
210.13	further] farther II–IV
211.32	autumn to autumn] season to season MS
213.18	sank] sunk I–IV, E[1-2]
214.2	intentness] intenseness II–IV
215.7	said] cried III–IV
215.18	Hollingsworth's] Hollingworth's III[a]
216.29	as me] as to me E[2]
218.9	at] by I–IV, E[1-2]
223.7	further] farther II–IV
223.13	back] back back MS
223.27–28	you happen] you may happen E[2]
223.33	hard] *omit* MS
225.27	can she] she can E[1-2]
230.5	quietly] quickly II–IV
230.7–8	out of my] out my III[a]
232.13	I am] I'm MS, E[1-2]
232.25	said Foster] said Silas Foster E[2]
233.19	up stream] up the stream E[2]
237.10	slowly] slow y I[1852-59]
242.13	at] of II[z]–IV
244.2	How much Nature] How Nature III–IV
244.5	of conscious] of a conscious III
247.4	Farther] Further I–IV, E[1-2]
247.24	in] to III–IV
247.26–32	I perceive . . . my face:–] *omit* MS

THE OHIO STATE UNIVERSITY LEAF

Purchased at auction from Parke-Bernet Galleries in November, 1962, a leaf from an earlier manuscript is preserved in the Ohio State University Libraries. This leaf is written on the recto of the same blue wove paper as the Pierpont Morgan Library manuscript. Its text runs from Morgan MS fol. 34, line 27, to fol. 35, line 36 (I, 56.28–58.14), which is Centenary 46.16–47.28 ("picion, and . . . glances as"). The following is a collation of every variant in this leaf against the Morgan MS, which in this passage is precisely reproduced by the Centenary text. The page-line references are Centenary; the reading to the left of the bracket is Centenary (i.e., Morgan) and that to the right is the early leaf.

46.18	be blown] get
19	a] *omit*
20	fill the social atmosphere] exist
21	filled it] existed
23	air before reaching it.] air, before they reached it.
27	subtle] subtile
28	system. The] system, when the
32	our companions] other persons
33	periods] times
33	upon] over
47.3	could observe] might have seen [*Morgan* 'could' *interlined above deleted* 'might']
4	deportment∧] ~ ,
4–5	commend itself as the utmost] seem the consummate
6	matron∧)] ~ ,)

10–11	Yet, sometimes,] ∼ ∧ ∼ ∧
11	conjectures. I acknowledged] conjectures, and acknowledged
16	avail] use
17	a wife] married
20–21	my mind reverted to] I dwelt upon
22–23	Zenobia . . . led me.] *omit*
24	she] Zenobia
26	eye-shot∧ in] eye-shot, during
26–27	of my mixing in] since I have mingled with

During the course of inscription the following alterations were made in the leaf:

46.24	repeat∧] *an original comma has been wiped out.*
26	intuition—] *the dash deletes an original comma.*
33	at such] 'at s' *written over erased* 'the'.
33	greater] 'er' *written over wiped-out* 'ly'.
34	a] *interlined with a caret.*
47.3	seen] *interlined above is wiped-out* 'her de', *and following* 'seen', *is deleted* 'though seemly and delightful in a'.
12	wicked] *interlined with a caret.*
15	Still] *written over wiped-out* 'Yet'.
18	folded] *what may be a following comma has been wiped out before the inscription of* 'petal'.
18	latent] *interlined with a caret.*

ALTERATIONS IN THE MANUSCRIPT

(NOTE: With the exceptions listed below, all alterations made in the manuscript during its inscription or review before submission (the two classes are ordinarily not distinguishable with certainty) are described here. The exceptions are as follows: (1) Letters or words that have been mended or traced-over for clarity without alteration of the original; (2) interlineations that repeat in a more clearly written form the identical original; and (3) deletions, mendings, or readings under alterations that could not be read. In the description, *above* means "interlined" and *over* means "in the same space." The presence of a caret is always noticed. Square brackets signify one or more illegible letters. Letters within square brackets are conjectural on some evidence but not wholly certain.)

1.1	In the] *follows deleted* 'Many readers will probably s'.
1.9	in the hope of giving] *interlined with a caret above deleted* 'to give'.
1.10	to] *written over wiped-out* 'be'.
2.4	a license with] *follows deleted* 'to' *and is written over wiped-out* 'to take a full lic'.
2.5	in view] 'in vi' *written over wiped-out* 'for th'.
2.5	every-day] *interlined with a caret.*
2.33	Woman] 'W' *mended from* 'w'.
2.35	tremulous] *written over wiped-out word, possibly* 'trembling'.
3.2–3	fervor—] *the dash written over a comma.*

3.4	by some accident] *interlined with a caret above* 'as it happened', *the caret in error to the right of the original comma after* 'accident'.
3.9–10	with whom . . . Institution] *interlined with a caret.*
3.11	others, whom he dares] 'whom he d' *written over wiped-out* 'such whom he', *and the* 's,' *added to original* 'other'.
3.17	Howadji] *the* 'a' *interlined with a caret.*
3.19	has since] *interlined with a caret.*
3.20	along the current] *interlined with a caret above deleted* 'on the shores'.
5.1	my departure] 'my d' *written over wiped-out* 'I en'.
5.4	elderly] *written over wiped-out* 'old man'.
5.21	profess] 'pro-	fess', *with* 'pro-' *written over wiped-out* 'af'.
6.2	arts] 'ts' *mended from* 't'.
6.3	contrasted] *interlined above deleted* 'contrived'.
6.13	was] 'w' *written over wiped-out* 't'.
7.25	three or four] *interlined above deleted* 'two or three'.
7.32	manner,] *the comma written below wiped-out double quotes.*
8.5	have] *written over what seems to be wiped-out* 'are y'.
8.28	wisest] 'i' *mended from* 'a'.
9.13	were] *mended from* 'are'.
10.23–24	and somewhat . . . demijohn—] *deleted, the comma after* 'box' *inadvertently being retained.*
11.4	scheme.] *following is an end-of-the-line dash.*
12.2	exhilarating] *first* 'a' *written over* 'i'.
12.3	ourselves] *interlined with a caret above deleted* 'us'.
12.23	good] *interlined with a caret.*
12.25	rude] 'rud' *written over wiped-out* 'good'.
13.4	over] *followed by* 'such' *deleted in pencil.*
13.9	Mrs.] *written over wiped-out* 'Silas'.
13.10	fair] *written over what seems to be wiped-out* 'good'.
13.29	thus] *interlined above deleted* 'so'.

14.13	one] *written over wiped-out* 'you'.
15.20	moment.] *following is an end-of-the-line dash.*
15.33	remarkably] *interlined with a caret.*
16.16	laugh—] *dash written over a comma.*
16.18	us] 'u' *written over wiped-out* 'h'.
16.32	degenerated] 'd' *written over wiped-out* 'f'.
17.14	a picture] 'a' *altered from* 'an', *and* 'picture' *interlined with a caret above deleted* 'image'.
17.15–16	I almost . . . it.] *deleted.*
17.30	gentleness] 'gentle' *written over wiped-out* 'grace'.
17.32	to have been] *written over wiped-out* 'to be refined'.
18.4	basket?] *following is an end-of-the-line dash.*
18.8	for] *mended over* 'from'.
19.3	—yes,] *originally* ';—yes', *but then a new dash deleted the semicolon, and* 'yes,' *written over wiped-out* '—yes'.
19.17	generosity—] *the dash written over a comma.*
19.30	both] *written over wiped-out* 'perpe'.
20.30	very] *written over wiped-out* 'soon'.
21.15	show] *follows wiped-out* 'ap-' *at end of preceding line.*
21.28	Yet] *follows wiped-out dash, and* 'Y' *mended from* 'y'.
24.7	she;] *the semicolon written over a dash.*
24.10	in] *interlined with a caret.*
25.33	at the threshold] *written over wiped-out* 'on the door-step'.
27.26	enough] *mended by wiping from* 'enouugh'.
28.20	to] *interlined with a caret.*
29.6	do me] 'do' *written over wiped-out* 'me'.
33.28	as] *written over wiped-out* 'of'.
35.11	thenceforth] *interlined with a caret above deleted* 'now'.
35.13	haunted] *follows repeated and deleted* 'had'.
36.11	caught] 'c' *written over wiped-out* 'h'.
36.19	heart] *follows deleted* 'own'.
36.34	our] 'o' *written over what seems to be an* 'n'.
37.18	a] *written over wiped-out* 'like'.
39.20	that] *interlined above deleted* 'which'.
39.21	between us] *interlined with a caret.*

40.6	town-residence] 'town' *written over wiped-out* 'city' *before the hyphen and* 'residence' *inscribed.*
40.27	banquet as] *written over wiped-out* 'feast as deli'.
40.30	pleased:—] *before the dash are two dots that are probably a colon.*
40.33	two yoke] *written over wiped-out* 'a dozen cows'.
44.2	poor little] *written over wiped-out* 'writings'.
44.15	naturally] *interlined with a caret.*
44.23	moreover,] *interlined with a caret and the comma added after* 'duty'.
45.6	I] *written over wiped-out* 'you'.
45.6	the] *written over wiped-out* 'only'.
45.29	that,] *the comma written over a dash.*
45.31	woman—] *the dash written over a comma.*
47.3	could] *interlined above deleted* 'might'.
47.16	upbraid] 'b' *interlined in pencil in different hand.*
47.16	myself] 'my' *mended over what seems to be* 'one'.
47.24	as she] *written over wiped-out* 'while'.
49.2	inquire] 'in' *mended from* 'en'.
49.7	her] *interlined with a caret.*
49.14	or] 'r' *mended over what seems to be an* 'f'.
50.8	the] 't' *written over wiped-out* 'p'.
50.12	was] *written over wiped-out* 'lik'.
51.14	admirably] *interlined above deleted* 'exquisitely'.
51.17	company] *follows deleted* 'the'.
51.29	resemblance] 'r' *written over what seems to be wiped-out* 'f'.
52.9	, and] *mended from* '. As'.
52.24	Sand's] 'd's' *mended from* 'ds'.
52.26	brought] *followed by wiped-out* 'with' *ending the line.*
53.24	disgust.] *followed by an end-of-the-line dash.*
54.16	seventy thousand] *just possibly hyphenated.*
54.18	sight!] *the exclamation point altered from a comma after an added exclamation point had been wiped out.*
55.8	fellows.] *followed by an end-of-the-line dash.*
55.32	identical] *written over wiped-out* 'very pursuit'.
56.17	strove to embody] *interlined with a caret above deleted* 'had embodied'.

56.18   kept] 'k' *written over wiped-out* 'h'.
59.27   we] *written over wiped-out* 'I'.
60.4   girl—] *the dash written over a wiped-out comma.*
60.11   of] *interlined with a caret.*
60.17   May-] 'M' *mended from* 'm'.
60.19   custom] *written over wiped-out* 'habit'.
60.30   airy] *seems to be written over wiped-out* 'airy
         tongues' *at the end of the line before* 'tongues'
         *was written to start the next line; but then both
         words wiped out and* 'airy' *traced over them.*
61.5–6   progressively] 'pr' *written over* 'gre'.
61.22   or] *written over wiped-out* 'gar'.
63.34   or] *written over wiped-out* 'and'.
64.3   epitome] *interlined above deleted* 'presentment'.
65.5   in] *written over* 'as'.
66.2   anticipated] 'ant' *written over wiped-out* 'expe'.
68.5   name!"] *following, and beginning a new para-
         graph, are the deleted words,* ' "I cannot con-
         ceive," observed Zenobia, with great emphasis;
         and, no doubt, she spoke fairly the feeling of
         the moment—"I cannot conceive of being, so con'.
68.13   a] *interlined with a caret before* 'slave'.
68.19   in] *written over wiped-out* 'ea'.
69.4   pretty] *interlined above deleted* 'almost'.
71.18   reality,] *the comma added before a wiped-out
         semicolon.*
72.5   wonder.] *the period added before a wiped-out
         semicolon.*
73.4   playful] 'play' *written over wiped-out* 'pathos'.
73.24   a] *written over wiped-out* 'b'.
74.2   sorrows∧] *a following comma is wiped out.*
74.19   she dropt] 'she' *written over wiped-out* 'and'.
75.19   laughing.] *following is an end-of-the-line dash.*
76.8   they] *interlined with a caret.*
76.9   I!] *the exclamation mark written over a wiped-
         out comma.*
76.19   taken] 't' *written over wiped-out* 'n'.
76.19   me] *interlined with a caret.*
77.1   me—] *the dash written over a comma.*
77.4   before they] *at the start of the next line repeated*
         'before they' *is deleted.*

77.5	them] *written over wiped-out* 'thither'.
79.22	Zenobia's] *written over wiped-out* 'her passion'.
80.15	at] *written over wiped-out* 'into'.
81.9	at] *written over wiped-out* 'from'.
81.16	absolutely] 'ab' *written over wiped-out* 'fu'.
82.1	cow-yards] *mended from* 'cowyards'.
82.19	the] *written over wiped-out* 'a ge'.
82.28	sidelong] *possibly* 'side long'.
84.27	they] *follows deleted* 'if'.
85.3	one] *written over wiped-out* 'thing'.
85.14	little] *the first* 'l' *written over wiped-out* 'g'.
85.22	perhaps] *interlined above deleted* 'because'.
85.34	is] *written over wiped-out* 'j'.
86.4	and] 'a' *written over wiped-out* 'h'.
86.5	gave] *followed by deleted* 'me'.
86.27	Zenobia!] *the exclamation mark written later than a comma.*
87.6	so as] *interlined above deleted* 'in order'.
87.26	tune] *follows deleted* 'the'.
87.34	any] *interlined above deleted* 'one'.
88.12	her too] 'her' *written over wiped-out* 'Zen'.
89.7	so] *interlined with a caret.*
89.22	me] *interlined with a caret.*
91.16	Æsthetic—] *a query preceding the dash seems to have been wiped out.*
92.3	But] *written over wiped-out* 'I[ ]'.
93.4	Indeed!] *the exclamation mark mended from a query.*
93.25	peculiar. Now] *mended from* 'peculiar; now'.
94.6	so] *written over wiped-out* '[ ]ff'.
95.10	with nothing] 'n' *written over wiped-out* 'out'.
95.13	contagion] *interlined above deleted* 'effect'.
95.34	the part of] *interlined with a caret.*
96.1	uncomfortable] *interlined with a caret.*
96.20	out] *written over wiped-out* 'of'.
96.28	it had] *written over wiped-out and very doubtful* 'by fate'.
99.24	turret] *following* 'turret$_\wedge$' *is deleted* 'of mine' *with an undeleted comma after it.*
101.17	disagreeable] *interlined with a caret above deleted* 'peculiar'.

101.28   with] *follows wiped-out* 'y'.
101.33   smothers] *interlined above deleted* 'murders'.
102.18   necessarily] 'nece' *written over wiped-out doubt-ful* '[ ]elo[ ]'.
103.5   no] 'n' *written over wiped-out* 'h'.
103.8   save] 'sa' *written over wiped-out* 'the'.
103.14   side] *interlined above deleted* 'part'.
104.21   inspired] *interlined with a caret above deleted* 'affected'.
105.1   subtilize] *interlined above deleted* 'convert'.
106.7   and charades] *interlined with a caret*.
106.18   Old Masters] 'Old M' *mended over wiped-out* 'old m'.
106.20   entreating] *interlined with a caret above deleted* 'pressing'.
108.1-2   From . . . for that.] *an addition, squeezed in.*
108.21   two of] 'of' *interlined with a caret.*
108.25   appeared] *written over wiped-out doubtful* 'showed her'.
109.12   only] *interlined with a caret.*
109.21   wine] *interlined above wiped-out* 'champagne'.
110.3   a corpse] 'a' *interlined with a caret.*
110.10   whom] *interlined with a caret.*
110.23   cried he,] *interlined with a caret.*
110.26   I am told,] *interlined with a caret.*
111.1   whither] *interlined with a caret above deleted* 'to which'.
111.9   sibylline] *interlined above deleted* 'oracular'.
111.12   heart] *interlined with a caret.*
111.21   life] *follows deleted* 'of'.
111.24   an] *interlined above deleted* 'unau'.
111.27   of] *interlined with a caret.*
111.32   the texture] 'the tex' *written over wiped-out* 'it seem'.
111.33   hiding] *interlined with a caret.*
111.33   that of] *interlined with a caret.*
112.5   a] *interlined above deleted* 'some'.
112.13   Thus] 'Th' *written over wiped-out* 'And'.
112.17   she] *written over wiped-out* 'with'.
113.6   and of the future world] *interlined with a caret.*
114.11   sight] *interlined with a caret.*

114.11   dim] *interlined with a caret above deleted* 'pale'.

114.18   essence,] *interlined with a caret.*

114.35   dark] *interlined with a caret above deleted* 'long'.

115.23   Lady'—] *the dash written over an exclamation mark.*

116.2   deep] *the second* 'deep' *is interlined with a caret.*

117.8   their] *written over wiped-out* 'the w'.

117.13   yoke-fellows] *the hyphen is an addition.*

118.5   together] 't' *written over wiped-out* 'g'.

118.12   and] *written over wiped-out* 'whi'.

119.1   out of] *written over wiped-out* 'into which'.

120.14   a] *written over wiped-out* 'f'.

120.22   of society] 'of s' *written over wiped-out* '[ ]t[ ]'.

121.11   motion] 'mot' *written over wiped-out* 'will'.

122.11   betrays] *followed by deleted* 'as' *or* 'us'.

123.33   only] *interlined above deleted* 'merely'.

124.15   An] *followed by wiped-out* 'pe', *the* 'n' *just written over the* 'p'.

125.10   been] *interlined above deleted* 'seemed'.

125.27   by her] *written over doubtful* '[ ]el[ ]'.

127.2   (plainly] *the parenthesis written over a comma.*

128.7   was] *a following comma appears to be deleted.*

130.11   I replied] 'I r' *written over wiped-out* 'repl'.

130.12   strong] 'str' *written over wiped-out* 'fair'.

131.10   is worth] 'is w' *written over wiped-out* 'worth'.

131.22   which] 'wh' *written over wiped-out* 'a th'.

132.10   it is] *written over wiped-out* 'she is'.

135.28   that] *interlined with a caret above deleted* 'as if'.

136.8   with one accord] *interlined with a caret which obscures the comma after* 'moments'.

137.3   a] *interlined with a caret.*

137.20   farm;—] *the dash written over wiped-out* 'an'.

138.5   Breath!] *the exclamation mark written over* 're'.

138.7   more?] *the query mended from an exclamation point.*

138.28   with] *beginning the next line is deleted* 'with'.

139.27   (though] *a comma preceding the parenthesis has been wiped out and then the parenthesis mended.*

140.6   the colonists of] *written over wiped-out* 'they be able to establish'.

140.14	ultimate] *interlined above deleted* 'ulterior'.
140.17	In] *written over wiped-out* 'It'.
140.34	of infinite space] *interlined with a caret.*
141.21	possess] *written over wiped-out* 'have'.
142.14	my] *written over wiped-out* 'affairs'.
143.2	to] *interlined in pencil with a caret in another hand.*
143.15	gave] 'g' *written over wiped-out* 'ha'.
146.11	so] *interlined with a caret.*
147.8	occurred] 'occ' *written over wiped-out* 'the'.
148.2	from the] *written over wiped-out* 'eastward;'.
148.11	a] *written over wiped-out* 'of'.
149.13	that] *interlined with a caret.*
149.16	its] *written over wiped-out* 'the'.
151.8	balustrade] *the first* 'a' *written over wiped-out* 'l'.
152.9	In the] *written over wiped-out* 'But the [p]'.
153.17	beholding] 'behold' *mended from* 'beholld'.
153.18	and left] *written over wiped-out* 'leaving'.
154.11	long ago] *interlined above deleted* 'recently'.
154.21	heart] *interlined with a caret.*
154.22	regard] *written over wiped-out* 'respect'.
155.11	sensible] 's' *written over a doubtful wiped-out* 'c'.
156.3	mood—] *the dash deletes a comma.*
156.12	requisite] 'requ' *written over wiped-out* 'that'.
156.29	old] 'o' *written over wiped-out* 'O'.
157.21	save] 's' *written over wiped-out* 'S'.
157.22	tenderness] 't' *written over wiped-out* 'f'.
157.35	a] *written over wiped-out* 'the'.
158.10	concern] *written over wiped-out* 'interest'.
158.20	circumspection] 'cu' *written over wiped-out* 'su'.
161.33	chamber] *interlined above deleted* 'room'.
163.12	to] 't' *written over wiped-out* 'f'.
164.1	flower,	though] 'flower' *written over wiped-out* ', though'; *starting the next line,* 'though' *written over very doubtful wiped-out* 'that'.
165.26	deem] *interlined above deleted* 'think'.
166.17	her] *a preceding* 'her' *ending the preceding line is deleted in pencil.*
167.22	the] *written over wiped-out* 'of'.
169.28	which] *interlined in pencil with a caret in another hand.*

169.28	her. She] *written over wiped-out* 'Priscilla'.
170.6	dreams] *interlined with a caret above deleted* 'thinks'.
170.32	except] 'ex' *written over doubtful wiped-out* 'sa'.
170.33	Providence] 'P' *written over wiped-out* 'p'.
171.6	bowed] *written over doubtful wiped-out* 'was bo'.
172.17	touches] *interlined with a caret.*
172.22	graciously] 'ly' *added in pencil in another hand.*
173.5	me,] *interlined with a caret.*
174.2	my] *interlined with a caret.*
175.1	my] 'm' *written over wiped-out* 'f'.
175.8	kindlier] 'lier' *written over wiped-out* 'er'.
175.11	unthought-of] *the hyphen doubtful.*
175.14	of tippling] *written over wiped-out* 'of drinking'.
176.17	those] 'tho' *written over wiped-out* 'Fl'.
176.20	joyously] 'joy' *written over wiped-out* 'for'.
176.20	quaffing] 'q' *written over wiped-out* 'f'.
176.35	men] 'm' *written over wiped-out* 'y'.
177.4	frothy] *interlined with a caret.*
178.14	tiny] *interlined with a caret above deleted* 'little'.
178.25	not] *interlined above deleted* 'never'.
179.11	according] 'accor' *written over wiped-out* 'he was'.
179.20	And he . . .] *originally,* 'man; and he	se', *which has been wiped out after* 'man' *and a period added.*
179.21	existence] 'exis-|tence', *with* 'tence' *interlined with a caret.*
180.28	a] *interlined with a caret.*
180.30	never] *interlined with a caret.*
181.9	trick—] *the dash written over a comma.*
181.11	look] 'k' *mended from wiped-out* 'ke'.
181.19	he began] 'he' *ends a line and the repeated* 'he' *at the start of the next has been deleted.*
181.21	when we first] *written over wiped-out* 'a few minutes ago'.
181.24	hardly any] 'hardly a' *written over wiped-out* 'very little'.
181.33	biographer.] *follows deleted* 'historian.'
182.3	call] *interlined with a caret.*
183.5	but] *written over wiped-out* 'only'.

183.26   The man] *written over wiped-out* 'Nor could'.
183.28   prosperity] *follows deleted* 'his'.
183.28   to] *interlined with a caret above deleted* 'into the'.
183.31   went far] *the first word of* 'far | far' *is wiped out.*
184.9   it] *interlined with a caret.*
184.28   sight] *written over wiped-out* 'eye'.
184.33   penury] *written over doubtful wiped-out* 'poverty'.
185.17   whether] 'w' *written over wiped-out* 'the'.
185.18   grandee] *interlined with a caret above deleted* 'man'.
186.21   purer] *written over doubtful wiped-out* 'higher'.
186.27   sombre] *interlined above deleted* 'outward'.
186.30   a] *interlined above deleted* 'some faint'.
186.33   cheerless] *interlined with a caret above deleted* 'squalid'.
188.17   spared Priscilla] *followed by deleted* 'spared Priscilla'.
189.13   triumphant] *interlined with a caret.*
189.34   careless] 'care' *written over wiped-out* 'puri'.
190.11   grief—] *the dash deletes a comma.*
190.14   her to Blithedale] *interlined with a caret.*
190.22   in the] *followed by* 'old' *which is wiped out and then deleted.*
190.22   old] 'o' *mended over wiped-out* 'O'.
190.23   a pause] *interlined with a caret; a partly formed caret appears after* 'There'.
190.24   lady's] *interlined above deleted* 'woman's'.
191.7   have been] *interlined with a caret above deleted* 'were'.
191.32–33 like lamps . . . temple] *interlined with a caret.*
192.2   state] *follows deleted* 'pride and'.
192.8   you?] *the query written over an exclamation mark.*
192.23   I know] 'I' *written over wiped-out* 'Yo'.
192.29–30 is all] *written over wiped-out* 'seem'.
195.19   only] *written over wiped-out* 'but'.
196.15   also] *interlined with a caret above deleted* 'too'.
196.33   autumnal] *interlined above deleted* 'September'.
197.27   irresistibly] 'is' *interlined with a caret.*

198.9	blue spectacles] 'blue s' *written over wiped-out* 'green sp'.
198.20	newly made] *mended currently from* 'new-m'.
198.27	utterly] *interlined above deleted* 'at once'.
198.30	all] *written over wiped-out* 'that'.
199.23	personage] *written over wiped-out* 'man'.
200.20	issuing] *written over doubtful wiped-out* 'stealing'.
200.22	of] *added in pencil in another hand.*
202.7	perpetrated] 'perp' *written over wiped-out* 'eff'.
202.8	reached] *written over wiped-out* 'been heard'.
202.20	sitting . . . hear the] *written over wiped-out* 'she could hear the desert-wind sweeping over the sands'.
202.26	persuade] *interlined above deleted* 'induce'.
202.30	mysterious] *interlined above deleted* 'visible'.
203.3	You] *originally* 'Your' *with the* 'r' *deleted in pencil.*
203.10	faith] *written over doubtful wiped-out* 'belie'.
203.14	as] *interlined with a caret.*
203.16	under the] 'under' *written over wiped-out* 'in the', *and* 'the' *interlined with a caret.*
205.14	that] *interlined with a caret above deleted* 'which'.
207.7	in] *interlined with a caret.*
207.25	a] *written over wiped-out* 'some'.
207.34–35	aslantwise] *written over wiped-out* 'leaning'.
208.32	fraternity] *written over wiped-out* 'brotherhood'.
209.9	proceeding . . . wood.] *interlined with a caret.*
210.2, 210.34	gipsy] *mended from* 'gipsey'.
210.5	broomstick in hand,] *interlined with a caret.*
210.8	leaned against a tree] *interlined with a caret.*
210.21	blended] *interlined above deleted* 'mingled'.
211.1	intruder!] *the exclamation mark written over a wiped-out comma.*
211.20	whole] *written over wiped-out* 'forthw'.
211.25	finally] 'fin' *written over wiped-out* 'soo'.
211.26	a] *written over wiped-out* 'h'.
212.9	voice—] *the dash written over a comma.*
212.10	something] 'thing' *interlined with a caret.*

213.8	resembled] *interlined above deleted* 'seemed'.
214.6	you] 'yo' *written over wiped-out* 'he'.
214.17	of the group to] 'of' *interlined with a caret;* 'the group to' *written over wiped-out* 'to another of'.
214.30	let] *interlined with a caret.*
215.5	part—] *the dash written over a comma.*
215.7	good!] *the exclamation added in place of an original comma.*
215.10	judge] *a following comma has been wiped out.*
215.13	judgment-seat that] *interlined with a caret; preceding is original* 'one' *deleted, and above* 'one' *is wiped-out interlined* 'the'; *another wiped-out interlined* 'the' *is found above* 'the only'.
215.16	and the] *written over wiped-out* 'the more'.
216.31	threatens to make] *interlined with a caret above deleted* 'has made'.
216.32	at least] 'at le' *written over wiped-out* 'as old'.
217.7	fully—] *the dash written over a comma.*
217.11	other] *written over wiped-out* 'question'.
218.20	whither] *interlined with a caret above deleted* 'to what'.
218.37	He was] 'H' *mended from* 'h'.
219.35	Priscilla—] *the dash written over a comma.*
220.2	We] 'W' *written over wiped-out* 'w'.
220.5	wished] *interlined above deleted* 'meant'.
220.5	which] 'w' *written over wiped-out* 'th'.
220.29	no] 'n' *written over wiped-out* 's'.
220.31	fault. That] *mended from* 'fault; that'.
222.11	it] *interlined with a caret.*
222.17	as] *written over wiped-out* 'Z'.
223.3	grief] *written over wiped-out* 'heart'.
223.20	an] *interlined with a caret above deleted* 'the'.
223.21	glance] *interlined with a caret above deleted* 'eyes'.
224.35	as] *interlined with a caret.*
225.27	looks] *interlined above deleted* 'eyes'.
225.28	scenes;] *the semicolon written over a dash.*
225.29	be] *interlined with a caret.*
225.30	secret;] *the semicolon written over a dash.*
225.30	uncomfortably;] *the semicolon written over a dash.*

225.31   of having] *interlined above deleted* 'that she had'.

226.17   discrowning] *the first 'n' interlined with a caret.*

226.19   Zenobia's sake] *interlined with a caret above deleted* 'me'.

226.28   The effect] 'The eff' *written over wiped-out* 'Her bea'.

227.10   very] *mended over wiped-out* 'veriest'.

228.16–17   left a] *original* 'had left an impressio' *is wiped out and* 'had left a br' *written over it; then* 'had' *is deleted.*

229.14   you] *interlined with a caret.*

230.30   cried.] *the period mended from a comma. Following is deleted,* 'with his eyes half out of his head, from mere surprise. "What on earth should the young woman do that for? Why, she has more means than she can use or waste, and lacks nothing to make her comfortable, but a husband—and that she could have, any day! There's some mistake about this, I tell you!" ' *This deleted passage is followed by,* ' "Come," said I, shuddering. . . . ' *Opposite the deletion, written vertically in the inner margin, is Hawthorne's direction,* 'Insert from blank page 188/2'. *The substitute passage,* 'I turned . . . I tell you!" ' *is inscribed at the foot of the verso of the next leaf, fol. 188.*

230.32   for?] *the query written over a wiped-out exclamation mark.*

231.17–18   A nameless . . . pulpit.] *interlined with a caret.*

231.27   on a Yankee last] 'on a' *and* 'last' *interlined, the first with a caret, above deleted* 'in' *and* 'land' *respectively.*

231.35   to me] *written over wiped-out* 'me F'.

232.13   I be] *written over wiped-out* 'I am'.

234.5   hereabouts,] *interlined with a caret above deleted* 'here'.

234.10   Zenobia—] *the dash written over a comma.*

234.14   grow] *interlined above deleted* 'become'.

234.21   overset] *written over doubtful wiped-out* 'upset th'.

235.2   I'm] *apostrophe and 'm' written over wiped-out 'm'.*

235.15   her body] *'her' written over wiped-out 'she', and 'body' interlined with a caret.*

235.15   the coffin] *'the' written over wiped-out 'her'.*

235.21   through] *written over wiped-out 'of her lips'.*

235.27   pool—] *the dash written over a comma.*

236.19   horror!] *followed by deleted* 'Being the woman that she was, could'.

236.21   Being] *follows deleted* 'Being the woman'.

236.23   her] *interlined with a caret.*

236.24   she] *mended from* 'the'.

237.3   that] *written over wiped-out* 'which'.

237.11   rock] *written over wiped-out* 'log'.

237.14   women] *written over wiped-out doubtful* 'beldames'.

237.15   it] *interlined with a caret.*

238.16   Blithedale colonists] *interlined with a caret.*

239.3   frippery] *interlined with a caret above deleted* 'foppery'.

239.12   spiritual] *interlined above deleted* 'eternal'.

239.22   horror] *'horr' written over wiped-out* 'eager'.

239.26   her—] *the dash written over a wiped-out semicolon.*

239.27   gone—] *the dash written over a wiped-out semicolon.*

239.29   Young as] *written over wiped-out* 'She had'.

240.14   which] *written over wiped-out* 'that other'.

240.20   all] *'a' written over wiped-out* 'th'.

241.4   Zenobia] *interlined above deleted* 'she'.

241.24   on one] *'on' written over wiped-out* 'one'.

241.35   see] *interlined above deleted* 'imagine'.

242.15–16 cottage, . . . retired,] *the commas written over dashes.*

242.17   encountering] *'en' written over doubtful wiped-out* 'see'.

242.20   Hollingsworth's face] *the apostrophe is an addition; 'face' interlined with a caret.*

242.29   Drawing nearer] *interlined with a caret above deleted* 'As they approached'.

243.1   begun!] *the exclamation mark mended from a comma.*

243.3   upbraiding] *'b' interlined with a caret.*

243.11–12 the tears . . . remembered &c.] *interlined with a caret between* 'Then' *and* 'I remembered the wild'.

243.19   admitting] *follows deleted* 'even'.

243.20   often] *interlined with a caret.*

243.21   perilous] *follows deleted* 'however most'.

245.17   be] *'b' written over wiped-out* 'p'.

246.4   dying,] *followed by deleted* 'I believe, of absolute starvation,'.

246.7   afield] *the 'a' is mended, but whether an original hyphen has been affected is doubtful; on the whole, the reading seems to be* 'afield', *as in 65.1.*

246.20   fair] *follows deleted* 'very'.

246.30   by no means] *interlined above deleted* 'do not exactly'.

247.9   Frostier] *interlined above deleted* 'Grayer'.

247.10   frostier] *interlined with a caret.*

247.10–11 have imbibed . . . and] *interlined with a caret above deleted* ', more worn, have'.

247.18   that] *written over wiped-out* 'which'.

COMPOSITORIAL STINTS IN THE
FIRST EDITION OF 1852

Unassigned	Preface
Henderson*	5.1–8.33 [The evening . . . for Blithedale.] MS 1–4. I, 9–13
Emery*	9.1–12.20 [There can . . . was one] MS 4–7. I, 14–17
Munn	12.20–16.24 [among the . . . themselves, it] MS 7–10. I, 18–22
Fox	16.25–21.22 [may be . . . sort of person] MS 10–14. I, 23–28.31
Emery	21.22–26.16 [to be turned . . . on the door-] MS 14–18. I, 28.32–33
Henderson	26.16–30.23 [step, just . . . pieces of] MS 18–22. I, 34–38
Munn	30.23–39.23 [dipt toast . . . prayerful habits,] MS 22–28. I, 39–48
Fox	40.1–44.5 [(except of . . . was made] MS 28–32. I, 49–53
Henderson	44.5–51.23 [(among a. . . . As I] MS 32–38. I, 54–62

* It is just possible that Henderson's stint ended, instead, at 7.22 [. . . man, sir!"] MS 3; I, 11, and Emery's stint began with 7.23 ["Does that . . .] MS 3; I, 12. There is a strong vertical pencil stroke in MS at this point unlike the lighter page-ending strokes, and Emery's name appears in pencil on the next leaf in the first available space, which was opposite the chapter heading, where it is suggested above that his stint began. If the strong vertical stroke had been a bracket, as found elsewhere, usually, to mark the start of a different compositor's work, the case would be certain.

Fox	51.23–55.28 [did not . . . nor scarcely] MS 38–42. I, 63–67
Emery†	55.28–60.21 [for the nutriment . . . midway] MS 42–45. I, 68–72
Munn†	60.21–63.34 [to Hollingsworth . . . waist at] MS 45–48. I, 73–76
Henderson	63.34–68.5 [every point . . . name!"] MS 48–52. I, 77–81
Emery	68.6–69.22 ["And how . . . business to] MS 52–54. I, 82–83
Henderson	69.23–74.31 [solve. Other . . . her new] MS 54–58. I, 84–89
Fox	74.32–77.7 [abode . . . learn, but] MS 58–61. I, 90–92
Emery	77.7–82.1 [cherish an . . . insomuch that our] MS 61–65. I, 93–98
Munn	82.1–86.10 [very cow-yards . . . yourself. But,] MS 65–68. I, 99–103
Fox	86.10–91.23 [come; we . . . any man.] MS 68–72. I, 104–9
Munn	91.24–95.2 ["I am . . . the excess] MS 72–75. I, 110–13
Henderson	95.2–101.20 [of his delight . . . sceptical and] MS 75–81. I, 114–21
Emery	101.20–106.23 [sneering view . . . frame; while] MS 81–84. I, 122–27
Fox	106.23–111.35 [at her feet . . . about the] MS 84–89. I, 128–33
Henderson	111.35–116.29 [room . . . conclusion.] MS 89–92. I, 134–39
Munn	117.1–120.20 [Our Sundays . . . woman in the] MS 93–96. I, 140–144.1
Innes	120.20–121.13 [world has . . . devolve into] MS 96. I, 144.2–144.32
Emery	121.13–125.17 [the hands . . . we must] MS 96–100. I, 145–49

† The end of Emery's stint and the beginning of Munn's between I, 72-73 is wrongly marked "72" in the manuscript, and the bracket is placed before "Hollingsworth" in error, instead of before "to". The pagination is corrected when Henderson's stint starts on page 77.

Fox	125.17–130.26 [make haste . . . "you will] MS 100–4. I, 150–55
Henderson	130.26–134.33 [die . . . kind of] MS 104–8. I, 156–60
Emery	134.33–140.20 [expression . . . that were] MS 108–12. I, 161–66
Munn	140.20–146.1 [wildest . . . my life.] MS 112–16. I, 167–72
Innes	146.1–148.18 [True . . . sheltered,] MS 116–19. I, 173–75
Fox	148.18–153.23 [and where . . . gloomy enough] MS 119–23. I, 176–81
Munn	153.23–158.4 [in town . . . times before,] MS 123–27. I, 182–86
Emery	158.4–163.19 [when she . . . terms of] MS 127–31. I, 187–92
Henderson§	163.19–167.30 [confidence. . . . Dear Priscilla!"] MS 131–34. I, 193–97
Munn§	168.1–172.12 [Priscilla . . . Wester-] MS 135–38. I, 198–202.28
Fox	172.12–178.6 [velt . . . world shall] MS 138–43. I, 202.29–207
Henderson	178.6–181.19 [endure . . . aspect of a] MS 143–46. I, 208–11
Emery	181.19–187.6 [decayed . . . earnest–] MS 146–50. I, 212–18
Munn	187.6–191.17 [that she . . . the mes-] MS 150–54. I, 219–23
Fox	191.17–196.24 [sage might . . . of per-] MS 154–58. I, 224–29
Munn	196.24–201.28 [son, in . . . faces encom-] MS 158–63. I, 230–235.30

§ Henderson's stint, as the book is now imposed, ends Chapter XIX on page 197, and Munn begins Chapter XX on page 198. However, the manuscript at the start of Munn's stint is marked "199". An extra line is added to pages 194-97; thus page 198 must originally have ended Chapter XIX, and page 199 begun Chapter XX, followed by an adjustment. Since erroneous pagination is marked in the manuscript for each successive stint to the very end of the book, it seems clear that on completion of the typesetting for the volume, the four-line page 198 was removed by relining pages 194-97, and fresh pagination was thereupon set in the headlines starting with page 199; 198 now began Chapter XX.

Henderson‡	201.28–205.30 [passing her . . . bitterness] MS 163–66. I, 235.31–239
Munn	205.30–209.35 [of self-scorn . . . and Revo-] MS 166–70. I, 240–44
Emery	219.33–224.26 ["True; we . . . sudden] MS 170–74. I, 245–50
Fox	215.23–219.32 [still mighty . . . it thus.] MS 174–78. I, 251–55
Emery	219.33–224.6 ["True; we . . . sudden] MS 178–82. I, 256–60
Henderson	224.26–229.21 [change . . . demanded.] MS 182–86. I, 261–66
Fox	229.21–234.1 ["Aha . . . retorted the] MS 186–90. I, 267–71
Munn	234.1–241.17 [yeoman . . . Zenobia's diver-] MS 190–96. I, 272–80
Fox	241.17–244.15 [sified capacity . . . valued.] MS 196–99. I, 281–84
Henderson	245.1–247.34 [It remains . . . END.] MS 199–201. I, 285–88

‡ The end of Chapter XXIII has produced some anomalies in that it must have run over several lines on first-edition page 238, whereupon the conclusion was moved to the foot of page 237, instead, by adding a thirty-third line to pages 234, 235, and 237. Some confusion still exists, however, in that the bracket and "238 Henderson" on manuscript folio 163 marks the presumable beginning of original page 236, not its modified beginning after the readjustments of type-lines necessary to tuck in the end of the chapter on page 237. However, if Munn's stint ended as marked by the bracket at the foot of page 235, the page would have been only thirty-one lines long, without typographical explanation. Thus the three (less likely the two) lines at the foot of page 235 are Henderson's typesetting, not Munn's, as the result of the altered make-up. The whole rearrangement must have been done when the runover was discovered on page 238 at the end of the chapter, since the faulty pagination in the manuscript continues still two in error and thus takes account of the adjustment. Because of the difficulty in knowing precisely whether two or three lines were transferred from the top of page 236 to the foot of page 235 as part of the rearrangement, a clear explanation for the anomalous thirty-two-line page 236 is not possible. The compositor could have inadvertently transferred the same number of lines (instead of a reduced number) to page 235 as he had added to page 236.

FANSHAWE

INTRODUCTION TO *FANSHAWE*

S HORTLY after Nathaniel Hawthorne's death, his
sister Elizabeth recalled, at his son Julian's request,
her brother's beginnings as a literary man:

It was while in college that he formed the design of becoming an author by profession. In a letter to me he says that
he had "made progress on my novel." I have already told you
that he wrote some tales to be called "Seven Tales of my
Native Land" . . . I read them and liked them. I think
they were better than "Fanshawe." . . . These "Seven Tales"
he attempted to publish; but one publisher, after keeping
them a long time, returned them with the acknowledgment
that he had not read them. It was the summer of 1825 [i.e.,
shortly after he graduated from Bowdoin] that he showed
them to me. One was a tale of witchcraft,—"Alice Doane,"
I believe it was called; and another was "Susan Grey." There
was much more of his peculiar genius in them than in
"Fanshawe." I recollect that he said, when he was still in
hopes to publish them, that he would write a story which
would make a smaller book, and get it published immediately
if possible, before the arrangements for bringing out the Tales
were completed. So he wrote "Fanshawe" and published it
at his own expense, paying $100 for that purpose. There
were a few copies sold, and he gave me one; but afterwards
he took possession of it, and no doubt burned it. We were
enjoined to keep the authorship a profound secret, and of
course we did, with one or two exceptions; for we were in
those days almost absolutely obedient to him. I do not quite

approve of either obedience or concealment. Your father kept his very existence a secret, as far as possible.[1]

Although Elizabeth's statement is not without its contradictions, it is tempting to assume that the "novel" and the "story which would make a smaller book" are both references to *Fanshawe*; yet she speaks of the "novel" as if Hawthorne had begun it in college, while she assigns the "smaller book" to a period during which he was hopeful of publishing the "Seven Tales," and those were written, according to her testimony in a letter to James T. Fields, "soon after Nathaniel left College."[2] Family tradition as recorded by Hawthorne's son-in-law is that "Seven Tales" was offered to Ferdinand Andrews, publisher of the *Salem Gazette*, who reluctantly returned the manuscript at Hawthorne's insistence.[3] Since Andrews left Salem before the end of 1826, it follows from Elizabeth's account that Hawthorne must have had *Fanshawe* in hand by this time. Exactly when he finished it and what vicissitudes accompanied its issuance we do not know. Especially puzzling is the matter of Hawthorne's financial underwriting of the volume. As a fledgling author he would almost certainly have been obliged to advance the publication costs, but in the economy of the late 1820's Elizabeth's figure of $100 seems doubtful; twice the amount would be a conservative guess.[4]

---

[1] Julian Hawthorne, *Nathaniel Hawthorne and His Wife* (Boston, 1884), I, 123-25.

[2] The letter is to James T. Fields, December 16, 1870 (postscript to her letter of December 13); in Randall Stewart, "Recollections of Hawthorne by His Sister Elizabeth," *American Literature*, XVI (January, 1945), 323.

[3] George Parsons Lathrop, *A Study of Hawthorne* (Boston, 1876), pp. 134-35; and Hubert H. Hoeltje, "Hawthorne as a Senior at Bowdoin," *Essex Institute Historical Collections*, XCIV (July, 1958), 205-28.

[4] By comparison, the printing bill for a slightly longer work of 1832, Feuerbach's *Caspar Hauser*, published by Allen and Ticknor in an edition of 1,000 copies, was $270, and this figure may not have included binding (see W. S. Tryon and William Charvat [eds.], *The Cost Books of Ticknor and Fields, 1832-1858* [New York, 1949], p. 4). The edition of *Fanshawe* was the same size and copies were bound. Hawthorne's sketch, "The Devil

Fanshawe was published by the Boston firm of Marsh and Capen in the last week of October, 1828,[5] and was actively promoted by a number of New England booksellers. It was advertised in the *Boston Statesman* six times between October 25 and December 13; in the *Boston Daily Advertiser,* every issue from October 28 through November 20 and from December 2 through 15; in the *Salem Gazette* twenty-nine times between November 4 and February 10, 1829; in the *Boston Semi-Weekly Courier* November 13; in the *Portsmouth Journal and Rockingham Gazette* December 13 and 20. The advertisements often simply list the title among books currently for sale. Yet a far from exhaustive newspaper search indicates a genuine attempt to gain a public for the anonymous author.[6]

Reviews of *Fanshawe* were for the most part favorable. The book was generally taken as increased evidence of the rise of a truly national literature. The *Yankee and Boston Literary Gazette,* November 6 (for 5), 1828, commented toward the end of a hundred-word note: "The story possesses considerable interest, and although the author has not yet added greatly to his country's literature, he should be encouraged to persevering efforts by a fair prospect of future success." The *Boston Weekly Messenger,* giving almost a thousand words to *Fanshawe* on November 13, declared:

---

in Manuscript," contains an allusion to a publisher who would "not absolutely decline" to issue a volume of tales on condition of the young author's "advancing half the cost of an edition, and giving bonds for the remainder." Such an arrangement would be consistent with the facts of the *Fanshawe* case as we know them.

[5] An announcement in the *Boston Daily Advertiser* for October 27 cited the book as "Published this day"; the *New England Galaxy* of October 31 stated that it had "just been published"; the *Boston Statesman* for November 4 equivocally included both the "this day" formula and the date October 25. We are indebted to Mr. Nolan Smith for searching out most of the contemporary notices discussed here.

[6] In accordance with then current trade practices, the booksellers may have stocked copies of *Fanshawe* on consignment. They may also have been given credit by the publishers for the cost of local advertisements, in which case Hawthorne would have been involved, at least passively, in promoting the book.

It is true to nature, and in no part does it shock us by a
violation of probability. Indeed, wherever there is a falling
off in the book, it is not in the design, but in the filling up—
in the throwing in of light and shade to give effect to the
picture. We attribute this, in some degree, to the author's
want of confidence in his own power. He is fearful of going
too far, and does not proceed far enough.

Mrs. Sarah J. Hale, editor of the *Ladies' Magazine,* wrote
in the issue for November, 1828: "Purchase it, reader. There
is but one volume, and trust me that it is worth placing in
your library." She praised the book briefly as an authentic
expression of American genius, and quoted some three
hundred of its words. A review in *The Critic,* November 22,
1828, although not happy with the characterization of Fanshawe himself, placed the anonymous author in the national-
istic pantheon. The notice concluded:

> We love to read, and love to review a work like this, where
> one can conscientiously shake hands with the author, and
> bid him, All hail, and be sure on leaving him, that no un-
> kindly feelings have been created, to rankle in his breast,
> making both the critic and the criticised unhappy. . . . Is it
> not quite possible that Willis wrote this book? We merely
> *guess.*

In the custom of the time, *The Critic* commentary was filled
out with a lengthy extract from the novel, as was the review
in the *Boston Statesman* for November 6, 1828. *The* [Boston]
Bower of Taste for November 8 and the *Philadelphia Album*
for November 26 both noted the book favorably, if in sum-
mary fashion.

High and conventional praise, then. Only one notice
damned the book. It appeared, October 31, 1828, in the
New England Galaxy and is presumably by the *Galaxy*
editor, Joseph Buckingham. In its entirety it reads:

> FANSHAWE. A love story with this title has just been pub-
> lished by Messrs. Marsh & Capen. It has, like ten thousand
> others, a mystery, an elopement, a villain, a father, a tavern,

almost a duel, a horrible death, and—Heaven save the mark!—
an end.

The *Galaxy* notice was picked up, credited to "Mr. Buckingham," by the *New York Mirror,* November 8, 1828. And
the *Connecticut Journal,* in noticing the November issue of
the *Ladies' Magazine,* said of its reviews that they were "all
praise." The editor added: "We do wish that Mrs. Hale's
kind and good feelings would not run away with her better
judgment." The *Boston Daily Advertiser* noted the publication of *Fanshawe* noncommitally November 12, 1828. In
the *North American Review* for January, 1829, there was
nothing but a books-received note in the New Publications
column.[7]

Fanshawe thus was on the whole cordially received—but
by gift-book ladies like Mrs. Hale. Indeed, the cordial reviewers together "placed" the book with some exactitude—
as did the bored Mr. Buckingham. It was a conventionally
compounded narrative, with appropriate echoes of Scott and
the Gothic romancers, "comical" interludes, conventional
hyperbolic passages on "nature," and the sort of plot in which
everything and everyone at the end assumed a proper place
in the American scheme of things. Harley College represents
Bowdoin,[8] and the rusticity of the scene is of a piece with the
rusticity of the minor characters. Against the scene and minor
characters are placed the benign college president, Dr. Melmoth; his beautiful ward, Ellen Langton; and her two suitors
—Edward Walcott, quintessentially the extrovert, and Fanshawe, quintessentially the introvert. (Is there an echo of
Hawthorne's own name in "Fanshawe"?) The problem is

[7] For a discussion of other reviews, see Bertha Faust, *Hawthorne's Con-
temporaneous Reputation* (Philadelphia, 1939).

[8] See Philip E. Burnham, "Hawthorne's *Fanshawe* and Bowdoin College," *Essex Institute Historical Collections,* LXXX (April, 1944), 131-38.
An interesting but not wholly convincing case for Dartmouth is made in
Robert Cantwell, *Nathaniel Hawthorne: The American Years* (New York
and Toronto, 1948), p. 119.

to bring Ellen and Fanshawe together and yet keep them apart, for it will not do to let a youth like Fanshawe, so anomalous in American society, win Ellen. The conventions of popular American fiction in the 1820's demanded that the man of deep thought and imagination be given his due but not his woman. The problem is solved by bringing in a villain (all the more deliciously villainous by virtue of the sentimental scene at his dying mother's bedside) who kidnaps Ellen, hoping thereby to secure her fortune, removes her to a mysterious cave, and seems to be threatening to rape her. Walcott is off in hot pursuit of the pair; but it is Fanshawe who saves her and witnesses the villain's accidental death. She offers her hand to him; but he knows he must decline it. Having done so, he returns to the life of study which is to hasten his death, while at the end Walcott marries Ellen, and life goes on as unterribly as so many of his contemporaries insisted it had to in America.

One can argue that *Fanshawe*, crude as it is, does contain the germ of much of Hawthorne's later work.[9] But, in view of Hawthorne's unhappiness over the book, it is important to observe how insistently *Fanshawe* is of a piece with the sort of fiction written by that "d——d mob of scribbling women" (Mrs. Hale was one of them) whose work later so infuriated him. For all its forced, wild inventiveness, it exhibits an incapacity to take the imaginative seriously, a defect which characterizes much popular fiction of the time.[10]

[9] See particularly Carl Bode, "Hawthorne's *Fanshawe*: The Promising of Greatness," *New England Quarterly*, XXIII (June, 1950), 235-42; Agostino Lombardo, "Il primo romanzo de Hawthorne," *Studi Americani*, I (1955), 73-95; and Robert Eugene Gross, "Hawthorne's First Novel: The Future of a Style," *PMLA*, LXXVIII (March, 1963), 60-68. Mr. Gross's study, centered mainly on matters of style, is the most sophisticated of these analyses, although at the outset he makes the strange error of confusing the date (1876) of the republication of *Fanshawe* with the date of Mrs. Hawthorne's denial (1864) that it was indeed Hawthorne's.

[10] See Terence Martin, *The Instructed Vision: Scottish Common Sense Philosophy and the Origins of American Fiction* (Bloomington, 1961), especially pp. 107-50.

The guess of *The Critic* reviewer was sound: *Fanshawe*, even though not by Willis, is nonetheless the sort of piece which Willis popularized. One has only to read through the two volumes of *The Legendary*, a miscellany Willis edited in 1828, to see compulsively reiterated the tone and motifs of *Fanshawe*. One piece, "Unwritten Philosophy," actually by Willis, demonstrates how a young scholar tutored a sweet ignorant girl until she was learned enough to become the wife of his bosom. In his own person, Willis comments that all marriages, unless based upon some such common ground as this, would be doomed to dullness and unhappiness after the initial passion and beauty were spent. In view of popular taste, such a philosophy *had* to be unwritten. Fanshawe was not allowed to tutor Ellen Langton thus, and in his scholarly honesty he knew that she should not be his. Thus, according to the requirements of popular fiction, the way was cleared for Walcott, the man of action—whom presumably marriage would gentle but would not cut off from the things of this world.

That at the beginning of his career Hawthorne could write such a novel is all the more interesting when we realize that, at roughly the same time, he could write a story like "Alice Doane"—which, perhaps with some modification, became the "Alice Doane's Appeal" published in *The Token* in 1835. "Alice Doane's Appeal" is crude but authentic Hawthorne. In it, the narrator takes two young ladies for a walk on Gallows Hill, hoping to bring them directly to a sense of their own history. In order to summon up for them specters of all the innocents who have been killed there, he reads to them from a manuscript he has brought along (presumably the original "Alice Doane"). And he stops only when his companions are dissolved in terror and tears. He can conclude: "And now the past had done all it could."

It is worth recalling "Alice Doane" here, in contrast with *Fanshawe*. In effect, the Fanshawe figure in the tale (unlike the hero of the novel) puts his imagination and his learning into action so that they make a vital difference in the lives of his companions. Might the introversion of Fanshawe explain why Hawthorne, even though he had at the very least allowed efforts to promote the novel, came so much to dislike it? It is possible that he wrote *Fanshawe* seriously and as well as he knew how to write at the time. But it is also possible that he deliberately aimed his book at the reader whose tastes went so much against the grain of his own. Perhaps he had hoped to try himself in two roles—as the "popular" writer in *Fanshawe* and as the "serious" writer in "Seven Tales." *Fanshawe,* then, may have been a deliberately calculated piece of hack-work: ironically enough, the sort of hack-work he would soon have to turn to in unhappy earnest. He had failed to get a publisher for the "Seven Tales," while by contrast *Fanshawe,* if the reviews count, was favorably received; was it in revulsion against such judgments that he set out systematically to dissociate himself from the novel?

The standard view, stemming from his sister's account and from his friend Bridge's recollections in the 1890's,[11] is that— to quote H. E. Scudder, editor of the Autograph Edition (1900) of Hawthorne's *Complete Writings*:

> Hawthorne quickly recognized the futility of his story, and when it failed, as it did almost from the beginning, he made an effort to call in all the copies that were within reach and to destroy them. He made his sister and his most intimate friend [Bridge] give up their copies to be burned, and he never referred to the misadventure. A dozen years after his death a copy was found by his family and reissued.[12]

Such evidence as we have refers only to Elizabeth Hawthorne's copy (which, she recalled, Hawthorne asked for in

---

[11] Horatio Bridge, *Personal Recollections of Nathaniel Hawthorne* (New York, 1893), p. 68.

[12] XVI, ix-x. Note the statement, p. 313 below, that Bridge himself burned his copy of the book.

December, 1832,[13] "and no doubt burned") and Bridge's copy (which he himself burned). Probably Hawthorne did not want his sister and his best friend to know him as only the author of a bit of hack-work. But the facts were not hidden from the Boston publisher Samuel G. Goodrich, who began to correspond with Hawthorne in 1829 after he had seen, as he later recalled, "some anonymous publication which seemed to indicate extraordinary powers," and had discovered through the publishers that the author was "N. Hawthorne."[14] On January 19, 1830, Goodrich wrote Hawthorne about some tales for his annual, *The Token,* and spoke explicitly of the book: "Had 'Fanshawe' been in the hands of more extensive dealers, I do believe it would have paid you a profit."[15] It is evident that Hawthorne had not yet successfully dissociated his name from *Fanshawe.*

Despite the destruction of Elizabeth Hawthorne's and Horatio Bridge's copies, the weight of the evidence is that Hawthorne wished not necessarily to suppress *Fanshawe,* but rather his connection with it. Confirmation of this point came in 1870 from Nahum Capen, one of the publishers of *Fanshawe,* who wrote the following letter to the *Boston Daily Advertiser*:

> An allusion is made in your paper of Tuesday last to a book entitled "Fanshawe" published by Marsh and Capen, 1828, in connection with the name of Hawthorne.
> It was the particular wish of Mr. Hawthorne that the authorship of this book should not be made public, and supposing that no one had the secret but myself, he enjoined me, not long before his death, not to disclose it to any one. I have a copy of the book, but in no way have I made known either its title or the name of the author.
> As the fact, however, has been published, I can with

---

[13] Elizabeth Hawthorne to Fields, January 28, 1871, in Stewart, "Recollections," p. 329.

[14] *Recollections of a Lifetime* (New York and Auburn, N. Y., 1857), II, 270.

[15] Julian Hawthorne, *op. cit.,* I, 132.

propriety correct the statement implying that the author attempted the suppression of the edition printed. This is not true. So far as he used any influence, it was to promote the sale of the book, not to destroy it.

When it was published, he felt that he could produce a superior work for a public beginning, and of the propriety of this he preferred to be his own judge.[16]

Then, a year later, Capen presented his copy of *Fanshawe* to the Boston Public Library. Now that the secret of its authorship was out, he declared in a covering letter, he felt that the Library should have the book. His letter is dated October 9, 1871. An endorsement dated October 10 and signed by Justin Winsor, the librarian, reads: "Mr. Capen stated to me orally that the Edition was 1000 copies, and that a portion of it was burned in his store on Washington St. It was kindly rec[d] as he says, but made no stir."[17]

Capen would seem to have been a responsible witness. He was by 1870 an important man in Boston, having been postmaster, a major figure in the Masonic order, and a crusader for copyright laws.[18] Self-interest could not have motivated his coming forward and testifying as he did. His declarations resolve at least one part of the *Fanshawe* puzzle: its rarity—which results not from Hawthorne's having "suppressed" it but from the fact that "a portion" of its stock was destroyed by fire, presumably in 1831 at the Marsh and Capen premises, 362 Washington Street.[19]

[16] October 15, 1870, p. 2, col. 3.

[17] MS, Boston Public Library. The existence of Capen's copy was first noted in an exhibition catalogue of the Grolier Club compiled by J. C. Chamberlain, *First Editions of the Works of Nathaniel Hawthorne* (New York, 1905), p. 4.

[18] John W. Moore (comp.), *Historical, Biographical, and Miscellaneous Gatherings* (Concord, N. H., 1886), pp. 465-66.

[19] We have found no record of the fire. But *Stimpson's Boston Directory* for 1831 shows the firm of Marsh, Capen and Lyon established at 362 Washington Street, while the *Directory* for 1832 gives the address as 131 Washington Street. Assuming fire as the cause of change in the firm's premises, it must have occurred before the issuance of the later directory. More explicitly, the publication date of both was May 20, but deadlines

When Evert Duyckinck was collecting material for the *Cyclopaedia of American Literature,* he acted upon a lead from Goodrich and inquired about *Fanshawe* of Fields, by then Hawthorne's publisher and friend. Fields wrote Duyckinck, December 10, 1850, that if possible, he would "unearth" the "'early book' talked of by Goodrich."[20] Fields wrote Hawthorne about it. The letter is missing from this sequence of Fields's letters to Hawthorne. In view of Hawthorne's reply, January 12, 1851, it is conceivable that he destroyed Fields's letter:

> You make an inquiry about some supposed former publication of mine. I cannot be sworn to make correct answers as to all the literary or other follies of my nonage; and I earnestly recommend you not to brush away the dust that may have gathered over them. Whatever might do me credit, you may be pretty sure that I should be ready enough to bring forward. Anything else, it is our mutual interest to conceal; and so far from assisting your researches in that direction, I especially enjoin it on you not to read any unacknowledged page which you may suppose to be mine.[21]

---

for directory copy must have been sufficiently earlier to make the calendar year of 1831 the likeliest span within which the fire occurred. In the view of Walter M. Whitehill of the Boston Athenaeum, the absence of publicity is not unusual: many important fires went unrecorded in the newspapers. Capen may have felt constrained to make up to Hawthorne for the loss incurred in the fire, for Hawthorne wrote Sophia Peabody, December 18, 1839, "I have a note to write to Mr. Capen, who torments me every now-and-then about a book he wants me to manufacture" (*Love Letters of Nathaniel Hawthorne, 1839-1863* [Chicago, 1907], I, 113). In 1838 (the letter is not precisely dated), Elizabeth Peabody wrote to Sophia: "I like to hear little items about Hawthorne. I had a nice talk with Mr. Capen about him to-day. He has him on his mind, and I hope it will come to some good purpose for the public" (Rose Hawthorne Lathrop, *Memories of Hawthorne* [Boston, 1897], p. 19). Capen could not have "tormented" Hawthorne after May 2, 1845, for on that date his firm (by then Marsh, Capen, Lyon and Webb) went into bankruptcy (Case No. 577, Insolvent Debtors, Suffolk County Court House, Boston).

20 MS, Duyckinck Collection, New York Public Library.

21 MS, Hawthorne-Fields Letter Book, Houghton Library, Harvard University. This is the letter which Fields published in his first "Our Whispering Gallery" essay on Hawthorne, *Atlantic Monthly,* XXVII (February, 1871), 249, and subsequently in *Yesterdays with Authors* (Boston, 1872), p. 48.

Fields may have been disingenuous in making his inquiry; for, as his wife later wrote, but without specifying dates, he himself had a copy of *Fanshawe* which he "put away and jealously guarded."[22] Nonetheless, he wrote Hawthorne, January 14, 1851:

> I regret you do not give me any clue to the Bk referred to in a former letter as pub[d] by Marsh & Capen. I wish to read all you have written, but do not press the matter.[23]

Naming Marsh and Capen, he betrayed the fact that he was not entirely ignorant of the "early book." We cannot know whether Hawthorne took note of this. In any case, he was almost successful in hushing up the matter of *Fanshawe* for the rest of his lifetime. The Duyckincks' *Cyclopaedia* contained no allusion to the work. But the *New American Cyclopaedia* (1858-63), edited by Hawthorne's Brook Farm colleagues George Ripley and Charles A. Dana, included a sentence calculated to pique curiosity at the same time that it misdated the volume:

> In 1832 [Hawthorne] published in Boston an anonymous romance which he has never since claimed, and which the public have not been able to identify.[24]

Soon after his death, the existence of the book was again tantalizingly confirmed—this time in an October, 1864, *North American Review* essay on his *Works* by his friend G. W. Curtis. The essay represents Curtis' attempt to "understand" Hawthorne's genius in such a way as to account for his dubious politics. For Hawthorne had annoyed his friends and admirers by his ambiguous attitude toward the Civil War and, of more immediate import, by his dedication of

[22] Annie Fields, *Nathaniel Hawthorne* (Boston, 1899), pp. 15-16.
[23] MS, Berg Collection, New York Public Library.
[24] VIII, 780. A close paraphrase of the statement is also to be found in *Chambers' Encyclopaedia* (London, 1860-68), V, 271.

Our Old Home to Franklin Pierce, who was then thought of as a lost leader. (Fields, ever loyal to Hawthorne, had declined Curtis' essay for the *Atlantic Monthly*.)[25] Curtis argued that Hawthorne's "disembodied intelligence" was unsuited to treat matters of day-to-day living and the realities of political issues. The essay expressed a view of many well-wishers who liked Hawthorne's work but condemned his political opinions; here is an important source of the myth of the "withdrawn" Hawthorne which recent biographers have labored hard to destroy. In Curtis' discussion *Fanshawe* served well as a foreshadowing of the Hawthorne whose work he had come to praise. The novel, wrote Curtis, without giving its name, "shows plainly the natural bent" of Hawthorne's mind. The fitfully kept secret of *Fanshawe* was once more incompletely disclosed. Ironically enough, Curtis was literally dragging *Fanshawe* into his argument; for it was, of course, not printed in the *Works* he was nominally reviewing.[26]

Most disturbed by Curtis' remarks on *Fanshawe* was Mrs. Hawthorne. Soon after the publication of Curtis' essay, she wrote Fields, October 3, 1864, to say that Horatio Bridge had told her—a month or more before—that he had long since burned his copy of "that novel or Romance which Mr Hawthorne so earnestly wished to be annihilated." She went on:

> I immediately thought I would ask you to burn the copy that you have, for Mr Hawthorne's sake, since he seemed to have such a great disgust at it. It is so wonderful that he never told me even that there was such a book printed,

[25] See Randall Stewart, *Nathaniel Hawthorne: A Biography* (New Haven, 1948), p. 239.

[26] XCIX (October, 1864), 539-57. Hawthorne's distaste for his own more "popular" works was no secret. When Curtis was about to become editor of *Putnam's Monthly Magazine*, he had asked Hawthorne for a suitable short piece, and Hawthorne had replied, October 28, 1852: "I have wasted far too much of my life, and done myself more than enough of moral and intellectual harm, with scribbling sketches for magazines" (MS, Houghton Library, Harvard University). From Curtis' point of view, such a writer would perforce have been a "disembodied intelligence."

so that when I read in the papers about a suppressed novel of his, I stoutly denied that there ever had been such a one. And it is amazing how any one should know it, is it not? If it does not equal his later works, and can do him no honor, I could wish there were no traces of it on the earth.[27]

Her wish was effective during most of her lifetime. But by October, 1870, two years after she had gone abroad to live, news of *Fanshawe* was stirring again. The *Boston Daily Advertiser* on October 4, 1870, noted that the editors of the *Williams* [College] *Review* had announced in their latest issue that they had got hold of and were going to print the Bowdoin "commencement parts" of Hawthorne, Longfellow, Pierce, and W. P. Fessenden, and further that "the wish is expressed that Hawthorne's juvenile novel, which the author destroyed after it was printed, might be discovered somewhere; but there is probably not a copy in existence."[28] Now, the editors of the *Review* were wrong; for the pieces they had were Latin exercises. (Hawthorne's was duly published in the October, 1870, issue of the *Review*.)[29] More important, the *Review* contains no reference to Hawthorne's "juvenile novel." So that the *Fanshawe* mystery is compounded. We have not been able to discover who was responsible for the newspaper note on *Fanshawe*, with the inference (however ambiguous) that it was part of the *Review* announcement. In any case, the *Advertiser* for October 11 stated that there were at least two copies of the novel in existence (was one of these Fields's?) and noted that Curtis had discussed it in the *North American Review* "six years ago"; in addition, a transcript of the *Fanshawe* title page was given.[30] Then on

[27] MS, Boston Public Library. That Mrs. Hawthorne learned about *Fanshawe* from "the papers" may indicate that she had read not the Curtis essay but a newspaper account of it, although we have found no such report.

[28] October 4, 1870, p. 2, col. 2.

[29] The brief composition (MS, Bowdoin College) is also printed as an appendix to Lathrop's *Study of Hawthorne*, p. 338.

[30] October 11, 1870, p. 2, col. 3.

October 15 came Nahum Capen's letter to the *Advertiser*, quoted above.

The flurry in the Boston newspaper seems to have alerted Fields. Perhaps it even precipitated his February, 1871, *Atlantic Monthly* "Our Whispering Gallery" essay on Hawthorne. For he made inquiry of Elizabeth Hawthorne concerning her brother's early work—an inquiry which resulted in her letter to him, December 13-16, 1870, followed by another letter, January 28, 1871, in which she corrected him in some details of his *Atlantic* essay. His main error was to have put the publication of *Fanshawe* in 1832, she said.[31] And it is a curious error, since Fields had a copy of the book and moreover was likely a reader of the *Advertiser*. His imprecise knowledge of *Fanshawe* is all the more puzzling because in the "Whispering Gallery" essay he recalled that Hawthorne spoke to him of *Fanshawe* "with great disgust," and that later, in answer to his query concerning an early novel about which he had heard, Hawthorne sent him the 1851 letter which began, "You make an inquiry. . . ."[32]

Thenceforth *Fanshawe* was mentioned regularly in accounts of Hawthorne, but until its republication in 1876 (some four years after Mrs. Hawthorne's death abroad) information about it derived from Fields's essay.[33] The novel was republished initially in both the Little Classics Edition and the Illustrated Library Edition of Hawthorne's works. Reviewing it in the *New York Daily Tribune*, Bayard Taylor could say only that it "is a work which derives its interest wholly from its author's later masterpieces. It has the slightest possible plot, the characters are imperfectly presented, the

[31] See note 13.

[32] *Atlantic Monthly*, XXVII (February, 1871), 248-49.

[33] See, for example, H. A. Page (pseud. of Alexander Japp), *Memoir of Nathaniel Hawthorne* (London, 1872), pp. 15-16; R. H. Stoddard, "Nathaniel Hawthorne," *Harper's Monthly*, XLV (October, 1872), 689; "Hawthorne," *The American Cyclopaedia* (New York, 1873-76), VIII, 535.

descriptions are commonplace to the verge of tameness, yet one who reads the story carefully will easily detect the weak and timid presence of all Hawthorne's peculiar powers."[34] And this is the tack which serious readers of *Fanshawe* have taken ever since, in order to remain serious. But the novel may be read as Hawthorne's attempt, at the outset of his career, to write for a popular audience—a calculated attempt to assume a role he later came so heartily to damn. His son-in-law George Parsons Lathrop was perhaps too much under his spell to say just this. Nonetheless, Lathrop's estimate of *Fanshawe* (at the end flatly contradicting Curtis' opinion of its place in Hawthorne's work) is juster than he knew.

> What separates [*Fanshawe*] from the rest of Hawthorne's works is an intricate plot, with passages of open humor, and a rather melodramatic tone in the conclusion. These are the result in part of the prevalent fashion of romance, and in part of a desire to produce effects not quite consonant with his native bent.[35]

R. H. P.

[34] July 7, 1876, p. 6, col. 1. The republished *Fanshawe* was reviewed that year in: *Boston Evening Transcript*, June 21; *Boston Daily Advertiser*, June 30; *Literary World*, VII (July 1, 1876), 19-20; *Connecticut Courant*, July 6, Supplement; *New Haven Morning Journal and Courier*, July 8; *New Haven Daily Palladium*, July 8; *Hartford Daily Courant*, July 12; *Independent*, XVIII (July 13, 1876), 11; *Springfield Daily Union*, July 13; *New York Times*, July 22; *Appleton's Journal*, n. s. I (August, 1876), 190. The comments on *Fanshawe*, usually coupled with discussion of *The Dolliver Romance* and miscellaneous pieces published at the same time, expressed opinions generally akin to Taylor's. Reviewers were on the whole unhappy about, but not surprised by, *Fanshawe*.

[35] *Op. cit.*, p. 131. Julian Hawthorne's characteristically self-indulgent anger at his brother-in-law Lathrop's book (see their exchange of letters in the *New York Daily Tribune*, July 8 and July 15, 1876) seems to involve, among many other things, Lathrop's having used private family papers to work out the story of the original publication of *Fanshawe*.
   In noticing the several works published in 1876, *Appleton's Journal* (see note 34) opened up another mystery. The anonymous reviewer wrote: "Perhaps not the least enjoyable of these works of Hawthorne's will be found in the two volumes of miscellaneous pieces which the fastidious author had suppressed and forgotten, and for the resurrection of which we are indebted, it is said, to the indefatigable researches of the late Mr. J. E. Babson." Babson (1830-75) was a minor essayist, litterateur, and bibliophile known in Boston by his occasional penname, Tom Folio. His precise connection with the republication of *Fanshawe* is yet to be discovered.

TEXTUAL INTRODUCTION: *FANSHAWE*

THE FIRST EDITION of *Fanshawe,* printed by Putnam and Hunt, was published, probably by the last week of October, 1828, by Marsh and Capen, 362 Washington Street, Boston. This firm had copyrighted the book at the District Clerk's Office on July 22. In 1871, Capen stated orally that 1,000 copies had been printed. The book collates, 12°: 1-12⁶; 172 leaves ($1, 3 signed), pp. [1-3] 4-141 [142-144]. The title page is on p. 1 and the copyright notice on p. 2. The text begins on p. 3 and concludes on p. 141 with an appended errata list headed: "The author requests the reader's favourable construction of several errors, chiefly of orthography and punctuation, which have escaped the press. The following affect the sense." Five items are listed for correction. Pages 142-44 are blank.

The characteristics of the documentary form of the first edition of 1828 (I) have been established for the purposes of the present edition by collation of the following five copies: Ohio State University, University of Virginia, Library of Congress, Yale University, and Huntington Library. In addition, eleven copies have been spot-checked by mail: Boston Athenaeum, Boston Public Library, British Museum, University of Buffalo, Harvard University, Morgan Library, Berg Collection of the New York Public Library (2), St.

Lawrence University, and University of Texas (2). Owing to the scarcity of this book, it proved impossible to assemble more than the Ohio State University and the University of Virginia copies for comparison on the Hinman Collating Machine; the other copies were collated by hand from photographic reproductions.

Only two minor variants, caused by dropped types, were discovered:

33.19	from	ViU
	rom	OU
52.34	has	OU
	ha	ViU

The binding up of the sheets with these variants produced four states of the book: *from-has, from-ha, rom-has, rom-ha*.[1]

Two non-textual differences between the University of Virginia and the Ohio State University copies have been noted. At 10.18–19 there is double spacing between the lines in ViU but single spacing in OU. At 102, lines 10–11, 13–14 are reset without textual change.

Two separate editions in different typesettings were published by James R. Osgood and Company in 1876. The first was *Fanshawe and Other Pieces*, which includes five "Biographical Sketches" with the romance. This edition (II[a]) is dated May 27 in the Cost Books and was printed in the format of the 1865 collected edition. For the Illustrated Library Edition these same plates were used in another combination (II[b]), dated September 12, 1876, in Osgood's Cost Books: *Fanshawe, The Dolliver Romance, and Other Pieces*. Machine collation of copies of the II[a] and II[b] printings in the Ohio State University Libraries discloses no alterations in the plates. The next edition (III), dated from August to September 1 in the Cost Books, was published also in

[1] See Matthew J. Bruccoli, "States of *Fanshawe*," *Papers of the Bibliographical Society of America*, LVIII (First Quarter, 1964), 32.

1876 by Osgood in the Little Classics series. The Riverside Edition of 1883 (IV) and the Autograph of 1900 (V) complete the list of collected editions that have been collated and their variants recorded for the Centenary text. No edition after the first has authority. The manuscript has not been preserved.

That more than one compositor set the 1828 first edition of *Fanshawe* is obvious from the variable spelling, capitalization, punctuation, and word-division characteristics found systematically in different groups of pages. Such marked differences are less unusual in early nineteenth-century American printing than later, when the enforcement of a printing-house style had an almost universal tendency among professional workmen to smooth out the texture of the original manuscript, or of individual compositors' anomalies in usage, and to impose what is often a completely uniform pattern. Thus compared with Metcalf and Co., the printers of *The Scarlet Letter* (1850), or Hobart and Robbins who printed *The House of the Seven Gables* (1851) and *The Blithedale Romance* (1852), Putnam and Hunt appear to have been little concerned with house-styling.

A rather considerable reconstruction of the stints of the five compositors who appear to have worked on *Fanshawe* is possible, therefore, from the evidence of their varying usage. No two workmen differ from each other in every respect in the evidence noticed. Moreover, the significant points of variance do not occur in the stints of every one of the compositors. Nevertheless, by observing the different combinations of twelve pieces of evidence selected as representing the general stylistic practice of an individual workman, but in each of which at least one other workman differs, some specific conjectures may be made despite the dearth of Hawthorne manuscripts from this period that would have assisted in identifying variants stemming from Hawthorne's own irregularities.

The main evidence is confined to nine spelling, capitalization, or punctuation variables: the ending of words in "-or" or in "-our", the spelling "gray" or "grey", the doublets "Doctor-doctor", "Widow-widow", "Dame-dame", "Master-master", "Inn-inn", "Heaven-heaven", and the presence or absence of quotation marks surrounding the epigraphs for each chapter. Occasional reference is made to the use of dashes at the end of sentences in narrative prose to justify the lines to the right margin. Some use can be made, also, of two particular anomalies in the placement of a final quotation mark in relation to other punctuation.

In the following account the page numbers refer to the pages of the first edition of 1828. The equation of these pages with the Centenary text will be found in an appendix.

Compositor A started the text with page 3 and composed pages 3-26, and possibly 27-30, either working alone or just possibly in some unknown combination with Compositor B. His next stint, which was his last, comprised pages 84-89, although he may have started with page 83. Compositor A never deviates from the "-or" ending. Thus we find forms of "honor", "favor", "neighbor" (page 4), "inferior" (5), "labor", "endeavor" (6), "parlor" (7), "favor" (10-12, 14), "labor" (15-16), "favor" (16-18), "endeavor" (19), "labor" (22), "endeavor" (24), "neighbor" (27), "parlor" (30), "favor" (84), "endeavor" (89). His spelling is always "gray" (19, 84, 87).

"Doctor" whether occurring alone or in "Doctor Melmoth" is capitalized without exception (5-8, 10-14, 17, 23, 30, 84-86). "Master" followed by a name is also capitalized on page 86, and one may note "Merchant Langton" on page 85. The titles accorded women, however, are invariably set without capitalization, as in "widow" (84-85) and "dame Crombie" (86). We find "inn" on page 4 but capitalized on page 85 in the conventional phrase "Hugh Crombie's Inn". "Heaven" is consistently capitalized (16, 21, 88). On the two occasions

(20, 89) when a semicolon occurs after a section of dialogue, the quotation mark is placed after the semicolon ($\sim$; ' $\sim$). These are the only two appearances of such usage in *Fanshawe* and they serve very neatly to link the two stints together. Correspondingly, in the two instances where a section of dialogue ends with a broken-off sentence marked by a dash, Compositor A sets the quotation mark and then a short dash. In the first instance (26) the quotation mark follows the final word without other punctuation ($\sim$ $_\wedge$ ' —), but in the second (88) a comma intervenes ($\sim$,' —). In his stints he does not use a justifying dash at the end of a line between sentences of narrative prose.

Since pages 27-30 contain only "neighbor" (27), "parlor" (30), and "Doctor Melmoth" (30), which are characteristics shared by Compositors A and B, no definite assignment can be made as between the two workmen.

Compositor B's identifiable stint begins with page 31 and continues to 41, resuming at page 45 to continue as far as 50, although perhaps not finishing until 53. Compositor B consistently uses "-or" forms: "vapor" (31), "endeavor" (32, 35), "neighbor" (38), "favor" (38, 40, 46). In contrast to A, he prefers the "grey" spelling (31, 41). "Doctor" is capitalized (32, 33). "Master" does not occur in his pages, but "Widow" is capitalized (45, 48) and "Dame Crombie" is set on page 47. "Inn" is also capitalized (37, 45, 47). On the contrary, "heaven" begins with lower-case (45). Compositor B does not use justifying dashes. On page 50 he sets "shew", and on page 48 "stedfastly".

The assignment to B of pages 51-53 is not inconsistent with his known characteristics in so far as there is evidence in "Widow" (52) and "favor" (53). On page 51 and again on 53 a broken-off sentence in dialogue ends with a period, followed by the quotation mark, and then a short dash ($\sim$. ' —). Whether this is a B usage cannot be known, for nowhere else in B's pages does another such sentence occur. Since these pages immediately follow a known B sequence, however, and are not inconsistent with his other characteristics, they may be conjecturally assigned to him.

In the sequence 3-30 the only compositorial evidence for a number of pages is the use of "-or" endings or of capitalized "Doctor", both of which are characteristics common to A and B. The possibility exists, therefore, that this set of pages might actually have been composed in alternating stints by the two compositors. But unless more refined evidence can be developed, this possibility must remain only a matter of conjecture. It is not necessarily significant that there are three different forms "sea-port" (6), "seaport" (11), and "sea port" (27), although something may be said for a connection between "Spring" on B's page 40 and "Spring and Summer" (15) in A's presumed stint since these are the only examples in *Fanshawe* of the capitalization of the seasons.[2] At the least, certain pages may be distinguished positively as A's whenever the characteristics of the two men are at odds. Thus there is no question that Compositor A set pages 16 ("Heaven"), 19 ("gray"), 20 (~ ;), and 21 ("Heaven"). If B did indeed set pages 51-53, then A doubtless set page 26 (~ ∧ '—). On the other hand, no identifiable B stylistic practices differing from A's are to be seen in pages 3-30.

Compositor C's identifiable work comes, oddly, only in three short stints of three pages each, in 42-44, 54-56, and 62-64. Although C agrees with A and B in ending words with "-or" ("honor", 42; "demeanor", 42; "honor", 64) and in capitalizing "Doctor" (55, 62, 63, 64), he differs from B

---

[2] The doubtful value of such isolated evidence from analogy, however, may be seen by comparing B's capitalized "Landlord" (38) with "Landlord" on page 85 of A's established sequence (the only capitalizations in *Fanshawe* of this common word). The evidence is apparently not reversible. Since "Spring" appears on page 40, B's "grey" on page 41, and C starts his three pages with page 42, no A sequence in B's pages 31-41 can be conjectured here.

in "inn" (42, 43, 54, 56, 63) and in "gray" (64). The distinction between C and A is less clear-cut. Both share "-or", "Doctor", and "gray". Compositor A's true preference for "inn" or for "Inn" is in doubt, but in contrast to "Crombie's Inn" on A's page 85, we have in C "Crombie's inn" on pages 56 and 63. A justifying dash, not known in A's work, appears on page 63. When on page 64 a broken-off dialogue requires a quotation mark and dash, the quotation mark follows a long dash (~ —'), instead of preceding a short one. It may perhaps be worthy of some notice that the only appearance in *Fanshawe* of Hawthorne's characteristic hyphen in a tree name comes in "elm-tree" on C's page 43, in contrast to A's "birch tree" (21), "oak tree" (26), and "elm tree" (85). On page 42 C sets "sabbath" and on page 62 "President" as against A's "Sabbath" (13) and "president" (5). However, the most striking, and indeed the really decisive difference comes in C's capitalization of "Widow" (43, 44) and of "Dame" (64) as against A's firm use of lower-case. It is clear that C is a separate workman and is not to be confused either with A or with B.

In C's work an error occurs that interestingly reveals one small detail about the manuscript. On page 44 appears the phrase "the Sun", which is corrected in the errata-list to "an Inn". We may accept the errata-list evidence that the intended article is "an" and not "the", and thus put "the" down to a compositorial sophistication required by his misreading of "Inn" as "Sun". But what is of interest is the fact that "inn" with a lower-case "i" in the manuscript could not be mistaken for an "s", let alone a capital "S", whereas an ill-formed capital "I" could be so mistaken. On this evidence, it seems clear that, assuming Hawthorne's consistency, Compositor A (once), B, and E were following copy in setting "Inn", whereas C and D were imposing their own style on the manuscript with lower-case "inn".

The only other characteristic of C's style that needs mention is his use of italic for the foreign phrase *en masse,* which is consistent with the italic of *lusus naturæ* on page 126 conjecturally assigned to D, and contrasts with the quotation marks about the roman settings of foreign phrases on pages 11 (A), 127 (unassigned), and 135 (unassigned).

Compositor D identifiably set pages 57-61, 65-82 (and perhaps 83), and 97-106. Alone among the four workmen, he put quotation marks about some epigraphs, specifically those heading Chapters VII and VIII (82, 104) though not the epigraph heading Chapter VI (73). He is unique, as well, in his almost invariable setting of "doctor" with a lower-case "d" (65, 66, 68, 69, 73-81, 97, 98, 103, 106), since "Doctor" appears only in the first line of page 65. His use of lower-case for titles is generally uniform: unlike A he sets "master" (61, 71, 72) although "Master" also occurs on page 61; like A he sets "widow" (58) and "dame" (57, 65, 66). He also prefers the "-or" ending ("endeavor", 69-70; "demeanor", 70; "parlor", 73-74; "endeavor", 77; "color", 101; "endeavor", 102), although "neighbour" is found on page 68, "parlour" on page 71, and "honour" on page 97. He is consistent in the form "inn" (58, 59, 66, 69, 70, 81, 99, 103, 106), and in "heaven" (57, 59, 72, 77, 79). "Gray-grey" does not occur in his stints. He uses a justifying dash on pages 66, 76, and 98. On pages 80, 81, and 101 he ends a broken-off dialogue sentence with no terminal punctuation other than a short dash followed by a quotation mark ($\sim$ $_\wedge$ $-$'). He spells "centre" on page 67 (according to Hawthorne's own style) but "centered" on page 106. When a short dash precedes the start of a sentence of dialogue within quotation marks, he has some tendency (unlike the other compositors) to omit punctuation before the dash (67, 78, 79, 103) as $\sim$ $_\wedge$ $-$'$\sim$ . . . instead of $\sim$,$-$'$\sim$. . . .

Compositor E identifiably set pages 90-96 and 107-17,

perhaps extending to 118-19. His most distinctive stylistic feature is his unique preference for "-our" endings ("ardour", 90; "endeavour", 92, 95; "demeanour", 94, 95; "endeavour", 109, 111; "demeanour", 113; "endeavour", 117) although he also sets "color" (90), "endeavor" (94), and "demeanor" (113). For the rest, in so far as other evidence appears, he spells "grey" (92, 94, 109, 116), and he capitalizes "Doctor" (91-96, 107, 108), "Widow" (90), "Inn" (108), and "Heaven" (92, 108, 115). Alone among the compositors he follows Hawthorne's style in setting "tomorrow" without a hyphen (111). "Recognise" occurs on page 110; he uses "Dr." once (93). The spelling "steadfast" occurs on page 94. Although his clearly identifiable second stint ends with page 117, on which appears "endeavour", it is possible that he also set pages 118-19. Page 120 with "heaven" is not likely to be his. Thus there may be some significance to the use of lower-case "n" in "nature" on page 119 as against the capitalized "Nature" found on page 123.

After page 119 the paucity of the stylistic evidence established as significant makes the development of any series of stints highly conjectural. Such evidence as there is suggests that Compositors D and E alternated or set simultaneously in short sequences up to the end of the book. In the analysis of the evidence that follows, it must be freely admitted that various of the characteristics cited might belong to A, B, or C. However, only for D and E do these minor pieces of evidence cohere to form any probable stints. We cannot suppose that all the compositors flung themselves upon this book after page 119, setting a page or two at random.

We may conjecture the setting of pages 120-26 by Compositor D on the basis of "heaven" (120, 124), and the relation of the quotation mark to the dash on page 126 ($\sim$ $_\wedge$ '$-$). Pages 127-28 are indifferent. It is true that the italicizing of the phrase *lusus naturæ* on page 125 contrasts with the use of single quotation marks about roman 'auri sacra fames' on page 127, but it is difficult to determine whether the fact is significant that the first appears in narrative and the second in dialogue. Compositor E may have set pages 129-30, on the evidence of "grey" (129) and "Heaven" (130). Yet "heaven" also appears on page 130, and the justifying dash on page 129 might suggest D. Since we do not know D's preferences in "gray-grey," it is not beyond possibility that D's stint stretched from 120 at least as far as 130. On the other hand, if E set these pages he very likely did not set page 134, with "gray". It is probably safer to keep to the known association of E with "grey" and to conjecture that D was a "gray" speller.

Pages 131 and 132 contain no identifiable evidence, but page 133 may be associated with D on the strength of "Widow Butler" and "Doctor Melmoth". If so, page 134 must follow 133 in D's stint. Page 135 has the quoted phrase 'quid pro quo' set in roman and occurring in narrative. Whether a connection can be established between this and the similarly quoted phrase in dialogue on page 127 is not to be determined. With page 136 containing "favoured" we seem to be firmly established with Compositor E, and "Heaven" on page 137 would suggest a sequence set by him. If page 139 is to be assigned conjecturally to D on the evidence of its "heaven", then the two occurrences on page 138 of broken-off dialogue with a quotation mark and short dash ($\sim$ $_\wedge$ '$-$) may prove to be significant as evidence for D's setting of pages 138-39. "Ardour" and "grey" on page 140 suggest that we are back with E; and we may note "favourable" in the errata instructions on page 141, although "heaven" in lower-case on the same page is anomalous in his setting.

For convenience of reference a chart of the major evidence utilized for the compositorial analysis is herewith appended, together with a chart of the conjectural page assignments.

COMPOSITORS

A	B	C	D	E
–or	–or	–or	–or/–our	–our/–or
gray	grey	gray	gray [?]	grey
Doctor	Doctor	Doctor	doctor	Doctor
Master	?	?	master	?
widow + name	Widow	Widow	widow	Widow
dame + name	Dame	?	dame	?
Inn/inn	Inn	inn	inn	Inn
Heaven	heaven	?	heaven	Heaven
~ ;'	?	?	?	?
~ ,'— ~ ‸ '—	~ .'— [?]	~ ‸ —'	~ ‸ —'	?
no justifying dashes	no	yes	yes	no
no quotation marks in epigraph	no	no	yes	?

CONJECTURAL ASSIGNMENT OF PAGES

A	B	C	B
⌈3–26 [27–30?]⌉	⌈[27–30?] 31–41⌉	⌈42–44⌉	⌈45–50⌉
B[?]	C	D	C
⌈51–53⌉	⌈54–56⌉	⌈57–61⌉	⌈62–64⌉
D	A	E	D
⌈65–82 [83?]⌉	⌈[83?] 84–89⌉	⌈90–96⌉	⌈97–106⌉
E	D[?]	[?]	E[?]
⌈107–17 [118–19?]⌉	⌈120–26⌉	⌈127–28⌉	⌈129–30⌉
[?]	D[?]	[?]	E[?]
⌈131–32⌉	⌈133–34⌉	⌈135⌉	⌈136–37⌉
	D[?]	E[?]	
	⌈138–39⌉	⌈140–41⌉	

When, as in *Fanshawe* or *The Scarlet Letter,* a Hawthorne first edition is the authority in the absence of a preserved manuscript, the house-styled accidentals (spelling, punctuation, capitalization, and word-division) must be thought of, in considerable part, as authoritative, in the sense that they constitute the evidence of the only documentary authority that exists for this particular work. Hence, when the print is consistent, as with the supplementary syntactical commas in parenthetical dash constructions in *The Scarlet Letter*, the knowledge that the lost manuscript would not have agreed cannot permit editorial emendation that would remove them. Any student of Hawthorne's manuscripts could in many respects restyle various of such first editions to enforce agreement with what clearly must have been a different manuscript usage. But no consistency is possible in a process like this, for only a part of the accidentals are susceptible of alteration with such certainty. A few notable and invariable Hawthorne characteristics might be emended, but much of the ordinary punctuation, for instance, could never be definitely distinguished as compositorial or authorial. Thus all internally consistent features of a first-edition copy-text must be retained in default of the evidence of its lost manuscript.

The case is altered, however, when the printed copy-text is not itself consistent, either because of compositorial slips or because of variable usage among the different compositors who set the book. Although in *The Scarlet Letter* different compositors rigidly followed house-style in what words were to be set with final "-or" and what with final "-our", for example, *Fanshawe* is by no means consistent in this or in many other matters affecting the accidentals and their forms. The bibliographical investigation that divides the book into typesetting by five compositors reveals that what we may suppose to have been the relatively consistent characteristics of the manuscript have been followed in different ways by the various workmen. Two, three, or four of them may agree in reproducing a known Hawthorne characteristic; on the other hand, four of them (as with the lack of hyphenation in tree names) may deal with some authorial usage after their own style, whereas only one may reproduce what the manuscript form almost certainly was.

Under these circumstances no one can defend the proposition that every such variable in the first edition of *Fanshawe* has other than technical authority. It follows that when variation is present, and when some one form can be established from manuscript (even though later) as representing Hawthorne's known characteristic, without ever forsaking documentary authority in the print an editor can go a long way by emendation of non-characteristic variants toward reconstructing with confidence some authentic feature of the lost manuscript. That is, when some one or more compositors in *Fanshawe* reproduce what can be determined from manuscripts to be a Hawthorne accidentals form (like "tomorrow" versus "to-morrow", or "aye" versus "ay"), this form is adopted throughout the Centenary text without regard for differences in the work of the other compositors. In this manner the edited text can actually be more authoritative in a number of details than the variable first edition, but never without reference to some authoritative reading within that edition. On the other hand, when all compositors are uniform, no authority exists within the print to justify emendation of the texture of the accidentals; and the first edition, the only documentary authority there is, has been faithfully followed without regard for its agreement or non-agreement with ascertained Hawthorne usage.

The Centenary text, therefore, represents a synthesis of first-edition documentary authority and is more faithful to what we may be sure were the characteristics of the lost manuscript of *Fanshawe* than is the first edition after each of the five compositors had altered the manuscript copy according to his own different ideas of styling. All such reconstructed emendations have been recorded so that a critic can always return to the exact form of the copy-text, except for such normalized typographical details as the length of dashes. The few abbreviations "Dr." and "Rev." have been silently expanded. In the present text, for uniformity with other volumes, the forms of chapter headings which in the print are "CHAPTER I." and so on have been normalized simply to the numeral "I".

F. B.

FANSHAWE

1

Our court shall be a little academy.
SHAKSPEARE

I N AN ANCIENT, though not very populous settlement, in a retired corner of one of the New-England States, arise the walls of a seminary of learning, which, for the convenience of a name, shall be entitled 'Harley College.' This institution, though the number of its years is inconsiderable, compared with the hoar antiquity of its European sisters, is not without some claims to reverence on the score of age; for an almost countless multitude of rivals, by many of which its reputation has been eclipsed, have sprung up since its foundation. At no time, indeed, during an existence of nearly a century, has it acquired a very extensive fame, and circumstances, which need not be particularized, have of late years involved it in a deeper obscurity. There are now few candidates for the degrees that the College is authorized to bestow. On two of its annual 'Commencement days,' there has been a total deficiency of Baccalaureates; and the lawyers and divines, on whom Doctorates in their respective professions are gratuitously inflicted, are not accustomed to consider the distinction as an honor. Yet the sons of this seminary have always maintained their full share of reputation, in whatever paths of life they trod. Few of them, perhaps, have been deep and finished scholars; but the College has supplied—what the emergencies of the country demanded—a set of men more useful in its present state, and whose deficiency in theoretical knowledge has not been found to imply a want of practical ability.

The local situation of the College, so far secluded from the sight and sound of the busy world, is peculiarly favorable to the moral, if not to the literary habits of its students; and this advantage probably caused the founders to overlook the inconveniences that were inseparably connected with it. The humble edifices rear themselves almost at the farthest extremity of a narrow vale, which, winding through a long extent of hill-country, is well nigh as inaccessible, except at one point, as the Happy Valley of Abyssinia. A stream, that farther on becomes a considerable river, takes its rise at a short distance above the College, and affords, along its wood-fringed banks, many shady retreats, where even study is pleasant, and idleness delicious. The neighborhood of the institution is not quite a solitude, though the few habitations scarcely constitute a village. These consist principally of farm-houses—of rather an ancient date, for the settlement is much older than the College—and of a little Inn, which, even in that secluded spot, does not fail of a moderate support. Other dwellings are scattered up and down the valley; but the difficulties of the soil will long avert the evils of a too dense population. The character of the inhabitants does not seem—as there was perhaps room to anticipate—to be in any degree influenced by the atmosphere of Harley College. They are a set of rough and hardy yeomen, much inferior, as respects refinement, to the corresponding classes in most other parts of our country. This is the more remarkable, as there is scarcely a family in the vicinity that has not provided, for at least one of its sons, the advantages of a 'liberal education.'

Having thus described the present state of Harley College, we must proceed to speak of it as it existed about eighty years since, when its foundation was recent and its prospects flattering. At the head of the institution, at this period, was a learned and orthodox Divine, whose fame was in all the churches. He was the author of several works which evinced much erudition and depth of research; and the public perhaps thought the more highly of his abilities from a singularity in the purposes to which he applied them, that added much to the curiosity of his labors, though little to their usefulness. But however fanciful might be his private pursuits, Doctor Melmoth, it was universally allowed, was diligent and successful in the arts of instruction. The young men of his charge prospered beneath his eye, and regarded him with an affection, that was strengthened by the little foibles which occasionally excited their ridicule. The President was assisted in the discharge of his duties by two inferior officers, chosen from the Alumni of the College, who, while they imparted to others the knowledge they had already imbibed, pursued the study of Divinity under the direction of their principal. Under such auspices the institution grew and flourished. Having at that time but two rivals in the country, (neither of them within a considerable distance,) it became the general resort of the youth of the province in which it was situated. For several years in succession, its students amounted to nearly fifty—a number which, relatively to the circumstances of the country, was very considerable.

From the exterior of the Collegians, an accurate observer might pretty safely judge how long they had been inmates of those classic walls. The brown cheeks and the rustic dress of some would inform him that they had but recently left the plough, to labor in a not less toilsome field. The grave look and the intermingling of garments of a more classic cut, would distinguish those who had begun to acquire the polish of their new residence;—and the air of superiority, the paler cheek, the less robust form, the spectacles of green, and the dress in general of threadbare black, would designate the highest class, who were understood to have acquired nearly all the science their Alma Mater could bestow, and to be on the point of assuming their stations in the world. There were, it is true, exceptions to this general description. A few young men had found their way hither from the distant sea-ports; and these were the models of fashion to their rustic companions, over whom they asserted a superiority in exterior accomplishments, which the fresh though unpolished intellect of the sons of the forest denied them in their literary competitions. A third class, differing widely from both the former, consisted of a few young descendants of the aborigines, to whom an impracticable philanthropy was endeavoring to impart the benefits of civilization.

If this institution did not offer all the advantages of elder and prouder seminaries, its deficiencies were compensated to its students by the inculcation of regular habits, and of a deep and awful sense of religion, which seldom deserted them in their course through life. The mild and gentle rule of Doctor Melmoth, like that of a father over his children, was more destructive to vice than a sterner sway; and though youth is never without its follies, they have seldom been more harmless than they were here. The students, indeed, ignorant of their own bliss, sometimes wished to hasten the time of their entrance on the business of life; but they found, in after years, that many of their happiest remembrances—many of the scenes which they would with least reluctance live over again—referred to the seat of their early studies. The exceptions to this remark were chiefly those whose vices had drawn down, even from that paternal government, a weighty retribution.

Doctor Melmoth, at the time when he is to be introduced to the reader, had borne the matrimonial yoke (and in his case it was no light burthen) nearly twenty years. The blessing of children, however, had been denied him—a circumstance which he was accustomed to consider as one of the sorest trials that chequered his path-way; for he was a man of a kind and affectionate heart, that was continually seeking objects to rest itself upon. He was inclined to believe, also, that a common offspring would have exerted a meliorating influence on the temper of Mrs. Melmoth, the character of whose domestic government often compelled him to call to mind such portions of the wisdom of antiquity, as relate to the proper endurance of the shrewishness of woman. But domestic comforts, as well as comforts of every other kind, have their draw-backs; and so long as the balance is on the side of happiness, a wise man will not murmur. Such was the opinion of Doctor Melmoth; and with a little aid from philosophy and more from religion, he journeyed on contentedly through life. When the storm was loud by the parlor hearth, he had always a sure and quiet retreat in his study, and there, in his deep though not always useful labors, he soon forgot whatever of disagreeable nature pertained to his situation. This small and dark apartment was the only portion of the house, to which, since one firmly repelled invasion, Mrs. Melmoth's omnipotence did not extend. Here (to reverse the words of Queen Elizabeth) there was 'but one Master and no Mistress'; and that man has little right to complain who possesses so much as one corner in the world, where he may be happy or miserable, as best suits him. In his study, then, the Doctor was accustomed to spend most of the hours that were unoccupied by the duties of his station. The flight of time was here as swift as the wind, and noiseless as the snow-flake; and it was a sure proof of real happiness, that night often came upon the student, before he knew it was mid-day.

Doctor Melmoth was wearing towards age, having lived nearly sixty years, when he was called upon to assume a character, to which he had as yet been a stranger. He had possessed, in his youth, a very dear friend, with whom his education had associated him, and who, in his early manhood, had been his chief intimate. Circumstances, however, had separated them for nearly thirty years, half of which had been spent by his friend, who was engaged in mercantile pursuits, in a foreign country. The Doctor had nevertheless retained a warm interest in the welfare of his old associate, though the different nature of their thoughts and occupations had prevented them from corresponding. After a silence of so long continuance, therefore, he was surprised by the receipt of a letter from his friend, containing a request of a most unexpected nature.

Mr. Langton had married rather late in life, and his wedded bliss had been but of short continuance. Certain misfortunes in trade, when he was a Benedict of three years standing, had deprived him of a large portion of his property, and compelled him, in order to save the remainder, to leave his own country for what he hoped would be but a brief residence in another. But though he was successful in the immediate objects of his voyage, circumstances occurred to lengthen his stay far beyond the period which he had assigned to it. It was difficult so to arrange his extensive concerns, that they could be safely trusted to the management of others; and when this was effected, there was another not less powerful obstacle to his return. His affairs, under his own inspection, were so prosperous, and his gains so considerable, that, in the words of the old ballad, 'He set his heart to gather gold,' and to this absorbing passion he sacrificed his domestic happiness. The death of his wife, about four years after his departure, undoubtedly contributed to give him a sort of dread of returning, which it required a strong effort to overcome. The welfare of his only child he knew would be little affected by this event; for she was under the protection of his sister, of whose tenderness he was well assured. But, after a few more years, this sister, also, was taken away by death; and then the father felt that duty imperatively called upon him to return. He realized, on a sudden, how much of life he had thrown away in the acquisition of what is only valuable as it contributes to the happiness of life, and how short a time was left him for life's true enjoyments. Still, however, his mercantile habits were too deeply seated to allow him to hazard his present prosperity by any hasty measures; nor was Mr. Langton, though capable of strong affections, naturally liable to manifest them violently. It was probable, therefore, that many months might yet elapse, before he would again tread the shores of his native country.

But the distant relative, in whose family, since the death of her aunt, Ellen Langton had remained, had been long at variance with her father, and had unwillingly assumed the office of her protector. Mr. Langton's request, therefore, to Doctor Melmoth, was, that his ancient friend (one of the few friends that time had left him) would be as a father to his daughter, till he could himself relieve him of the charge.

The Doctor, after perusing the epistle of his friend, lost no time in laying it before Mrs. Melmoth, though this was, in truth, one of the very few occasions on which he had determined that his will should be absolute law. The lady was quick to perceive the firmness of his purpose; and would not (even had she been particularly averse to the proposed measure) hazard her usual authority by a fruitless opposition. But, by long disuse, she had lost the power of consenting graciously to any wish of her husband's.

'I see your heart is set upon this matter,' she observed; 'and, in truth, I fear we cannot decently refuse Mr. Langton's request. I see little good of such a friend, Doctor, who never lets one know he is alive, till he has a favor to ask.'

'Nay, but I have received much good at his hand,' replied Doctor Melmoth; 'and if he asked more of me, it should be done with a willing heart. I remember in my youth, when my worldly goods were few and ill-managed, (I was a bachelor, then, dearest Sarah, with none to look after my household,)

how many times I have been beholden to him. And see—in
his letter he speaks of presents, of the produce of the country,
which he has sent both to you and me.'

'If the girl were country-bred,' continued the lady, 'we
might give her house-room, and no harm done. Nay, she
might even be a help to me; for Esther, our maid-servant,
leaves us at the month's end. But I warrant she knows as
little of household matters as you do yourself, Doctor.'

'My friend's sister was well grounded in the *re familiari*,'
answered her husband; 'and doubtless she hath imparted
somewhat of her skill to this damsel. Besides, the child is of
tender years, and will profit much by your instruction and
mine.'

'The child is eighteen years of age, Doctor,' observed Mrs.
Melmoth, 'and she has cause to be thankful that she will have
better instruction than yours.'

This was a proposition that Doctor Melmoth did not choose
to dispute; though he perhaps thought, that his long and
successful experience in the education of the other sex might
make him an able coadjutor to his wife, in the care of
Ellen Langton. He determined to journey in person to the
sea-port, where his young charge resided, leaving the concerns
of Harley College to the direction of the two tutors. Mrs.
Melmoth, who indeed anticipated with pleasure the arrival
of a new subject to her authority, threw no difficulties in the
way of his intention. To do her justice, her preparations for
his journey, and the minute instructions with which she
favored him, were such as only a woman's true affection could
have suggested. The traveller met with no incidents important to this tale; and, after an absence of about a fortnight, he
and Ellen Langton alighted from their steeds (for on horseback had the journey been performed) in safety at his
own door.

If pen could give an adequate idea of Ellen Langton's
loveliness, it would achieve what pencil (the pencils at least

of the Colonial artists who attempted it) never could; for though the dark eyes might be painted, the pure and pleasant thoughts that peeped through them could only be seen and felt. But descriptions of beauty are never satisfactory. It must therefore be left to the imagination of the reader to conceive of something not more than mortal—nor, indeed, quite the perfection of mortality—but charming men the more, because they felt, that, lovely as she was, she was of like nature to themselves.

From the time that Ellen entered Doctor Melmoth's habitation, the sunny days seemed brighter and the cloudy ones less gloomy, than he had ever before known them. He naturally delighted in children; and Ellen, though her years approached to womanhood, had yet much of the gaiety and simple happiness, because the innocence, of a child. She consequently became the very blessing of his life—the rich recreation that he promised himself for hours of literary toil. On one occasion, indeed, he even made her his companion in the sacred retreat of his study, with the purpose of entering upon a course of instruction in the learned languages. This measure, however, he found inexpedient to repeat; for Ellen, having discovered an old romance among his heavy folios, contrived, by the charm of her sweet voice, to engage his attention therein, till all more important concerns were forgotten.

With Mrs. Melmoth, Ellen was not, of course, so great a favorite as with her husband; for women cannot, so readily as men, bestow upon the offspring of others those affections that nature intended for their own; and the Doctor's extraordinary partiality was anything rather than a pledge of his wife's. But Ellen differed so far from the idea she had previously formed of her, as a daughter of one of the principal merchants, who were then, as now, like nobles in the land, that the stock of dislike which Mrs. Melmoth had provided, was found to be totally inapplicable. The young stranger strove so hard, too, (and undoubtedly it was a pleasant labor,) to win her love, that she was successful, to a degree of which the lady herself was not perhaps aware. It was soon seen that her education had not been neglected in those points which Mrs. Melmoth deemed most important. The nicer departments of cookery, after sufficient proof of her skill, were committed to her care; and the Doctor's table was now covered with delicacies, simple indeed, but as tempting on account of their intrinsic excellence as of the small white hands that made them. By such arts as these—which in her were no arts, but the dictates of an affectionate disposition—by making herself useful where it was possible, and agreeable on all occasions, Ellen gained the love of every one within the sphere of her influence.

But the maiden's conquests were not confined to the members of Doctor Melmoth's family. She had numerous admirers among those, whose situation compelled them to stand afar off and gaze upon her loveliness; as if she were a star, whose brightness they saw, but whose warmth they could not feel. These were the young men of Harley College, whose chief opportunities of beholding Ellen were upon the Sabbaths, when she worshipped with them in the little chapel, which served the purposes of a church to all the families of the vicinity. There was, about this period, (and the fact was undoubtedly attributable to Ellen's influence,) a general and very evident decline in the scholarship of the college—especially in regard to the severer studies. The intellectual powers of the young men seemed to be directed chiefly to the construction of Latin and Greek verse, many copies of which, with a characteristic and classic gallantry, were strewn in the path where Ellen Langton was accustomed to walk. They however produced no perceptible effect; nor were the aspirations of another ambitious youth, who celebrated her perfections in Hebrew, attended with their merited success.

But there was one young man, to whom circumstances, independent of his personal advantages, afforded a superior opportunity of gaining Ellen's favor. He was nearly related to Doctor Melmoth, on which account he received his education at Harley College, rather than at one of the English Universities, to the expenses of which his fortune would have been adequate. This connexion entitled him to a frequent and familiar access to the domestic hearth of the dignitary— an advantage of which, since Ellen Langton became a member of the family, he very constantly availed himself.

Edward Walcott was certainly much superior, in most of the particulars of which a lady takes cognizance, to those of his fellow students who had come under Ellen's notice. He was tall, and the natural grace of his manners had been improved (an advantage which few of his associates could boast) by early intercourse with polished society. His features, also, were handsome, and promised to be manly and dignified, when they should cease to be youthful. His character as a scholar was more than respectable, though many youthful follies, sometimes perhaps approaching near to vices, were laid to his charge. But his occasional derelictions from discipline were not such as to create any very serious apprehensions respecting his future welfare; nor were they greater than perhaps might be expected from a young man who possessed a considerable command of money, and who was, besides, the fine gentleman of the little community of which he was a member—a character, which generally leads its possessor into follies that he would otherwise have avoided.

With this youth Ellen Langton became familiar, and even intimate; for he was her only companion, of an age suited to her own, and the difference of sex did not occur to her as an objection. He was her constant companion, on all necessary and allowable occasions, and drew upon himself, in consequence, the envy of the college.

II

Why, all delights are vain, but that most vain,
Which, with pain purchased, doth inherit pain;
  As painfully to pore upon a book,
   To seek the light of truth, while truth the while
Doth falsely blind the eye-sight of his look.

SHAKSPEARE

O N ONE of the afternoons which afforded to the students a relaxation from their usual labors, Ellen was attended by her cavalier in a little excursion over the rough bridle roads that led from her new residence. She was an experienced equestrian—a necessary accomplishment at that period, when vehicles of every kind were rare. It was now the latter end of spring; but the season had hitherto been backward, with only a few warm and pleasant days. The present afternoon, however, was a delicious mingling of Spring and Summer, forming, in their union, an atmosphere so mild and pure, that to breathe was almost a positive happiness. There was a little alternation of cloud across the brow of heaven, but only so much as to render the sunshine more delightful.

The path of the young travellers lay sometimes among tall and thick standing trees, and sometimes over naked and desolate hills, whence man had taken the natural vegetation, and then left the soil to its barrenness. Indeed, there is little inducement to a cultivator to labor among the huge stones, which there peep forth from the earth, seeming to form a continued ledge for several miles. A singular contrast to this unfavored tract of country is seen in the narrow but luxuriant, though sometimes swampy, strip of interval, on both sides of the stream, that, as has been noticed, flows down the valley. The light and buoyant spirits of Edward Walcott and Ellen rose higher as they rode on, and their way was enlivened, wherever its roughness did not forbid, by their conversation and pleasant laughter. But at length Ellen drew her bridle, as they emerged from a thick portion of the forest, just at the foot of a steep hill.

'We must have ridden far,' she observed—'farther than I thought. It will be near sunset before we can reach home.'

'There are still several hours of daylight,' replied Edward Walcott, 'and we will not turn back without ascending this hill. The prospect from the summit is beautiful, and will be particularly so now, in this rich sunlight. Come Ellen—one light touch of the whip:—your pony is as fresh as when we started.'

On reaching the summit of the hill, and looking back in the direction in which they had come, they could see the little stream, peeping forth many times to the daylight, and then shrinking back into the shade. Farther on, it became broad and deep, though rendered incapable of navigation, in this part of its course, by the occasional interruption of rapids.

'There are hidden wonders, of rock, and precipice, and cave, in that dark forest,' said Edward, pointing to the space between them and the river. 'If it were earlier in the day, I should love to lead you there. Shall we try the adventure now, Ellen?'

'Oh, no!' she replied; 'let us delay no longer. I fear I must even now abide a rebuke from Mrs. Melmoth, which I have surely deserved. But who is this, who rides on so slowly before us?'

She pointed to a horseman, whom they had not before observed. He was descending the hill; but, as his steed seemed to have chosen his own pace, he made a very inconsiderable progress.

'Oh! do you not know him?—But it is scarcely possible you

should,' exclaimed her companion. 'We must do him the good office, Ellen, of stopping his progress, or he will find himself at the village, a dozen miles farther on, before he resumes his consciousness.'

'Has he then lost his senses?' inquired Miss Langton.

'Not so, Ellen—if much learning has not made him mad,' replied Edward Walcott. 'He is a deep scholar and a noble fellow, but I fear we shall follow him to his grave, ere long. Doctor Melmoth has sent him to ride in pursuit of his health. He will never overtake it, however, at this pace.'

As he spoke, they had approached close to the subject of their conversation, and Ellen had a moment's space for observation, before he started from the abstraction, in which he was plunged. The result of her scrutiny was favorable, yet very painful.

The stranger could scarcely have attained his twentieth year, and was possessed of a face and form, such as Nature bestows on none but her favorites. There was a nobleness on his high forehead, which time would have deepened into majesty; and all his features were formed with a strength and boldness, of which the paleness, produced by study and confinement, could not deprive them. The expression of his countenance was not a melancholy one;—on the contrary, it was proud and high—perhaps triumphant—like one who was a ruler in a world of his own, and independent of the beings that surrounded him. But a blight, of which his thin, pale cheek and the brightness of his eye were alike proofs, seemed to have come over him ere his maturity.

The scholar's attention was now aroused by the hoof-tramps at his side, and starting, he fixed his eyes on Ellen, whose young and lovely countenance was full of the interest he had excited. A deep blush immediately suffused his cheek, proving how well the glow of health would have become it. There was nothing awkward, however, in his manner; and soon recovering his self-possession, he bowed to her and would have rode on.

'Your ride is unusually long, to-day, Fanshawe,' observed Edward Walcott. 'When may we look for your return?'

The young man again blushed, but answered, with a smile that had a beautiful effect upon his countenance, 'I was not, at the moment, aware in which direction my horse's head was turned. I have to thank you for arresting me in a journey, which was likely to prove much longer than I intended.'

The party had now turned their horses, and were about to resume their ride, in a homeward direction; but Edward perceived that Fanshawe, having lost the excitement of intense thought, now looked weary and dispirited.

'Here is a cottage close at hand,' he observed. 'We have ridden far, and stand in need of refreshment. Ellen, shall we alight?'

She saw the benevolent motive of his proposal, and did not hesitate to comply with it. But as they paused at the cottage door, she could not but observe, that its exterior promised few of the comforts which they required. Time and neglect seemed to have conspired its ruin, and but for a thin curl of smoke from its clay chimney, they could not have believed it to be inhabited. A considerable tract of land, in the vicinity of the cottage, had evidently been, at some former period, under cultivation, but was now overrun by bushes and dwarf pines, among which many huge gray rocks, ineradicable by human art, endeavored to conceal themselves. About half an acre of ground was occupied by the young blades of Indian corn, at which a half-starved cow gazed wistfully, over the mouldering log fence. These were the only agricultural tokens. Edward Walcott nevertheless drew the latch of the cottage door, after knocking loudly, but in vain.

The apartment, which was thus opened to their view, was quite as wretched, as its exterior had given them reason to

anticipate. Poverty was there, with all its necessary, and unnecessary concomitants. The intruders would have retired,
had not the hope of affording relief detained them.

The occupants of the small and squalid apartment were
two women, both of them elderly, and, from the resemblance
of their features, appearing to be sisters. The expression of
their countenances, however, was very different. One, evidently the younger, was seated on the farther side of the large
hearth, opposite to the door, at which the party stood. She
had the sallow look of long and wasting illness, and there
was an unsteadiness of expression about her eyes, that immediately struck the observer. Yet her face was mild and
gentle, therein contrasting widely with that of her companion.

The other woman was bending over a small fire of decayed
branches, the flame of which was very disproportionate to the
smoke, scarcely producing heat sufficient for the preparation
of a scanty portion of food. Her profile, only, was visible to
the strangers, though, from a slight motion of her eye, they
perceived that she was aware of their presence. Her features
were pinched and spare, and wore a look of sullen discontent, for which the evident wretchedness of her situation
afforded a sufficient reason. This female, notwithstanding her
years and the habitual fretfulness, that is more wearing than
time, was apparently healthy and robust, with a dry, leathery
complexion. A short space elapsed before she thought proper
to turn her face towards her visiters, and she then regarded
them with a lowering eye, without speaking or rising from
her chair.

'We entered,' Edward Walcott began to say, 'in the hope';
—but he paused, on perceiving that the sick woman had risen
from her seat, and with slow and tottering footsteps was
drawing near to him. She took his hand in both her own, and,
though he shuddered at the touch of age and disease, he did
not attempt to withdraw it. She then perused all his features,
with an expression at first of eager and hopeful anxiety, which

faded by degrees into disappointment. Then, turning from him, she gazed into Fanshawe's countenance with the like eagerness, but with the same result. Lastly, tottering back to her chair, she hid her face, and wept bitterly. The strangers, though they knew not the cause of her grief, were deeply affected; and Ellen approached the mourner with words of comfort, which, more from their tone than their meaning, produced a transient effect.

'Do you bring news of him?' she inquired, raising her head. 'Will he return to me? Shall I see him before I die?' Ellen knew not what to answer, and ere she could attempt it, the other female prevented her.

'Sister Butler is wandering in her mind,' she said, 'and speaks of one she will never behold again. The sight of strangers disturbs her, and you see we have nothing here to offer you.'

The manner of the woman was ungracious, but her words were true. They saw that their presence could do nothing towards the alleviation of the misery they witnessed, and they felt that mere curiosity would not authorize a longer intrusion. So soon, therefore, as they had relieved, according to their power, the poverty that seemed to be the least evil of this cottage, they emerged into the open air.

The breath of heaven felt sweet to them, and removed a part of the weight from their young hearts, which were saddened by the sight of so much wretchedness. Perceiving a pure and bright little fountain, at a short distance from the cottage, they approached it, and using the bark of a birch-tree as a cup, partook of its cool waters. They then pursued their homeward ride with such diligence, that, just as the sun was setting, they came in sight of the humble wooden edifice, which was dignified with the name of Harley College. A golden ray rested upon the spire of the little chapel, the bell of which sent its tinkling murmur down the valley, to summon the wanderers to evening prayers.

Fanshawe returned to his chamber, that night, and lit his lamp as he had been wont to do. The books were around him, which had hitherto been to him like those fabled volumes of Magic, from which the reader could not turn away his eye, till death were the consequence of his studies. But there were unaccustomed thoughts in his bosom, now; and to these, leaning his head on one of the unopened volumes, he resigned himself.

He called up in review the years, that, even at his early age, he had spent in solitary study—in conversation with the dead—while he had scorned to mingle with the living world, or to be actuated by any of its motives. He asked himself, to what purpose was all this destructive labor, and where was the happiness of superior knowledge? He had climbed but a few steps of a ladder that reached to infinity—he had thrown away his life in discovering, that, after a thousand such lives, he should still know comparatively nothing. He even looked forward with dread—though once the thought had been dear to him—to the eternity of improvement that lay before him. It seemed now a weary way, without a resting place, and without a termination; and, at that moment, he would have preferred the dreamless sleep of the brutes that perish, to man's proudest attribute, of immortality.

Fanshawe had hitherto deemed himself unconnected with the world, unconcerned in its feelings, and uninfluenced by it in any of his pursuits. In this respect he probably deceived himself. If his inmost heart could have been laid open, there would have been discovered that dream of undying fame, which, dream as it is, is more powerful than a thousand realities. But at any rate, he had seemed, to others and to himself, a solitary being, upon whom the hopes and fears of ordinary men were ineffectual.

But now he felt the first thrilling of one of the many ties, that, so long as we breathe the common air (and who shall say how much longer?) unite us to our kind. The sound of a soft, sweet voice—the glance of a gentle eye—had wrought a change upon him, and, in his ardent mind, a few hours had done the work of many. Almost in spite of himself, the new sensation was inexpressibly delightful. The recollection of his ruined health—of his habits, so much at variance with those of the world—all the difficulties that reason suggested— were inadequate to check the exulting tide of hope and joy.

III

And let the aspiring youth beware of love,—
Of the smooth glance, beware; for 'tis too late,
When on his heart the torrent softness pours.
Then wisdom prostrate lies, and fading fame
Dissolves in air away.

THOMSON

A FEW MONTHS passed over the heads of Ellen Langton and her admirers, unproductive of events, that, separately, were of sufficient importance to be related. The summer was now drawing to a close, and Doctor Melmoth had received information that his friend's arrangements were nearly completed, and that, by the next homebound ship, he hoped to return to his native country. The arrival of that ship was daily expected.

During the time that had elapsed since his first meeting with Ellen, there had been a change, yet not a very remarkable one, in Fanshawe's habits. He was still the same solitary being, so far as regarded his own sex, and he still confined himself as sedulously to his chamber, except for one hour— the sunset hour—of every day. At that period, unless prevented by the inclemency of the weather, he was accustomed to tread a path that wound along the banks of the stream. He had discovered that this was the most frequent scene of Ellen's walks, and this it was that drew him thither.

Their intercourse was at first extremely slight. A bow on the one side, a smile on the other, and a passing word from both—and then the student hurried back to his solitude. But, in course of time, opportunities occurred for more extended conversation; so that, at the period with which this chapter is concerned, Fanshawe was, almost as constantly as Edward Walcott himself, the companion of Ellen's walks.

His passion had strengthened, more than proportionably to the time that had elapsed since it was conceived; but the first glow and excitement which attended it, had now vanished. He had reasoned calmly with himself and rendered evident to his own mind the almost utter hopelessness of success. He had also made his resolution strong, that he would not even endeavor to win Ellen's love, the result of which, for a thousand reasons, could not be happiness. Firm in this determination, and confident of his power to adhere to it—feeling, also, that time and absence could not cure his own passion, and having no desire for such a cure—he saw no reason for breaking off the intercourse that was established between Ellen and himself. It was remarkable, that, notwithstanding the desperate nature of his love, that, or something connected with it, seemed to have a beneficial effect upon his health. There was now a slight tinge of color in his cheek, and a less consuming brightness in his eye. Could it be that hope, unknown to himself, was yet alive in his breast?—that a sense of the possibility of earthly happiness was redeeming him from the grave?

Had the character of Ellen Langton's mind been different, there might perhaps have been danger to her from an intercourse of this nature, with such a being as Fanshawe; for he was distinguished by many of those asperities around which a woman's affection will often cling. But she was formed to walk in the calm and quiet paths of life, and to pluck the flowers of happiness from the way-side, where they grow. Singularity of character, therefore, was not calculated to win her love. She undoubtedly felt an interest in the solitary student, and perceiving, with no great exercise of vanity, that her society drew him from the destructive intensity of his studies, she perhaps felt it a duty to exert her influence. But it did not occur to her, that her influence had been sufficiently strong to change the whole current of his thoughts and feelings.

Ellen and her two lovers (for both, though perhaps not equally, deserved that epithet) had met, as usual, at the close of a sweet summer day, and were standing by the side of the stream, just where it swept into a deep pool. The current, undermining the bank, had formed a recess which, according to Edward Walcott, afforded at that moment a hiding place to a trout of noble size.

'Now would I give the world,' he exclaimed, with great interest, 'for a hook and line—a fish spear, or any piscatorial instrument of death! Look, Ellen, you can see the waving of his tail from beneath the bank.'

'If you had the means of taking him, I should save him from your cruelty, thus,' said Ellen, dropping a pebble into the water, just over the fish. 'There! he has darted down the stream. How many pleasant caves and recesses there must be, under these banks, where he may be happy! May there not be happiness in the life of a fish?' she added, turning with a smile to Fanshawe.

'There may,' he replied, 'so long as he lives quietly in the caves and recesses of which you speak. Yes, there may be happiness, though such as few would envy;—but then the hook and line——'

'Which, there is reason to apprehend, will shortly destroy the happiness of our friend the trout,' interrupted Edward, pointing down the stream. 'There is an angler on his way towards us, who will intercept him.'

'He seems to care little for the sport, to judge by the pace at which he walks,' said Ellen.

'But he sees, now, that we are observing him, and is willing to prove that he knows something of the art,' replied Edward Walcott. 'I should think him well acquainted with the stream; for, hastily as he walks, he has tried every pool and ripple, where a fish usually hides. But that point will be decided when he reaches yonder old bare oak-tree.'

'And how is the old tree to decide the question?' inquired Fanshawe. 'It is a species of evidence of which I have never before heard.'

'The stream has worn a hollow under its roots,' answered Edward—'a most delicate retreat for a trout. Now, a stranger would not discover the spot; or, if he did, the probable result of a cast would be the loss of hook and line—an accident that has occurred to me more than once. If, therefore, this angler takes a fish from thence, it follows that he knows the stream.'

They observed the fisher, accordingly, as he kept his way up the bank. He did not pause when he reached the old leafless oak, that formed with its roots an obstruction very common in American streams; but throwing his line with involuntary skill, as he passed, he not only escaped the various entanglements, but drew forth a fine large fish.

'There, Ellen, he has captivated your protégé, the trout— or at least one very like him in size,' observed Edward. 'It is singular,' he added, gazing earnestly at the man.

'Why is it singular?' inquired Ellen Langton. 'This person perhaps resides in the neighborhood, and may have fished often in the stream.'

'Do but look at him, Ellen, and judge whether his life can have been spent in this lonely valley,' he replied. 'The glow of many a hotter sun than ours has darkened his brow; and his step and air have something foreign in them, like what we see in sailors, who have lived more in other countries than in their own. Is it not so, Ellen?—for your education in a sea-port must have given you skill in these matters. But, come—let us approach nearer.'

They walked towards the angler, accordingly, who still remained under the oak, apparently engaged in arranging his fishing tackle. As the party drew nigh, he raised his head and threw one quick, scrutinizing glance towards them, disclosing, on his part, a set of bold and rather coarse features, weather beaten, but indicating the age of the owner to be not above thirty. In person he surpassed the middle size, was well set, and evidently strong and active.

'Do you meet with much success, Sir?' inquired Edward Walcott, when within a convenient distance for conversation.

'I have taken but one fish,' replied the angler, in an accent which his hearers could scarcely determine to be foreign, or the contrary. 'I am a stranger to the stream, and have doubt-less passed over many a likely place for sport.'

'You have an angler's eye, Sir,' rejoined Edward. 'I observed that you made your casts as if you had often trod these banks, and I could scarcely have guided you better myself.'

'Yes, I have learnt the art, and I love to practise it,' replied the man. 'But will not the young lady try her skill?' he con-tinued, casting a bold eye on Ellen. 'The fish will love to be drawn out by such white hands as those.'

Ellen shrank back, though almost imperceptibly, from the free bearing of the man. It seemed meant for courtesy, but its effect was excessively disagreeable. Edward Walcott, who perceived and coincided in Ellen's feelings, replied to the stranger's proposal.

'The young lady will not put the gallantry of the fish to the proof, Sir,' he said, 'and she will therefore have no occa-sion for your own.'

'I shall take leave to hear my answer from the young lady's own mouth,' answered the stranger, haughtily. 'If you will step this way, Miss Langton'—here he interrupted himself—'if you will cast the line by yonder sunken log, I think you will meet with success.'

Thus saying, the angler offered his rod and line to Ellen. She at first drew back—then hesitated—but finally held out her hand to receive them. In thus complying with the stranger's request, she was actuated by a desire to keep the peace, which, as her notice of Edward Walcott's crimsoned cheek and flashing eye assured her, was considerably endangered. The angler led the way to the spot which he had pointed out, which, though not at such a distance from Ellen's companions but that words in a common tone could be distinguished, was out of the range of a lowered voice.

Edward Walcott and the student remained by the oak, the former biting his lip with vexation; the latter, whose abstraction always vanished where Ellen was concerned, regarding her and the stranger with fixed and silent attention. The young men could at first hear the words that the angler addressed to Ellen. They related to the mode of managing the rod; and she made one or two casts under his direction. At length, however, as if to offer his assistance, the man advanced close to her side, and seemed to speak; but in so low a tone, that the sense of what he uttered was lost, before it reached the oak. But its effect upon Ellen was immediate, and very obvious. Her eye flashed, and an indignant blush rose high on her cheek, giving to her beauty a haughty brightness, of which the gentleness of her disposition in general deprived it. The next moment, however, she seemed to recollect herself, and restoring the angling rod to its owner, she turned away, calmly, and approached her companions.

'The evening breeze grows chill, and mine is a dress for a summer day,' she observed. 'Let us walk homeward.'

'Miss Langton, is it the evening breeze, alone, that sends you homeward?' inquired Edward.

At this moment, the angler, who had resumed and seemed to be intent upon his occupation, drew a fish from the pool which he had pointed out to Ellen.

'I told the young lady,' he exclaimed, 'that if she would listen to me a moment longer, she would be repaid for her trouble;—and here is the proof of my words.'

'Come, let us hasten towards home,' cried Ellen, eagerly; and she took Edward Walcott's arm, with a freedom that, at another time, would have enchanted him. He at first seemed inclined to resist her wishes; but complied, after exchanging, unperceived by Ellen, a glance with the stranger, the meaning of which the latter appeared perfectly to understand. Fanshawe also attended her. Their walk towards Doctor Melmoth's dwelling was almost a silent one, and the few words that passed between them, did not relate to the adventure which occupied the thoughts of each. On arriving at the house, Ellen's attendants took leave of her, and retired.

Edward Walcott, eluding Fanshawe's observation with little difficulty, hastened back to the old oak-tree. From the intelligence with which the stranger had received his meaning glance, the young man had supposed that he would here await his return. But the banks of the stream, upward and downward, so far as his eye could reach, were solitary. He could see only his own image in the water, where it swept into a silent depth; and could hear only its ripple, where stones and sunken trees impeded its course. The object of his search might indeed have found concealment among the tufts of alders, or in the forest that was near at hand; but thither it was in vain to pursue him. The angler had apparently set little store by the fruits of his assumed occupation; for the last fish that he had taken lay yet alive on the bank, gasping for the element to which Edward was sufficiently compassionate to restore him. After watching him as he glided down the stream, making feeble efforts to resist its current, the youth turned away, and sauntered slowly towards the College.

Ellen Langton, on her return from her walk, found Doctor Melmoth's little parlor unoccupied, that gentleman being deeply engaged in his study, and his lady busied in her domestic affairs. The evening, notwithstanding Ellen's remark concerning the chillness of the breeze, was almost sultry, and the windows of the apartment were thrown open. At one of these, which looked into the garden, she seated herself, listening almost unconsciously to the monotonous music of a thousand insects, varied, occasionally, by the voice of a whippoorwill, who, as the day departed, was just commencing his song. A dusky tint, as yet almost imperceptible, was beginning to settle on the surrounding objects, except where they were opposed to the purple and golden clouds, which the vanished sun had made the brief inheritors of a portion of his brightness. In these gorgeous vapors, Ellen's fancy, in the interval of other thoughts, pictured a fairy land, and longed for wings to visit it.

But as the clouds lost their brilliancy, and assumed first a dull purple, and then a sullen gray tint, Ellen's thoughts recurred to the adventure of the angler, which her imagination was inclined to invest with an undue singularity. It was, however, sufficiently unaccountable, that an entire stranger should venture to demand of her a private audience; and she assigned, in turn, a thousand motives for such a request, none of which were in any degree satisfactory. Her most prevailing thought, though she could not justify it to her reason, inclined her to believe that the angler was a messenger from her father. But wherefore he should deem it necessary to communicate any intelligence, that he might possess, only by means of a private interview, and without the knowledge of her friends, was a mystery she could not solve. In this view of the matter, however, she half regretted that her instinctive delicacy had impelled her so suddenly to break off their conference, admitting, in the secrecy of her own mind, that, if an opportunity were again to occur, it might not again be shunned. As if that unuttered thought had power to conjure up its object, she now became aware of a form, standing in the garden, at a short distance from the window, where she sat. The dusk had deepened, during Ellen's abstraction, to such a degree, that the man's features were not perfectly distinguishable; but the maiden was not long in doubt of his identity, for he approached, and spoke in the same low tone in which he had addressed her, when they stood by the stream.

'Do you still refuse my request, when its object is but your own good, and that of one who should be most dear to you?' he asked.

Ellen's first impulse had been, to cry out for assistance—her second was, to fly;—but rejecting both these measures, she determined to remain, endeavoring to persuade herself that she was safe. The quivering of her voice, however, when she attempted to reply, betrayed her apprehensions.

'I cannot listen to such a request from a stranger,' she said. 'If you bring news from—from my father, why is it not told to Doctor Melmoth?'

'Because what I have to say is for your ear alone,' was the reply; 'and if you would avoid misfortune now, and sorrow hereafter, you will not refuse to hear me.'

'And does it concern my father?' asked Ellen, eagerly.

'It does—most deeply,' answered the stranger.

She meditated a moment, and then replied, 'I will not refuse—I will hear—but speak quickly.'

'We are in danger of interruption in this place—and that would be fatal to my errand,' said the stranger. 'I will await you in the garden.'

With these words, and giving her no opportunity for reply, he drew back, and his form faded from her eyes. This precipitate retreat from argument was the most probable method, that he could have adopted, of gaining his end. He had awakened the strongest interest in Ellen's mind, and he calculated justly, in supposing that she would consent to an interview upon his own terms.

Doctor Melmoth had followed his own fancies in the mode of laying out his garden; and, in consequence, the plan that had undoubtedly existed in his mind, was utterly incomprehensible to every one but himself. It was an intermixture of kitchen and flower garden—a labyrinth of winding paths, bordered by hedges and impeded by shrubbery. Many of the original trees of the forest were still flourishing among the exotics, which the Doctor had transplanted thither. It was not without a sensation of fear, stronger than she had ever before experienced, that Ellen Langton found herself in this artificial wilderness, and in the presence of the mysterious stranger. The dusky light deepened the lines of his dark, strong features, and Ellen fancied that his countenance wore a wilder and a fiercer look, than when she had met him by the stream. He perceived her agitation, and addressed her in the softest tones of which his voice was capable.

'Compose yourself,' he said, 'you have nothing to fear from me. But we are in open view from the house, where we now stand; and discovery would not be without danger, to both of us.'

'No eye can see us here,' said Ellen, trembling at the truth of her own observation, when they stood beneath a gnarled, low-branched pine, which Doctor Melmoth's ideas of beauty had caused him to retain in his garden. 'Speak quickly; for I dare follow you no farther.'

The spot was indeed sufficiently solitary, and the stranger delayed no longer to explain his errand.

'Your father,' he began—'Do you not love him? Would you do aught for his welfare?'

'Every thing that a father could ask, I would do,' exclaimed Ellen, eagerly. 'Where is my father; and when shall I meet him?'

'It must depend upon yourself, whether you shall meet him in a few days or never.'

'Never!' repeated Ellen. 'Is he ill?—Is he in danger?'

'He is in danger,' replied the man; 'but not from illness. Your father is a ruined man. Of all his friends, but one remains to him. That friend has travelled far, to prove if his daughter has a daughter's affection.'

'And what is to be the proof?' asked Ellen, with more calmness than the stranger had anticipated; for she possessed a large fund of plain sense, which revolted against the mystery of these proceedings. Such a course, too, seemed discordant with her father's character, whose strong mind and almost cold heart were little likely to demand, or even to pardon, the romance of affection.

'This letter will explain,' was the reply to Ellen's question. 'You will see that it is in your father's hand; and that may gain your confidence, though I am doubted.'

She received the letter, and many of her suspicions of the stranger's truth were vanquished by the apparent openness of his manner. He was preparing to speak further, but paused— for a footstep was now heard, approaching from the lower part of the garden. From their situation, at some distance from the path, and in the shade of the tree, they had a fair chance of eluding discovery from any unsuspecting passenger; and when Ellen saw that the intruder was Fanshawe, she hoped that his usual abstraction would assist their concealment.

But, as the student advanced along the path, his air was not that of one, whose deep, inward thoughts withdrew his attention from all outward objects. He rather resembled the hunter, on the watch for his game; and while he was yet at a distance from Ellen, a wandering gust of wind waved her white garment and betrayed her.

'It is as I feared,' said Fanshawe to himself. He then drew nigh, and addressed Ellen with a calm authority that became him well, notwithstanding that his years scarcely exceeded her own. 'Miss Langton,' he inquired, 'what do you here, at such an hour, and with such a companion?'

Ellen was sufficiently displeased at what she deemed the unauthorized intrusion of Fanshawe in her affairs; but his imposing manner and her own confusion prevented her from replying.

'Permit me to lead you to the house,' he continued, in the words of a request, but in the tone of a command. 'The dew hangs dank and heavy on these branches, and a longer stay would be more dangerous than you are aware.'

Ellen would fain have resisted; but, though the tears hung as heavy on her eye lashes, between shame and anger, as the dew upon the leaves, she felt compelled to accept the arm that he offered her. But the stranger, who, since Fanshawe's approach, had remained a little apart, now advanced.

'You speak as one in authority, young man,' he said. 'Have you the means of compelling obedience? Does your power extend to men?—Or do you rule only over simple girls? Miss Langton is under my protection, and, till you can bend me to your will, she shall remain so.'

Fanshawe turned, calmly, and fixed his eye on the stranger. 'Retire, Sir,' was all he said.

Ellen almost shuddered, as if there were a mysterious and unearthly power in Fanshawe's voice; for she saw that the stranger endeavored in vain, borne down by the influence of a superior mind, to maintain the boldness of look and bearing, that seemed natural to him. He at first made a step forward—then muttered a few half audible words;—but, quailing at length beneath the young man's bright and steady eye, he turned and slowly withdrew.

Fanshawe remained silent, a moment, after his opponent had departed; and when he next spoke, it was in a tone of depression. Ellen observed, also, that his countenance had lost its look of pride and authority; and he seemed faint and exhausted. The occasion that called forth his energies had passed; and they had left him.

'Forgive me, Miss Langton,' he said, almost humbly, 'if my eagerness to serve you has led me too far. There is evil in this stranger, more than your pure mind can conceive. I know not what has been his errand; but let me entreat you to put confidence in those to whose care your father has entrusted you. Or if I—or—or Edward Walcott;—but I have no right to advise you; and your own calm thoughts will guide you best.'

He said no more; and, as Ellen did not reply, they reached the house, and parted in silence.

IV

The seeds by nature planted
Take a deep root i' th' soil, and though for a time
The trenchant share and tearing harrow may
Sweep all appearance of them from the surface,
Yet, with the first warm rains of Spring, they'll shoot,
And with their rankness smother the good grain.
Heaven grant, it mayn't be so with him.

RICHES

THE SCENE of this tale must now be changed to the little Inn, which at that period, as at the present, was situated in the vicinity of Harley College. The site of the modern establishment is the same with that of the ancient, but every thing of the latter, that had been built by hands, has gone to decay and been removed, and only the earth, beneath and around it, remains the same. The modern building, a house of two stories, after a lapse of twenty years, is yet unfinished. On this account, it has retained the appellation of the 'new Inn,' though, like many who have frequented it, it has grown old ere its maturity. Its dingy whiteness and its apparent superfluity of windows (many of them being closed with rough boards) give it somewhat of a dreary look, especially in a wet day.

The ancient Inn was a house, of which the eaves approached within about seven feet of the ground, while the roof, sloping gradually upward, formed an angle at several times that height. It was a comfortable and pleasant abode to the weary traveller, both in summer and winter; for the frost never ventured within the sphere of its huge hearths; and it was protected from the heat of the sultry season by three large elms that swept the roof with their long branches and seemed to create a breeze where there was not one. The device upon the sign, suspended from one of these trees, was a Hand, holding a long necked Bottle, and was much more appropriate than the present unmeaning representation, of a Black Eagle. But it is necessary to speak rather more at length of the landlord, than of the house over which he presided.

Hugh Crombie was one, for whom most of the wise men, who considered the course of his early years, had predicted the gallows as an end, before he should arrive at middle age. That these prophets of ill had been deceived was evident from the fact, that the doomed man had now past the fortieth year, and was in more prosperous circumstances than most of those who had wagged their tongues against him. Yet the failure of their forebodings was more remarkable than their fulfilment would have been.

He had been distinguished almost from his earliest infancy by those precocious accomplishments, which, because they consist in an imitation of the vices and follies of maturity, render a boy the favorite plaything of men. He seemed to have received from nature the convivial talents, which, whether natural or acquired, are a most dangerous possession; and before his twelfth year he was the welcome associate of all the idle and dissipated of his neighborhood, and especially of those who haunted the tavern of which he had now become the landlord. Under this course of education Hugh Crombie grew to youth and manhood; and the lovers of good words could only say in his favor, that he was a greater enemy to himself than to any one else, and that, if he should reform, few would have a better chance of prosperity than he.

The former clause of this modicum of praise (if praise it may be termed) was indisputable; but it may be doubted, whether, under any circumstances where his success depended on his own exertions, Hugh would have made his way well through the world. He was one of those unfortunate persons, who, instead of being perfect in any single art or occupation, are superficial in many, and who are supposed to possess a larger share of talent than other men, because it consists of numerous scraps instead of a single mass. He was partially acquainted with most of the manual arts that gave bread to others; but not one of them, nor all of them, would give bread to him. By some fatality, the only two of his multifarious accomplishments, in which his excellence was generally conceded, were both calculated to keep him poor rather than to make him rich. He was a musician and a poet.

There are yet remaining, in that portion of the country, many ballads and songs—set to their own peculiar tunes— the authorship of which is attributed to him. In general, his productions were upon subjects of local and temporary interest, and would consequently require a bulk of explanatory notes, to render them interesting or intelligible to the world at large. A considerable proportion of the remainder are Anacreontics—though, in their construction, Hugh Crombie imitated neither the Teian nor any other bard. These latter have generally a coarseness and sensuality, intolerable to minds even of no very fastidious delicacy. But there are two or three simple little songs, into which a feeling and a natural pathos have found their way, that still retain their influence over the heart. These, after two or three centuries, may perhaps be precious to the collectors of our early poetry. At any rate, Hugh Crombie's effusions, tavern-haunter and vagrant though he was, have gained a continuance of fame (confined, indeed, to a narrow section of the country) which many, who called themselves poets then, and would have scorned such a brother, have failed to equal.

During the long winter evenings, when the farmers were idle round their hearths, Hugh was a courted guest; for none could while away the hours more skilfully than he. The winter therefore was his season of prosperity; in which respect he differed from the butterflies and useless insects, to which he otherwise bore a resemblance. During the cold months, a very desirable alteration for the better, appeared in his outward man. His cheeks were plump and sanguine, his eyes bright and cheerful, and the tip of his nose glowed with a Bardolphian fire—a flame, indeed, which Hugh was so far a vestal as to supply with its necessary fuel, at all seasons of the year. But as the spring advanced, he assumed a lean and sallow look, wilting and fading in the sunshine, that brought life and joy to every animal and vegetable except himself. His winter patrons eyed him with an austere regard, and some even practised upon him the modern and fashionable courtesy of the 'cut direct.'

Yet, after all, there was good, or something that Nature intended to be so, in the poor outcast—some lovely flowers, the sweeter even for the weeds that choked them. An instance of this was his affection for an aged father, whose whole support was the broken reed—his son. Notwithstanding his own necessities, Hugh contrived to provide food and raiment for the old man—how, it would be difficult to say, and perhaps as well not to inquire. He also exhibited traits of sensitiveness to neglect and insult, and of gratitude for favors; both of which feelings a course of life like his is usually quick to eradicate.

At length the restraint, for such his father had ever been, upon Hugh Crombie's conduct, was removed by his death; and then the wise men and the old began to shake their heads; and they who took pleasure in the follies, vices, and misfortunes of their fellow-creatures, looked for a speedy gratification. They were disappointed, however; for Hugh had apparently determined, that, whatever might be his catastrophe, he would meet it among strangers, rather than at home. Shortly after his father's death, he disappeared altogether from the vicinity; and his name became, in the course of years, an unusual sound, where once the lack of other topics of interest had given it a considerable degree of notoriety. Sometimes, however, when the winter blast was loud round the lonely farm-house, its inmates remembered him who had so often chased away the gloom of such an hour, and, though with little expectation of its fulfilment, expressed a wish to behold him again.

Yet that wish, formed perhaps because it appeared so desperate, was finally destined to be gratified. One summer evening, about two years previous to the period of this tale, a man of sober and staid deportment, mounted upon a white horse, arrived at the Hand and Bottle, to which some civil or military meeting had chanced that day to draw most of the inhabitants of the vicinity. The stranger was well, though plainly dressed, and anywhere but in a retired country town, would have attracted no particular attention; but here, where a traveller was not of every day occurrence, he was soon surrounded by a little crowd, who, when his eye was averted, seized the opportunity diligently to peruse his person. He was rather a thick-set man, but with no superfluous flesh; his hair was of iron-gray; he had a few wrinkles; his face was so deeply sun burnt, that, excepting a half smothered glow on the tip of his nose, a dusky yellow was the only apparent hue. As the people gazed, it was observed that the elderly men, and the men of substance, gat themselves silently to their steeds, and hied homeward with an unusual degree of haste; till at length the Inn was deserted, except by a few wretched objects to whom it was a constant resort. These, instead of retreating, drew closer to the traveller, peeping anxiously into his face, and asking, ever and anon, a question, in order to discover the tone of his voice. At length, with one consent, and as if the recognition had at once burst upon them, they hailed their old boon companion, Hugh Crombie, and leading him into the Inn, did him the honor to partake of a cup of welcome at his expense.

But, though Hugh readily acknowledged the not very reputable acquaintances, who alone acknowledged him, they speedily discovered that he was an altered man. He partook with great moderation of the liquor, for which he was to pay; he declined all their flattering entreaties for one of his old songs; and, finally, being urged to engage in a game at all-fours, he calmly observed, almost in the words of an old clergyman, on a like occasion, that his principles forbade a profane appeal to the decision by lot.

On the next Sabbath, Hugh Crombie made his appearance at public worship, in the chapel of Harley College, and here his outward demeanor was unexceptionably serious and devout—a praise, which, on that particular occasion, could be bestowed on few besides. From these favorable symptoms, the old established prejudices against him began to waver; and, as he seemed not to need, and to have no intention to ask, the assistance of any one, he was soon generally acknowledged by the rich, as well as by the poor. His account of his past life and of his intentions for the future was brief, but not unsatisfactory. He said, that, since his departure, he had been a sea-faring man, and that, having acquired sufficient property to render him easy in the decline of his days, he had returned to live and die in the town of his nativity.

There was one person, and the one whom Hugh was most interested to please, who seemed perfectly satisfied of the verity of his reformation. This was the landlady of the Inn, whom, at his departure, he had left a gay, and, even at thirty-five, a rather pretty wife, and whom, on his return, he found a widow of fifty, fat, yellow, wrinkled, and a zealous member of the church. She, like others, had at first cast a cold eye on the wanderer; but it shortly became evident, to close observers, that a change was at work in the pious matron's sentiments, respecting her old acquaintance. She was now careful to give him his morning dram from her own peculiar bottle—to fill his pipe from her private box of Virginia—and to mix for him the sleeping cup, in which her late husband had delighted. Of all these courtesies Hugh Crombie did partake, with a wise and cautious moderation, that, while it proved them to be welcome, expressed his fear of trespassing on her kindness. For the sake of brevity, it shall suffice to say, that, about six weeks after Hugh's return, a writing appeared on one of the elm-trees in front of the tavern, (where, as the place of greatest resort, such notices were usually displayed,) setting forth, that marriage was intended between Hugh Crombie and the Widow Sarah Hutchins. And the ceremony, which made Hugh a landholder, a householder, and a substantial man, in due time took place.

As a landlord, his general conduct was very praiseworthy. He was moderate in his charges, and attentive to his guests; he allowed no gross and evident disorders in his house, and practised none himself; he was kind and charitable to such as needed food and lodging, and had not wherewithal to pay—for with these his experience had doubtless given him a fellow feeling. He was also sufficiently attentive to his wife; though it must be acknowledged that the religious zeal, which had had a considerable influence in gaining her affections, grew, by no moderate degrees, less fervent. It was whispered, too, that the new landlord could, when time, place, and company were to his mind, upraise a song as merrily, and drink a glass as jollily as in the days of yore. These were the weightiest charges that could now be brought against him; and wise men thought, that, whatever might have been the evil of his past life, he had returned with a desire (which years of vice, if they do not sometimes produce, do not always destroy) of being honest if opportunity should offer;—and Hugh had certainly a fair one.

On the afternoon previous to the events related in the last chapter, the personage, whose introduction to the reader has occupied so large a space, was seated under one of the elms, in front of his dwelling. The bench which now sustained him, and on which were carved the names of many former occupants, was Hugh Crombie's favorite lounging place, unless when his attentions were required by his guests. No demand had that day been made upon the hospitality of

the Hand and Bottle, and the landlord was just then murmuring at the unfrequency of employment. The slenderness
of his profits, indeed, were no part of his concern; for the
Widow Hutchins' chief income was drawn from her farm,
nor was Hugh ever miserly inclined. But his education and
habits had made him delight in the atmosphere of an Inn,
and in the society of those who frequented it; and of this
species of enjoyment his present situation certainly did not
afford an overplus.

Yet had Hugh Crombie an enviable appearance of indolence and ease, as he sat under the old tree, polluting the
sweet air with his pipe, and taking occasional draughts from
a brown jug, that stood near at hand. The basis of the
potation contained in this vessel, was harsh old cider, from
the Widow's own orchard; but its coldness and acidity were
rendered innocuous by a due proportion of yet older brandy.
The result of this mixture was extremely felicitous, pleasant
to the taste, and producing a tingling sensation on the coats
of the stomach, uncommonly delectable to so old a toper
as Hugh.

The landlord cast his eye, ever and anon, along the road
that led down the valley in the direction of the village; and
at last, when the sun was wearing westward, he discovered
the approach of a horseman. He immediately replenished
his pipe, took a long draught from the brown jug, summoned
the ragged youth who officiated in most of the subordinate
departments of the Inn, and who was now to act as ostler;
and then prepared himself for confabulation with his guest.

'He comes from the sea-coast,' said Hugh to himself, as
the traveller emerged into open view on the level road. 'He
is two days in advance of the post, with its news of a fortnight
old. Pray Heaven, he prove communicative!' Then as the
stranger drew nigher, 'One would judge that his dark face
had seen as hot a sun as mine. He has felt the burning breeze
of the Indies, East and West, I warrant him. Ah, I see we

shall send away the evening merrily! Not a penny shall
come out of his purse—that is, if his tongue runs glibly. Just
the man I was praying for—Now may the devil take me if he
is!' interrupted Hugh, in accents of alarm, and starting from
his seat. He composed his countenance, however, with the
power that long habit and necessity had given him over his
emotions, and again settled himself quietly on the bench.

The traveller, coming on at a moderate pace, alighted
and gave his horse to the ragged ostler. He then advanced
towards the door near which Hugh was seated, whose agitation was manifested by no perceptible sign, except by the
shorter and more frequent puffs with which he plied his pipe.
Their eyes did not meet till just as the stranger was about to
enter, when he started apparently with a surprise and alarm
similar to those of Hugh Crombie. He recovered himself,
however, sufficiently to return the nod of recognition with
which he was favored, and immediately entered the house,
the landlord following.

'This way, if you please, Sir,' said Hugh. 'You will find
this apartment cool and retired.'

He ushered his guest into a small room, the windows of
which were darkened by the creeping plants that clustered
round them. Entering and closing the door, the two gazed
at each other, a little space, without speaking. The traveller
first broke silence.

'Then this is your living self, Hugh Crombie?' he said. The
landlord extended his hand as a practical reply to the question.
The stranger took it, though with no especial appearance of
cordiality.

'Aye, this seems to be flesh and blood,' he said, in the tone
of one who would willingly have found it otherwise. 'And
how happens this, friend Hugh? I little thought to meet
you again in this life. When I last heard from you, your
prayers were said, and you were bound for a better world.'

'There would have been small danger of your meeting me there,' observed the landlord, dryly.

'It is an unquestionable truth, Hugh,' replied the traveller. 'For which reason I regret that your voyage was delayed.'

'Nay, that is a hard word to bestow on your old comrade,' said Hugh Crombie. 'The world is wide enough for both of us, and why should you wish me out of it?'

'Wide as it is,' rejoined the stranger, 'we have stumbled against each other—to the pleasure of neither of us, if I may judge from your countenance. Methinks I am not a welcome guest at Hugh Crombie's Inn.'

'Your welcome must depend on the cause of your coming and the length of your stay,' replied the landlord.

'And what if I come to settle down among these quiet hills where I was born?' inquired the other. 'What if I, too, am weary of the life we have led—or afraid, perhaps, that it will come to too speedy an end? Shall I have your good word, Hugh, to set me up in an honest way of life? Or will you make me a partner in your trade, since you know my qualifications? A pretty pair of publicans should we be, and the quart pot would have little rest between us.'

'It may be as well to replenish it now,' observed Hugh, stepping to the door of the room and giving orders accordingly. 'A meeting between old friends should never be dry. But for the partnership, it is a matter in which you must excuse me. Heaven knows, I find it hard enough to be honest, with no tempter but the Devil and my own thoughts; and if I have you also to contend with, there is little hope of me.'

'Nay, that is true. Your good resolutions were always like cobwebs, and your evil habits like five inch cables,' replied the traveller. 'I am to understand, then, that you refuse my offer?'

'Not only that—but if you have chosen this valley as your

place of rest, Dame Crombie and I must look through the world for another. But, hush—here comes the wine.'

The ostler, in the performance of another part of his duty, now appeared, bearing a measure of the liquor that Hugh had ordered. The wine of that period, owing to the comparative lowness of the duties, was of more moderate price than in the mother country, and of purer and better quality than at the present day.

'The stuff is well chosen, Hugh,' observed the guest, after a draught large enough to authorize an opinion. 'You have most of the requisites for your present station, and I should be sorry to draw you from it. I trust there will be no need.'

'Yet you have a purpose in your journey hither,' observed his comrade.

'Yes—and you would fain be informed of it,' replied the traveller. He arose and walked once or twice across the room; then seeming to have taken his resolution, he paused and fixed his eye stedfastly on Hugh Crombie. 'I could wish, my old acquaintance,' he said, 'that your lot had been cast any-where rather than here. Yet if you choose it, you may do me a good office, and one that shall meet with a good reward. Can I trust you?'

'My secrecy, you can,' answered the host, 'but nothing farther. I know the nature of your plans, and whither they would lead me, too well to engage in them. To say the truth, since it concerns not me, I have little desire to hear your secret.'

'And I as little to tell it, I do assure you,' rejoined the guest. 'I have always loved to manage my affairs myself, and to keep them to myself. It is a good rule, but it must sometimes be broken. And now, Hugh, how is it that you have become possessed of this comfortable dwelling and of these pleasant fields?'

'By my marriage with the Widow Sarah Hutchins,' replied

Hugh Crombie, staring at a question, which seemed to have little reference to the present topic of conversation.

'It is a most excellent method of becoming a man of substance,' continued the traveller—'attended with little trouble, and honest withal.'

'Why, as to the trouble,' said the landlord, 'it follows such a bargain, instead of going before it. And for honesty—I do not recollect that I have gained a penny more honestly these twenty years.'

'I can swear to that,' observed his comrade. 'Well, mine host, I entirely approve of your doings; and, moreover, have resolved to prosper after the same fashion myself.'

'If that be the commodity you seek,' replied Hugh Crombie, 'you will find none here to your mind. We have widows in plenty, it is true, but most of them have children and few have houses and lands. But now to be serious—and there has been something serious in your eye, all this while—what is your purpose in coming hither? You are not safe here. Your name has had a wider spread than mine, and if discovered it will go hard with you.'

'But who would know me, now?' asked the guest.

'Few—few indeed,' replied the landlord, gazing at the dark features of his companion, where hardship, peril, and dissipation had each left their traces. 'No, you are not like the slender boy of fifteen, who stood on the hill by moonlight, to take a last look at his father's cottage. There were tears in your eyes, then; and as often as I remember them, I repent that I did not turn you back, instead of leading you on.'

'Tears, were there? Well, there have been few enough since,' said his comrade, pressing his eyelids firmly together, as if even then tempted to give way to the weakness that he scorned. 'And for turning me back, Hugh, it was beyond your power. I had taken my resolution, and you did but shew me the way to execute it.'

'You have not inquired after those you left behind,' observed Hugh Crombie.

'No—no;—nor will I have aught of them,' exclaimed the traveller, starting from his seat, and pacing rapidly across the room. 'My father, I know, is dead, and I have forgiven him. My mother—What could I hear of her, but misery?—I will hear nothing.'

'You must have passed the cottage, as you rode hitherward,' said Hugh. 'How could you forbear to enter?'

'I did not see it,' he replied. 'I closed my eyes and turned away my head.'

'Oh, if I had had a mother—a loving mother—if there had been one being in the world, that loved me or cared for me, I should not have become an utter cast away,' exclaimed Hugh Crombie.

The landlord's pathos—like all pathos that flows from the wine cup—was sufficiently ridiculous; and his companion, who had already overcome his own brief feelings of sorrow and remorse, now laughed aloud.

'Come, come, mine host of the Hand and Bottle,' he cried, in his usual hard, sarcastic tone; 'be a man, as much as in you lies. You had always a foolish trick of repentance; but, as I remember, it was commonly of a morning, before you had swallowed your first dram. And now, Hugh, fill the quart pot again, and we will to business.'

When the landlord had complied with the wishes of his guest, the latter resumed in a lower tone than that of his ordinary conversation.

'There is a young lady, lately become a resident hereabouts. Perhaps you can guess her name; for you have a quick apprehension in these matters.'

'A young lady?' repeated Hugh Crombie. 'And what is your concern with her? Do you mean Ellen Langton, daughter of the old Merchant Langton, whom you have some cause to remember?'

'I do remember him; but he is where he will speedily be forgotten,' answered the traveller. 'And this girl—I know your eye has been upon her, Hugh. Describe her to me.'

'Describe her,' exclaimed Hugh, with much animation. 'It is impossible, in prose; but you shall have her very picture, in a verse of one of my own songs.'

'Nay, mine host, I beseech you to spare me. This is no time for quavering,' said the guest. 'However, I am proud of your approbation, my old friend—for this young lady do I intend to take to wife. What think you of the plan?'

Hugh Crombie gazed into his companion's face, for the space of a moment, in silence. There was nothing in its expression that looked like a jest. It still retained the same hard, cold look, that, except when Hugh had alluded to his home and family, it had worn through their whole conversation.

'On my word, comrade,' he at length replied, 'my advice is, that you give over your application to the quart pot, and refresh your brain by a short nap. And yet, your eye is cool and steady. What is the meaning of this?'

'Listen, and you shall know,' said the guest. 'The old man, her father, is in his grave——'

'Not a bloody grave, I trust,' interrupted the landlord, starting, and looking fearfully into his comrade's face.

'No, a watery one,' he replied, calmly. 'You see, Hugh, I am a better man than you took me for. The old man's blood is not on my head, though my wrongs are on his. Now listen. He had no heir but this only daughter; and to her, and to the man she marries, all his wealth will belong. She shall marry me. Think you her father will rest easy in the ocean, Hugh Crombie, when I am his son-in-law?'

'No, he will rise up to prevent it, if need be,' answered the landlord. 'But the dead need not interpose to frustrate so wild a scheme.'

'I understand you,' said his comrade. 'You are of opinion that the young lady's consent may not be so soon won as asked. Fear not for that, mine host. I have a winning way with me, when opportunity serves; and it shall serve with Ellen Langton. I will have no rivals in my wooing.'

'Your intention, if I take it rightly, is to get this poor girl into your power, and then to force her into a marriage,' said Hugh Crombie.

'It is; and I think I possess the means of doing it,' replied his comrade. 'But methinks, friend Hugh, my enterprise has not your good wishes.'

'No; and I pray you to give it over,' said Hugh Crombie, very earnestly. 'The girl is young, lovely, and as good as she is fair. I cannot aid in her ruin. Nay, more—I must prevent it.'

'Prevent it!' exclaimed the traveller, with a darkening countenance. 'Think twice before you stir in this matter, I advise you. Ruin, do you say? Does a girl call it ruin, to be made an honest wedded wife? No, no, mine host; nor does a widow either—else have you much to answer for.'

'I gave the Widow Hutchins fair play, at least; which is more than poor Ellen is like to get,' observed the landlord. 'My old comrade, will you not give up this scheme?'

'My old comrade, I will not give up this scheme,' returned the other, composedly. 'Why, Hugh, what has come over you, since we last met? Have we not done twenty worse deeds of a morning, and laughed over them at night?'

'He is right there,' said Hugh Crombie, in a meditative tone. 'Of a certainty, my conscience has grown unreasonably tender, within the last two years. This one small sin, if I were to aid in it, would add but a trifle to the sum of mine. But then the poor girl——'

His companion overheard him thus communing with himself, and having had much former experience of his infirmity of purpose, doubted not that he should bend him to his will.

In fact, his arguments were so effectual, that Hugh at length, though reluctantly, promised his co-operation. It was necessary that their motions should be speedy; for, on the second day thereafter, the arrival of the post would bring intelligence of the shipwreck, by which Mr. Langton had perished.

'And after the deed is done,' said the landlord, 'I beseech you never to cross my path again. There have been more wicked thoughts in my head, within the last hour, than for the whole two years that I have been an honest man.'

'What a saint art thou become, Hugh!' said his comrade. 'But fear not that we shall meet again. When I leave this valley, it will be to enter it no more.'

'And there is little danger that any other, who has known me, will chance upon me here,' observed Hugh Crombie. 'Our trade was unfavorable to length of days, and I suppose most of our old comrades have arrived at the end of theirs.'

'One, whom you knew well, is nearer to you than you think,' answered the traveller; 'for I did not travel hitherward entirely alone.'

V

A naughty night to swim in.
SHAKSPEARE

THE EVENING of the day succeeding the adventure
of the angler, was dark and tempestuous. The rain descended almost in a continued sheet, and occasional
powerful gusts of wind drove it hard against the north-eastern
windows of Hugh Crombie's Inn. But at least one apartment
of the interior presented a scene of comfort, and of apparent
enjoyment; the more delightful from its contrast with the ele-
mental fury that raged without. A fire, which the chillness of
the evening, though a summer one, made necessary, was burning brightly on the hearth; and in front was placed a small
round table, sustaining wine and glasses. One of the guests,
for whom these preparations had been made, was Edward
Walcott. The other was a shy, awkward young man, distinguished, by the union of classic and rural dress, as having
but lately become a student of Harley College. He seemed
little at his ease—probably from a consciousness that he was
on forbidden ground, and that the wine, of which he nevertheless swallowed a larger share than his companion, was an
unlawful draught.

In the catalogue of crimes, provided against by the laws
of Harley College, that of tavern-haunting was one of the
principal. The secluded situation of the seminary, indeed,
gave its scholars but a very limited choice of vices; and this

was therefore the usual channel by which the wildness of youth discharged itself. Edward Walcott, though naturally temperate, had been not an unfrequent offender in this respect; for which a superfluity both of time and money might plead some excuse. But since his acquaintance with Ellen Langton he had rarely entered Hugh Crombie's doors; and an interruption in that acquaintance was the cause of his present appearance there.

Edward's jealous pride had been considerably touched on Ellen's compliance with the request of the angler. He had by degrees, imperceptible perhaps to himself, assumed the right of feeling displeased with her conduct; and she had as imperceptibly accustomed herself to consider what would be his wishes, and to act accordingly. He would, indeed, in no contingency, have ventured an open remonstrance; and such a proceeding would have been attended by a result, the reverse of what he desired. But there existed between them a silent compact (acknowledged perhaps by neither, but felt by both) according to which they had regulated the latter part of their intercourse. Their lips had yet spoken no word of love; but some of love's rights and privileges had been assumed on the one side, and at least not disallowed on the other.

Edward's penetration had been sufficiently quick to discover that there was a mystery about the angler—that there must have been a cause for the blush that rose so proudly on Ellen's cheek; and his quixotism had been not a little mortified, because she did not immediately appeal to his protection. He had however paid his usual visit, the next day, at Doctor Melmoth's, expecting that, by a smile of more than common brightness, she would make amends to his wounded feelings—such having been her usual mode of reparation, in the few instances of disagreement that had occurred between them. But he was disappointed. He found her cold, silent, and abstracted, inattentive when he spoke, and indisposed to speak herself. Her eye was sedulously averted from his; and the casual meeting of their glances, only proved, that there were feelings in her bosom which he did not share. He was unable to account for this change in her deportment; and, added to his previous conceptions of his wrongs, it produced an effect upon his rather hasty temper, that might have manifested itself violently, but for the presence of Mrs. Melmoth. He took his leave in very evident displeasure; but, just as he closed the door, he noticed an expression in Ellen's countenance, that, had they been alone, and had not he been quite so proud, would have drawn him down to her feet. Their eyes met—when, suddenly, there was a gush of tears into those of Ellen, and a deep sadness, almost despair, spread itself over her features. He paused a moment, and then went his way; equally unable to account for her coldness, or for her grief. He was well aware, however, that his situation in respect to her, was unaccountably changed—a conviction so disagreeable, that, but for a hope that is latent, even in the despair of youthful hearts, he could have been sorely tempted to shoot himself.

The gloom of his thoughts—a mood of mind the more intolerable to him, because so unusual—had driven him to Hugh Crombie's Inn, in search of artificial excitement. But even the wine had no attractions; and his first glass stood now almost untouched before him, while he gazed in heavy thought into the glowing embers of the fire. His companion perceived his melancholy, and essayed to dispel it by a choice of such topics of conversation, as he conceived would be most agreeable.

'There is a lady in the house,' he observed. 'I caught a glimpse of her in the passage, as we came in. Did you see her, Edward?'

'A lady,' repeated Edward carelessly. 'What know you of ladies? No, I did not see her; but I will venture to say that it was Dame Crombie's self, and no other.'

'Well, perhaps it might,' said the other, doubtingly. 'Her head was turned from me, and she was gone like a shadow.'

'Dame Crombie is no shadow, and never vanishes like one,' resumed Edward. 'You have mistaken the slip-shod servant girl for a lady.'

'Aye, but she had a white hand, a small white hand,' said the student, piqued at Edward's contemptuous opinion of his powers of observation—'as white as Ellen Langton's.' He paused, for the lover was offended by the profanity of the comparison, as was made evident by the blood that rushed to his brow.

'We will appeal to the landlord,' said Edward, recovering his equanimity, and turning to Hugh, who just then entered the room—'Who is this angel, mine host, that has taken up her abode in the Hand and Bottle?'

Hugh cast a quick glance from one to another, before he answered, 'I keep no angels here, gentlemen. Dame Crombie would make the house any thing but Heaven, for them and me.'

'And yet Glover has seen a vision in the passage way—a lady with a small white hand.'

'Ah! I understand—a slight mistake of the young gentleman's,' said Hugh, with the air of one who could perfectly account for the mystery. 'Our passage way is dark—or perhaps the light had dazzled his eyes. It was the Widow Fowler's daughter, that came to borrow a pipe of tobacco for her mother. By the same token, she put it into her own sweet mouth, and puffed as she went along.'

'But the white hand,' said Glover, only half convinced.

'Nay, I know not,' answered Hugh, 'but her hand was at least as white as her face; that I can swear. Well, gentlemen, I trust you find every thing in my house to your satisfaction. When the fire needs renewing, or the wine runs low, be pleased to tap on the table. I shall appear with the speed of a sunbeam.'

After the departure of the landlord, the conversation of the young men amounted to little more than monosyllables. Edward Walcott was wrapped in his own contemplations, and his companion was in a half slumberous state, from which he started every quarter of an hour, at the chiming of the clock that stood in a corner. The fire died gradually away, the lamps began to burn dim, and Glover, rousing himself from one of his periodical slumbers, was about to propose a return to their chambers. He was prevented, however, by the approach of footsteps along the passage way; and Hugh Crombie, opening the door, ushered a person into the room, and retired.

The new comer was Fanshawe. The water, that poured plentifully from his cloak, evinced that he had but just arrived at the Inn; but whatever was his object, he seemed not to have attained it, in meeting with the young men. He paused near the door, as if meditating whether to retire.

'My intrusion is altogether owing to a mistake, either of the landlord's, or mine,' he said; 'I came hither to seek another person; but as I could not mention his name, my inquiries were rather vague.'

'I thank Heaven for the chance that sent you to us,' replied Edward, rousing himself; 'Glover is wretched company, and a duller evening have I never spent. We will renew our fire, and our wine, and you must sit down with us. And for the man you seek,' he continued in a whisper, 'he left the Inn within a half hour after we encountered him. I inquired of Hugh Crombie, last night.'

Fanshawe did not express his doubts of the correctness of the information on which Edward seemed to rely. Laying aside his cloak, he accepted his invitation to make one of the party, and sat down by the fireside.

The aspect of the evening now gradually changed. A strange wild glee spread from one to another of the party, which, much to the surprise of his companions, began with,

and was communicated from, Fanshawe. He seemed to
overflow with conceptions, inimitably ludicrous, but so singular, that, till his hearers had imbibed a portion of his own
spirit, they could only wonder at, instead of enjoying them.
His applications to the wine were very unfrequent; yet his
conversation was such as one might expect from a bottle of
champagne, endowed by a fairy with the gift of speech. The
secret of this strange mirth lay in the troubled state of his
spirits, which, like the vexed ocean at midnight, (if the simile
be not too magnificent,) tossed forth a mysterious brightness.
The undefined apprehensions, that had drawn him to the
Inn, still distracted his mind; but mixed with them, there
was a sort of joy, not easily to be described. By degrees, and
by the assistance of the wine, the inspiration spread, each one
contributing such a quantity, and such quality of wit and
whim, as was proportioned to his genius; but each one, and
all, displaying a greater share of both, than they had ever been
suspected of possessing.

At length, however, there was a pause—the deep pause of
flagging spirits, that always follows mirth and wine. No one
would have believed, on beholding the pensive faces, and
hearing the involuntary sighs, of the party, that from these,
but a moment before, had arisen so loud and wild a laugh.
During this interval, Edward Walcott, (who was the poet
of his class,) volunteered the following song, which, from
its want of polish, and from its application to his present
feelings, might charitably be taken for an extemporaneous
production.

> The wine is bright, the wine is bright,
>   And gay the drinkers be;
> Of all that drain the bowl to-night,
>   Most jollily drain we.
> Oh, could one search the weary earth,
>   The earth from sea to sea,—
> He'd turn and mingle in our mirth,
>   For we're the merriest three.

Yet there are cares, oh, heavy cares,—
    We know that they are nigh;
When forth each lonely drinker fares,
    Mark then his altered eye.
Care comes upon us when the jest,
    And frantic laughter, die;
And care will watch the parting guest,—
    Oh late, then, let us fly!

Hugh Crombie, whose early love of song and minstrelsy was still alive, had entered the room at the sound of Edward's voice, in sufficient time to accompany the second stanza on the violin. He now, with the air of one who was entitled to judge in these matters, expressed his opinion of the performance.

'Really, Master Walcott, I was not prepared for this,' he said, in the tone of condescending praise, that a great man uses to his inferior, when he chooses to overwhelm him with excess of joy. 'Very well, indeed, young gentleman. Some of the lines, it is true, seem to have been dragged in by the head and shoulders; but I could scarcely have done much better myself, at your age. With practice, and with such instruction as I might afford you, I should have little doubt of your becoming a distinguished poet. A great defect in your seminary, gentlemen—the want of due cultivation in this heavenly art.'

'Perhaps, Sir,' said Edward, with much gravity, 'you might yourself be prevailed upon to accept the Professorship of Poetry?'

'Why, such an offer would require consideration,' replied the landlord. 'Professor Hugh Crombie, of Harley College;— it has a good sound, assuredly. But I am a public man, Master Walcott, and the public would be loath to spare me from my present office.'

'Will Professor Crombie favor us with a specimen of his productions?' inquired Edward.

'Ahem, I shall be happy to gratify you, young gentleman,'

answered Hugh. 'It is seldom, in this rude country, Master Walcott, that we meet with kindred genius; and the opportunity should never be thrown away.'

Thus saying, he took a heavy draught of the liquor by which he was usually inspired, and the praises of which were the prevailing subject of his song. Then, after much hemming, thrumming, and prelusion, and with many queer gestures and gesticulations, he began to effuse a lyric, in the following fashion.

> I've been a jolly drinker, this five and twenty year,
> And still a jolly drinker, my friends, you see me here;
> I sing the joys of drinking;—bear a chorus every man,
> With pint pot, and quart pot, and clattering of can.

The sense of the Professor's first stanza, was not in exact proportion to the sound; but being executed with great spirit, it attracted universal applause. This, Hugh appropriated with a condescending bow and smile; and making a signal for silence, he went on—

> King Solomon of old, boys, (a jolly king was he,)—

But here he was interrupted by a clapping of hands, that seemed a continuance of the applause bestowed on his former stanza. Hugh Crombie, who, as is the custom of many great performers, usually sang with his eyes shut, now opened them, intending gently to rebuke his auditors for their unseasonable expression of delight. He immediately perceived, however, that the fault was to be attributed to neither of the three young men; and following the direction of their eyes, he saw, near the door, in the dim back-ground of the apartment, a figure in a cloak. The hat was flapped forward, the cloak muffled round the lower part of the face, and only the eyes were visible.

The party gazed a moment in silence, and then rushed *en masse* upon the intruder, the landlord bringing up the rear, and sounding a charge upon his fiddle. But as they drew nigh, the black cloak began to assume a familiar look—the hat, also, was an old acquaintance;—and these being removed, from beneath them shone forth the reverend face and form of Doctor Melmoth.

The President, in his quality of clergyman, had, late in the preceding afternoon, been called to visit an aged female, who was supposed to be at the point of death. Her habitation was at the distance of several miles from Harley College; so that it was night-fall before Doctor Melmoth stood at her bed-side. His stay had been lengthened beyond his anticipation, on account of the frame of mind in which he found the dying woman; and after essaying to impart the comforts of religion to her disturbed intellect, he had waited for the abatement of the storm, that had arisen while he was thus engaged. As the evening advanced, however, the rain poured down in undiminished cataracts; and the Doctor, trusting to the prudence, and sure-footedness of his steed, had, at length, set forth on his return. The darkness of the night, and the roughness of the road, might have appalled him, even had his horsemanship and his courage been more considerable than they were; but by the special protection of Providence, as he reasonably supposed, (for he was a good man, and on a good errand,) he arrived safely as far as Hugh Crombie's Inn. Doctor Melmoth had no intention of making a stay there; but as the road passed within a very short distance, he saw lights in the windows, and heard the sound of song and revelry. It immediately occurred to him, that these midnight rioters were, probably, some of the young men of his charge, and he was impelled, by a sense of duty, to enter and disperse them. Directed by the voices, he found his way, with some difficulty, to the apartment, just as Hugh concluded his first stanza, and amidst the subsequent applause, his entrance had been unperceived.

There was a silence of a moment's continuance, after the

discovery of Doctor Melmoth, during which he attempted to clothe his round, good-natured face, in a look of awful dignity. But, in spite of himself, there was a little twisting of the corners of his mouth, and a smothered gleam in his eye.

'This has apparently been a very merry meeting, young gentlemen,' he at length said; 'but I fear my presence has cast a damp upon it.'

'Oh, yes! your reverence's cloak is wet enough to cast a damp upon anything,' exclaimed Hugh Crombie, assuming a look of tender anxiety. 'The young gentlemen are affrighted for your valuable life. Fear deprives them of utterance; permit me to relieve you of these dangerous garments.'

'Trouble not yourself, honest man,' replied the Doctor, who was one of the most gullible of mortals. 'I trust I am in no danger, my dwelling being near at hand. But for these young men——'

'Would your reverence but honor my Sunday suit—the gray broadcloth coat, and the black velvet small-clothes, that have covered my unworthy legs but once? Dame Crombie shall have them ready in a moment,' continued Hugh, beginning to divest the Doctor of his garments.

'I pray you to appease your anxiety,' cried Doctor Melmoth, retaining a firm hold on such parts of his dress as yet remained to him. 'Fear not for my health. I will but speak a word to those misguided youth, and begone.'

'Misguided youth, did your reverence say?' echoed Hugh, in a tone of utter astonishment. 'Never were they better guided, than when they entered my poor house. Oh! had your reverence but seen them, when I heard their cries, and rushed forth to their assistance. Dripping with wet were they, like three drowned men at the resurrec—ahem!' interrupted Hugh, recollecting that the comparison he meditated might not suit the Doctor's ideas of propriety.

'But why were they abroad on such a night?' inquired the President.

'Ah! Doctor, you little know the love these good young gentlemen bear for you,' replied the landlord. 'Your absence— your long absence—had alarmed them; and they rushed forth through the rain and darkness to seek you.'

'And was this indeed so?' asked the Doctor in a softened tone, and casting a tender and grateful look upon the three students. They, it is but justice to mention, had simultaneously made a step forward, in order to contradict the egregious falsehoods, of which Hugh's fancy was so fertile; but he assumed an expression of such ludicrous entreaty, that it was irresistible.

'But methinks their anxiety was not of long continuance,' observed Doctor Melmoth, looking at the wine, and remembering the song that his entrance had interrupted.

'Ah! your reverence disapproves of the wine, I see,' answered Hugh Crombie. 'I did but offer them a drop, to keep the life in their poor young hearts. My dame advised strong waters; but, Dame Crombie, says I, would ye corrupt their youth? And in my zeal for their good, Doctor, I was delighting them, just at your entrance, with a pious little melody of my own, against the sin of drunkenness.'

'Truly, I remember something of the kind,' observed Doctor Melmoth; 'and, as I think, it seemed to meet with good acceptance.'

'Aye, that it did,' said the landlord. 'Will it please your reverence to hear it?

King Solomon of old, boys, (a wise man I'm thinking,)
Has warned you to beware of the horrid vice of drinking—

But why talk I of drinking, foolish man that I am! and all this time, Doctor, you have not sipped a drop of my wine. Now, I entreat your reverence, as you value your health, and the peace and quiet of these youth.'

Doctor Melmoth drank a glass of wine, with the benevolent

intention of allaying the anxiety of Hugh Crombie and the students. He then prepared to depart; for a strong wind had partially dispersed the clouds, and occasioned an interval in the cataract of rain. There was, perhaps, a little suspicion yet remaining in the good man's mind, respecting the truth of the landlord's story;—at least, it was his evident intention, to see the students fairly out of the Inn, before he quitted it himself. They therefore proceeded along the passage way in a body. The lamp that Hugh Crombie held, but dimly en-lightened them, and the number and contiguity of the doors, caused Doctor Melmoth to lay his hand upon the wrong one.

'Not there, not there, Doctor! It is Dame Crombie's bed-chamber,' shouted Hugh, most energetically. 'Now Belzebub defend me,' he muttered to himself, perceiving that his ex-clamation had been a moment too late.

'Heavens! what do I see?' ejaculated Doctor Melmoth, lifting his hands, and starting back from the entrance of the room. The three students pressed forward;—Mrs. Crombie and the servant girl had been drawn to the spot, by the sound of Hugh's voice; and all their wondering eyes were fixed on poor Ellen Langton.

The apartment, in the midst of which she stood, was dimly lighted by a solitary candle, at the farther extremity; but Ellen was exposed to the glare of the three lamps, held by Hugh, his wife, and the servant girl. Their combined rays seemed to form a focus exactly at the point where they reached her; and the beholders, had any been sufficiently calm, might have watched her features, in their agitated workings, and frequent change of expression, as perfectly as by the broad light of day. Terror had at first blanched her as white as a lily, or as a marble statue, which for a moment she resembled, as she stood motionless in the centre of the room. Shame next bore sway; and her blushing countenance, covered by her slender white fingers, might fantastically be compared to a variegated rose, with its alternate stripes of white and red. The next instant, a sense of her pure and innocent intentions gave her strength and courage; and her attitude and look had now something of pride and dignity. These, however, in their turn gave way; for Edward Walcott pressed forward, and attempted to address her.

'Ellen, Ellen,' he said in an agitated and quivering whisper; —but what was to follow cannot be known, for his emotion checked his utterance. His tone, and look, however, again overcame Ellen Langton, and she burst into tears. Fanshawe advanced and took Edward's arm; 'She has been deceived,' he whispered—'she is innocent. You are unworthy of her if you doubt it.'

'Why do you interfere, Sir?' demanded Edward, whose passions, thoroughly excited, would willingly have wreaked themselves on any one. 'What right have you to speak of her innocence? Perhaps,' he continued, an undefined and ridiculous suspicion arising in his mind, 'perhaps you are acquainted with her intentions. Perhaps you are the deceiver.'

Fanshawe's temper was not naturally of the meekest character; and having had a thousand bitter feelings of his own to overcome, before he could attempt to console Edward, this rude repulse had almost aroused him to fierceness. But his pride, of which a more moderate degree would have had a less peaceable effect, came to his assistance, and he turned calmly and contemptuously away.

Ellen, in the meantime, had been restored to some degree of composure. To this effect, a feeling of pique against Edward Walcott had contributed. She had distinguished his voice in the neighboring apartment—had heard his mirth and wild laughter, without being aware of the state of feeling that produced them. She had supposed that the terms on which they parted in the morning, (which had been very grievous to herself,) would have produced a corresponding sadness in him. But while she sat in loneliness and in tears, her bosom distracted by a thousand anxieties and sorrows, of many of which Edward was the object, his reckless gaiety had seemed to prove the slight regard in which he held her. After the first outbreak of emotion, therefore, she called up her pride, (of which, on proper occasions, she had a reasonable share,) and sustained his upbraiding glance with a passive composure, which women have more readily at command than men.

Doctor Melmoth's surprise had, during this time, kept him silent and inactive. He gazed alternately from one to another, of those who stood around him, as if to seek some explanation of so strange an event. But the faces of all were as perplexed as his own;—even Hugh Crombie had assumed a look of speechless wonder—speechless, because his imagination, prolific as it was, could not supply a plausible falsehood.

'Ellen, dearest child,' at length said the Doctor, 'what is the meaning of this?'

Ellen endeavored to reply; but, as her composure was merely external, she was unable to render her words audible. Fanshawe spoke in a low voice to Doctor Melmoth, who appeared grateful for his advice.

'True, it will be the better way,' he replied. 'My wits are utterly confounded, or I should not have remained thus long. Come, my dear child,' he continued, advancing to Ellen, and taking her hand, 'let us return home, and defer the explanation till the morrow. There, there; only dry your eyes, and we will say no more about it.'

'And that will be your wisest way, old gentleman,' muttered Hugh Crombie.

Ellen at first exhibited but little desire—or, rather, an evident reluctance—to accompany her guardian. She hung back, while her glance passed almost imperceptibly over the faces that gazed so eagerly at her; but the one she sought was not visible among them. She had no alternative, and suffered herself to be led from the Inn.

Edward Walcott, alone, remained behind—the most

wretched being, (at least such was his own opinion,) that breathed the vital air. He felt a sinking and sickness of the heart, and alternately a feverish frenzy, neither of which his short and cloudless existence had heretofore occasioned him to experience. He was jealous of, he knew not whom, and he knew not what. He was ungenerous enough to believe that Ellen—his pure and lovely Ellen—had degraded herself; though from what motive, or by whose agency, he could not conjecture. When Doctor Melmoth had taken her in charge, Edward returned to the apartment where he had spent the evening. The wine was still upon the table, and in the desperate hope of stupifying his faculties, he unwisely swallowed huge successive draughts. The effect of his imprudence was not long in manifesting itself; though insensibility, which at another time would have been the result, did not now follow. Acting upon his previous agitation, the wine seemed to set his blood in a flame; and for the time being, he was a perfect madman.

A phrenologist would probably have found the organ of destructiveness in strong development, just then, upon Edward's cranium; for he certainly manifested an impulse to break and destroy whatever chanced to be within his reach. He commenced his operations by upsetting the table and breaking the bottles and glasses. Then, seizing a tall heavy chair in each hand, he hurled them, with prodigious force, one through the window, and the other against a large looking-glass, the most valuable article of furniture in Hugh Crombie's Inn. The crash and clatter of these outrageous proceedings, soon brought the master, mistress, and maid-servant to the scene of action; but the two latter, at the first sight of Edward's wild demeanor and gleaming eyes, retreated with all imaginable expedition. Hugh chose a position behind the door, from whence protruding his head, he endeavored to mollify his inebriated guest. His interference, however, had nearly been productive of most unfortunate consequences; for a massive andiron, with round brazen head, whizzed past him, within a hair's breadth of his ear.

'I might as safely take my chance in a battle,' exclaimed Hugh, withdrawing his head, and speaking to a man who stood in the passage way. 'A little twist of his hand to the left would have served my turn, as well as if I stood in the path of a forty-two pound ball. And here comes another broadside,' he added, as some other article of furniture rattled against the door.

'Let us return his fire, Hugh,' said the person whom he addressed, composedly lifting the andiron. 'He is in want of ammunition; let us send him back his own.'

The sound of this man's voice produced a most singular effect upon Edward. The moment before, his actions had been those of a raving maniac; but when the words struck his ear, he paused, put his hand to his forehead, seemed to recollect himself, and finally advanced with a firm and steady step. His countenance was dark and angry, but no longer wild.

'I have found you, villain,' he said to the angler. 'It is you who have done this.'

'And having done it, the wrath of a boy—his drunken wrath—will not induce me to deny it,' replied the other scornfully.

'The boy will require a man's satisfaction,' returned Edward —'and that speedily.'

'Will you take it now?' inquired the angler, with a cool, derisive smile, and almost in a whisper. At the same time he produced a brace of pistols, and held them towards the young man.

'Willingly,' answered Edward, taking one of the weapons. 'Choose your distance.'

The angler stepped back a pace; but before their deadly intentions, so suddenly conceived, could be executed, Hugh Crombie interposed himself between them.

'Do you take my best parlor for the cabin of the Black Andrew, where a pistol shot was a nightly pastime?' he inquired of his comrade. 'And you, Master Edward, with what sort of a face will you walk into the chapel, to morning prayers, after putting a ball through this man's head, or receiving one through your own?—Though in this last case, you will be past praying for, or praying, either.'

'Stand aside—I will take the risk. Make way, or I will put the ball through your own head,' exclaimed Edward, fiercely; for the interval of rationality, that circumstances had produced, was again giving way to intoxication.

'You see how it is,' said Hugh to his companion, unheard by Edward. 'You shall take a shot at me, sooner than at the poor lad in his present state. You have done him harm enough already, and intend him more. I propose,' he continued aloud, and with a peculiar glance towards the angler, 'that this affair be decided tomorrow, at nine o'clock, under the old oak, on the bank of the stream. In the meantime I will take charge of these pop-guns, for fear of accidents.'

'Well, mine host, be it as you wish,' said his comrade. 'A shot, more or less, is of little consequence to me.' He accordingly delivered his weapon to Hugh Crombie, and walked carelessly away.

'Come, Master Walcott, the enemy has retreated. Victoria! And now, I see, the sooner I get you to your chamber, the better,' added he aside; for the wine was at last beginning to produce its legitimate effect, in stupifying the young man's mental and bodily faculties.

Hugh Crombie's assistance, though not perhaps quite indispensable, was certainly very convenient to our unfortunate hero, in the course of the short walk that brought him to his chamber. When arrived there, and in bed, he was soon locked in a sleep, scarcely less deep than that of death.

The weather, during the last hour, had appeared to be on

the point of changing;—indeed, there were every few minutes, most rapid changes. A strong breeze sometimes drove the clouds from the brow of heaven, so as to disclose a few of the stars; but, immediately after, the darkness would again become Egyptian, and the rain rush like a torrent from the sky.

VI

About her neck a packet-mail
Fraught with advice, some fresh, some stale,
Of men that walked when they were dead.

HUDIBRAS

SCARCELY a word had passed between Doctor Melmoth and Ellen Langton, on their way home; for, though the former was aware that his duty towards his ward would compel him to inquire into the motives of her conduct, the tenderness of his heart prompted him to defer the scrutiny to the latest moment. The same tenderness induced him to connive at Ellen's stealing secretly up to her chamber, unseen by Mrs. Melmoth; to render which measure practicable, he opened the house door very softly, and stood before his half-sleeping spouse, (who waited his arrival in the parlor,) without any previous notice. This act of the Doctor's benevolence was not destitute of heroism; for he was well assured, that, should the affair come to the lady's knowledge through any other channel, her vengeance would descend not less heavily on him for concealing, than on Ellen for perpetrating, the elopement. That she had, thus far, no suspicion of the fact, was evident from her composure, as well as from the reply to a question, which, with more than his usual art, her husband put to her respecting the non-appearance of his ward. Mrs. Melmoth answered that Ellen had complained of indisposition, and, after drinking, by her prescription, a large cup of herb-tea, had retired to her chamber, early in the evening. Thankful that all was yet safe, the Doctor laid his head upon his pillow; but, late as was the hour, his many anxious thoughts long drove sleep from his eyelids.

The diminution in the quantity of his natural rest, did not, however, prevent Doctor Melmoth from rising at his usual hour, which, at all seasons of the year, was an early one. He found, on descending to the parlor, that breakfast was nearly in readiness; for the lady of the house, (and, as a corollary, her servant girl,) was not accustomed to await the rising of the sun, in order to commence her domestic labors. Ellen Langton, however, who had heretofore assimilated her habits to those of the family, was this morning invisible— a circumstance imputed by Mrs. Melmoth to her indisposition of the preceding evening, and by the Doctor to mortification, on account of her elopement, and its discovery.

'I think I will step into Ellen's bed-chamber,' said Mrs. Melmoth, 'and inquire how she feels herself. The morning is delightful after the storm, and the air will do her good.'

'Had we not better proceed with our breakfast? If the poor child is sleeping, it were a pity to disturb her,' observed the Doctor; for, besides his sympathy with Ellen's feelings, he was reluctant, as if he were the guilty one, to meet her face.

'Well, be it so. And now sit down, Doctor, for the hot cakes are cooling fast. I suppose you will say they are not so good as those Ellen made, yesterday morning. I know not how you will bear to part with her; though the thing must soon be.'

'It will be a sore trial, doubtless,' replied Doctor Melmoth —'like tearing away a branch that is grafted on an old tree. And yet there will be a satisfaction in delivering her safe into her father's hands.'

'A satisfaction for which you may thank me, Doctor,' observed the lady. 'If there had been none but you to look after the poor thing's doings, she would have been enticed away long ere this, for the sake of her money.'

Doctor Melmoth's prudence could scarcely restrain a smile

at the thought, that an elopement, as he had reason to believe, had been plotted, and partly carried into execution, while Ellen was under the sole care of his lady; and had been frustrated only by his own despised agency. He was not accustomed, however—nor was this an eligible occasion—to dispute any of Mrs. Melmoth's claims to superior wisdom.

The breakfast proceeded in silence—or, at least, without any conversation material to the tale. At its conclusion, Mrs. Melmoth was again meditating on the propriety of entering Ellen's chamber; but she was now prevented by an incident, that always excited much interest both in herself and her husband.

This was the entrance of the servant, bearing the letters and newspaper, with which, once a fortnight, the mail-carrier journeyed up the valley. Doctor Melmoth's situation, at the head of a respectable seminary, and his character, as a scholar, had procured him an extensive correspondence among the learned men of his own country; and he had even exchanged epistles with one or two of the most distinguished dissenting clergymen of Great Britain. But, unless when some fond mother enclosed a one pound note, to defray the private expenses of her son at College—it was frequently the case, that the packets addressed to the Doctor, were the sole contents of the mail bag. In the present instance, his letters were very numerous, and, to judge from the one he chanced first to open, of an unconscionable length. While he was engaged in their perusal, Mrs. Melmoth amused herself with the newspaper—a little sheet of about twelve inches square, which had but one rival in the country. Commencing with the title, she labored on, through advertisements, old and new, through poetry, lamentably deficient in rhythm and rhymes—through essays, the ideas of which had been trite since the first week of the creation;—till she finally arrived at the department that, a fortnight before, had contained the latest news from all quarters. Making such remarks upon these items as to her seemed good, the dame's notice was at length attracted by an article, which her sudden exclamation proved to possess uncommon interest. Casting her eye hastily over it, she immediately began to read aloud to her husband; but he, deeply engaged in a long and learned letter, instead of listening to what she wished to communicate, exerted his own lungs in opposition to hers—as is the custom of abstracted men, when disturbed. The result was as follows.

'A brig just arrived in the outer harbor,' began Mrs. Melmoth, 'reports, that on the morning of the 25th ult.'—here the Doctor broke in, 'wherefore I am compelled to differ from your exposition of the said passage, for those reasons, of the which I have given you a taste; provided'—the lady's voice was now most audible—'ship bottom upward, discovered by the name on her stern to be the Ellen of'—'and in the same opinion are Hooker, Cotton, and divers learned divines of a later date.'

The Doctor's lungs were deep and strong, and victory seemed to incline toward him; but Mrs. Melmoth now made use of a tone, whose peculiar shrillness, as long experience had taught her husband, argued a mood of mind not to be trifled with.

'On my word, Doctor,' she exclaimed, 'this is most unfeeling and unchristian conduct! Here am I, endeavoring to inform you of the death of an old friend, and you continue as deaf as a post.'

Doctor Melmoth, who had heard the sound, without receiving the sense, of these words, now laid aside the letter in despair, and submissively requested to be informed of her pleasure.

'There—read for yourself,' she replied, handing him the paper, and pointing to the passage containing the important intelligence. 'Read, and then finish your letter, if you have a mind.'

He took the paper, unable to conjecture how the dame

could be so much interested in any part of its contents; but, before he had read many words, he grew pale as death. 'Good Heavens, what is this?' he exclaimed. He then read on, 'being the vessel wherein that eminent son of New-England, John Langton, Esquire, had taken passage for his native country, after an absence of many years.'

'Our poor Ellen, his orphan child!' said Doctor Melmoth, dropping the paper. 'How shall we break the intelligence to her? Alas! her share of the affliction causes me to forget my own.'

'It is a heavy misfortune, doubtless, and Ellen will grieve as a daughter should,' replied Mrs. Melmoth, speaking with the good sense of which she had a competent share. 'But she has never known her father, and her sorrow must arise from a sense of duty, more than from strong affection. I will go and inform her of her loss. It is late, and I wonder if she be still asleep?'

'Be cautious, dearest wife,' said the Doctor.—'Ellen has strong feelings, and a sudden shock might be dangerous.'

'I think I may be trusted, Doctor Melmoth,' replied the lady, who had a high opinion of her own abilities as a comforter, and was not averse to exercise them.

Her husband, after her departure, sat listlessly turning over the letters, that yet remained unopened, feeling little curiosity, after such melancholy intelligence, respecting their contents. But by the hand writing of the direction on one of them, his attention was gradually arrested, till he found himself gazing earnestly on those strong, firm, regular characters. They were perfectly familiar to his eye; but from what hand they came, he could not conjecture. Suddenly, however, the truth burst upon him; and, after noticing the date, and reading a few lines, he rushed hastily in pursuit of his wife. He had arrived at the top of his speed, and at the middle of the stair-case, when his course was arrested by the lady whom he sought, who came, with a velocity equal to his own, in an opposite direction. The consequence was, a concussion between the two meeting masses, by which Mrs. Melmoth was seated securely on the stairs, while the Doctor was only preserved from precipitation to the bottom, by clinging desperately to the balustrade. As soon as the pair discovered that they had sustained no material injury by their contact, they began eagerly to explain the cause of their mutual haste, without those reproaches, which, on the lady's part, would, at another time, have followed such an accident.

'You have not told her the bad news, I trust?' cried Doctor Melmoth, after each had communicated his and her intelligence, without obtaining audience of the other.

'Would you have me tell it to the bare walls?' inquired the lady, in her shrillest tone. 'Have I not just informed you that she has gone, fled, eloped? Her chamber is empty, and her bed has not been occupied.'

'Gone!' repeated the Doctor—'and when her father comes to demand his daughter of me, what answer shall I make?'

'Now, Heaven defend us from the visits of the dead and drowned!' cried Mrs. Melmoth. 'This is a serious affair, Doctor; but not, I trust, sufficient to raise a ghost.'

'Mr. Langton is yet no ghost,' answered he; 'though this event will go near to make him one. He was fortunately prevented, after he had made every preparation, from taking passage in the vessel that was lost.'

'And where is he now,' she inquired.

'He is in New-England. Perhaps he is at this moment, on his way to us,' replied her husband. 'His letter is dated nearly a fortnight back, and he expresses an intention of being with us in a few days.'

'Well, I thank Heaven for his safety,' said Mrs. Melmoth; 'but truly, the poor gentleman could not have chosen a better time to be drowned, nor a worse one to come to life, than this. What we shall do, Doctor, I know not; but, had you locked the doors, and fastened the windows, as I advised, the misfortune could not have happened.'

'Why, the whole country would have flouted us,' answered the Doctor. 'Is there a door in all the province, that is barred or bolted, night or day? Nevertheless, it might have been advisable last night, had it occurred to me.'

'And why at that time, more than at all times?' she inquired. 'We had surely no reason to fear this event.'

Doctor Melmoth was silent; for his worldly wisdom was sufficient to deter him from giving his lady the opportunity, which she would not fail to use to the utmost, of laying the blame of the elopement at his door. He now proceeded, with a heavy heart, to Ellen's chamber, to satisfy himself with his own eyes, of the state of affairs. It was deserted, too truly; and the wild flowers with which it was the maiden's custom, daily, to decorate her premises, were drooping, as if in sorrow, for her who had placed them there. Mrs. Melmoth, on this second visit, discovered on the table a note, addressed to her husband, and containing a few words of gratitude from Ellen, but no explanation of her mysterious flight. The Doctor gazed long on the tiny letters, which had evidently been traced with a trembling hand, and blotted with many tears.

'There is a mystery in this—a mystery that I cannot fathom,' he said. 'And now, I would I knew what measures it would be proper to take.'

'Get you on horseback, Doctor Melmoth, and proceed as speedily as may be, down the valley to the town,' said the dame, the influence of whose firmer mind was sometimes, as in the present case, most beneficially exerted over his own. 'You must not spare for trouble—no, nor for danger—now, oh! if I were a man——'

'Oh that you were,' murmured the Doctor, in a perfectly inaudible voice. 'Well, and when I reach the town, what then?'

'As I am a christian woman, my patience cannot endure you,' exclaimed Mrs. Melmoth—'oh, I love to see a man with the spirit of a man; but you——' and she turned away in utter scorn.

'But, dearest wife,' remonstrated the husband, who was really at a loss how to proceed, and anxious for her advice, 'your worldly experience is greater than mine, and I desire to profit by it. What should be my next measure, after arriving at the town?'

Mrs. Melmoth was appeased by the submission with which the Doctor asked her counsel; though, if the truth must be told, she heartily despised him for needing it. She condescended, however, to instruct him in the proper method of pursuing the runaway maiden, and directed him, before his departure, to put strict inquiries to Hugh Crombie, respecting any stranger who might lately have visited his Inn. That there would be wisdom in this, Doctor Melmoth had his own reasons for believing; and, still without imparting them to his lady, he proceeded to do as he had been bid.

The veracious landlord acknowledged that a stranger had spent a night and day at his Inn, and was missing that morning; but he utterly denied all acquaintance with his character, or privity to his purposes. Had Mrs. Melmoth, instead of her husband, conducted the examination, the result might have been different. As the case was, the Doctor returned to his dwelling but little wiser than he went forth; and, ordering his steed to be saddled, he began a journey, of which he knew not what would be the end.

In the meantime, the intelligence of Ellen's disappearance circulated rapidly, and soon sent forth hunters more fit to follow the chase than Doctor Melmoth.

VII

There was racing and chacing o'er Cannobie Lee.

WALTER SCOTT

WHEN Edward Walcott awoke, the next morning, from his deep slumber, his first consciousness was, of a heavy weight upon his mind, the cause of which, he was unable, immediately, to recollect. One by one, however, by means of the association of ideas, the events of the preceding night came back to his memory; though those of latest occurrence were dim as dreams. But one circumstance was only too well remembered—the discovery of Ellen Langton. By a strong effort, he next attained to an uncertain recollection, of a scene of madness and violence, followed, as he at first thought, by a duel. A little farther reflection, however, informed him that this event was yet among the things of futurity; but he could by no means recall the appointed time or place. As he had not the slightest intention (praiseworthy and prudent as it would unquestionably have been) to give up the chance of avenging Ellen's wrongs, and his own, he immediately arose and began to dress, meaning to learn from Hugh Crombie those particulars which his own memory had not retained. His chief apprehension was, that the appointed time had already elapsed; for the early sunbeams of a glorious morning were now peeping into his chamber.

More than once, during the progress of dressing, he was

• 407 •

inclined to believe, that the duel had actually taken place, and been fatal to him, and that he was now in those regions, to which, his conscience told him, such an event would be likely to send him. This idea resulted from his bodily sensations, which were in the highest degree uncomfortable. He was tormented by a raging thirst, that seemed to have absorbed all the moisture of his throat and stomach; and in his present agitation, a cup of icy water would have been his first wish, had all the treasures of earth and sea been at his command. His head, too, throbbed almost to bursting, and the whirl of his brain, at every movement, promised little accuracy in the aim of his pistol when he should meet the angler. These feelings, together with the deep degradation of his mind, made him resolve that no circumstances should again, draw him into an excess of wine. In the meantime, his head was perhaps still too much confused to allow him fully to realize his unpleasant situation.

Before Edward was prepared to leave his chamber, the door was opened by one of the College bed-makers, who, perceiving that he was nearly dressed, entered and began to set the apartment in order. There were two of these officials pertaining to Harley College; each of them being, and for obvious reasons this was an indispensable qualification, a model of perfect ugliness in her own way. One was a tall, raw-boned, huge-jointed, double-fisted giantess, admirably fitted to sustain the part of Glumdalca, in the tragedy of Tom Thumb. Her features were as excellent as her form, appearing to have been rough hewn with a broad axe, and left unpolished. The other was a short, squat figure, about two thirds the height and three times the circumference of ordinary females. Her hair was gray, her complexion of a deep yellow, and her most remarkable feature was a short snub nose, just discernible amid the broad immensity of her face. This latter lady was she who now entered Edward's chamber. Notwithstanding her deficiency in personal attractions, she was rather a favorite of the students, being good natured, anxious for their comfort, and, when duly encouraged, very communicative. Edward perceived, as soon as she appeared, that she only waited his assistance in order to disburden herself of some extraordinary information; and more from compassion than curiosity, he began to question her.

'Well, Dolly, what news this morning?'

'Why, let me see—oh, yes. It had almost slipped my memory,' replied the bed-maker. 'Poor Widow Butler died last night, after her long sickness. Poor woman! I remember her forty years ago, or so, as rosy a lass as you could set eyes on.'

'Ah! Has she gone?' said Edward, recollecting the sick woman of the cottage, which he had entered with Ellen and Fanshawe. 'Was she not out of her right mind, Dolly?'

'Yes; this seven years,' she answered. 'They say she came to her senses, a bit, when Doctor Melmoth visited her yesterday, but was raving mad when she died. Ah! That son of hers, if he is yet alive.—Well, well.'

'She had a son, then?' inquired Edward.

'Yes, such as he was. The Lord preserve me from such a one,' said Dolly. 'It was thought he went off with Hugh Crombie, that keeps the tavern now. That was fifteen years ago.'

'And have they heard nothing of him since?' asked Edward.

'Nothing good, nothing good,' said the bed-maker. 'Stories did travel up the valley, now and then; but for five years there has been no word of him. They say Merchant Langton, Ellen's father, met him in foreign parts and would have made a man of him; but there was too much of the wicked one in him for that. Well, poor woman! I wonder who'll preach her funeral sermon.'

'Doctor Melmoth, probably,' observed the student.

'No, no; the Doctor will never finish his journey in time. And who knows but his own funeral will be the end of it,' said Dolly with a sagacious shake of her head.

'Doctor Melmoth gone a journey!' repeated Edward. 'What do you mean? For what purpose?'

'For a good purpose enough, I may say,' replied she. 'To search out Miss Ellen, that was run away with, last night.'

'In the Devil's name, woman, of what are you speaking?' shouted Edward, seizing the affrighted bed-maker forcibly by the arm.

Poor Dolly had chosen this circuitous method of communicating her intelligence, because she was well aware, that, if she first told of Ellen's flight, she should find no ear for her account of the Widow Butler's death. She had not calculated, however, that the news would produce so violent an effect upon her auditor; and her voice faltered as she recounted what she knew of the affair. She had hardly concluded, before Edward, who as she proceeded, had been making hasty preparations, rushed from his chamber, and took the way towards Hugh Crombie's Inn. He had no difficulty in finding the landlord; who had already occupied his accustomed seat, and was smoking his accustomed pipe, under the elm-tree.

'Well, Master Walcott, you have come to take a stomach reliever, this morning, I suppose,' said Hugh, taking the pipe from his mouth. 'What shall it be? a bumper of wine with an egg?—or a glass of smooth, old, oily brandy, such as Dame Crombie and I keep for our own drinking? Come, that will do it, I know.'

'No, no;—neither,' replied Edward, shuddering, involuntarily, at the bare mention of wine and strong drink. 'You know well, Hugh Crombie, the errand on which I come.'

'Well, perhaps I do,' said the landlord. 'You come to order me to saddle my best horse. You are for a ride, this fine morning.'

'True, and I must learn of you in what direction to turn my horse's head,' replied Edward Walcott.

'I understand you,' said Hugh, nodding and smiling. 'And now, Master Edward, I really have taken a strong liking to you; and if you please to hearken to it, you shall have some of my best advice.'

'Speak,' said the young man, expecting to be told in what direction to pursue the chase.

'I advise you, then,' continued Hugh Crombie, in a tone, in which some real feeling mingled with assumed carelessness—'I advise you to forget that you have ever known this girl—that she has ever existed; for she is as much lost to you, as if she never had been born, or as if the grave had covered her. Come, come, man;—toss off a quart of my old wine, and keep up a merry heart. This has been my way, in many a heavier sorrow than ever you have felt; and you see I am alive and merry yet.' But Hugh's merriment had failed him just as he was making his boast of it; for Edward saw a tear in the corner of his eye.

'Forget her? Never, never!' said the student, while his heart sank within him, at the hopelessness of pursuit, which Hugh's words implied. 'I will follow her to the ends of the earth.'

'Then so much the worse for you, and for my poor nag—on whose back you shall be in three minutes,' rejoined the landlord. 'I have spoken to you as I would to my own son, if I had such an incumbrance. Here you ragamuffin, saddle the gray and lead him round to the door.'

'The gray? I will ride the black,' said Edward, 'I know your best horse, as well as you do yourself, Hugh.'

'There is no black horse in my stable; I have parted with him to an old comrade of mine,' answered the landlord, with a wink of acknowledgment to what he saw were Edward's suspicions. 'The gray is a stout nag, and will carry you a round pace, though not so fast as to bring you up with them you seek. I reserved him for you, and put Mr. Fanshawe off with the old white, on which I travelled hitherward, a year or two since.'

'Fanshawe? Has he then the start of me?' asked Edward.

'He rode off about twenty minutes ago,' replied Hugh; 'but you will overtake him within ten miles, at farthest. But if mortal man could recover the girl, that fellow would do it— even if he had no better nag than a broomstick, like the witches of old times.'

'Did he obtain any information from you as to the course?' inquired the student.

'I could give him only this much,' said Hugh, pointing down the road, in the direction of the town. 'My old comrade trusts no man farther than is needful, and I ask no unnecessary questions.'

The ostler now led up to the door the horse which Edward was to ride. The young man mounted with all expedition; but as he was about to apply the spurs, his thirst, which the bed-maker's intelligence had caused him to forget, returned most powerfully upon him.

'For Heaven's sake, Hugh, a mug of your sharpest cider— and let it be a large one,' he exclaimed. 'My tongue rattles in my mouth like——'

'Like the bones in a dice-box,' said the landlord, finishing the comparison and hastening to obey Edward's directions. Indeed, he rather exceeded them, by mingling with the juice of the apple, a jill of his old brandy, which, his own experience told him, would at that time have a most desirable effect upon the young man's internal system.

'It is powerful stuff, mine host, and I feel like a new man already,' observed Edward, after draining the mug to the bottom.

'He is a fine lad, and sits his horse most gallantly,' said Hugh Crombie to himself, as the student rode off. 'I heartily wish him success. I wish to Heaven my conscience had suffered me to betray the plot before it was too late. Well, well—a man must keep his mite of honesty.'

The morning was now one of the most bright and glorious, that ever shone for mortals; and, under other circumstances, Edward's bosom would have been as light, and his spirit would have sung as cheerfully, as one of the many birds that warbled around him. The rain-drops of the preceding night hung like glittering diamonds on every leaf of every tree, shaken and rendered more brilliant by occasional sighs of wind, that removed from the traveller the superfluous heat of an unclouded sun. In spite of the adventure, so mysterious and vexatious, in which he was engaged, Edward's elastic spirit (assisted perhaps by the brandy he had unwittingly swallowed) rose higher as he rode on, and he soon found himself endeavoring to accommodate the tune of one of Hugh Crombie's ballads to the motion of the horse. Nor did this reviving cheerfulness argue anything against his unwavering faith, and pure and fervent love for Ellen Langton. A sorrowful and repining disposition is not the necessary accompaniment of a 'leal and loving heart'; and Edward's spirits were cheered, not by forgetfulness, but by hope, which would not permit him to doubt of the ultimate success of his pursuit. The uncertainty itself, and the probable danger of the expedition, were not without their charm to a youthful and adventurous spirit. In fact, Edward would not have been altogether satisfied to recover the errant damsel, without first doing battle in her behalf.

He had proceeded but a few miles, before he came in sight of Fanshawe, who had been accommodated by the landlord with a horse much inferior to his own. The speed to which he had been put, had almost exhausted the poor animal, whose best pace was now but little beyond a walk. Edward drew his bridle, as he came up with Fanshawe.

'I have been anxious to apologize,' he said to him, 'for the hasty and unjust expressions of which I made use, last evening. May I hope, that, in consideration of my mental distraction, and the causes of it, you will forget what has past?'

'I had already forgotten it,' replied Fanshawe, freely offering his hand. 'I saw your disturbed state of feeling, and it would have been unjust, both to you and to myself, to remember the errors it occasioned.'

'A wild expedition this,' observed Edward, after shaking warmly the offered hand. 'Unless we obtain some farther information at the town, we shall hardly know which way to continue the pursuit.'

'We can scarcely fail, I think, of lighting upon some trace of them,' said Fanshawe. 'Their flight must have commenced after the storm subsided, which would give them but a few hours the start of us. May I beg,' he continued, noticing the superior condition of his rival's horse, 'that you will not attempt to accommodate your pace to mine?'

Edward bowed and rode on, wondering at the change which a few months had wrought in Fanshawe's character. On this occasion, especially, the energy of his mind had communicated itself to his frame. The color was strong and high in his cheek, and his whole appearance was that of a gallant and manly youth, whom a lady might love, or a foe might fear. Edward had not been so slow as his mistress in discovering the student's affection, and he could not but acknowledge in his heart that he was a rival not to be despised, and might yet be a successful one, if by his means Ellen Langton were restored to her friends. This consideration caused him to spur forward with increased ardour; but all his speed could not divest him of the idea, that Fanshawe would finally overtake him, and attain the object of their mutual pursuit. There was certainly no apparent ground for this imagination; for every step of his horse increased the advantage which Edward had gained, and he soon lost sight of his rival.

Shortly after overtaking Fanshawe, the young man passed the lonely cottage, formerly the residence of the Widow

Butler, who now lay dead within. He was at first inclined to alight and make inquiries respecting the fugitives; for he observed, through the windows, the faces of several persons, whom curiosity or some better feeling had led to the house of mourning. Recollecting, however, that this portion of the road must have been passed by the angler and Ellen at too early an hour to attract notice, he forbore to waste time by a fruitless delay.

Edward proceeded on his journey, meeting with no other noticeable event, till, arriving at the summit of a hill, he beheld, a few hundred yards before him, the Reverend Doctor Melmoth. The worthy President was toiling onward, at a rate unexampled in the history either of himself or his steed, the excellence of the latter consisting in sure-footedness, rather than rapidity. The rider looked round, seemingly in some apprehension, at the sound of hoof-tramps behind him, but was unable to conceal his satisfaction on recognizing Edward Walcott.

In the whole course of his life, Doctor Melmoth had never been placed in circumstances so embarrassing as the present. He was altogether a child in the ways of the world, having spent his youth and early manhood in abstracted study, and his maturity in the solitude of these hills. The expedition, therefore, on which fate had now thrust him, was an entire deviation from the quiet path-way of all his former years, and he felt like one who sets forth over the broad ocean, without chart or compass. The affair would undoubtedly have been perplexing to a man of far more experience than he; but the Doctor pictured to himself a thousand difficulties and dangers, which, except in his imagination, had no existence. The perturbation of his spirit had compelled him, more than once since his departure, to regret that he had not invited Mrs. Melmoth to a share in the adventure; this being an occasion where her firmness, decision, and confident sagacity—which made her a sort of domestic hedge-hog—would have been peculiarly appropriate. In the absence of such a counsellor, even Edward Walcott—young as he was, and indiscreet as the Doctor thought him—was a substitute not to be despised; and it was singular and rather ludicrous to observe how the gray-haired man unconsciously became as a child to the beardless youth. He addressed Edward with an assumption of dignity, through which his pleasure at the meeting was very obvious.

'Young gentleman, this is not well,' he said. 'By what authority have you absented yourself from the walls of Alma Mater, during term-time?'

'I conceived that it was unnecessary to ask leave, at such a conjuncture, and when the head of the institution was himself in the saddle,' replied Edward.

'It was a fault, it was a fault,' said Doctor Melmoth, shaking his head; 'but, in consideration of the motive, I may pass it over. And now, my dear Edward, I advise that we continue our journey together, as your youth and inexperience will stand in need of the wisdom of my gray head. Nay, I pray you, lay not the lash to your steed. You have ridden fast and far, and a slower pace is requisite for a season.'

And, in order to keep up with his young companion, the Doctor smote his own gray nag; which unhappy beast, wondering what strange concatenation of events had procured him such treatment, endeavored to obey his master's wishes. Edward had sufficient compassion for Doctor Melmoth (especially as his own horse now exhibited signs of weariness) to moderate his pace to one attainable by the former.

'Alas, youth! These are strange times,' observed the President, 'when a Doctor of Divinity and an under graduate set forth, like a knight-errant and his squire, in search of a stray damsel. Methinks I am an epitome of the church militant, or a new species of polemical divinity. Pray Heaven, however, there be no encounter in store for us: for I utterly forgot to provide myself with weapons.'

'I took some thought for that matter, reverend knight,' replied Edward, whose imagination was highly tickled by Doctor Melmoth's chivalrous comparison.

'Aye, I see that you have girded on a sword,' said the Divine. 'But wherewith shall I defend myself?—my hand being empty, except of this golden-headed staff, the gift of Mr. Langton.'

'One of these, if you will accept it,' answered Edward, exhibiting a brace of pistols, 'will serve to begin the conflict, before you join the battle hand to hand.'

'Nay, I shall find little safety in meddling with that deadly instrument, since I know not accurately from which end proceeds the bullet,' said Doctor Melmoth. 'But were it not better, seeing we are so well provided with artillery, to betake ourselves, in the event of an encounter, to some stone wall or other place of strength?'

'If I may presume to advise,' said the squire, 'you, as being most valiant and experienced, should ride forward, lance in hand, (your long staff serving for a lance,) while I annoy the enemy from afar.'

'Like Teucer behind the shield of Ajax,' interrupted Doctor Melmoth, 'or David with his stone and sling. No, no, young man; I have left unfinished in my study a learned treatise, important not only to the present age, but to posterity, for whose sakes I must take heed to my safety. But, lo! who ride yonder?' he exclaimed, in manifest alarm, pointing to some horsemen upon the brow of a hill, at a short distance before them.

'Fear not, gallant leader,' said Edward Walcott, who had already discovered the objects of the Doctor's terror. 'They are men of peace, as we shall shortly see. The foremost is somewhere near your own years, and rides like a grave, substantial citizen—though what he does here, I know not. Behind come two servants, men likewise of sober age and pacific appearance.'

'Truly, your eyes are better than mine own. Of a verity, you are in the right,' acquiesced Doctor Melmoth, recovering his usual quantum of intrepidity. 'We will ride forward courageously, as those who, in a just cause, fear neither death nor bonds.'

The reverend knight-errant and his squire, at the time of discovering the three horsemen, were within a very short distance of the town, which was, however, concealed from their view by the hill, that the strangers were descending. The road from Harley College, through almost its whole extent, had been rough and wild, and the country thin of population; but now, standing frequent amid fertile fields on each side of the way, were neat little cottages, from which groups of white-headed children rushed forth to gaze upon the travellers. The three strangers, as well as the Doctor and Edward, were surrounded, as they approached each other, by a crowd of this kind, plying their little bare legs most pertinaciously, in order to keep pace with the horses.

As Edward gained a nearer view of the foremost rider, his grave aspect and stately demeanor struck him with involuntary respect. There were deep lines of thought across his brow, and his calm, yet bright gray eye, betokened a stedfast soul. There was also an air of conscious importance, even in the manner in which the stranger sat his horse, which a man's good opinion of himself, unassisted by the concurrence of the world in general, seldom bestows. The two servants rode at a respectable distance in the rear; and the heavy portmanteaus at their backs intimated that the party had journeyed from afar. Doctor Melmoth endeavored to assume the dignity that became him, as the head of Harley College; and with a gentle stroke of his staff upon his wearied steed, and a grave nod to the principal stranger, was about to commence the ascent of the hill, at the foot of which they were. The gentleman, however, made a halt.

'Doctor Melmoth, am I so fortunate as to meet you?' he exclaimed, in accents expressive of as much surprise and pleasure, as were consistent with his staid demeanor. 'Have you then forgotten your old friend?'

'Mr. Langton! Can it be?' said the Doctor, after looking him in the face a moment. 'Yes, it is my old friend, indeed! Welcome, welcome! Though you come at an unfortunate time.'

'What say you? How is my child? Ellen, I trust, is well?' cried Mr. Langton; a father's anxiety overcoming the coldness and reserve that were natural to him, or that long habit had made a second nature.

'She is well in health. She was so, at least, last night,' replied Doctor Melmoth, unable to meet the eye of his friend. 'But—but I have been a careless shepherd, and the lamb has strayed from the fold while I slept.'

Edward Walcott, who was a deeply interested observer of this scene, had anticipated that a burst of passionate grief would follow the disclosure. He was, however, altogether mistaken. There was a momentary convulsion of Mr. Langton's strong features, as quick to come and go as a flash of lightning; and then his countenance was as composed—though perhaps a little sterner—as before. He seemed about to inquire into the particulars of what so nearly concerned him; but changed his purpose on observing the crowd of children, who, with one or two of their parents, were endeavoring to catch the words that passed between the Doctor and himself.

'I will turn back with you to the village,' he said, in a steady voice; 'and, at your leisure, I shall desire to hear the particulars of this unfortunate affair.'

He wheeled his horse accordingly, and, side by side with Doctor Melmoth, began to ascend the hill. On reaching the summit, the little country town lay before them, presenting a cheerful and busy spectacle. It consisted of one long, regular street, extending parallel to, and at a short distance from the river; which here, enlarged by a junction with another stream, became navigable, not indeed for vessels of burthen, but for rafts of lumber and boats of considerable size. The houses, with peaked roofs and jutting stories, stood at wide intervals along the street; and the commercial character of the place was manifested by the shop door and windows, that occupied the front of almost every dwelling. One or two mansions, however, surrounded by trees and standing back at a haughty distance from the road, were evidently the abodes of the aristocracy of the village. It was not difficult to distinguish the owners of these—self-important personages, with canes and well-powdered periwigs—among the crowd of meaner men, who bestowed their attention upon Doctor Melmoth and his friend, as they rode by. The town being the nearest mart of a large extent of back country, there were many rough farmers and woodsmen, to whom the cavalcade was an object of curiosity and admiration. The former feeling, indeed, was general throughout the village. The shop-keepers left their customers and looked forth from the doors—the female portion of the community thrust their heads from the windows—and the people in the street formed a lane, through which, with all eyes concentrated upon them, the party rode onward to the tavern. The general aptitude that pervades the populace of a small country town, to meddle with affairs not legitimately concerning them, was increased on this occasion by the sudden return of Mr. Langton, after passing through the village. Many conjectures were afloat respecting the cause of this retrograde movement; and, by degrees, something like the truth, though much distorted, spread generally among the crowd—communicated, probably, from Mr. Langton's servants. Edward Walcott, incensed at the uncourteous curiosity of which he, as well as his companions, was the object, felt a frequent impulse, (though fortunately for himself, resisted,) to make use of his riding switch in clearing a passage.

On arriving at the tavern, Doctor Melmoth recounted to his friend the little he knew beyond the bare fact of Ellen's disappearance. Had Edward Walcott been called to their conference, he might, by disclosing the adventure of the angler, have thrown a portion of light upon the affair; but, since his first introduction, the cold and stately merchant had honored him with no sort of notice.

Edward, on his part, was not well pleased at the sudden appearance of Ellen's father, and was little inclined to co-operate in any measures that he might adopt for her recovery. It was his wish to pursue the chase on his own responsibility, and as his own wisdom dictated; he chose to be an independent ally, rather than a subordinate assistant. But, as a step pre-liminary to his proceedings of every other kind, he found it absolutely necessary, having journeyed far and fasting, to call upon the landlord for a supply of food. The viands that were set before him, were homely, but abundant; nor were Edward's griefs and perplexities so absorbing, as to overcome the appetite of youth and health.

Doctor Melmoth, and Mr. Langton, after a short private conversation, had summoned the landlord, in the hope of obtaining some clue to the developement of the mystery. But no young lady, nor any stranger answering to the description the Doctor had received from Hugh Crombie (which was indeed a false one) had been seen to pass through the village since day-break. Here, therefore, the friends were entirely at a loss in what direction to continue the pursuit. The village was the focus of several roads, diverging to widely distant portions of the country; and which of these the fugitives had taken, it was impossible to determine. One point, however, might be considered certain—that the village was the first stage of their flight; for it commanded the only outlet from the valley, except a rugged path among the hills, utterly impassable by horse. In this dilemma, expresses were sent by each of the different roads; and poor Ellen's imprudence, the tale no wise decreasing as it rolled along, became known to a wide extent of country. Having thus done every thing in his power to recover his daughter, the merchant exhibited a composure which Doctor Melmoth admired, but could not equal. His own mind, however, was in a far more comfortable state, than when the responsibility of the pursuit had rested upon himself.

Edward Walcott, in the meantime, had employed but a very few moments in satisfying his hunger; after which his active intellect alternately formed and relinquished a thousand plans for the recovery of Ellen. Fanshawe's observation, that her flight must have commenced after the subsiding of the storm, recurred to him. On inquiry, he was informed that the violence of the rain had continued, with a few momentary intermissions, till near daylight. The fugitives must, therefore, have passed through the village, long after its inhabitants were abroad; and how, without the gift of invisibility, they had contrived to elude notice, Edward could not conceive.

'Fifty years ago,' thought Edward, 'my sweet Ellen would have been deemed a witch, for this trackless journey. Truly, I could wish I were a wizard, that I might bestride a broomstick, and follow her.'

While the young man, involved in these perplexing thoughts, looked forth from the open window of the apartment, his attention was drawn to an individual, evidently of a different, though not of a higher class, than the countrymen among whom he stood. Edward now recollected that he had noticed his rough, dark face, among the most earnest of those who had watched the arrival of the party. He had then taken him for one of the boatmen, of whom there were many in the village, and who had much of a sailor-like dress and appearance. A second, and more attentive observation, however, convinced Edward that this man's life had not been spent upon fresh water; and had any stronger evidence, than the nameless marks which the ocean impresses upon its sons, been necessary, it would have been found in his mode of locomotion. While Edward was observing him, he beat slowly up to one of Mr. Langton's servants, who was standing near the door of the Inn. He seemed to question the man with affected carelessness; but his countenance was dark and perplexed, when he turned to mingle again with the crowd. Edward lost no time in ascertaining from the servant the nature of his inquiries. They had related to the elopement of Mr. Langton's daughter; which was, indeed, the prevailing, if not the sole subject of conversation in the village.

The grounds for supposing that this man was in any way connected with the angler, were, perhaps, very slight; yet, in the perplexity of the whole affair, they induced Edward to resolve to get at the heart of his mystery. To attain this end, he took the most direct method—by applying to the man himself.

He had now retired apart from the throng and bustle of the village, and was seated upon a condemned boat that was drawn up to rot upon the banks of the river. His arms were folded, and his hat drawn over his brows. The lower part of his face, which alone was visible, evinced gloom and depression, as did also the deep sighs, which, because he thought no one was near him, he did not attempt to restrain.

'Friend, I must speak with you,' said Edward Walcott, laying his hand upon his shoulder, after contemplating the man a moment, himself unseen.

He started at once from his abstraction and his seat, apparently expecting violence, and prepared to resist it; but perceiving the youthful and solitary intruder upon his privacy, he composed his features with much quickness.

'What would you with me?' he asked.

'They tarry long—or you have kept a careless watch,' said Edward, speaking at a venture.

For a moment there seemed a probability of obtaining such a reply to this observation, as the youth had intended to elicit. If any trust could be put in the language of the stranger's countenance, a set of words, different from those to which he subsequently gave utterance, had risen to his lips. But he seemed naturally slow of speech; and this defect was now, as is frequently the case, advantageous, in giving him space for reflection.

'Look you, youngster;—crack no jokes on me,' he at length said, contemptuously. 'Away!—back whence you came, or——' and he slightly waved a small rattan, that he held in his right hand.

Edward's eyes sparkled, and his color rose. 'You must change this tone, fellow, and that speedily,' he observed. 'I order you to lower your hand, and answer the questions that I shall put to you.'

The man gazed dubiously at him; but finally adopted a more conciliatory mode of speech.

'Well, master, and what is your business with me?' he inquired. 'I am a boatman out of employ. Any commands in my line?'

'Pshaw! I know you, my good friend, and you cannot deceive me,' replied Edward Walcott. 'We are private here,' he continued, looking around. 'I have no desire or intention to do you harm; and, if you act according to my directions, you shall have no cause to repent it.'

'And what if I refuse to put myself under your orders?' inquired the man. 'You are but a young captain, for such an old hulk as mine.'

'The ill consequences of a refusal would all be on your own side,' replied Edward. 'I shall, in that case, deliver you up to justice; if I have not the means of capturing you myself,' he continued, observing the seaman's eye to wander rather scornfully over his youthful and slender figure, 'there are hundreds within call whom it will be in vain to resist.

Besides, it requires little strength to use this,' he added, laying his hand on a pistol.

'If that were all, I could suit you there, my lad,' muttered the stranger. He continued aloud, 'Well, what is your will with me? D—d ungenteel treatment, this!—But put your questions; and to oblige you, I may answer them;—if so be that I know any thing of the matter.'

'You will do wisely,' observed the young man. 'And now to business. What reason have you to suppose that the persons for whom you watch are not already beyond the village?'

The seaman paused long before he answered, and gazed earnestly at Edward, apparently endeavoring to ascertain from his countenance, the amount of his knowledge. This he probably overrated, but, nevertheless, hazarded a falsehood.

'I doubt not they passed before midnight,' he said. 'I warrant you they are many a league towards the sea-coast, ere this.'

'You have kept watch, then, since midnight?' asked Edward.

'Aye, that have I. And a dark and rough one it was,' answered the stranger.

'And you are certain that if they passed at all, it must have been before that hour?'

'I kept my walk across the road, till the village was all astir,' said the seaman. 'They could not have missed me. So, you see, your best way is to give chase; for they have a long start of you, and you have no time to lose.'

'Your information is sufficient, my good friend,' said Edward, with a smile. 'I have reason to know that they did not commence their flight before midnight. You have made it evident that they have not passed since. Ergo, they have not passed at all. An indisputable syllogism. And now will I retrace my footsteps.'

'Stay, young man,' said the stranger, placing himself full in Edward's way, as he was about to hasten to the Inn—'you have drawn me in to betray my comrade; but before you leave this place, you must answer a question or two of mine. Do you mean to take the law with you?—or will you right your wrongs, if you have any, with your own right hand?'

'It is my intention to take the latter method. But if I choose the former, what then?' demanded Edward.

'Nay, nothing;—only, you or I might not have gone hence alive,' replied the stranger. 'But as you say he shall have fair play——'

'On my word, friend,' interrupted the young man. 'I fear your intelligence has come too late to do either good or harm. Look towards the Inn; my companions are getting to horse, and my life on it, they know whither to ride.'

So saying, he hastened away, followed by the stranger. It was indeed evident that news, of some kind or other, had reached the village. The people were gathered in groups, conversing eagerly; and the pale cheeks, uplifted eye-brows, and outspread hands of some of the female sex, filled Edward's mind with undefined, but intolerable apprehensions. He forced his way to Doctor Melmoth, who had just mounted, and seizing his bridle, peremptorily demanded if he knew aught of Ellen Langton.

VIII

Full many a miserable year hath past—
She knows him as one dead,—or worse than dead;
And many a change her varied life hath known,
But her heart none.

MATURIN

SINCE her interview with the angler, which was interrupted by the appearance of Fanshawe, Ellen Langton's hitherto calm and peaceful mind, had been in a state of insufferable doubt and dismay. She was imperatively called upon—at least, she so conceived—to break through the rules which nature and education impose upon her sex, to quit the protection of those whose desire for her welfare was true and strong—and to trust herself, for what purpose she scarcely knew, to a stranger, from whom the instinctive purity of her mind would involuntarily have shrunk, under whatever circumstances she had met him. The letter which she had received from the hands of the angler, had seemed to her inexperience, to prove beyond a doubt, that the bearer was the friend of her father, and authorized by him, if her duty and affection were stronger than her fears, to guide her to his retreat. The letter spoke vaguely of losses and misfortunes, and of a necessity for concealment on her father's part, and secrecy on hers; and to the credit of Ellen's not very romantic understanding, it must be acknowledged, that the mystery of the plot had nearly prevented its success. She did not, indeed, doubt that the letter was from her father's hand; for every line and stroke, and even many of its phrases, were familiar to her. Her apprehension was, that his misfortunes, of what nature soever they were, had affected his intellect, and that, under such an influence, he had commanded her to take a step, which nothing less than such a command could justify. Ellen did not, however, remain long in this opinion; for when she re-perused the letter, and considered the firm, regular characters, and the style—calm and cold, even in requesting such a sacrifice—she felt that there was nothing like insanity here. In fine, she came gradually to the belief, that there were strong reasons, though incomprehensible by her, for the secrecy that her father had enjoined.

Having arrived at this conviction, her decision lay plain before her. Her affection for Mr. Langton was not, indeed— nor was it possible—so strong, as that she would have felt for a parent who had watched over her from her infancy. Neither was the conception, she had unavoidably formed of his character, such as to promise, that in him she would find an equivalent for all she must sacrifice. On the contrary, her gentle nature and loving heart, which otherwise would have rejoiced in a new object of affection, now shrank with something like dread from the idea of meeting her father—stately, cold, and stern, as she could not but imagine him. A sense of duty was, therefore, Ellen's only support, in resolving to tread the dark path that lay before her.

Had there been any person of her own sex, in whom Ellen felt confidence, there is little doubt that she would so far have disobeyed her father's letter, as to communicate its contents, and take counsel as to her proceedings. But Mrs. Melmoth was the only female—excepting, indeed, the maid-servant—to whom it was possible to make the communication; and though Ellen at first thought of such a step, her timidity and her knowledge of the lady's character, did not permit her to venture upon it. She next reviewed her acquaintances of the other sex; and Doctor Melmoth first presented himself, as, in every respect but one, an unexceptionable confidant. But the single exception was equivalent to many. The maiden, with the highest opinion of the Doctor's learning and talents, had sufficient penetration to know, that in the ways of the world, she was herself the better skilled of the two. For a moment she thought of Edward Walcott; but he was light and wild, and—which her delicacy made an insurmountable objection—there was an untold love between them. Her thoughts finally centred on Fanshawe. In his judgment, young and inexperienced though he was, she would have placed a firm trust, and his zeal, from whatever cause it arose, she could not doubt.

If, in the short time allowed her for reflection, an opportunity had occurred for consulting him, she would, in all probability, have taken advantage of it. But the terms on which they had parted, the preceding evening, had afforded him no reason to hope for her confidence; and he felt that there were others who had a better right to it than himself. He did not, therefore, throw himself in her way, and poor Ellen was consequently left without an adviser.

The determination that resulted from her own unassisted wisdom, has been seen. When discovered by Doctor Melmoth at Hugh Crombie's Inn, she was wholly prepared for flight, and but for the intervention of the storm, would, ere then, have been far away.

The firmness of resolve, that had impelled a timid maiden upon such a step, was not likely to be broken by one defeat; and Ellen, accordingly, confident that the stranger would make a second attempt, determined that no effort on her part should be wanting to its success. On reaching her chamber, therefore, instead of retiring to rest, (of which, from her sleepless thoughts of the preceding night, she stood greatly in need,) she sat watching for the abatement of the storm. Her meditations were now calmer, than at any time since her first meeting with the angler. She felt as if her fate was decided. The stain had fallen upon her reputation—she was no longer the same pure being, in the opinion of those whose approbation she most valued.

One obstacle to her flight—and, to a woman's mind, a most powerful one—had thus been removed. Dark and intricate as was the way, it was easier, now, to proceed, than to pause; and her desperate and forlorn situation gave her a strength, which, hitherto, she had not felt.

At every cessation in the torrent of rain that beat against the house, Ellen flew to the window, expecting to see the stranger's form beneath it. But the clouds would again thicken, and the storm re-commence, with its former violence; and she began to fear, that the approach of morning would compel her to meet the now dreaded face of Doctor Melmoth. At length, however, a strong and steady wind, supplying the place of the fitful gusts of the preceding part of the night, broke and scattered the clouds from the broad expanse of the sky. The moon commencing her late voyage not long before the sun, was now visible, setting forth like a lonely ship from the dark line of the horizon, and touching at many a little silver cloud, the islands of that aerial deep. Ellen felt that now the time was come; and with a calmness, wonderful to herself, she prepared for her final departure.

She had not long to wait, ere she saw, between the vacancies of the trees, the angler, advancing along the shady avenue that led to the principal entrance of Doctor Melmoth's dwelling. He had no need to summon her, either by word or signal; for she had descended, emerged from the door, and stood before him, while he was yet at some distance from the house.

'You have watched well,' he observed, in a low, strange tone. 'As saith the scripture, many daughters have done virtuously, but thou excellest them all.'

He took her arm, and they hastened down the avenue.

Then leaving Hugh Crombie's Inn on their right, they found its master, in a spot so shaded that the moonbeams could not enlighten it. He held by the bridle two horses, one of which the angler assisted Ellen to mount. Then, turning to the landlord, he pressed a purse into his hand; but Hugh drew back, and it fell to the ground.

'No; this would not have tempted me, nor will it reward me,' he said. 'If you have gold to spare, there are some that need it more than I.'

'I understand you, mine host. I shall take thought for them, and enough will remain for you and me,' replied his comrade. 'I have seen the day when such a purse would not have slipped between your fingers. Well, be it so. And now, Hugh, my old friend, a shake of your hand; for we are seeing our last of each other.'

'Pray Heaven, it be so; though I wish you no ill,' said the landlord, giving his hand. He then seemed about to approach Ellen, who had been unable to distinguish the words of this brief conversation; but his comrade prevented him. 'There is no time to lose,' he observed. 'The moon is growing pale already, and we should have been many a mile beyond the valley, ere this.' He mounted, as he spoke, and guiding Ellen's rein till they reached the road, they dashed away.

It was now that she felt herself completely in his power; and with that consciousness, there came a sudden change of feeling, and an altered view of her conduct. A thousand reasons forced themselves upon her mind, seeming to prove that she had been deceived; while the motives, so powerful with her but a moment before, had either vanished from her memory, or lost all their efficacy. Her companion, who gazed searchingly into her face, where the moonlight, coming down between the pines, allowed him to read its expression, probably discerned somewhat of the state of her thoughts.

'Do you repent so soon?' he inquired. 'We have a weary

way before us. Faint not ere we have well entered upon it.'

'I have left dear friends behind me, and am going I know not whither,' replied Ellen tremblingly.

'You have a faithful guide,' he observed; turning away his head, and speaking in the tone of one who endeavors to smother a laugh.

Ellen had no heart to continue the conversation; and they rode on in silence, and through a wild and gloomy scene. The wind roared heavily through the forest, and the trees shed their rain-drops upon the travellers. The road, at all times rough, was now broken into deep gullies, through which streams went murmuring down, to mingle with the river. The pale moonlight combined with the gray of the morning to give a ghastly and unsubstantial appearance to every object.

The difficulties of the road had been so much increased by the storm, that the purple eastern clouds gave notice of the near approach of the sun, just as the travellers reached the little lonesome cottage which Ellen remembered to have visited several months before. On arriving opposite to it, her companion checked his horse, and gazed with a wild earnestness at the wretched habitation. Then, stifling a groan that would not altogether be repressed, he was about to pass on. But, at that moment, the cottage door opened, and a woman, whose sour, unpleasant countenance Ellen recognized, came hastily forth. She seemed not to heed the travellers; but the angler, his voice thrilling and quivering with indescribable emotion, addressed her.

'Woman, whither do you go?' he inquired.

She started; but, after a momentary pause, replied, 'There is one within at the point of death. She struggles fearfully, and I cannot endure to watch alone by her bed-side. If you are christians, come in with me.'

Ellen's companion leaped hastily from his horse, assisted her also to dismount, and followed the woman into the cottage, having first thrown the bridles of the horses carelessly over the branch of a tree. Ellen trembled at the awful scene she would be compelled to witness; but, when death was so near at hand, it was more terrible to stand alone in the dim morning light, than even to watch the parting of soul and body. She therefore entered the cottage.

Her guide, his face muffled in his cloak, had taken his stand at a distance from the death-bed, in a part of the room, which neither the increasing daylight nor the dim rays of a solitary lamp, had yet enlightened. At Ellen's entrance, the dying woman lay still, and apparently calm, except that a plaintive, half articulate sound occasionally wandered through her lips.

'Hush! For mercy's sake, silence!' whispered the other woman to the strangers. 'There is good hope now, that she will die a peaceable death; but, if she is disturbed, the boldest of us will not dare to stand by her bed-side.'

The whisper, by which her sister endeavored to preserve quiet, perhaps reached the ears of the dying female; for she now raised herself in bed, slowly, but with a strength superior to what her situation promised. Her face was ghastly and wild, from long illness, approaching death, and disturbed intellect; and a disembodied spirit could scarcely be a more fearful object, than one whose soul was just struggling forth. Her sister, approaching with the soft and stealing step appropriate to the chamber of sickness and death, attempted to replace the covering around her, and to compose her again upon the pillow. 'Lie down and sleep, sister,' she said; 'and when the day breaks, I will waken you. Methinks your breath comes freer, already. A little more slumber, and tomorrow you will be well.'

'My illness is gone, I am well,' said the dying woman, gasping for breath. 'I wander where the fresh breeze comes sweetly over my face, but a close and stifled air has choked my lungs.'

'Yet a little while and you will no longer draw your breath

in pain,' observed her sister, again replacing the bed-clothes, which she continued to throw off.

'My husband is with me,' murmured the widow. 'He walks by my side, and speaks to me as in old times; but his words come faintly on my ear; cheer me and comfort me, my husband; for there is a terror in those dim, motionless eyes, and in that shadowy voice.'

As she spoke thus, she seemed to gaze upon some object that stood by her bed-side, and the eyes of those who witnessed this scene could not but follow the direction of hers. They observed that the dying woman's own shadow was marked upon the wall, receiving a tremulous motion from the fitful rays of the lamp, and from her own convulsive efforts. 'My husband stands gazing on me,' she said, again; 'but my son—where is he?—and as I ask, the father turns away his face. Where is our son? For his sake I have longed to come to this land of rest. For him I have sorrowed many years. Will he not comfort me now?'

At these words, the stranger made a few hasty steps towards the bed; but, ere he reached it, he conquered the impulse that drew him thither, and, shrouding his face more deeply in his cloak, returned to his former position. The dying woman, in the meantime, had thrown herself back upon the bed; and her sobbing and wailing, imaginary as was their cause, were inexpressibly affecting.

'Take me back to earth,' she said; 'for its griefs have followed me hither.'

The stranger advanced, and, seizing the lamp, knelt down by the bed-side, throwing the light full upon his pale and convulsed features.

'Mother, here is your son,' he exclaimed.

At that unforgotten voice, the darkness burst away at once from her soul. She arose in bed, her eyes and her whole countenance beaming with joy, and threw her arms about his neck. A multitude of words seemed struggling for utterance;

but they gave place to a low moaning sound, and then to the silence of death. The one moment of happiness, that recompensed years of sorrow, had been her last. Her son laid the lifeless form upon the pillow, and gazed with fixed eyes on his mother's face.

As he looked, the expression of enthusiastic joy, that parting life had left upon the features, faded gradually away, and the countenance, though no longer wild, assumed the sadness which it had worn through a long course of grief and pain. On beholding this natural consequence of death, the thought perhaps occurred to him, that her soul, no longer dependant on the imperfect means of intercourse possessed by mortals, had communed with his own, and become acquainted with all its guilt and misery. He started from the bed-side, and covered his face with his hands, as if to hide it from those dead eyes.

Such a scene as has been described could not but have a powerful effect upon any one, who retained aught of humanity; and the grief of the son, whose natural feelings had been blunted, but not destroyed, by an evil life, was much more violent than his outward demeanor would have expressed. But his deep repentance, for the misery he had brought upon his parent, did not produce in him a resolution to do wrong no more. The sudden consciousness of accumulated guilt made him desperate. He felt as if no one had thenceforth a claim to justice or compassion at his hands, when his neglect and cruelty had poisoned his mother's life, and hastened her death. Thus it was that the Devil wrought with him to his own destruction, reversing the salutary effect, which his mother would have died, exultingly, to produce upon his mind. He now turned to Ellen Langton, with a demeanor singularly calm and composed.

'We must resume our journey,' he said, in his usual tone of voice. 'The sun is on the point of rising, though but little light finds its way into this hovel.'

Ellen's previous suspicions as to the character of her companion had now become certainty, so far as to convince her that she was in the power of a lawless and guilty man; though what fate he intended for her, she was unable to conjecture. An open opposition to his will, however, could not be ventured upon; especially as she discovered, on looking round the apartment, that, with the exception of the corpse, they were alone.

'Will you not attend your mother's funeral?' she asked, trembling, and conscious that he would discover her fears.

'The dead must bury their dead,' he replied; 'I have brought my mother to her grave;—and what can a son do more? This purse, however, will serve to lay her in the earth, and leave something for the old hag. Whither is she gone?' interrupted he, casting a glance round the room in search of the old woman. 'Nay, then, we must speedily to horse. I know her of old.'

Thus saying, he threw the purse upon the table, and without trusting himself to look again towards the dead, conducted Ellen out of the cottage. The first rays of the sun at that moment gilded the tallest trees of the forest.

On looking towards the spot where the horses had stood, Ellen thought that Providence, in answer to her prayers, had taken care for her deliverance. They were no longer there, a circumstance easily accounted for, by the haste with which the bridles had been thrown over the branch of the tree. Her companion, however, imputed it to another cause.

'The hag! She would sell her own flesh and blood by weight and measure,' he muttered to himself. 'This is some plot of hers, I know well.'

He put his hand to his forehead, for a moment's space, seeming to reflect on the course most advisable to be pursued. Ellen, perhaps unwisely, interposed.

'Would it not be well to return?' she asked, timidly. 'There is now no hope of escaping; but I might yet reach home undiscovered.'

'Return!' repeated her guide, with a look and smile from which she turned away her face. 'Have you forgotten your father and his misfortunes? No, no, sweet Ellen; it is too late for such thoughts as these.'

He took her hand, and led her towards the forest, in the rear of the cottage. She would fain have resisted; but they were all alone, and the attempt must have been both fruitless and dangerous. She therefore trod with him a path, so devious, so faintly traced, and so overgrown with bushes and young trees, that only a most accurate acquaintance in his early days could have enabled her guide to retain it. To him, however, it seemed so perfectly familiar, that he was not once compelled to pause, though the numerous windings soon deprived Ellen of all knowledge of the situation of the cottage. They descended a steep hill, and proceeding parallel to the river—as Ellen judged by its rushing sound—at length found themselves at what proved to be the termination of their walk.

Ellen now recollected a remark of Edward Walcott's, respecting the wild and rude scenery, through which the river here kept its way; and, in less agitating circumstances, her pleasure and admiration would have been great. They stood beneath a precipice, so high that the loftiest pine tops (and many of them seemed to soar to heaven) scarcely surmounted it. This line of rock has a considerable extent, at unequal heights and with many interruptions, along the course of the river, and it seems probable, that, at some former period, it was the boundary of the waters, though they are now confined within far less ambitious limits. The inferior portion of the crag, beneath which Ellen and her guide were standing, varies so far from the perpendicular as not to be inaccessible by a careful footstep; but only one person has been known to

attempt the ascent of the superior half, and only one the
descent, yet steep as is the height, trees and bushes of various
kinds have clung to the rock, wherever their roots could gain
the slightest hold—thus seeming to prefer the scanty and
difficult nourishment of the cliff, to a more luxurious life in
the rich interval that extends from its base to the river. But,
whether or no these hardy vegetables have voluntarily chosen
their rude resting place, the cliff is indebted to them for much
of the beauty that tempers its sublimity. When the eye is
pained and wearied by the bold nakedness of the rock, it
rests with pleasure on the cheerful foliage of the birch, or
upon the darker green of the funereal fir. Just at the termination of the accessible portion of the crag, these trees are
so numerous, and their foliage so dense, that they completely
shroud from view a considerable excavation, formed, probably, hundreds of years since, by the fall of a portion of the
rock. The detached fragment still lies at a little distance from
the base, gray and moss-grown, but corresponding, in its
general outline, to the cavity from which it was rent.

But the most singular and beautiful object in all this scene,
is a tiny fount of chrystal water, that gushes forth from the
high, smooth forehead of the cliff. Its perpendicular descent
is of many feet; after which it finds its way, with a sweet,
diminutive murmur, to the level ground.

It is not easy to conceive, whence the barren rock procures
even the small supply of water, that is necessary to the existence of this stream; it is as unaccountable, as the gush of
gentle feeling which sometimes proceeds from the hardest
heart; but there it continues to flow and fall, undiminished
and unincreased. The stream is so slender, that the gentlest
breeze suffices to disturb its descent, and to scatter its pure
sweet waters over the face of the cliff. But, in that deep
forest, there is seldom a breath of wind: so that, plashing
continually upon one spot, the fount has worn its own little
channel of white sand, by which it finds its way to the river.

Alas, that the Naiades have lost their old authority; for what a Deity of tiny loveliness must once have presided here!

Ellen's companion paused not to gaze either upon the loveliness or the sublimity of this scene, but assisting her where it was requisite, began the steep and difficult ascent of the lower part of the cliff. The maiden's ingenuity in vain endeavored to assign reasons for this movement; but when they reached the tuft of trees, which, as has been noticed, grew at the ultimate point where mortal footstep might safely tread, she perceived through their thick branches the recess in the rock. Here they entered; and her guide pointed to a mossy seat, in the formation of which, to judge from its regularity, art had probably a share.

'Here you may remain in safety,' he observed, 'till I obtain the means of proceeding. In this spot you need fear no intruder; but it will be dangerous to venture beyond its bounds.'

The meaning glance that accompanied these words, intimated to poor Ellen, that, in warning her against danger, he alluded to the vengeance with which he would visit any attempt to escape. To leave her thus alone, trusting to the influence of such a threat, was a bold, yet a necessary and by no means a hopeless measure. On Ellen, it produced the desired effect; and she sat in the cave as motionless, for a time, as if she had herself been a part of the rock. In other circumstances, this shady recess would have been a delightful retreat, during the sultry warmth of a summer's day. The dewy coolness of the rock kept the air always fresh, and the sunbeams never thrust themselves so as to dissipate the mellow twilight through the green trees with which the chamber was curtained. Ellen's sleeplessness and agitation, for many preceding hours, had perhaps deadened her feelings; for she now felt a sort of indifference creeping upon her, an inability to realize the evils of her situation, at the same time that she was perfectly aware of them all. This torpor of mind increased, till her eyelids began to grow heavy, and the cave and trees to swim before her sight. In a few moments more, she would probably have been in dreamless slumber; but, rousing herself by a strong effort, she looked round the narrow limits of the cave, in search of objects to excite her worn-out mind.

She now perceived, wherever the smooth rock afforded place for them, the initials, or the full length names, of former visitants of the cave. What wanderer on mountain-tops, or in deep solitudes, has not felt the influence of these records of humanity, telling him, when such a conviction is soothing to his heart, that he is not alone in the world? It was singular, that, when her own mysterious situation had almost lost its power to engage her thoughts, Ellen perused these barren memorials with a certain degree of interest. She went on repeating them aloud, and starting at the sound of her own voice, till at length, as one name passed through her lips, she paused, and then, leaning her forehead against the letters, burst into tears. It was the name of Edward Walcott; and it struck upon her heart, arousing her to a full sense of her present misfortunes and dangers, and, more painful still, of her past happiness. Her tears had, however, a soothing, and at the same time a strengthening effect upon her mind; for, when their gush was over, she raised her head and began to meditate on the means of escape. She wondered at the species of fascination that had kept her, as if chained to the rock, so long, when there was, in reality, nothing to bar her path-way. She determined, late as it was, to attempt her own deliverance; and for that purpose began slowly and cautiously to emerge from the cave.

Peeping out from among the trees, she looked and listened with most painful anxiety, to discover if any living thing were in that seeming solitude, or if any sound disturbed the heavy stillness. But she saw only Nature, in her wildest forms, and heard only the plash and murmur (almost inaudible, because continual) of the little waterfall, and the quick, short throbbing of her own heart, against which she pressed her hand, as if to hush it. Gathering courage, therefore, she began to descend; and, starting often at the loose stones that even her light footstep displaced and sent rattling down, she at length reached the base of the crag in safety. She then made a few steps in the direction, as nearly as she could judge, by which she arrived at the spot; but paused, with a sudden revulsion of the blood to her heart, as her guide emerged from behind a projecting part of the rock. He approached her deliberately, an ironical smile writhing his features into a most disagreeable expression, while in his eyes there was something that seemed a wild, fierce joy. By a species of sophistry of which oppressors often make use, he had brought himself to believe that he was now the injured one, and that Ellen, by her distrust of him, had fairly subjected herself to whatever evil it consisted with his will and power to inflict upon her. Her only restraining influence over him, the consciousness in his own mind that he possessed her confidence, was now done away. Ellen, as well as her enemy, felt that this was the case. She knew not what to dread; but she was well aware that danger was at hand, and that, in the deep wilderness, there was none to help her, except that Being, with whose inscrutable purposes it might consist, to allow the wicked to triumph for a season, and the innocent to be brought low.

'Are you so soon weary of this quiet retreat?' demanded her guide, continuing to wear the same sneering smile. 'Or has your anxiety for your father induced you to set forth alone, in quest of the afflicted old man?'

'Oh, if I were but with him!' exclaimed Ellen. 'But this place is lonely and fearful, and I cannot endure to remain here.'

'Lonely, is it, sweet Ellen?' he rejoined, 'am I not with you? Yes, it is lonely—lonely as guilt could wish. Cry aloud,

Ellen, and spare not. Shriek, and see if there be any among these rocks and woods to hearken to you!'

'There is—there is one,' exclaimed Ellen, shuddering and affrighted at the fearful meaning of his countenance. 'He is here—He is there.' And she pointed to heaven.

'It may be so, dearest,' he replied. 'But if there be an ear that hears, and an eye that sees all the evil of the earth, yet the arm is slow to avenge. Else why do I stand before you, a living man?'

'His vengeance may be delayed for a time, but not forever,' she answered, gathering a desperate courage from the extremity of her fear.

'You say true, lovely Ellen; and I have done enough, ere now, to insure its heaviest weight. There is a pass, when evil deeds can add nothing to guilt, nor good ones take anything from it.'

'Think of your mother—of her sorrow through life, and perhaps even after death,' Ellen began to say. But as she spoke these words, the expression of his face was changed, becoming suddenly so dark and fiend-like, that she clasped her hands and fell on her knees before him.

'I have thought of my mother,' he replied, speaking very low, and putting his face close to hers. 'I remember the neglect—the wrong—the lingering and miserable death, that she received at my hands. By what claim can either man or woman henceforth expect mercy from me? If God will help you, be it so; but by those words you have turned my heart to stone.'

At this period of their conversation, when Ellen's peril seemed most imminent, the attention of both was attracted by a fragment of rock, which, falling from the summit of the crag, struck very near them. Ellen started from her knees, and, with her false guide, gazed eagerly upward; he in the fear of interruption, she in the hope of deliverance.

IX

At length, he cries, behold the fated spring!
Yon rugged cliff conceals the fountain blest,
Dark rocks it's chrystal source o'ershadowing.

PSYCHE

THE TALE now returns to Fanshawe, who, as will be recollected, after being overtaken by Edward Walcott, was left with little apparent prospect of aiding in the deliverance of Ellen Langton.

It would be difficult to analyze the feelings with which the student pursued the chase, or to decide whether he was influenced and animated by the same hopes of successful love, that cheered his rival. That he was conscious of such hopes, there is little reason to suppose; for the most powerful minds are not always the best acquainted with their own feelings. Had Fanshawe, moreover, acknowledged to himself the possibility of gaining Ellen's affections, his generosity would have induced him to refrain from her society, before it was too late. He had read her character with accuracy, and had seen how fit she was to love, and to be loved by a man who could find his happiness in the common occupation of the world; and Fanshawe never deceived himself so far, as to suppose that this would be the case with him. Indeed, he often wondered at the passion, with which Ellen's simple loveliness of mind and person had inspired him, and which seemed to be founded on the principle of contrariety, rather than of sympathy. It was the yearning of a soul, formed by Nature in a peculiar mould, for communion with those to whom it bore a resemblance, yet of whom it was not. But there was no reason to suppose that Ellen, who differed from the multitude only as being purer and better, would cast away her affections on the one, of all who surrounded her, least fitted to make her happy. Thus Fanshawe reasoned with himself, and of this he believed that he was convinced. Yet, ever and anon, he found himself involved in a dream of bliss, of which Ellen was to be the giver and the sharer. Then would he rouse himself, and press upon his mind the chilling consciousness, that it was, and could be, but a dream. There was also another feeling, apparently discordant with those which have been enumerated. It was a longing for rest—for his old retirement, that came at intervals so powerfully upon him, as he rode on, that his heart sickened of the active exertion on which fate had thrust him.

After being overtaken by Edward Walcott, Fanshawe continued his journey with as much speed as was attainable by his wearied horse, but at a pace infinitely too slow for his earnest thoughts. These had carried him far away, leaving him only such a consciousness of his present situation as to make diligent use of the spur, when a horse's tread, at no great distance, struck upon his ear. He looked forward, and behind; but, though a considerable extent of the narrow, rocky, and grass-grown road was visible, he was the only traveller there. Yet again he heard the sound, which, he now discovered, proceeded from among the trees that lined the road-side. Alighting, he entered the forest, with the intention, if the steed proved to be disengaged and superior to his own, of appropriating him to his own use. He soon gained a view of the object he sought; but the animal rendered a closer acquaintance unattainable, by immediately taking to his heels. Fanshawe had however made a most interesting discovery; for the horse was accoutred with a side-saddle; and who, but Ellen Langton, could have been his rider? At this conclusion, though his perplexity was thereby in no degree diminished, the student immediately arrived. Returning to the road, and perceiving on the summit of the hill a cottage, which he recognized as the one he had entered with Ellen and Edward Walcott, he determined there to make inquiry respecting the objects of his pursuit.

On reaching the door of the poverty-stricken dwelling, he saw that it was not now so desolate of inmates as on his previous visit. In the single inhabitable apartment were several elderly women, clad evidently in their well-worn and well-saved Sunday clothes, and all wearing a deep-grievous expression of countenance. Fanshawe was not long in deciding, that death was within the cottage, and that these aged females were of the class who love the house of mourning, because to them it is a house of feasting. It is a fact, disgusting and lamentable, that the disposition which Heaven for the best of purposes has implanted in the female breast—to watch by the sick and comfort the afflicted—frequently becomes depraved into an odious love of scenes of pain, and death and sorrow. Such women are like the Gouls of the Arabian Tales, whose feasting was among tombstones, and upon dead carcasses.

(It is sometimes, though less frequently, the case, that this disposition to make a 'joy of grief' extends to individuals of the other sex. But in us it is even less excusable and more disgusting, because it is our nature to shun the sick and afflicted; and, unless restrained by principles other than we bring into the world with us, men might follow the example of many animals in destroying the infirm of their own species. Indeed, instances of this nature might be adduced among savage nations.) Sometimes, however, from an original *lusus naturæ,* or from the influence of circumstances, a man becomes a haunter of death-beds—a tormentor of afflicted hearts —and a follower of funerals. Such an abomination now appeared before Fanshawe, and beckoned him into the cottage. He was considerably beyond the middle age, rather corpulent, with a broad, fat, tallow complexioned countenance. The student obeyed his silent call, and entered the room, through the open door of which he had been gazing.

He now beheld, stretched out upon the bed, where she had so lately laid in life, though dying, the yet uncoffined corpse of the aged woman, whose death has been described. How frightful it seemed!—that fixed countenance of ashy paleness, amid its decorations of muslin and fine linen—as if a bride were decked for the marriage chamber—as if death were a bridegroom, and the coffin a bridal bed. Alas, that the vanity of dress should extend even to the grave!

The female, who, as being the near and only relative of the deceased, was supposed to stand in need of comfort, was surrounded by five or six of her own sex. These continually poured into her ear the stale, trite maxims, which, where consolation is actually required, add torture insupportable to the wounded heart. Their present object, however, conducted herself with all due decorum, holding her handkerchief to her tearless eyes, and answering with very grievous groans to the words of her comforters. Who could have imagined that there was joy in her heart, because, since her sister's death, there was but one remaining obstacle between herself and the sole property of that wretched cottage?

While Fanshawe stood silently observing this scene, a low, monotonous voice was uttering some words in his ear, of the meaning of which his mind did not immediately take note. He turned, and saw that the speaker was the person who had invited him to enter.

'What is your pleasure with me, Sir?' demanded the student.

'I made bold to ask,' replied the man, 'whether you would choose to partake of some creature comfort, before joining in prayer with the family and friends of our deceased sister?'

As he spoke, he pointed to a table, on which was a moderate sized stone jug, and two or three broken glasses; for then, as now, there were few occasions of joy or grief, on which ardent spirits were not considered indispensable, to heighten the one, or to alleviate the other.

'I stand in no need of refreshment,' answered Fanshawe; 'and it is not my intention to pray at present.'

'I pray your pardon, reverend Sir,' rejoined the other; 'but your face is pale, and you look wearied. A drop from yonder vessel is needful to recruit the outward man. And for the prayer, the sisters will expect it, and their souls are longing for the outpouring of the spirit. I was intending to open my own mouth, with such words as are given to my poor ignorance, but——'

Fanshawe was here about to interrupt this address, which proceeded on the supposition, arising from his black dress and thoughtful countenance, that he was a clergyman. But one of the females now approached him, and intimated that the sister of the deceased was desirous of the benefit of his conversation. He would have returned a negative to this request, but, looking towards the afflicted woman, he saw her withdraw her handkerchief from her eyes, and cast a brief, but penetrating and most intelligent, glance upon him. He immediately expressed his readiness to offer such consolation as might be in his power.

'And in the meantime,' observed the lay-preacher, 'I will give the sisters to expect a word of prayer and exhortation, either from you or from myself.'

These words were lost upon the supposed clergyman, who was already at the side of the mourner. The females withdrew out of ear-shot, to give place to a more legitimate comforter than themselves.

'What know you respecting my purpose?' inquired Fanshawe, bending towards her.

The woman gave a groan—the usual result of all efforts at consolation—for the edification of the company; and then replied in a whisper, which reached only the ear for which it was intended. 'I know whom you come to seek—I can direct you to them. Speak low, for God's sake,' she continued, observing that Fanshawe was about to utter an exclamation. She then resumed her groans, with greater zeal than before.

'Where—where are they?' asked the student, in a whisper which all his efforts could scarcely keep below his breath. 'I adjure you to tell me.'

'And if I should, how am I like to be bettered by it?' inquired the old woman, her speech still preceded and fol-lowed by a groan.

'Oh God!—The *auri sacra fames!*' thought Fanshawe with a sickening heart, looking at the motionless corpse upon the bed, and then at the wretched being, whom the course of Nature, in comparatively a moment of time, would reduce to the same condition.

He whispered again, however, putting his purse into the hag's hand. 'Take this. Make your own terms when they are discovered. Only tell me where I must seek them—and speedily, or it may be too late.'

'I am a poor woman and am afflicted,' said she, taking the purse, unseen by any who were in the room. 'It is little that worldly goods can do for me, and not long can I enjoy them,' and here she was delivered of a louder, and a more heartfelt groan, than ever. She then continued, 'Follow the path behind the cottage, that leads to the river side. Walk along the foot of the rock, and search for them near the water-spout; keep a slow pace till you are out of sight,' she added, as the student started to his feet.

The guests of the cottage did not attempt to oppose Fan-shawe's progress, when they saw him take the path towards the forest, imagining, probably, that he was retiring for the purpose of secret prayer. But the old woman laughed behind the handkerchief with which she veiled her face.

'Take heed to your steps, boy,' she muttered; 'for they are leading you whence you will not return. Death, too, for the slayer. Be it so.'

Fanshawe, in the meanwhile, contrived to discover, and, for awhile, to retain, the narrow and winding path that led to the river side. But it was originally no more than a track, by which the cattle belonging to the cottage went down to their watering place; and by these four-footed passengers it had long been deserted. The fern bushes, therefore, had grown over it, and in several places, trees of considerable size had shot up in the midst. These difficulties could scarcely have been surmounted by the utmost caution; and as Fanshawe's thoughts were too deeply fixed upon the end, to pay a due regard to the means, he soon became desperately bewildered, both as to the locality of the river, and of the cottage. Had he known, however, in which direction to seek the latter, he would not probably have turned back; not that he was infected by any chivalrous desire to finish the adventure alone; but because he would expect little assistance from those he had left there. Yet he could not but wonder— though he had not in his first eagerness taken notice of it— at the anxiety of the old woman that he should proceed singly, and without the knowledge of her guests, on the search. He nevertheless continued to wander on—pausing often to listen for the rush of the river, and then starting forward, with fresh rapidity, to rid himself of the sting of his own thoughts, which became painfully intense, when undisturbed by bodily motion. His way was now frequently interrupted by rocks, that thrust their huge gray heads from the ground, compelling him to turn aside, and thus depriving him, fortunately perhaps, of all remaining idea of the direction he had intended to pursue.

Thus he went on—his head turned back, and taking little heed to his footsteps—when, perceiving that he trod upon a smooth, level rock, he looked forward, and found himself almost on the utmost verge of a precipice.

After the throbbing of the heart that followed this narrow escape had subsided, he stood gazing down where the sunbeams slept so pleasantly at the roots of the tall old trees, with whose highest tops he was upon a level. Suddenly he seemed to hear voices—one well remembered voice—ascending from beneath; and approaching to the edge of the cliff, he saw at its base the two whom he sought.

He saw and interpreted Ellen's look and attitude of entreaty, though the words, with which she sought to soften the ruthless heart of her guide, became inaudible, ere they reached the height where Fanshawe stood. He felt that Heaven had sent him thither, at the moment of her utmost need, to be the preserver of all that was dear to him, and he paused only to consider the mode in which her deliverance was to be effected. Life he would have laid down willingly—exultingly;—his only care was, that the sacrifice should not be in vain.

At length, when Ellen fell upon her knees, he lifted a small fragment of rock, and threw it down the cliff. It struck so near the pair, that it immediately drew the attention of both.

When the betrayer—at the instant in which he had almost defied the power of the Omnipotent to bring help to Ellen—became aware of Fanshawe's presence, his hardihood failed him for a time, and his knees actually tottered beneath him. There was something awful, to his apprehension, in the slight form that stood so far above him, like a being from another sphere, looking down upon his wickedness. But his half superstitious dread endured only a moment's space; and then, mustering the courage that in a thousand dangers had not deserted him, he prepared to revenge the intrusion by which Fanshawe had a second time interrupted his designs.

'By Heaven, I will cast him down at her feet!' he muttered through his closed teeth. 'There shall be no form nor likeness of man left in him. Then let him rise up, if he is able, and defend her.'

Thus resolving, and overlooking all hazard, in his eager hatred, and desire for vengcance, he began a desperate attempt to ascend the cliff. The space, which only had hitherto been deemed accessible, was quickly past, and in a moment more he was half way up the precipice, clinging to trees, shrubs, and projecting portions of the rock, and escaping through hazards which seemed to menace inevitable destruction.

Fanshawe, as he watched his upward progress, deemed that every step would be his last; but when he perceived that more than half, and, apparently, the most difficult part of the ascent was surmounted, his opinion changed. His courage, however, did not fail him, as the moment of need drew nigh. His spirits rose buoyantly, his limbs seemed to grow firm and strong, and he stood on the edge of the precipice, prepared for the death-struggle which would follow the success of his enemy's attempt.

But that attempt was not successful. When within a few feet of the summit, the adventurer grasped at a twig, too slenderly rooted to sustain his weight. It gave way in his hand, and he fell backward down the precipice. His head struck against the less perpendicular part of the rock, whence the body rolled heavily down to the detached fragment, of which mention has heretofore bccn made. There was no life left in him. With all the passions of hell alive in his heart, he had met the fate that he intended for Fanshawe.

The student paused not, then, to shudder at the sudden and awful overthrow of his enemy, for he saw that Ellen lay motionless at the foot of the cliff. She had, indeed, fainted, at the moment she became aware of her deliverer's presence— and no stronger proof could she have given of her firm reliance upon his protection.

Fanshawe was not deterred by the danger, of which he had just received so fearful an evidence, from attempting to descend to her assistance; and whether owing to his advantage in lightness of frame, or to superior caution, he arrived safely at the base of the precipice.

He lifted the motionless form of Ellen in his arms, and resting her head against his shoulder, gazed on her cheek of lily paleness, with a joy—a triumph—that rose almost to madness. It contained no mixture of hope, it had no reference to the future—it was the perfect bliss of a moment—an insulated point of happiness. He bent over her and pressed a kiss —the first, and he knew it would be the last—on her pale lips; then bearing her to the fountain, he sprinkled its waters profusely over her face, neck, and bosom. She at length opened her eyes, slowly and heavily; but her mind was evidently wandering, till Fanshawe spoke.

'Fear not, Ellen; you are safe,' he said.

At the sound of his voice, her arm, which was thrown over his shoulder, involuntarily tightened its embrace, telling him, by that mute motion, with how firm a trust she confided in him. But, as a fuller sense of her situation returned, she raised herself to her feet, though still retaining the support of his arm. It was singular, that, although her insensibility had commenced before the fall of her guide, she turned away her eyes, as if instinctively, from the spot where the mangled body lay; nor did she inquire of Fanshawe the manner of her deliverance.

'Let us begone from this place,' she said, in faint, low accents, and with an inward shudder.

They walked along the precipice, seeking some passage by which they might gain its summit, and at length arrived at that by which Ellen and her guide had descended. Chance—for neither Ellen nor Fanshawe could have discovered the path—led them, after but little wandering, to the cottage. A messenger was sent forward to the town, to inform Doctor Melmoth of the recovery of his ward; and the intelligence thus received had interrupted Edward Walcott's conversation with the seaman.

It would have been impossible, in the mangled remains of Ellen's guide, to discover the son of the Widow Butler, except from the evidence of her sister, who became by his death the sole inheritrix of the cottage. The history of this evil and unfortunate man must be comprised within very narrow limits. A harsh father, and his own untameable disposition, had driven him from home in his boyhood, and chance had made him the temporary companion of Hugh Crombie. After two years of wandering, when in a foreign country and in circumstances of utmost need, he attracted the notice of Mr. Langton. The merchant took his young countryman under his protection, afforded him advantages of education, and, as his capacity was above mediocrity, gradually trusted him in many affairs of importance. During this period, there was no evidence of dishonesty on his part. On the contrary, he manifested a zeal for Mr. Langton's interest, and a respect for his person, that proved his strong sense of the benefits he had received. But he unfortunately fell into certain youthful indiscretions, which, if not entirely pardonable, might have been palliated by many considerations, that would have occurred to a merciful man. Mr. Langton's justice, however, was seldom tempered by mercy; and on this occasion, he shut the door of repentance against his erring protégé, and left him in a situation not less desperate, than that from which he had relieved him. The goodness and the nobleness, of which his heart was not destitute, turned, from that time, wholly to evil, and he became irrecoverably ruined and irreclaimably depraved. His wandering life had led him, shortly before the period of this tale, to his native country. Here the erroneous intelligence of Mr. Langton's death had reached him, and suggested the scheme, which circumstances seemed to render practicable, but the fatal termination of which has been related.

The body was buried where it had fallen, close by the huge, gray, moss-grown fragment of rock—a monument on which centuries can work little change. The eighty years that have elapsed since the death of the widow's son, have, however, been sufficient to obliterate an inscription, which some one was at the pains to cut in the smooth surface of the stone. Traces of letters are still discernible; but the writer's many efforts could never discover a connected meaning. The grave, also, is overgrown with fern bushes, and sunk to a level with the surrounding soil. But the legend, though my version of it may be forgotten, will long be traditionary in that lonely spot, and give to the rock, and the precipice, and the fountain, an interest thrilling to the bosom of the romantic wanderer.

X

Sitting then in shelter shady
To observe and mark his mone
Suddenly I saw a Lady
Hasting to him all alone,
    Clad in maiden-white and green:
    Whom I judg'd the Forrest Queen.
                    THE WOOD-MAN'S BEAR

D URING several weeks succeeding her danger and
deliverance, Ellen Langton was confined to her
chamber, by illness, resulting from the agitation she
had endured. Her father embraced the earliest opportunity
to express his deep gratitude to Fanshawe for the inestimable
service he had rendered, and to intimate a desire to requite
it, to the utmost of his power. He had understood that the
student's circumstances were not prosperous, and, with the
feeling of one who was habituated to give and receive a *quid
pro quo,* he would have rejoiced to share his abundance
with the deliverer of his daughter. But Fanshawe's flushed
brow and haughty eye, when he perceived the thought that
was stirring in Mr. Langton's mind, sufficiently proved to
the discerning merchant, that money was not in the present
instance a circulating medium. His penetration, in fact, very
soon informed him of the motives by which the young man
had been actuated, in risking his life for Ellen Langton; but
he made no allusion to the subject—concealing his intentions,
if any he had, in his own bosom.

During Ellen's illness, Edward Walcott had manifested
the deepest anxiety respecting her; he had wandered around
and within the house, like a restless ghost, informing himself
of the slightest fluctuation in her health, and thereby grad-

uating his happiness or misery. He was at length informed
that her convalescence had so far progressed, that on the
succeeding day she would venture below. From that time,
Edward's visits to Doctor Melmoth's mansion were relinquished;—his cheek grew pale, and his eye lost its merry
light—but he resolutely kept himself a banished man. Multifarious were the conjectures to which this course of conduct
gave rise; but Ellen understood and approved his motives.
The maiden must have been far more blind than ever woman
was, in such a matter, if the late events had not convinced
her of Fanshawe's devoted attachment; and she saw that
Edward Walcott, feeling the superior, the irresistible strength
of his rival's claim, had retired from the field. Fanshawe,
however, discovered no intention to pursue his advantage.
He paid her no voluntary visit, and even declined an invitation to tea, with which Mrs. Melmoth, after extensive preparations, had favored him. He seemed to have resumed all
the habits of seclusion, by which he was distinguished previous to his acquaintance with Ellen—except that he still
took his sunset walk, on the banks of the stream.

On one of these occasions, he staid his footsteps by the old
leafless oak, which had witnessed Ellen's first meeting with
the angler. Here he mused upon the circumstances that had
resulted from that event, and upon the rights and privileges—
for he was well aware of them all—which those circumstances
had given him. Perhaps the loveliness of the scene, and the
recollections connected with it—perhaps the warm and mellow sunset—perhaps a temporary weakness in himself, had
softened his feelings, and shaken the firmness of his resolution, to leave Ellen to be happy with his rival. His strong
affections rose up against his reason, whispering that bliss—
on earth and in Heaven, through time and Eternity—might
yet be his lot with her. It is impossible to conceive of the
flood of momentary joy, which the bare admission of such a
possibility sent through his frame; and just when the tide was

highest in his heart, a soft little hand was laid upon his own, and, starting, he beheld Ellen at his side.

Her illness, since the commencement of which, Fanshawe had not seen her, had wrought a considerable, but not a disadvantageous change in her appearance. She was paler and thinner—her countenance was more intellectual—more spiritual—and a spirit did the student almost deem her, appearing so suddenly in that solitude. There was a quick vibration of the delicate blood in her cheek, yet never brightening to the glow of perfect health; a tear was glittering on each of her long dark eye lashes; and there was a gentle tremor through all her frame, which compelled her, for a little space, to support herself against the oak. Fanshawe's first impulse was, to address her in words of rapturous delight; but he checked himself, and attempted—vainly, indeed—to clothe his voice in tones of calm courtesy. His remark merely expressed pleasure at her restoration to health; and Ellen's low and indistinct reply had as little relation to the feelings that agitated her.

'Yet I fear,' continued Fanshawe, recovering a degree of composure, and desirous of assigning a motive (which he felt was not the true one) for Ellen's agitation—'I fear that your walk has extended too far for your strength.'

'It would have borne me farther, with such a motive,' she replied, still trembling—'to express my gratitude to my preserver.'

'It was needless, Ellen, it was needless; for the deed brought with it its own reward,' exclaimed Fanshawe, with a vehemence that he could not repress. 'It was dangerous, for——'

Here he interrupted himself, and turned his face away.

'And wherefore was it dangerous?' inquired Ellen, laying her hand gently on his arm; for he seemed about to leave her.

'Because you have a tender and generous heart, and I a weak one,' he replied.

'Not so,' answered she, with animation. 'Yours is a heart, full of strength and nobleness; and if it have a weakness——'

'You know well that it has, Ellen—one that has swallowed up all its strength,' said Fanshawe. 'Was it wise, then, to tempt it thus—when, if it yield, the result must be your own misery?'

Ellen did not affect to misunderstand his meaning. On the contrary, with a noble frankness, she answered to what was implied, rather than expressed.

'Do me not this wrong,' she said, blushing, yet earnestly. 'Can it be misery—will it not be happiness to form the tie that shall connect you to the world?—to be your guide—a humble one, it is true, but the one of your choice—to the quiet paths, from which your proud and lonely thoughts have estranged you? Oh! I know that there will be happiness in such a lot, from these and a thousand other sources.'

The animation with which Ellen spoke, and, at the same time, a sense of the singular course to which her gratitude had impelled her, caused her beauty to grow brighter and more enchanting with every word. And when, as she concluded, she extended her hand to Fanshawe, to refuse it was like turning from an angel, who would have guided him to Heaven. But, had he been capable of making the woman he loved a sacrifice to her own generosity, that act would have rendered him unworthy of her. Yet the struggle was a severe one, ere he could reply.

'You have spoken generously and nobly, Ellen,' he said. 'I have no way to prove that I deserve your generosity, but by refusing to take advantage of it. Even if your heart were yet untouched—if no being, more happily constituted than myself, had made an impression there—even then, I trust, a selfish passion would not be stronger than my integrity. But now——' He would have proceeded, but the firmness, which had hitherto sustained him, gave way. He turned aside to hide the tears, which all the pride of his nature could not restrain, and which, instead of relieving, added to his anguish. At length he resumed. 'No, Ellen, we must part now and forever. Your life will be long and happy. Mine will be short, but not altogether wretched—nor shorter than if we had never met. When you hear that I am in my grave, do not imagine that you have hastened me thither. Think that you scattered bright dreams around my path-way—an ideal happiness, that you would have sacrificed your own to realize.'

He ceased; and Ellen felt that his determination was unalterable. She could not speak; but taking his hand, she pressed it to her lips; and they saw each other no more. Mr. Langton and his daughter, shortly after, returned to the sea-port, which, for several succeeding years, was their residence.

After Ellen's departure, Fanshawe returned to his studies with the same absorbing ardour, that had formerly characterized him. His face was as seldom seen among the young and gay;—the pure breeze and the blessed sunshine as seldom refreshed his pale and weary brow; and his lamp burned as constantly from the first shade of evening, till the gray morning light began to dim its beams. Nor did he, as weak men will, treasure up his love in a hidden chamber of his breast. He was in reality the thoughtful and earnest student that he seemed. He had exerted the whole might of his spirit over itself—and he was a conqueror. Perhaps, indeed, a summer breeze of sad and gentle thoughts would sometimes visit him; but, in these brief memories of his love, he did not wish that it should be revived, or mourn over its event.

There were many who felt an interest in Fanshawe; but the influence of none could prevail upon him to lay aside the habits, mental and physical, by which he was bringing himself to the grave. His passage thither was consequently rapid—terminating just as he reached his twentieth year. His fellow students erected to his memory a monument of rough-hewn granite, with a white marble slab, for the inscription.

This was borrowed from the grave of Nathanael Mather, whom, in his almost insane eagerness for knowledge and in his early death, Fanshawe resembled.

THE ASHES OF A HARD STUDENT AND A GOOD SCHOLAR

MANY tears were shed over his grave; but the thoughtful and the wise, though turf never covered a nobler heart, could not lament that it was so soon at rest. He left a world for which he was unfit; and we trust, that, among the innumerable stars of heaven, there is one where he has found happiness.

Of the other personages of this tale—Hugh Crombie, being exposed to no strong temptations, lived and died an honest man. Concerning Doctor Melmoth, it is unnecessary here to speak. The reader, if he have any curiosity upon the subject, is referred to his life, which, together with several sermons and other productions of the Doctor, was published by his successor in the Presidency of Harley College, about the year 1768.

It was not till four years after Fanshawe's death, that Edward Walcott was united to Ellen Langton. Their future lives were uncommonly happy. Ellen's gentle, almost imperceptible, but powerful influence, drew her husband away from the passions and pursuits that would have interfered with domestic felicity; and he never regretted the worldly distinction of which she thus deprived him. Theirs was a long life of calm and quiet bliss;—and what matters it, that, except in these pages, they have left no name behind them?

TEXTUAL NOTES

333.14 College] The general intention of the first edition seems to be to capitalize "College" as an institution (as at 333.23 or 334.4) but to distinguish the "college" as a collective designation for an association of students (as at 342.26 and 343.34). The emendation necessary to make uniform this distinction has not been extensive, since it has concerned only 334.20 and 335.15 in addition to 334.14.

334.19-20 farm-houses— . . . College—] The use of dashes to replace syntactical commas in parenthetical constructions is common with Hawthorne; and in the manuscripts the ordinary house style of comma plus dash, as in the first edition here, is not found. Since the print is inconsistent and occasionally admits Hawthorne's own usage (as at 342.10-11, 367.10, 376.16-17, 383.21-22, 428.6-7, 428.12-13, 437.18), all such house-styled punctuation has been normalized to conform to the characteristics of Hawthorne's manuscripts.

334.20 Inn] The capitalization or non-capitalization of "Inn" is in some part demonstrably compositorial, although the manuscript may not have been entirely consistent. That Hawthorne intended the capital is clear, however, from the explicit use in the erratum note upon 372.6, "for 'atmosphere of the Sun,' read 'atmosphere of an Inn.'" Moreover, the only explanation for the compositorial misreading "Sun" would be manuscript "Inn" with the majuscule. Hence the text has been made uniform throughout by emendation.

335.19-20 country, . . . distance,)] Hawthorne's manuscript usage in respect to parentheses was the opposite of that for parenthetical dashes. Whereas his dashes replaced all other punctuation, he was remarkably consistent in placing necessary syntactical commas before the opening parenthesis and then after the final word immediately before the closing parenthesis. Since syntactical commas are required in the present reading, and since the styling of the first edition is inconsistent according to the compositor, Hawthorne's manuscript usage has been adopted by emendation throughout when required. However, unnecessary commas, where he himself would probably not have employed them, have not been inserted in such places as 337.19-20, 339.13-14, 340.30-31, or 340.34-341.1.

335.22 fifty—] Although the house style of the time required a comma before a dash introducing a phrase or clause ending a sentence, Hawthorne's manuscripts habitually omit the comma. Since the practice in the first edition is not uniform, and Hawthorne's own system is occasionally seen (as at 368.15, 376.7, 378.2, 379.14, 382.25, 390.17, 401.22, 401.31, 405.24, 407.8, 441.35), the Centenary text normalizes throughout according to Hawthorne's manuscript style. However, as may be seen in such manuscripts as *The House of the Seven Gables*, Hawthorne accepted a semicolon plus dash in this construction, and thus this particular punctuation has been retained in such appearances as at 335.32.

344.13 heaven] Hawthorne's manuscripts are consistent in distinguishing "heaven" as the sky from "Heaven" as a divine locale. The correct use is occasionally found in the first edition (as at 398.3, 460.9 "heaven" and 412.21 and 456.32 "Heaven"), but often the form is at the mercy of the compositors. Consistent emendation in the Centenary text enforces the manuscript distinction.

349.28 birch-tree] Hawthorne's manuscript practice of hyphenating tree names is reproduced in "elm-trees" at 371.3; hence all tree names have been normalized to fit this authorial characteristic.

383.35 Dame] Little uniformity exists in the first edition in respect to capitalizing "dame," "widow," "master," and "doctor" when used as titles, although all are capitalized with some regularity by at least one compositor. As evidenced by the manuscripts, Hawthorne's usual practice was to capitalize; hence the adjustments have been made throughout the Centenary text to secure uniformity. (The first appearances of each with a capital are "Dame" 375.1, "Widow" 371.6, "Master" 387.30, and "Doctor" 335.8.)

389.24 Inn.] The dash that follows the period in the first edition is a justifying device, the various occurrences of which have been omitted at 389.24, 392.9, 401.29, 422.13, and 449.22 since they are compositorial.

390.8 reverence's] Apparently the compositor's sense of propriety led him to capitalize "Reverence" on its first appearance here although he then followed copy when he set it three more times on the same page uncapitalized. That the copy indeed was written with a minuscule may be suggested by the appearance of the word set in lower-case by another compositor in the next two pages of the first edition, Centenary 391.

393.29 neighboring] With the exception of "ardour," which appears twice only and in the same form, all -our spellings in the first edition are paralleled according to the compositors by -or forms of the same word. Since manuscripts show Hawthorne to have been a consistent -or speller before he went to England, all -our forms have been normalized when a variation exists within the text, which is to say all words save "ardour."

397.17 tomorrow] Hawthorne's invariable manuscript practice in respect to "tomorrow" is reproduced not by the hyphenated form emended here but by "tomorrow" at 433.30, which contrasts with his invariably hyphenated "to-day."

404.28 New-England] This hyphen, as emended here, is found in the first edition at 3.2 and 77.25, Centenary 333.2 and 403.4. A few such hyphens also appear sporadically in the manuscript of *The House of the Seven Gables* without distinction as to noun or adjectival use. Hence in the first edition the hyphen would appear to be authorial and to represent a practice that Hawthorne gradually discarded. At this date, however, the odds favor the hypothesis that "New-England" represented a fairly consistent usage in the lost *Fanshawe* manuscript.

415.17 recognizing] Although Hawthorne's dictionary listed the spelling "recognise" as found in the text here and at 432.24-25, the form with "z" as in 445.4 is standard in the manuscripts. However, the distinction between an "s" and a "z" is not always very clear in Hawthorne's script; hence the reading would be much at the compositor's option.

418.25-26 stedfast] The first edition of *The Scarlet Letter* exhibits the same inconsistency of spelling "stedfast" or "steadfast" as does *Fanshawe*, although interestingly a significant change made by some agent other than Hawthorne altered "stedfastly" in *The Scarlet Letter* at Centenary 208.9 in the standing type to "steadfastly" in preparation for the second edition. Later manuscripts like *The Blithedale Romance* and *The House of the Seven Gables* are not consistent but frequently employ the "stedfast" spelling. The odds are that Hawthorne started with "stedfast" and then sporadically modernized to "steadfast" over the passage of years.

420.24 concentrated] Given the typical Hawthorne use of "concentred" in *The Scarlet Letter* at Centenary 57.2 (altered by the compositor of the second edition to "concentrated") and MS "concentred" in *The House of the Seven Gables* 254.19 (altered by the first-edition compositor to "concentrated"), a certain temptation exists to emend; but at this early date Hawthorne's use of "concentred" is not established and so "concentrated" here may not be a hidden compositorial corruption.

EDITORIAL EMENDATIONS IN THE COPY-TEXT

For the key to the edition-symbols, see the headnote to Historical Collation, below.

*333.14,   College] CENTENARY; college I–V
334.20,
335.15

*334.19   farm-houses ∧ — . . . College ∧ —] CENTENARY;
          ∼ ,— . . . ∼ ,— I; ∼ , . . . (for . . . college),
          II–V

*334.20, 369.22, 369.29, 370.22, 381.5, 383.23, 385.15,
385.26, 386.12, 389.24, 392.7, 394.34, 395.28, 406.16,
406.21, 423.6, 425.34, 426.11, 429.22   Inn] CENTENARY;
inn I–V

335.13   President] CENTENARY; president I–V

*335.19–20 country, . . . distance,) ∧] CENTENARY; ∼ ∧
          . . . ∼ ∧) ∧ I; ∼ ∧ . . . ∼ ∧), II–V

*335.22   fifty ∧ —] CENTENARY; ∼ ,—I–V

336.24–26 remembrances ∧ — . . . again ∧ —] CENTENARY;
          ∼ ,— . . . ∼ ,— I; ∼ , ∧ . . . ∼ , ∧ II–V

336.33   him ∧ —] CENTENARY; ∼ ,— I–V

336.35   path-way] CENTENARY; ∼ ∧ ∼ I; pathway II–V

339.33   ill-managed, . . . household,) ∧] CENTENARY;
          ∼ ∧ . . . ∼ ∧) ∧ I; ∼ ∧ . . . ∼ ∧), II–V

340.1   see ∧ —] II; ∼ ,— I

340.9   ∧ re familiari, ∧ '] II; 're familiari,' ' I

340.22   sea-port] CENTENARY; seaport I–V

• 465 •

341.7   mortality ∧ —] CENTENARY; ~ ,— I; ~ , ∧ II–V
341.16   life ∧ —] CENTENARY; ~ ,— I–V
342.1   labor,)∧] CENTENARY; ~ ∧) ∧ I; ~ ∧), II–V
342.25   influence,)∧] IV; ~ ∧) ∧ I; ~ ∧), II–III
342.26   college∧—] CENTENARY; ~ ,— I; ~ , ∧ II–V
343.8   dignitary∧—] CENTENARY; ~ ,— I–V
343.27   member∧—] CENTENARY; ~ ,— I–V
344.5   equestrian∧—] CENTENARY; ~ ,— I–V
*344.13,   heaven] II; Heaven I
   349.24,
   437.26

345.8   observed ∧ —] CENTENARY; ~ ,— I–V
345.13,   Ellen ∧ —] CENTENARY; ~ ,— I–V
   346.6
348.8   squalid] II; squallid I
348.29   hope' ;—] CENTENARY; ~;'— I; ~,"— II; ~∧—"
         III; ~∧"— IV–V
*349.28   birch-tree] II; ~ ∧ ~ I
350.10–11   study∧— . . . dead∧—] CENTENARY; ~ ,— . . .
         ~ ,— I; ~ , ∧ . . . ~ , ∧ II–V
350.15   infinity∧—] CENTENARY; ~ ,— I–V
351.1   voice∧— . . . eye∧—] CENTENARY; ~ ,— . . .
         ~ ,— I; ~ , ∧ . . . ~ , ∧ II–V
351.5–6   health∧— . . . world∧— . . . suggested∧—]
         CENTENARY; ~ ,— . . . ~ ,— . . . ~ ,— I;
         ~ , ∧ of his habits (so much . . . ~),— . . .
         ~ , ∧ II–IV; ~ , ∧ of his habits (so much . . .
         ~),— . . . ~ ∧ ∧ V
352.21   both∧—] CENTENARY; ~ ,— I; ~ ; ∧ II–V
353.11–13   it∧— . . . cure∧—] CENTENARY; ~ ,— . . . ~
         ,— I; ~ ; ∧ . . . ~ ,— II–V
354.3–4   perhaps∧ . . . equally,] II; ~ , . . . ~ ∧ I
354.11   line∧—] CENTENARY; ~ ,— I; ~ , ∧ II–V
354.24   line——'] III; ~ '— I–II
355.2   oak-tree] II; ~ ∧ ~ I
355.7   Edward∧—] CENTENARY; ~ ,— I–V
355.9   line∧—] CENTENARY; ~ ,— I–V
355.18   protégé] III; protegée I; protégée II
355.18   trout∧—] CENTENARY; ~ ,— I; ~ , ∧ II–V
355.30   sea-port] CENTENARY; ~ ∧ ~ I; seaport II–V

355.31   come∧–] CENTENARY; ~ ,– I; ~ , ∧ II–V

356.29   himself∧–] CENTENARY; ~ ,– I; ~) ,– II–V

356.33   back∧– . . . hesitated∧–] CENTENARY; ~ ,–
. . . ~ ,– I; ~ , ∧ . . . ~ , ∧ II–V

358.11   oak-tree] II; ~ ∧ ~ I

359.12, 416.19, 416.23, 418.25, 432.13, 438.13, 438.18,
   449.31, 459.20   gray] II; grey I

360.21   refuse∧–] CENTENARY; ~ ,– I; ~ , ∧ II–V

360.22   place∧–] CENTENARY; ~ ,– I; ~ , ∧ II–V

361.1   garden∧–] CENTENARY; ~ ,– I; ~ , ∧ II–V

361.24   began∧–] CENTENARY; ~ ,– I–V

362.13   paused∧–] CENTENARY; ~ ,– I; ~ , ∧ II–V

363.22   forward∧–] CENTENARY; ~ ,– I; ~ , ∧ II–V

363.31   'if] II; ∧ ~ I

363.33   I∧–] II; ~ ,– I

366.5,   landlord] II; Landlord I
410.21

367.16   Anacreontics∧–] CENTENARY; ~ ,– I; ~ ; ∧ II–V

367.24   tavern-haunter] II; ~ ∧ ~ I

368.3   fire∧–] CENTENARY; ~ ,– I–V

368.5   spring] II; Spring I

368.12   outcast∧–] CENTENARY; ~ ,– I–V

368.17   man∧–] CENTENARY; ~ ,– I; ~ : ∧ II–V

369.16   iron-gray] II; iron-grey I

370.5   Sabbath] II; sabbath I

370.8   devout∧–] CENTENARY; ~ ,– I–V

370.10   symptoms] II; symptons I

370.31   bottle∧– . . . Virginia∧–] CENTENARY; ~ ,–
. . . ~ ,– I; ~ , ∧ . . . ~ , ∧ II–V

371.5   displayed,)∧] CENTENARY; ~ ∧) ∧ I, IV; ~ ∧),
II–III, V

371.13   pay∧–] CENTENARY; ~ ,– I–V

372.6   an Inn] I (errata); the Sun I (text); the inn
II–V

372.32, 385.22, 404.20, 404.32, 445.16, 451.3   Heaven]
  II; heaven I

372.33   One] II; one I

373.2   purse∧–] CENTENARY; ~ ,– I–V

373.9   frequent] III; frequented I–II

373.30, 384.6, 417.6, 425.19   Aye] CENTENARY; Ay I–V

374.4   delayed.'] II; ~ . ∧ I
374.9   other∧—] CENTENARY; ~ ,— I–V
374.16   led∧—] II; ~ ,— I
374.27   Devil] II; devil I
374.34   that∧—] CENTENARY; ~ ,— I; ~ ; ∧ II–V
375.2   hush∧—] CENTENARY; ~ ,— I; ~ ! ∧ II–V
375.15   Yes∧—] CENTENARY; ~ ,— I; ~ ; ∧ II–V
375.19   anywhere] II; any where I
376.4   traveller∧—] CENTENARY; ~ ,— I; ~ ; ∧ II–V
376.22   Few∧—] CENTENARY; ~ ,— I; ~ , ∧ II–V
376.23   peril,] II; ~ ∧ I
377.3   No∧—] II; ~ ,— I
377.12   mother∧—if] CENTENARY; ~ ,— ~ I; ~ ! ~ II–V
377.16–17   pathos∧— . . . cup∧—] CENTENARY; ~ ,— . . .
         ~ ,— I; ~ , ∧ . . . ~ , ∧ II–V
378.9   friend∧—] CENTENARY; ~ ,— I; ~ ; ∧ II–V
378.22   grave∧—'] CENTENARY; ~ .'— I; ~ .' ∧ II–V
379.14   Nay,] II; ~ ∧ I
379.19   either∧—] CENTENARY; ~ ,— I; ~ , ∧ II–V
379.31   girl∧—'] CENTENARY; ~ .'— I; ~ !" ∧ II–V
381.16   ease∧—] CENTENARY; ~ ,— I; ~ , ∧ II–V
381.22   seminary] II; Seminary I
382.31   feelings∧—] CENTENARY; ~ ,— I; ~ ; ∧ II–V
382.34   disappointed] II; diappointed I
383.12   met∧—] CENTENARY; ~ ,— I; ~ , ∧ II–V
383.17   changed∧—] CENTENARY; ~ ,— I–V
*383.35, 391.18, 392.12, 410.28   Dame] II; dame I
384.18,   Heaven] CENTENARY; heaven I–V
  458.23
384.20   way∧—] CENTENARY; ~ ,— I–V
384.22   understand∧—] CENTENARY; ~ ,— I; ~ ! ∧ II–V
384.24   dark∧—] CENTENARY; ~ ,— I; ~ ; ∧ II–V
384.25, 409.10, 410.14, 453.9   Widow] II; widow I
384.34   sunbeam.'] III; ~ . ∧ I–II
385.23   'Glover] II; ∧ ~ I
386.5   applications] II; application I
386.10   magnificent,) ∧] CENTENARY; ~ ∧) ∧ I; ~ ∧),
         II–V
386.10   mysterious] II; myterious I
386.19   pause∧—] CENTENARY; ~ ,— I–V

387.8   Oh] II; O I
387.14,   Master] II; master I
  397.3,
  397.24
387.23   gentlemen$_\wedge$–] CENTENARY; $\sim$,– I–V
389.2   look$_\wedge$–] CENTENARY; $\sim$,– I; $\sim$; $_\wedge$ II–V
*389.24   Inn. $_\wedge$] II; inn.– I
*390.8   reverence's] II; Reverence's I
391.1, 391.5, 391.19, 391.30, 392.12, 394.15, 399.23, 400.13,
  400.20, 400.22, 400.31, 401.23, 402.11, 402.23, 403.18,
  404.4, 404.18, 404.22, 404.35, 405.4, 405.21, 405.33,
  406.11, 406.25, 421.26   Doctor] CENTENARY; doctor I–V
391.13, 391.22, 392.11, 392.16, 394.19, 395.9, 399.1, 400.4,
  400.27, 403.7, 403.20, 404.11, 405.27, 406.17, 406.31,
  421.3, 422.6, 426.19, 428.33, 429.21   Doctor] II (Dr.);
  doctor I
391.26   it?$_\wedge$] III; $\sim$?' I–II
391.28   drinking$_\wedge$–] III; $\sim$ $_\wedge$ –" I; $\sim$ $_\wedge$ "– II
391.29   talk I] II; I talk I
392.9   body.] II; $\sim$.– I
393.9   into] II; to I
393.10   She] II; she I
*393.29   neighboring] II; neighbouring I
393.29   apartment$_\wedge$–] CENTENARY; $\sim$,– I; $\sim$, $_\wedge$
             II–V
394.4   pride,] CENTENARY; $\sim$ $_\wedge$ I–V
394.13   wonder$_\wedge$–] CENTENARY; $\sim$,– I–V
394.35   behind$_\wedge$–] CENTENARY; $\sim$,– I; $\sim$, $_\wedge$ II–V
396.10   Hugh,'] II; $\sim$, $_\wedge$ I
396.24–25   Edward$_\wedge$–] CENTENARY; $\sim$;– I; $\sim$, $_\wedge$ II–V
397.1   parlor] II; parlour I
397.8   aside$_\wedge$–] CENTENARY; $\sim$,– I; $\sim$: $_\wedge$ II–V
*397.17   tomorrow] CENTENARY; to-morrow I–V
397.20   'A] II; $_\wedge$ $\sim$ I
399.11,   Doctor's] CENTENARY; doctor's I–V
  402.18
399.15   perpetrating,] II; $\sim$ $_\wedge$ | I
400.11   invisible$_\wedge$–] CENTENARY; $\sim$,– I–V
400.32   lady.] II; $\sim$, I

• 469 •

401.5   however∧— . . . occasion∧—] CENTENARY; ∼ ,—
       . . . ∼ ,— I–V
401.7   silence∧—] CENTENARY; ∼ ,— I; ∼ , ∧ II–V
401.26   unconscionable] II; unconscienable I
401.28   newspaper∧—] CENTENARY; ∼ ,— I–V
401.29   country.∧] II; ∼ .– I
402.7   hers∧—] CENTENARY; ∼ ,— I; ∼ , ∧ II–V
402.23   word,] II; ∼ ∧ I
402.31   There∧—] CENTENARY; ∼ ,— I; ∼ , ∧ II–V
402.35   ∧He] III; ' ∼ I–II
403.3   Heavens] II; heavens I
403.18   Doctor.—] CENTENARY; ∼ ∧ – I; ∼ . ∧ II–V
*404.28 New-England] CENTENARY; ∼ ∧ ∼ I–V
407.17   own, he] II; own. He I
407.21, sunbeams] II; sun-beams I
  450.6
408.26   Glumdalca] CENTENARY; Glumdalea I (errata);
      Gleardallen I (text); Glumdalia II–V
409.9   see∧—] CENTENARY; ∼ ,— I–V
409.20   Well, well] II; ∼ ∧ Well I
409.27   Edward.∧] II; ∼ .' I
409.28   ¶| 'Nothing] II; no indention I
410.4   Edward.] II; ∼ , I
410.8   Devil's] III; devil's I–II
410.23   elm-tree] II; ∼ ∧ ∼ I
410.30   neither,'] II; ∼ ;' I
410.33   'You] II; ∧ ∼ I
411.10–11 carelessness∧—] CENTENARY; ∼ ,— I–V
411.12   girl∧—] CENTENARY; ∼ ,— I; ∼ , ∧ II–V
411.24   nag∧—] CENTENARY; ∼ ,— I; ∼ , ∧ II–V
411.31   stable;] CENTENARY; ∼ , I; ∼ . II–V
411.31   'There] II; ∧ ∼ I
412.5   'but] II; ∧ ∼ I
412.7   it∧—] CENTENARY; ∼ ,— I; ∼ , ∧ II–V
412.13   'My] II; ∧ ∼ I
412.13–14 comrade trusts] II; comrade, trust I
412.15   questions.'] II; ∼ . ∧ I
412.21   cider∧—] CENTENARY; ∼ ,— I; ∼ ; ∧ II–IV;
      ∼ ! ∧ V
412.23   like∧——'] III; ∼ ,— ∧ I; ∼ ∧ '– II

412.34	off.] II; ⁓ , I
413.2	well₍ₐ₎–] CENTENARY; ⁓ ,– I; ⁓ , ₐII–V
413.20	heart';] III; ⁓ ;' I–II
414.22	foe] I (errata); fool I (text)
*415.17	recognizing] II; recognising I
416.5	gray-haired] II; grey-haired I
416.25,	endeavored] II; endeavoured I
433.17,	
439.7	
417.7	myself?–my] CENTENARY; ⁓ ?–My I; ⁓ , my
	II–V
417.21	lance,)ₐ] CENTENARY; ⁓ ₐ) ₐ I; ⁓ ₐ), II–V
418.1	citizenₐ–] CENTENARY; ⁓ ,– I–V
418.23,	demeanor] II; demeanour I
419.5,	
435.31	
*418.25–26	stedfast] CENTENARY; steadfast I–V
419.17	Butₐ–] II; ⁓ ,– I
419.28	endeavoring] II; endeavouring I
420.6	jutting] I (errata); pitting I (text)
420.13–14	theseₐ– . . . periwigsₐ–] II; ⁓ ,– . . . ⁓ ,– I
420.22–23	doorsₐ– . . . windowsₐ–] CENTENARY; ⁓ ,–
	. . . ⁓ ,– I; ⁓ ; ₐ . . . ⁓ ; ₐ II–V
*420.24	concentrated] stet
420.32	crowdₐ–] CENTENARY; ⁓ ,– I; ⁓ , ₐ II–V
421.9	honored] II; honoured I
421.33	certainₐ–] CENTENARY; ⁓ ,– I–V
422.13	Ellen.ₐ] II; ⁓ .–	I
422.17	daylight] II; day light I
422.23–24	broomstick] II; broom-stick I
423.17	methodₐ–] II; ⁓ ,– I
423.34	longₐ–] CENTENARY; ⁓ ,– I–V
424.18	speech.] II; ⁓ ₐ I
425.4	Well] II; well I
427.5	conceivedₐ–] II; ⁓ ,– I
427.8	strongₐ–] CENTENARY; ⁓ ,– I; ⁓ , ₐ II–V
427.18	hers] II; her's I
428.20	fatherₐ–] CENTENARY; ⁓ ,– I–V
428.27	take] II; takc I
428.28	maid-servant] II; ⁓ ₐ ⁓ I

429.2   Doctor's] CENTENARY; doctor's I–V
429.8   centred] III; centered I–II
429.30   rest,] II; ~ ∧ I
430.1   reputation∧–] CENTENARY; ~ ,– I; ~ : ∧ II–V
430.11   stranger's] CENTENARY; stranger I–V
431.2   moonbeams] II; moon-beams I
431.8   me,'] II; ~ , ∧ I
431.8   'If] II; ∧ ~ I
432.5   endeavors] II; endeavours I
432.10   rain-drops] CENTENARY; ~ ∧ ~ I; raindrops II–V
432.24–25 recognized] II; recognised I
432.31   bed-side] CENTENARY; bedside I–V
433.8   daylight] II; day light I
434.15   son∧–] II; ~ ,– I
438.4   hold∧–] CENTENARY; ~ ,– I; ~ ; ∧ II–V
438.12   fir] CENTENARY; fire I; pine II–V
438.34   upon] II; up-|en I
439.15   proceeding.] II; ~ , I
440.34   Nature] II; nature I
442.17   mother∧–] CENTENARY; ~ ,– I–V
444.5   her,] II; ~ ∧ I
444.13   rest∧–] CENTENARY; ~ ,– I; ~ , ∧ II–V
444.25   grass-grown] II; ~ ∧ ~ I
444.26   there.] II; ~ ∧ I
445.18   afflicted∧–] III; ~ , ∧ I; ~ ,– II
445.33   death-beds∧– . . . hearts∧–] CENTENARY; ~ ,–
         . . . ~ ,– I; ~ , ∧ . . . ~ , ∧ II–V
446.9–10 linen∧– . . . chamber∧–] CENTENARY; ~ ,–
         . . . ~ ,– I; ~ , ∧ . . . ~ , ∧ II–V
447.8   Sir] CENTENARY; sir I–V
447.14   but——'] III; ~ '– I–II
448.4   seek∧–] CENTENARY; ~ ∧– I; ~ : ∧ II–V
448.14   *auri sacra fames!*'] II; 'auri sacra fames!' I
448.17   Nature] II; nature I
448.22   them∧–] II; ~ ,– I
449.4   Death,] II; ~ ∧ I
449.6   contrived] I (*errata*); continued I (*text*)
449.22   there.∧] II; ~ .– | I
449.26   on∧–] CENTENARY; ~ ,– I–V
452.2   presence∧–] CENTENARY; ~ ,– I; ~ ; ∧ II–V

452.14 future∧– . . . moment∧–] CENTENARY; ~ ,–
. . . ~ ,– I; ~ : ∧ . . . ~ ,– II–V
453.2–3 Chance∧– . . . path∧–] II; ~ ,– . . . ~ ,– I
453.30 protégé] II; protegéé I
454.7 rock∧–] CENTENARY; ~ ,– I–V
455.9–10 ∧*quid pro quo,*∧] II; 'quid pro quo,' I
455.18 subject∧–] CENTENARY; ~ ,– I; ~ , ∧ II–V
456.6 light∧–] CENTENARY; ~ ,– I; ~ ; ∧ II–V
456.17 favored] II; favoured I
456.19 Ellen∧–] CENTENARY; ~ ,– I; ~ , ∧ II
456.27–28 it∧– . . . sunset∧–] CENTENARY; ~ ,– . . . ~
,– I; ~ , ∧ . . . ~ , ∧ II–V
456.31–32 bliss∧– . . . Eternity∧–] II; ~ ,– . . . ~ ,– I
457.6–7 thinner∧– . . . spiritual∧–] CENTENARY; ~ ,–
. . . ~ ,– I; ~ ; ∧ . . . ~ ; ∧ II–V
457.22 agitation∧–] CENTENARY; ~ ,– I–V
457.25 trembling∧–] CENTENARY; ~ ,– I–V
457.27 needless,] II; ~ ∧ I
457.30 for——'] III; ~ '– I–II
458.2 weakness——'] III; ~ '– I–II
458.3 Ellen∧–] CENTENARY; ~ ,– I–V
458.30–31 untouched∧– . . . there∧–] CENTENARY; ~ ,–
. . . ~ ,– I; ~ , ∧ . . . ~ , ∧ II–V
458.33 now——'] CENTENARY; ~ , '– I; ~ ∧ "– II,
IV–V; ~ –' III
459.4 wretched∧–] CENTENARY; ~ ,– I; ~ , ∧ II–V
459.7 path-way∧–] CENTENARY; ~ ,– I–IV
459.18 sunshine] II; sun-shine I
459.25 itself∧–] CENTENARY; ~ ,– I; ~ , ∧ II–V
459.33 rapid∧–] CENTENARY; ~ ,– I; ~ , ∧ II–V
460.4 SCHOLAR∧] V; ~ . I–IV
460.11 tale∧–] CENTENARY; ~ ,– I–V

WORD-DIVISION

1. End-of-the-Line Hyphenation in the Centenary Edition

(NOTE: No hyphenation of a possible compound at the end of a line in the Cententary text is present except for the following, which are hyphenated within the line in the 1828 first-edition copy-text. Hyphenated compounds in which both elements are capitalized are not included.)

334.14	wood-|fringed
337.34	man-|hood
340.31	horse-|back
352.6	home-|bound
353.15	notwith-|standing
358.14	down-|ward
375.19	any-|where ('any where' *emended to* 'anywhere' *in copy-text, p. 48.17.*)
392.12	bed-|chamber
395.26	looking-|glass
399.9	half-|sleeping
414.29	over-|take
422.23	broom-|stick ('broomstick' *emended to* 'broom-stick' *in copy-text, p. 99.8.*)
440.9	mountain-|tops
445.10	well-|saved
450.6	sun-|beams ('sun-beams' *emended to* 'sunbeams' *in copy-text, p. 129.30.*)
459.34	rough-|hewn

2. *End-of-the-Line Hyphenation in the First Edition*

(NOTE: The following compounds, or possible compounds, are hyphenated at the end of the line in the 1828 first-edition copy-text. The form in which they have been transcribed in the Centenary Edition, as listed below, represents the practice of the first edition as ascertained by other appearances. Hawthorne's manuscripts closest to this period have been consulted when evidence was not available in the print.)

334.19	farm-|houses
345.13	sun-|light
345.18	day-|light
346.29	hoof-|tramps
347.1	self-|possession
348.31	footsteps
352.6	home-|bound
357.25	homeward
371.9	praiseworthy
377.29	hereabouts
385.32	fireside
390.18	small-|clothes
411.32	landlord
415.25	path-|way
415.35	hedge-|hog
416.4	grey-|haired (*emended to* 'gray-haired' *in copy-text, p. 92.2.*)
418.17	white-|headed
421.20	overcome
424.33	seaman's
425.16	sea-|coast
425.32	footsteps
426.16	uplifted
440.1	eyelids
444.28	road-|side
445.21	tombstones
446.6	uncoffined

451.22	death-	struggle
453.18	countryman
456.28	sunset

3. Special Cases

(NOTE: The following compound, or possible compound, is hyphenated at the end of the line in the 1828 first edition and in the Centenary Edition.)

| 352.6 | home-|bound |

HISTORICAL COLLATION

The following editions (new typesettings) have been collated and their variants recorded: I, 1828 first edition; II^a, 1876 untitled first collected edition (begun in 1865), and II^b, 1876 Illustrated Library Edition; III, 1876 Little Classics Edition; IV, 1883 Riverside Edition; and V, 1900 Autograph Edition.

The plates for II were used in the editions of 1879 Fireside, 1880 Globe, 1884 Globe (Crowell), and 1886 New Fireside; those of III, for 1891 Popular, 1894 Salem, and 1899 Concord; and plates of IV, for 1884 Wayside, 1884–85 Complete Works (London), 1891 Standard Library, 1902 New Wayside, and 1909 Fireside. Machine collations of first and last printings of II, III, and IV were made, but no printing of V after the 1900 Autograph was collated. For variants occurring in plates III and IV, the superior a indicates first printing while z indicates last printing; no attempt has been made to record the printing in which the variant first appeared.

333	(*epigraph*) academy] academe III^z; Academe IV, V
333.2	New-England] $\sim_{\wedge}\sim$ II^a–V
334.11	well nigh] wellnigh IV
336.32	burthen] burden III–V
338.12	years standing] $\sim,\sim$ III; years' $_{\wedge}\sim$ IV, V
339.17	perusing] persuing II$^{a\text{-}b}$
347.2	rode] ridden IV^z–V
348.4	squalid] squallid I
350.1	lit] lighted II–V

354.29 towards] toward II–V
355.18 protégé] protegēe I; protégée II[a-b]
357.18 eye] eyes II–V
363.15 eye] eyes II–V
366.10 past] passed II–V
368.22 removed by his death] removed by death IV, V
370.10 symptoms] symptons I
372.4 Hutchins'] Hutchins's II–V
372.6 an Inn] *errata* I; the Sun I; the inn II–V
372.27 ostler] hostler II[a]–V
373.9 frequent] frequented I, II
375.19 anywhere] any where I
375.24 farther] further III–V
376.35 shew] show II[a]–V
381.3 continued] continuous III–V
382.34 disappointed] diappointed I
383.19 could] would III–V
386.5 applications] application I
386.10 mysterious] myterious I
390.25 begone] be gone III–V
391.29 why talk I] why I talk I
392.13 Belzebub] Beelzebub II[a]–V
393.9 into tears] to tears I
401.26 unconscionable] unconscienable I
402.14 most] almost III–V
402.21 argued] augured III–V
407.11 farther] further II[a]–V
408.26 Glumdalca] *errata* I; Gleardallen I; Glumdalia
        II[a]–V
411.15 keep] kept IV[a]
412.13–14 comrade trusts] comrade, trust I
413.21 forgetfulness, but by hope, which] forgetfulness,
        by hope, but which II[a-b]
414.2 past] passed III–V
414.8 farther] further II[a]–V
414.22 foe] *errata* I; fool I
417.7 Divine] divine II[a]–V
418.2 come] came III
419.11 Ellen, I trust] Ellen, I I trust II[a-b]
420.5 burthen] burden III–V

420.6	jutting] *errata* I; pitting I
420.18	were] are IV[a]
427	(*epigraph*) past] passed II[a]–V
427.18	hers] her's I
430.11	stranger's] stranger I–V
434.28	down by] down down by II[a-b]
435.12	dependant] dependent II[a]–V
436.22	where] were IV
437.26	heaven] Heaven I
438.12	fir] firē I; pine II–V
438.34	upon] up-|en I
439.34	same time that] same that II[a-b]
442.6–7	ear . . . eye] Ear . . . Eye II[a]–V
442.8	arm] Arm II[a]–V
443.16	occupation] occupations III–V
446.6	laid] lain IV–V
446.32	made] make II[a]–V
449.6	contrived] *errata* I; continued I
451.10	past] passed II[a]–V
451.31	passion] passions II[a-b], III, IV
453.30	protégé] protegéé I
456.21	staid] stayed III–V
460.1	Nathanael] Nathaniel V

THE CENTENARY TEXTS:
EDITORIAL PRINCIPLES

T HE CENTENARY EDITION of Hawthorne provides for the first time established texts of the romances, tales, and associated shorter works. The general procedures governing this establishment are outlined here, whereas the specific problems for each text are treated in the separate Textual Introductions.

The text itself is a critical unmodernized reconstruction. It is critical in that it is not necessarily an exact reprint of any individual document: the print or manuscript chosen as copy-text (i.e., as the basis for this edition) may be emended by reference to other authorities or by editorial decision. The Centenary text, in short, has been established by the application of bibliographical and analytical criticism to the evidence of the various early documentary forms in which the text has appeared.[1] It is unmodernized in that every effort has been made to present the text in as close a form to Hawthorne's own inscription as the surviving documents for each work permit of such reconstruction, subject to normal editorial procedure.

The first step in the establishment of a critical text is the determination of the exact forms of the texts in the early docu-

[1] Various terms used here are discussed at length in Fredson Bowers, "Established Texts and Definitive Editions," *Philological Quarterly*, XLI (1962), 1-17.

ments and of the facts about their relationship to one another. When manuscripts are extant, the establishment of the texts of these documents involves the checking of the written form of all words and the determination of the texture of their spelling, capitalization, word-division, and punctuation, i.e., the "accidentals" of a text as distinguished from its "substantives," or the forms of the words as distinguished from the words themselves. Any manuscript alteration of the initial inscription is noticed, and whenever possible the author's rejected forms are reconstructed from the available evidence and recorded.

Since the first editions printed from Hawthorne's preserved manuscripts have a supplementary authority, the duty is placed on an editor to identify and analyze any variation in the readings of the printed texts that have primary or supplementary authority. To this end a number of copies of the first—and of any other edition possessing authority—have been mechanically compared for variation on the Hinman Collating Machine. Previously unknown differences that developed in the text during the course of printing have been discovered by this process, as well as such major variation within editions as the duplicate typesetting of the last gathering of the first and of the preliminary gathering of the second edition of *The Scarlet Letter*. Although it is too much to hope that every minor variant in an impression has been discovered by the extensive multiple collation, one can state with some confidence that the majority have probably been noticed; unknown major variation, at least, is not likely to exist in unseen copies of the editions examined by this method. Hence, the readings of the text in the authoritative documents, even in relatively minor respects of form, have been substantially established from the evidence of the machine comparison by superimposition of a number of exemplars, letter for letter and word for word.

The forms of other editions chosen for examination have

also been established by multiple collation of copies on the Hinman Machine. Technically, an edition comprises a particular typesetting, without regard for the number of different printings made at various times from this typesetting or its plates.[2] Since most Hawthorne book editions after the first (and often the first, too) were printed from stereotype plates, the history of the usual edition is the history of the textual variation in its set of plates throughout the various printings. Plates were occasionally altered between impressions, at times to correct errors in the edition-typesetting, at times to incorporate editorial normalizations and fancied improvements, and at times to repair plate damage caused by handling accidents and normal wear on the press. Therefore, in order to establish the exact forms of the editions (in respect to the history of their plates), the first impression from the plates of any edition-typesetting has been compared on the Hinman Machine against the last ascertained impression (in the Boston line of publication), and those variants affecting substantives have been recorded as between the early and late states of the plates. However, only when changes in plates were made before 1865 (Hawthorne died in 1864) have the individual variants been tracked down through the intermediate impressions in order to establish the dates of their first appearances. Finally, no attempt has been made to record variation in the plates in respect to non-verbal alteration. In punctuation readings, for instance, actual alterations are often impossible to distinguish from anomalies caused by plate wear and damage; moreover, for the purposes of the present edition non-verbal variants in unauthoritative prints have no textual significance, interesting as they might prove to a historian of printing practice.

Following the establishment of the variant documentary

[2] In the Centenary Edition the use of the bibliographical terms "edition," "impression" (or "printing"), "issue," and "state" follows that recommended in Fredson Bowers, *Principles of Bibliographical Description* (Princeton, 1949), pp. 379-426.

forms of all editions chosen as significant in the history of Hawthorne's text, these different edition-typesettings have been individually hand-collated against the first edition; and all substantive, or word, variants recorded, as well as such occasional variants among the accidentals as might bear on the question of the authority of any of the documents by which the texts were transmitted. From this evidence, printed in the Historical Collation appended to each edited work, the line of textual transmission can be traced from document to document and the general authority of each edition can thus be determined. This evidence, also, determines in large part the specific authority of any document, since bibliographical and critical analysis of the textual variants has demonstrated which are mere reprint editions—that is, editions in which the cumulative transmitted error was never corrected systematically but, instead, largely by chance. Evidence of this nature indicates that no comparison of the printer's copy had been made against any authoritative document, and thus that the various alterations observed (when not mechanical corrections) were in their turn corruptions and could not represent, in some manner, an editorial return to a purer version of the text.

On internal evidence like this, combined sometimes with external evidence, one can determine, usually with precision, the printed texts that have Hawthorne's immediate authority as against the number that are simply derived reprints without authority. In this connection, authority is defined as resident in any document printed directly from a Hawthorne manuscript or from some other document, such as another edition, that had been corrected or revised by Hawthorne or by some other person utilizing a Hawthorne manuscript. Such authoritative texts are called substantive, as contrasted with derived. Only substantive texts have been used as documentary sources of revisory emendation, although occasional correction may be drawn, for convenience, from derived editions.

After the derived reprints have been isolated, the next step in the editorial process is the selection of the copy-text from among the established substantive texts. In practice, the selection may differ from literary work to literary work according to the distinctive conditions, but the theory is firm: whenever practicable the copy-text selected is that form of the text, no matter how it may subsequently have been revised, that is nearest to the primary authority of Hawthorne's manuscript.

Obviously, when the manuscript is no longer in existence, the copy-text must be the first printed edition that was set directly from such a manuscript, since only this edition can preserve in any authoritative form such characteristics of the manuscript as have escaped the normalization of printing-house style imposed on the copy. If Hawthorne never intervened to revise or correct this text in any subsequent edition, the first edition remains the sole authority. However, if—as happened in *The Marble Faun*—Hawthorne did introduce corrections and revisions to a later edition (the first American edition, typeset from corrected sheets of the first English edition), the claims of more than the single, or copy-text authority must be considered.

The editorial procedure in such cases follows the principles laid down by Sir Walter Greg.[3] That is, a double authority is recognized. The copy-text remains the supreme authority for the accidentals, since it alone was set directly from Hawthorne's manuscript. On the other hand, the substantive variants in other texts not thought to be printer's errors must be taken to represent Hawthorne's revisions, and to these must be added such alterations in the accidentals as appear to derive from the author, although this last is a much more difficult matter to determine. Hence the resulting critical Centenary text will incorporate in the first-edition copy-text such variants

[3] "The Rationale of Copy-Text," *Studies in Bibliography*, III (1950-51), 19-36. See also Fredson Bowers, "Current Theories of Copy-Text," *Modern Philology*, LXVIII (1950), 12-20.

from later demonstrably authoritative editions as pass the editorial tests for authorial alterations. In effect this procedure attempts to reproduce the lost marked-up printer's copy that Hawthorne furnished for the revised text, and in this reconstruction to filter out the unauthorized printing-house variants that creep into any reprint and are thus found in the printed form even of a revised edition. Despite the fact that he "accepted" them (provided he read the proof for a revised edition), Hawthorne did not authorize these printing-house variants; hence they can have no place in the pure text that the Centenary Edition endeavors to establish.

Correspondingly, when Hawthorne's manuscript of a work has been preserved, this manuscript becomes the copy-text. In each case this manuscript has been collated against the first printed edition and all details of substantive variance have been recorded. However, the printing-house style imposed on the authoritative manuscript has been rejected except for necessary corrections,[4] and only those variants from the manuscript in substantives or in accidentals that appear to have been inserted by Hawthorne in the proof have been accepted and incorporated in the critical text. Thereafter, the determination of the history of the text and of the authority of all variants in editions after the first follows the regular procedures outlined above.

Hawthorne's shorter works that might have been published in periodical and gift-book form several times before collection present a special problem. In general, the Greg theory of copy-text holds, and an attempt has been made to separate the authority of the substantives from that of the accidentals in the different versions of the text and thus to establish the

[4] When in such a text as *The House of the Seven Gables* the printer of the first edition made on an average about fifteen alterations per page in conformity with house style, the cumulative effect on Hawthorne's own modes of expression as seen in the manuscript is very serious indeed. Only the manuscript contains the full record of the subtleties of Hawthorne's parenthetical expression and emphasis.

most authoritative form of each in a critical text that may fairly be said to synthesize the most authoritative versions. Only when one can determine that a later edition was set from an independent manuscript (not from marked-up copy of an earlier print) or was so thoroughly revised from printed sheets as to make distinction impossible between Hawthorne's and the printer's alterations, has the copy-text been shifted from the earliest printing from manuscript to a later substantive edition.

To repeat, the purpose of the Centenary Edition is to establish the text in as close a form, in all details, to Hawthorne's final intentions as the preserved documents of each separate work permit. This aim compels the editors to treat each work as a unit, with its own separate textual problems. That is, no attempt is made between texts to secure a uniformity of style that is not authorized from those documents for the texts in question that establish their most authoritative preserved forms. It follows that the texture of accidentals in a work like *The House of the Seven Gables,* established from authorial manuscript, will differ from that in a work like *The Scarlet Letter,* established from the first printed edition.

In the latter, the printing-house style imposed on the text removes it in various respects from conformity with Hawthorne's known practices in spelling, punctuation, capitalization, and word-division as seen in his manuscripts of about the same date. One might be able to alter some of these forms in *The Scarlet Letter* to bring the critical text, in theory, into a closer relationship with what one may reasonably suppose to have been certain of the details of the lost manuscript. But interesting as such an experiment might be, the result could never be wholly consistent and could not lead to any demonstrably established form of the text. Hence, each work in the Centenary Edition rests as a separate unit on the evidence of its own preserved documents, and represents a faithfulness to Hawthorne's full intentions in varying degrees of exactitude according to the authority of this evidence.

Editorial treatment of the text, then, is primarily concerned with synthesizing the evidence of all manuscripts and authoritative printed editions in order to arrive at Hawthorne's detailed final intentions as nearly as may be determined from the documents. In this situation any alteration believed to be Hawthorne's must be adopted, regardless of critical estimate of its literary worth, although, of course, an editor's literary judgment is one of the various criteria that operate to establish any alteration as a Hawthorne variant instead of the printer's. On the other hand, not all Hawthorne revisions are literary in their nature. When Hawthorne softened his original satire, or excised sections for personal reasons as with the passage on saloons in *The Blithedale Romance* revised in the print, presumably in deference to his wife's prejudices, the unrevised version has been retained in the established text as more faithfully representing Hawthorne's true intentions than the results of censorship even though self-imposed.

Revision of the copy-text, therefore, can be admitted only from the evidence of authoritative documents. On the other hand, correction may be drawn from any source, whether a substantive or reprint edition, or from independent editorial judgment. Indeed, no correction from an unauthoritative document can have any more validity than editorial correction; hence reprint editions are noted as sources for emendation only as a convenience and not because there is any secondary value in the fact that the chosen emendation first originated in them.

Editorial correction is of five kinds. First, since Hawthorne appears to have been a rapid and far from accurate proofreader,[5] he did not catch in proof all of the printer's errors

---

[5] For some information on this and other matters affecting the text, see Fredson Bowers, "Hawthorne's Text," in *Hawthorne Centenary Essays*, ed. Roy Harvey Pearce (Columbus, O., 1964), pp. 401-25.

that manifestly need setting right; hence some substantive emendation has proved necessary.

Second, inconsistencies may be present in the manuscripts in respect to spelling, capitalization, and division of words that were regularized in the prints. Such regularization of a manuscript has generally been accepted when the printer's version appears to coincide with Hawthorne's usual practice; however, if the print regularizes anomalies in opposition to Hawthorne's more habitual practice, or else fails to normalize an irregularity, independent emendation has been admitted.

Third, if Hawthorne's own usual practice cannot be determined (as in his frequent undifferentiated use of "subtle" and "subtile" and sometimes of "farther" and "further"), the variant forms are retained in the established text unless normalization seems justified on the authority of the dictionary that Hawthorne used—*A New Critical Pronouncing Dictionary of the English Language . . . By an American Gentleman* (Burlington, N. J.: Allinson, 1813).[6]

Fourth, whereas all characteristic spellings are followed in our unmodernized text when they are acceptable variants of more common forms and are regular in the literary text in question, misspellings, like Hawthorne's habitual manuscript "cieling", are always corrected.

Fifth, word-division is regularized according to the practice in the most authoritative documents for each text. If the matter is in doubt within a given text, the form has been adopted that agrees with parallels within the text or that is most characteristic of manuscripts closest in date to the print. When in the original documents a possible compound is hyphenated at the break between two lines, the editorial decision whether to establish the word in the Centenary Edition as a hyphenated compound or as a single word conforms to the same principle.

6 This Hawthorne family dictionary was identified and described in Carroll A. Wilson, *Thirteen Author Collections of the Nineteenth Century and Five Centuries of Familiar Quotations*, ed. Jean C. S. Wilson and David A. Randall (New York, 1950), I, 154.

No attempt has been made in the Centenary Edition to reproduce the typographical details of the original documents such as the lineation, the number of lines of indentation for display capitals and the number of capitalized text-letters following them, or the capitals or lower-case in running-titles and chapter headings. For instance, the customary periods after running-titles, and chapter numbers and headings, have been omitted, and old-fashioned wide spacing like "I 'll" or "that 's" (not always uniform in Hawthorne's manuscripts) has been ignored. Although the text has been scrupulously treated, its appurtenances have been modernized.

In every other respect, however, the Centenary Edition reproduces the features of the copy-text or else notes an alteration. No variation of any kind from the copy-text (other than those enumerated above) has gone unreported; hence, the interested reader at any point can reconstruct the copy-text from the Centenary print in tandem with its records of emendation. These records are contained in an appendix to each literary work, where specialists may consult the details at leisure. The basis for the record is the page and line number in the Centenary text; *viz.*, 42.15 means page 42, line 15.

The usual textual appendix contains the following sections:

Textual Notes: Whenever an emendation of the copy-text, or a refusal to emend, seems to require special notice, a brief comment upon the reading is provided.

Editorial Emendations: All alterations to the copy-text made in the present edition are recorded, together with the immediate source of the approved reading, always the first appearance of the emendation in the editions consulted in the preparation of the particular text. Since the purpose of this emendations list is to present at a view only the departures from the copy-text, and the origin for each reading of the correction or revision, the history of the copy-text reading up to the point of emendation is provided, but not its subsequent history. For substantives, this last can be found in the Historical Collation.

The basic note provides, first, the precise form of the emended reading in the Centenary text. Following the square bracket appears the identification of the earliest source of the emendation in the editions collated. A semicolon succeeds this notation, and following this appears the rejected copy-text reading with the sigla of editions that provide its history up to the point of emendation. In these notations certain arbitrary symbols appear. When the variant to be noted is one of punctuation, a wavy dash ∼ takes the place of the repeated word associated with the pointing. An inferior caret ∧ calls attention to the absence of punctuation either in the copy-text or in the early edition from which the alteration was drawn. Three dots indicate one or more omitted words in a series. The sigla for denoting the editions recorded are explained in the Textual Introduction for each work. In general, editions listed by their dates are those set from type, whereas roman numbers are used to identify the stereotype plates first put into use from a new typesetting in the listed edition. If a second edition were printed in the same year from a different setting of type, the two would be differentiated as in 1850^1 and 1850^2. All editions are American unless otherwise noted. English editions are identified as E. The notation (r) indicates reset type, and (s) standing type. Unless specifically excepted, the reading listed as originating in a plated edition comes from the original state of the plates and is constant in all recorded impressions made from these plates. An emendation assigned to CENTENARY is made for the first time in the present edition if by "the first time" is understood "the first time in respect to the listed editions chosen for collation."

The following examples are from *The Scarlet Letter*:

133.33   broad,] E, III; ∼ ∧ $1850^{1-2(r)}$

Here the copy-text first edition in 1850 (1850^1) places no punctuation after "broad", and the lack of punctuation is followed in the second edition of 1850, this reading occurring in one of the reset pages. The necessary comma, adopted in the Centenary text, was first inserted in the third American edition, printed from plates 1850; and it is also found in the first English edition of 1851. Since this English edition was set from a copy of 1850^2 independently, its sigla are placed for convenience before that of III in order not to interrupt the sequence of American plated editions beginning with III.

> *262.25   sombre-hued] CENTENARY; sobre-hued 1850$^{1-2(s)}$, E, L; sober-hued III–VII

In the above the Centenary original emendation of "sombre-" substitutes for the copy-text (1850^1) misprint "sobre-" followed in the standing type of the second edition (1850^2), by the first English edition, and by the Levin 1960 Riverside paperback, but sophisticated to "sober-" in the third edition (III) and repeated in this form by all subsequent texts collated, including the 1900 Autograph Edition (VII). The asterisk preceding the reference indicates that a Textual Note discusses this reading. Discussion of a reading that has not been emended is indicated in the emendations list as in the following, with the editions noted in which the unemended reading appears:

> *221.29   such personage] *stet* 1850^1–III

Word-Division: Hyphenation of a possible compound at the end of a line in the Centenary Edition poses a problem for the reader as to the exact form in the copy-text. Moreover, end-of-the-line hyphenation in the copy-text itself requires editorial decision whether the reading should be reproduced in the Centenary text as one word or as a hyphenated compound. This double problem is faced in the appendix section on Word-Division, which is designed to record all the essential facts about the forms of possible compounds both in the Centenary and in the copy-text.

No hyphen at the end of a line in the Centenary text is present in the copy-text unless listed in this section of the apparatus, as in the form:

6.21   grizzly-|bearded

This notation indicates that "grizzly-", ending the line in the Centenary Edition, page 6, line 21, is printed as part of a hyphenated compound within the line in the copy-text.

Since many hyphens ending lines in the copy-text may actually break an original hyphenated compound, not just the syllables of a single word, the second part of this appendix section lists all occurrences of established hyphenated compounding and of possible compounding broken at the end of a line in the copy-text itself, except when the hyphen joins capitalized units and there can be no ambiguity. Here the reading is that of the Centenary Edition; whether the compound is hyphenated or unhyphenated in the listing is in accord with the determined practice of the copy-text or (failing this evidence) of the manuscripts closest in date. It is to be understood that each reading was broken in the copy-text at the point of the hyphen, or where one would normally have occurred if the compound had been hyphenated.

3.18   lifemates
7.21   slop-sellers

Here the copy-text readings were, respectively, "life-|mates" and "slop-|sellers".

The third section lists those rarer examples when, by chance, the same compound reading is broken at the hyphenation in both the copy-text and the Centenary Edition. Within parentheses, the established correct form is thereupon provided for the information of the reader.

These precautions being observed, anyone may transcribe a passage from the Centenary Edition with no ambiguity about word-division in the copy-text.

Historical Collation: A list is provided of all substantive variants from the Centenary text in the editions chosen for collation. Variant readings in the accidentals are ignored because of their copiousness and their basic lack of significance save when they affect the sense in a substantive manner and thus qualify for listing, or for some special reason in connection with the tracing of the family tree of textual derivation. Moreover, the various accidental forms in different editions of a recorded substantive reading are ignored.

The first reading, to the left of the bracket, is that of the Centenary Edition, which will not necessarily be that of the copy-text if emendation has taken place. To the right of the bracket is placed the variant and the sigla for the specific collated editions in which it appears. The reading is that of the Centenary text in any such edition not listed.

21.29   all of his] all his IV–VII

This example from *The Scarlet Letter* signifies that the first three American editions, the first English edition, and the Levin text read with the Centenary Edition "all of his" but that the variant "all his" appears first in the Little Classics Edition of 1875 (IV) and continues through the intervening collated editions, the Red-Line of 1878 (V), the Riverside of 1883 (VI), and the Autograph of 1900 (VII) and all their collated platings.

In this Historical Collation an attempt is made to distinguish the states of the plates of the various editions in respect to substantive readings. Thus in *The Scarlet Letter*, for example,

50.30   They] Thed III[a]

records the fact that the first impression made from the plates of the third edition, in 1850, misprinted "They" as "Thed" at page 50, line 30, of the present edition; but that the error was corrected in the 1851 second impression of these plates.[7] For each work the special sigla identifying the plates and their printings are explained in a headnote preceding the Historical Collation. The entry

26.12   make] made III[e-g]; have made IV–VII

indicates that as part of a repair of the third-edition plates for the Illustrated Library Edition of 1871 (e), "make" was inadvertently altered to "made", a reading that was reproduced in the 1876 Illustrated Library Edition state of the plates (f) and the c. 1880 Globe Edition state (g) including the last impression of this state to be collated, the undated (c. 1886) New Fireside Edition. This error was sophisticated to "have made" when type was set for the Little Classics Edition of 1875, a reading that persisted through the Autograph typesetting (VII) but not in the Levin text (L).

An attempt is made in this Historical Collation to be complete and accurate in respect to this substantive plate variation in the several editions and their numerous impressions. Additional plate variants, discovered after a Centenary volume has gone to press, will be recorded in the Descriptive Bibliography of Hawthorne that will be appended to the Centenary Edition.

Variants in the First Edition: Any differences in the typesetting or plates that appear during the course of printing the first edition, or any other substantive edition, are recorded and identified in respect to the collated copies.

[7] If the error had appeared in all the impressions of the third-edition plates, the notation would read simply: They] Thed III.

Special Lists: Whenever the textual situation warrants the addition of further information than that supplied in the standard sections of the textual appendix, special lists record the necessary data.

For example, in *The Scarlet Letter* the variants in the standing type of the second edition seem to have been ordered by the publisher and not by the author; thus, they have not been regularly incorporated as part of the establishment of the Centenary text. In addition, the variants in the reset pages of the second edition must represent a mixture of printer's divergences from copy and the publisher's markings for alteration similar to those made in standing type. Since a difficult and not wholly demonstrable decision about authority has had to be a matter of editorial judgment, the whole list is provided so that the reader may be in possession of all the evidence in the event that he wishes to make an independent study of the problem.

Also, when the manuscript of a Hawthorne text has been preserved, an appendix list details the facts of revision or alteration in the inscription of this manuscript insofar as recovery can be made from a close examination of the documents.

On the other hand, a full record of the differences between the manuscript and the first edition printed from it would usually run to quite extraordinary length: about five thousand items, for instance, for *The House of the Seven Gables.* As a consequence, the editors' early hope that every variant between the manuscript copy-texts and the initial prints could be recorded has had to be abandoned, regretfully, in respect to the accidentals. However, all substantive variation will be found recorded in the Historical Collation for such works, with the Editorial Emendations list indicating those readings in which the manuscript copy-text has been altered by reference to a variant in the prints.

In order to secure a common ground for collation of the different Hawthorne works, the following procedures have been adopted.

Multiple copies (usually eight or more) of the first appearances in print and of any later substantive editions[8] have been mechanically collated on the Hinman Machines at the Ohio State University and the University of Virginia where extensive collections of Hawthorne have been gathered in the Ohio State University Libraries Special Collections and in the University of Virginia's Alderman Library, including the Clifton Waller Barrett Collection.

The establishment of the text has then proceeded by the determination of the family tree and of the authority or non-authority of editions after the first. These facts are recorded in the Historical Collation appended to each work. The following collected editions have always been collated against the copy-text: Little Classics (1875), Riverside (1883), and Autograph (1900). These are the only collected editions in the Boston line of publishers to Houghton Mifflin Company that represent different typesettings.[9]

For each of these editions the latest identified impression

[8] Only substantive editions printed from type metal (and hence subject to change during impression) have been collated from multiple copies on the Hinman Machine, for the chances are infinitesimal that the plates of an edition would be altered during the course of an impression of a sheet. Nevertheless, since accidents will happen, the editors have taken certain precautions against such an occurrence, however remote the possibility. When hand collation of the copy-text edition is made against later editions for the record of the Historical Collation, different copies of the primary edition are used as the basis for the comparison of every subsequent edition. In this manner, plate variation if present in the copy-text should be reflected in variant readings of a kind that are automatically checked.

[9] The succession of the publishers is as follows: Allen and Ticknor (1832-34); William D. Ticknor (1834-43); William D. Ticknor and Company (1843-49); Ticknor, Reed, and Fields (1849-54); Ticknor and Fields (1854-68); Fields, Osgood and Company (1868-71); James R. Osgood and Company (1871-78); Houghton, Osgood and Company (1878-80); Houghton, Mifflin and Company (1880-1908); Houghton Mifflin Company (1908——).

made from the edition-plates has been collated on the Hinman Machine against the first impression in order to secure the maximum information about the changes made in the history of the plates. But only the blue-bound form of the Autograph Edition has been collated (not the form with the signed illustrations), and no further account of its plates has been provided beyond this one impression.

Within the limits of the information about impressions available at the time of editing each text, an attempt has been made to identify the exact printing in which each plate-variant originated up to 1865. Thereafter, only the last known impression has been collated against the first, the differences being recorded without specifying the impression in which they originated. *The Scarlet Letter* has been given fuller treatment than other texts, in that plate variation has been identified in specific impressions later than 1865.

As well as the collected editions issued by Hawthorne's Boston publishers and their successors to the present Houghton Mifflin Company, all separate editions representing different typesettings put out by these publishers before 1900, and a few later, have also been collated and their variants noted. For each work the first English edition has also been collated, in part to establish its derivation, and in part to determine whether authoritative alterations were made in the American sheets sent to England to serve as copy. When a work was first published in England, something of the English history of the text has been investigated by collation of later editions; the usual history of the American line of the text has, of course, also been established.

This extensive collation has been carried forward well beyond 1864, the year of Hawthorne's death, in order to insure against the possibility (however faint) that fresh authority has entered a text if it was compared with an authoritative manuscript by some conscientious editor; and partly to provide for its own sake the history of the text, in detail, in the standard editions up to the present.

The textual record is a sad one of pyramiding corruption, sometimes trivial but often serious. Yet occasionally a purpose may be served in this section by demonstrating in detail that the editions commonly used by scholars and critics for analysis and quotation are unreliable. More important, the Historical Collation provides for the reader the total substantive evidence for textual transmission available to the textual editor, who has been chiefly responsible for the establishment of the text. All the cards are on the table, face up.

To insure maximum accuracy, all hand collation of the different typesettings of later editions against the copy-text was duplicated by individual workers at the Ohio State University and the University of Virginia, the results conflated, differences checked, and every variant wherever noted was rechecked through the whole list of editions. This process should have produced exactness of fact unless the collators of an edition at both universities simultaneously passed over a variant unique to that edition, in which case no system of double checking could catch the error. All proofs have been read at least five times and by three or more editors.

F. B.

THE BLITHEDALE ROMANCE
and
FANSHAWE

Volume III in the Centenary Edition of the Works of Nathaniel Hawthorne.

Published by the Ohio State University Press, Columbus.

The texts of the novel are set in eleven-point Fairfield, with Goudy Old Style initial capitals. Chapter headings are set in fourteen-point Caledonia capitals.

Composition, presswork, and binding by the F. J. Heer Printing Company, Columbus, Ohio.

Paper for the Centenary Edition is sixty-pound Permalife Text, manufactured by the Standard Paper Manufacturing Company of Richmond, Virginia.

Binding cloth for the Edition is Colonial Linen, manufactured by the Columbia Mills, Inc., Syracuse, New York.

Preliminary pages designed by Turck and Reinfeld, Inc., New York City.